Geert Spillebeen lives in Belgium and is a journalist. His first book, *Kipling's Choice*, was a 2006 ALA Best Book for Young Adults.

Terese Edelstein lived in Holland for many years. She now teaches in Michigan, where she lives with her husband. She translated Geert Spillebeen's previous book, *Kipling's Choice*.

A Son

> *My son was killed while laughing at some jest. I would I knew*
> *What it was, and it might serve me in a time when jests are few.*

Rudyard Kipling

John Condon groped for a chair. He was in shock. Now he knew for sure that not only was he dead and buried, but someone had even dug him up again ...

He had already been dead for nine years. At the end of May 1915, he learned of his own death from the British Military Government. Coldly they informed him through a telegram that he was missing "somewhere on the battlefield" and was "presumed dead." It had been an enormous blow for his mother. She thought that her youngest son had been safely playing soldier in an Irish barracks, certainly not at the front. And what about himself? Strange, but during that time of all-out war, John didn't really want to acknowledge the fact that he was gone, "killed in action" somewhere in Belgium. He had heard countless fellows report this kind of information. Every day the newspaper published a list of missing or dead boys. Occasionally a paragraph would appear about a missing soldier who had returned. Thus the news of his own demise had not actually come as a complete surprise. You learned to live with death during those years. How many comrades had he lost? When the Great War ended in 1918, the population of Waterford consisted primarily of old men. Ireland and all of Great Britain were bursting with young widows and grieving girls.

But today, the blow was a hard one for John Condon, even after all these years. They had finally found his body. With trembling hands he lay the letter down on the table. It had a proper military letterhead, but the contents were much too hastily penned by some bored military clerk. *What a gruesome way to inform me,* he thought. *Almost worse than the Great War itself.* He read the little wad of paper yet again:

Officer i/c
Infantry Record Office

Warwick, 5 January 1924

Dear Sir,

The undernamed article listed below that was found on the body of the late No. 6322, soldier John Condon (Royal Irish Regiment), has been received here. Please inform me if you wish it sent to you or whether it may be destroyed.

Subject in question: "one piece of boot."

I have no record of place of burial, though this information may be obtained by you from The Chairman of the Imperial War Graves Commission, 82 Baker Street, London W.1.

Stamped and addressed envelope enclosed for your reply.

Yours faithfully,
Captain D. Jones
By order of the Colonel,
Office i/c of the Infantry Record Office

So it's true—I'm really dead, thought John Condon. In a daze he shuffled to the kitchen cupboard and pulled out a drawer. The little box was still there. He opened it and examined the two medals inside. "British War and Victory Medal," he read on one. He let the colourful ribbons glide over his shaking palm. "1914–1915 Star" was engraved on the other. John would never forget how odd it had felt to sign for these posthumous decorations when they arrived: *Patrick Condon.* The real Patrick was dead; he had reported to the front as John. Patrick had given his older brother's name because he himself was too young to be a soldier. He died in Flanders a few weeks before his fourteenth birthday. *In Flanders Fields. Where the poppies blow,* John thought. *Perhaps there are poppies growing on my grave. My little brother's grave. Somewhere in Flanders there is a cross or a headstone that bears my name.*

THIRTEEN YEARS EARLIER

1911

WATERFORD

Farewell, School Days

"Give that bag here, you little rotter!" Patrick Condon shouted.

With such a voice one could chase blue flies off horse manure, which always lay in piles on the gleaming cobblestones of the back harbour.

It was a young, crazy voice in the crossing, a boy's voice that constantly wavered between soprano and bass. Patrick Condon was obviously in a cheerful mood, for most of the time he would have barely opened his mouth for such a trifle. If he really wanted something, the other ragamuffins stepped aside of their own accord. Patrick stood head and shoulders above everyone and thus looked older than ten. His rough hands were as big as coal shovels and usually just as black. But no one could say for sure whether he had actually thrashed anyone.

"Like a trick that never fails, Patrick Condon's tough as nails!" he roared, but immediately tried to look serious. "You should be ashamed, Rogers! Raising hell for a dozen bruised apples! Where did you steal them from, anyway? Or was O'Sullivan in on it, too?" He waved mightily with one fist, and with his other he swept the bulging sack of fruit above their heads.

"We'll share." Patrick grabbed the stolen booty and threw the apples at the snickering bystanders, one by one. He put two apples into his pocket and threw the last two onto the cobblestones in front of O'Sullivan and Rogers. "And now get out of here!"

The two boys sped away.

"He always has to be the boss. God bless the day he leaves school," whispered O'Sullivan, afraid that Patrick would hear him.

"You can say that again," said Rogers, nudging his friend.

"You don't get it, Rog."

Rogers stopped, frowned, and looked searchingly at O'Sullivan. "You don't mean it?"

"It's true," O'Sullivan answered. "He has a job. But don't ask me what it is or how he got it."

Bewildered, Rogers looked back at Patrick's disappearing silhouette. He saw the broad shoulders against the light of the setting sun and the drawn-out shadow that danced behind him. "Shit collector in Ballybricken," he blurted out all of a sudden.

A few pennies could sometimes be earned by picking up manure at the pig and cattle market of Ballybricken, the district where Patrick Condon lived.

"There's been gossip about it for a while already. His brother John spilled the beans this afternoon." O'Sullivan was chattering away now. "But I didn't get anything more out of him. I'm sure he was afraid that someone would steal the job from Patrick."

"Or that his strong little brother would let him have it," Rogers sneered. "You know what he's like, that Patrick . . ." He winked and punched the air with his fists.

"Actually, he wants to be a soldier."

"Yes, we know that, Sully. But first let him practice on the pigs!"

They walked on the cobblestones along the River Suir toward home.

Patrick Condon marched with his nose in the air. He was in high spirits. The still air above the water made the black hairs on his sturdy forearms stand up. Ropes and pulleys tapped against the sea of masts along the quay. He made this detour whenever possible. The ships in Waterford inspired him to dream away. He wanted to sail over the water to the continent someday. To "*la douce France*," or to Germany, a country that Mr. Baldwin had talked about at school. "Germany is growing dangerously large, it's becoming an industrial state, a glutton that's lying in wait for our crown," his teacher had said.

"What crown?" the slow-witted Jimmy Salt had asked.

Chuckling, Patrick heaved a sigh at the memory.

"What crown? What crown do you think? The English crown, you idiot!" the teacher had barked. "King George the Fifth's crown. What else?"

"Isn't there an Irish crown, then?" Salty asked. His blubbery face looked puzzled. "Daddy says that the English king makes lots of promises to us Irish but that there—"

"Enough!" Mr. Baldwin roared. "Maths lesson! Condon, come to the board!"

"Stupid schoolteacher," Patrick thought good-humoredly now as he walked briskly along. "I'm finally rid of that yapping goody-goody!"

The dark, low tones of an ocean steamer caught Patrick's attention. It sailed out of the inlet, leaving a long white plume behind it. Perhaps it was going to America. He thought about Paddy Stone, a boy from his street who, like so many others, had left for the promised land. Patrick wanted to cross the ocean someday, too.

He turned onto Wheelbarrow Lane. The common man in Waterford thought that was a better name than the official one, the overly chic Thomas's Avenue. Patrick's street wasn't wide enough to be considered an avenue by anyone's standards, certainly not by those who had to pass through with a handcart or a cattle wagon.

He approached the low brick house at number two and opened the door. He could tell he was home by the smell. His mother had a pot of mutton stew on the fire. Mollie, the wife of his oldest brother, Peter, sat in a corner, nursing her newborn baby. They lived in the little house, too. Mollie turned away, embarrassed.

"Ready for the big day tomorrow?" called his mother, glancing at him.

Patrick bent forward to pass through the doorway. His broad shoulders blocked the outside light. "Yup!" was his curt reply.

Farewell, Childhood

Patrick was out of bed at four in the morning. He hadn't slept a wink. He rubbed his eyes as he carefully unbolted the front door. He had to hurry over the cobblestones to keep up with his father and two brothers. The first horse carts, laden with pigs, were already rattling through the streets of Ballybricken, right on time for the market. Four shadows of various sizes, with hunched shoulders and caps draped over one ear, walked on the other side of the street toward the Waterford harbour. On the way the Condons had to continually step aside to avoid the small herds of cows being driven in their direction by black-smocked men wielding large sticks. Now and then Patrick saw in the half darkness a rough-looking face illuminated by the glow of a cigarette. The rank smell of fresh cow dung penetrated his cold nose. Gradually he found the rhythm for keeping pace with the other three. After ten minutes, his oldest brother turned left toward O'Sullivan's Brewery, where he had found work.

"Bye!" Peter was barely audible.

"See you tonight?" Patrick shouted. Peter didn't answer.

They walked past the back harbour and followed the Suir downriver, toward Waterford. Patrick was familiar with this area along the river. In his mind he could see a few kilometres farther to the magnificent convergence of the Three Sisters: the rivers Suir, Barrow, and Nore. During his summer holidays he had often romped on the fertile green slopes. He knew that just beyond them lay the bay, then the St. George's Channel and the Irish Sea.

Three sisters, thought Patrick. *Two sisters are enough*

for me. But now there's Mollie and the baby. They're still sleeping, and so is Mother. He wondered what his first day of work would be like. He would show them what he could do with his hands, at any rate. Better that than being in the schoolroom, hearing the unbearable yammering of those brats in Mr. Baldwin's class.

Far behind them the clock-tower chimes of the Holy Trinity interrupted his thoughts. Four thirty. Ten seconds later the Protestant Christ Church Cathedral chimed, too. Patrick could unerringly distinguish between the sounds of the two clocks, but now he thought they sounded different than usual, one here in the dark and one so far across the water.

"You'll keep your trap shut when I'm with you, understand?" Father broke the silence. The rough voice indicated that he was in a foul mood.

"Yes."

"You're fourteen when I'm not there with you. Got it?"

"But, Pa," John protested. "Patrick is ten—"

"From now on Patrick is fourteen. See? Or do you want to get him fired right away? We can use those few pennies he'll earn."

"Yes, Pa."

Archibald Hook was an enormous plum pudding of a man, with three hairy rolls of blubber around his bull-neck. He held up his immense trousers with a rope that ran between the folds of fat on his tremendous belly. His nickname, "Fatso," was well deserved. But the worst thing was his rancid odour. His hair hung in strings that stuck to his tiny skull and disappeared behind his ears. Even in the morning he sweated so profusely that it seemed as though he had smeared his entire body with a smelly hair tonic.

"This is him, Archie. My youngest son." The friendliness in Father's voice seemed exaggerated.

Patrick knew that Pa was groveling before this monster. The boy looked directly into Archibald Hook's face.

"Name?" the big man growled.

"Patrick," answered his father. "And Condon, just like me. And—"

"How old are you, boy?"

Patrick held his tongue. Even in the morning darkness he could see the blood vessels pulsing through the man's eyes. And that breath—a mix of garlic and gin—was enough to make him gag.

"He just turned fourteen!" Father hastened to say. "So it's no problem, is it, Archie?"

"That remains to be seen," Mr. Hook snapped. "Little blokes *are* problems. You know that from experience." He dabbed his forehead with a gray rag and pointed to the *Caesar,* an empty steamship that towered above the quay. "He can go sweep the hold right away. Peanuts—that'll keep him busy."

Peanuts. *That's a good beginning* flashed through Patrick's head. *Maybe I can start up a business from this. As long as I don't come across that monkey face of Archie the Fatso too often.*

"Okay, thanks, Archie," said Father, and he turned to Patrick. "Let's go, boy." He winked at his other son to follow him.

"Just a moment, Condon!" The giant planted a filthy claw onto Father's shoulder. "Cash in hand!" he growled. "For the first week the boy works for me. After that I get ten percent of his wages."

Dirty swindler, thought Patrick with a shudder. *I barely know this fellow, but he's already making me sick.*

"One day's work for free is what you said, Archie," his father protested. "That was the agreement, wasn't it?"

"And today I want a whole week," the fat man snickered. "But all right, Condon." He turned to a group of boys a bit farther up. "There's no end of candidates, I tell you . . ."

"Fine." Father hesitated. "A week, then."

"And payment in advance, Condon. Now!" Mr. Hook tightened his grip. Patrick looked about and exchanged glances with John, who was looking around as well. The lowlifes at the scene felt a fight coming on and were sizing up the situation. Patrick knew that his father would have absolutely no trouble shaking off Mr. Hook. But the big man had power—the power to rob a person blind.

Father snatched a few coins from his pocket and counted them in his hand. "I can't give you any more now—you know that."

"Bring the rest tomorrow morning straightaway; otherwise Port Láirge will be too small for the both of us!" Mr. Hook roared.

We'll see about that, thought Patrick. He was seething.

Monkey in the Peanuts

Patrick had never seen a ship so close up before, let alone the belly of such a mastodon. *Jonah in the whale,* he thought. He could count the happy memories at his school desk on one hand, but the lessons in religious history would certainly be among them. When Mr. Baldwin had related the unbelievable adventures of those Bible figures, the otherwise noisy class had hung on every word. Patrick could still hear his teacher's voice resonating in the classroom. "Is anyone here?" Patrick called out. He was startled by the sound of his own voice, which rolled through the ship's hold and echoed back to him.

Mr. Hook had directed him to the gangway of the *Caesar*. "You'll see what you have to do with the nuts below," he had snarled. "I'll come later to check on how you're doing. Now get going!"

Patrick had crossed the gangplank and steel steps. Luckily he'd been able to make his way deep down into the bowels of the deserted ship. He had reached the cargo hold; that was certain. It smelled like rancid butter. The first rays of sun were white as snow and streamed obliquely in through three high portholes. Slowly his eyes grew used to the contrast of light and darkness. *There's no shortage of peanuts,* he thought when he saw the remnants of the cargo on the floor. The layer of nuts wasn't any thicker than a centimetre or two, but this iron whale of a ship was probably as long as a soccer field.

"Is anyone here?" he called, more carefully this time. He thought he heard a distant shout rise above his echoes.

"Here in front!" he seemed to have heard. A tiny

voice was coming from the left. Patrick stepped cautiously onto the ledge that ran in a bow along the side of the hold and walked toward the nose of the boat.

He discovered that the voice was coming from the very front of the hold. It belonged to a gaunt little fellow who looked at Patrick with suspicion. He was lying on a heap of burlap sacks piled on top of a long crate. Apparently the forecastle served as a storage area for bags and chests and as a place to sleep, too.

"Do *you* sleep here?" Patrick asked in surprise.

"You noticed," the boy replied. "It's still a lucky break, this ship. At least it's dry." He patted down his reddish hair and rubbed the sleep from his eyes, yawning.

He doesn't look well, Patrick thought when he saw the bags under his eyes.

"I'm Seamus," the boy said as he threw a heavy sack off his legs. He jumped up.

Patrick was confused. Because of the boy's small stature, Patrick had taken Seamus to be thirteen or fourteen. But now that Patrick had a better look and could see the sunken cheeks, Seamus seemed much older.

"Seamus," the boy repeated. "Welcome."

"Oh . . . I'm Patrick . . . Condon . . . Uh, I was sent here by Fatso—I mean, Mr. Hook. You know him, don't you?"

"Better than you think!"

Patrick noticed the bitterness in Seamus's voice. "Are any other . . . uh, men coming to work here?" he inquired. "Dockworkers, I mean."

Seamus sighed. "Hook prefers to keep the boys separated from the men."

"Maybe it's better that way," Patrick said.

"It depends on how you look at it. Yes, it's better for *him!*" Seamus rolled his eyes and shrugged his shoulders in disdain. "So you've come to pick up peanuts, Patrick. Fatso likes it when boys bend forward and scrape their knees for him."

Patrick had no idea what Seamus meant, but he fervently agreed with the boy that Archibald Hook was a real bastard.

"You can begin in the meantime," Seamus said. "Fill the sacks. Here they are." He pointed to a pile of burlap bags.

"What about you?"

"I'm going to pee over the railing and get myself a hunk of bread. I'll only be gone ten minutes. It would be better for you to have a brush or shovel handy when Fatso makes his rounds, otherwise he'll put *you* in the sack," Seamus warned, and he snickered.

Patrick wasn't especially clumsy, but filling that first sack turned out to be more difficult than he expected. *Luckily no one is around to see me botch this,* he thought. He held his heavy spade in one hand, and with the other hand he opened the mouth of the shapeless bag and shovelled peanuts in. Just as many nuts landed outside the bag as inside.

Seamus returned fifteen minutes later. He laughed himself silly when he saw that Patrick had scarcely begun to fill his second bag. "You won't even be halfway through by next year, Patrick!" he chuckled. "Look, this is the way you have to do it." From a corner in his improvised sleeping quarters he pulled out an iron stand, a sort of giant hat rack, and moved it to their work area. He hung two sacks upon it, then effortlessly aimed his first shovelful of peanuts into an open sack. Patrick spit into his hands and followed Seamus's example. A glance from one was taken as a challenge by the other, and each filled a bag in no time.

They spent hours working in one area that morning. It was like a contest, and Patrick could hold his own. He seemed to be stronger, but Seamus was handier. Seamus needed to take a drink of water every now and then—he had some trouble with his lungs, and the dust in the boat did him no good. But he was obviously enjoying the company of his new colleague. And despite the heavy work, Patrick was in high spirits as a brand-new dockworker. When Seamus stopped to catch his breath, Patrick amused him with his silly antics, swinging from one spanning to another near the top of the loading area. By midday they had filled about a hundred large sacks that were one and one-half metres in length and had grouped them neatly together. Soon those sacks would be hoisted up through a hatch.

"It's nice work," Seamus said, pointing to the bags, "because we can eat in between loadings."

"Isn't there a lunch break?" Patrick asked, wiping the dust from his eyelashes.

"Not for you, Condon!" a deep voice crackled right behind him.

Patrick turned around and looked directly at Archibald Hook's fat stomach. The sweet aroma of peanuts was overpowered by the stench of beer and sweat. Mr. Hook thrust his belly forward and threw him a nasty punch. Patrick flew two metres back and tumbled against the wall of the hold.

"*You* come with me!" Mr. Hook beckoned to Seamus as he pointed to the sleeping quarters. During this whole time the boy had been cowering like a beaten dog. Slavishly he followed Mr. Hook's command.

"And you, Condon," the big man said, slurring his words, "go to the crane operator on the wharf and say that in a half hour we'll bring this freight up."

Patrick scurried away as fast as he could. The giant called after him, "And bring me a big bottle of cold beer from the Skipper, that cafe not far from here."

Patrick hesitated. "But I have no money."

"Have them put it on my tab, damn it! Now get out of my sight!"

That slave driver Archibald Hook had an odd concept of "not far," for Patrick had walked for at least fifteen minutes. He found the Skipper to be more like a plush theatre than a cafe. It was even darker inside than in the belly of the ship, and there were many strange women walking about, all heavily perfumed and scantily dressed. The customers weren't used to seeing boys his age on the premises, and they looked up in surprise when he entered. But the owner of the cafe knew Mr. Hook and didn't make trouble.

Patrick hurried back to the wharf, convinced that he'd be scolded for being late. Breathlessly he dove down the last stairwell to the forecastle. Suddenly a strange feeling overcame him.

Rising above his own panting were sounds from the half darkness, stifled, panic-stricken cries from Seamus and snorting growls from a furious Fatso. Chests and planks were crashing against the walls. Patrick crept closer and hid behind the filled bales.

His heart was beating in his throat. Seamus was across from him; wild-eyed, he was waving a shovel defiantly at Mr. Hook. Patrick had never seen a face so filled with hate and despair. Mr. Hook was standing with his back against the sacks. Sweat ran in streams among the folds of his neck.

"You'll be sorry for this, you little shit!" he roared, taking a step forward.

It was then that Patrick noticed the unbelievably huge, white, hairy backside of the man. At the same time he realised that the rags piled on top of the sacks were Mr. Hook's trousers.

I don't want to lose my job, not on the first day. Patrick's thoughts were racing. *My father will kill me if I come to blows with that bum. Where would we find other work?* His heart was beating like a sledgehammer. For a moment he exchanged glances with Seamus. The boy straightened his shoulders with newfound courage and tightened his grip on the shovel.

"Get back, you pig!" Seamus shouted. "I have nothing more to lose!" He swung the shovel, grazing the buttons on the man's shirt.

Carefully Patrick lifted his head above the sacks

and gestured to Seamus to calm down. Then he raised his thumbs high and scampered to the stairs.

"Okay, all the hatches can be opened!" Patrick called to the crane operator and the handful of dockhands who had been brought to help. Immediately the operator led the way and pulled open one of the panels.

Never had there been a more beautiful spectacle in any Waterford theater than the farce that had played out in the hold of the *Caesar* that day. The grand finale had been the monster's escape. Mr. Hook had run across the cobblestones of the wharf with a jute sack wrapped around his middle.

"And where are his trousers?" asked Seamus, when he heard about what had happened.

"I've no idea," Patrick answered, winking.

When they were through hoisting up the last of the bales from the ship, only an enormous wad of cloth remained on the floor. For a long time afterward those trousers were kept behind the bar of a local pub. Every once in a while they were brought out and displayed like a trophy.

TWO YEARS LATER
June 1913

Goodbye, Waterford?

Patrick looked across the rusty-brown backs of four oxen. The midday sun shone on their gleaming withers. He whistled as he passed his stick over their backs to chase away the flies, which swarmed the cattle market of Ballybricken on warm days. He liked this job. Whenever he and his brothers couldn't find work at the harbour in the mornings, they headed home right away. They could always charm a few cattle dealers into letting them tend their stock while negotiating a sale or clinching a deal in the nearby cafes. And if the brothers couldn't find work at the market, they could always offer a hand at O'Sullivan's, the brewery in the centre of the city. But the job of dockworker paid the best. Sometimes they could also do business in lost goods or cargo remnants, but that was back-breaking labour, even for a tough, sturdy fellow like Patrick.

"In a year or two or three, you'll be stronger and faster than all of us," the dockhands said generously. "But you'll have to grow a head taller." The men at the wharf had taken a liking to him, but when jobs were scarce, it was every man for himself.

Patrick couldn't wait another two years. He had very quickly settled down in the harbour and felt good among those strapping men. Besides, anything was better than school. But before long, his old flame came knocking again—he wanted to become a soldier, and he let everyone know it. He could talk forever about the drummer boys and buglers who had accompanied the Duke of Marlborough to the European battlefields in days gone by; or about the powder monkeys, who had had to supply the cannons for Lord Nelson's fleet in the Battle of Trafalgar; or about the fourteen-year-old boys who served in Queen Elizabeth's Royal Navy. He knew it all. Whenever navy boats were moored in the area, you couldn't tear him away. Not long before he had gone missing for two days, until his father dragged him from a frigate and kicked him back to Ballybricken.

One thing was drummed into his ear during that adventure: "You must be sixteen to join the army." *If my father lets me lie about my age to get work, then I can add a few years for the army, too,* Patrick mused. He was hatching a plan.

I should have left a note, certainly for my mother, Patrick thought. But writing was not his strongest suit. He kept a brisk pace and pursued his tall skipping shadow in a westward direction. It would soon become completely light. His eyes followed the winding dirt road to where the towers of Fiddown loomed above the rising mist in the distance. The grass along the shoulders gradually gained more colour from the stark-white chervil and the bright-red poppies. On the slopes, the yellow tracts of coleseed now pierced through the haze. The birds in the shrubs twittered to one another. Patrick breathed deeply, taking in the smells of the herbs that grew here.

He could tell by the milky-white sunlight penetrating through the mist that it was going to be a glorious day.

Patrick was beginning to relax. He had succeeded in slipping away from home without having been seen. He couldn't go back now. A vague mix of relief and remorse crept over him. He had cut the cord, but he had disappeared like a thief in the night, without saying goodbye. He didn't want to hurt his mother and two sisters, although he strongly suspected that they had known he was up to something. *If all goes well, I'll write them a letter, even if it's just a short one,* he thought to comfort himself.

"Louder!" shouted the man with a red mustache.

"Sorry, *sir!*" said Patrick, a bit more forcefully now. Quickly he removed his hat and put it under his arm.

"Don't say sorry!" barked the man, red-faced. "Name?"

Patrick felt his shoes pinching his aching feet. The thirty-mile trek to Clonmel had not agreed with him. He was terribly tired and flustered, and now this little tyrant was breaking his eardrums.

"John Condon, *sir!*"

"John? *John!* Is that your name?"

Patrick's heart skipped a beat. *This man can't possibly know my real name,* he was thinking.

"John, eh?" roared the little man, who was right in front of his face now.

Patrick felt the tips of their shoes touch. The man's breath was horrible. And what a strange, filthy brown uniform he was wearing! Patrick had heard about these new khaki outfits of the professional army, but he didn't think much of them.

"Hear that, Corporal? His name is John!" The awful face turned to the man at the writing table. "And surely Condon is his first name?" he snickered.

The corporal forced himself to appear amused. He shrugged his shoulders. "Uh, my name is Condon, *sir.*" Patrick could barely finish his sentence.

"HOLD! YOUR! TONGUE!" roared the corporal with renewed energy. "Has ANYONE asked you?"

"No, sir." Patrick hardly dared to answer. It had been a long time since he'd had a crying fit, but he could feel one coming on now.

"And stop calling me *sir!*" The whiskered man put one of his sleeves forward. "Three stripes and another two under them. That's sergeant major. And *sir*—that's for officers. Is that clear?"

"Yes, Sergeant Major," Patrick ventured to say. Ever since he'd been a toddler, he had known all the ranks, stars, and stripes by heart, even the complicated sleeve piping of the navy. And Patrick certainly was aware that this man was a noncommissioned officer. But how was *he* to know what to call him?

The corporal finally wrote down Patrick's name and address. Then came the most sensitive subject of all.

"Age?" barked the sergeant as he circled him.

Patrick pulled his shoulders up a bit more in order to appear heavier. He knew that this man, who had experience with recruits, was assessing him. The boy shut his eyes and hesitated a little. "Seventeen, Sergeant Major," he finally answered boldly.

For a moment it was quiet. Patrick had added on five years. Would they fall for it? His brother John was exactly five years older than he. Thus they could safely check the office of records in Waterford.

"Do you have a letter of recommendation with you, Condon?"

"I hadn't thought to get one, Sergeant Major," Patrick lied. He was trying to hide his relief over his previous lie. Everything was going to be all right!

"Come back tomorrow for the physical, Condon. If you pass it, I see no reason why you can't be placed on the recruit list for part-time soldiers. Okay, dismissed!" the sergeant major commanded. He turned to the corporal. "Next!"

As Patrick was heading for the door, the sergeant major called to him. "Oh, Condon, one more thing . . ."

Here it comes, thought Patrick. *He's on to me.*

The man removed his cap and pointed to his close-cropped head. "From now on, comb that lousy hair of yours. It's full of straw." He could barely suppress a smile.

Patrick breathed with relief, yet he was confused. *Idiot,* he reproached himself. That morning he had carefully brushed off his clothes after crawling out of the haystack, hadn't he? He reached up to touch his hair—he apparently had forgotten to tend to the straw up there. He smiled back, thanked the sergeant, and limped out the door. His eyes were filled with tears, which were as much from happiness as from the terrible blisters his worn-out shoes had given him.

A Soldier at Last

Patrick had never before been as far as Clonmel. Once he and his mother had travelled to Dunmore East, a cozy little fishermen's harbour half a day's walk to the south. There they had visited his mother's sister, who was gravely ill. She lived in an earthen hut on the west bank of the St. George's Channel, near the Irish Sea. Aunt Ella . . . They weren't a moment too soon, for she died the next day.

And here he was, a full day's journey from Waterford, all alone, on the border of County Tipperary. What would his family think? "One less mouth to feed," his father would growl, but also, "A wage earner gone, and a nuisance, too." Father probably wasn't very upset. His mother, on the other hand—she usually remained silent in family disputes, to keep the peace, but he knew she'd be concerned.

My worries are short-lived, in any case, Patrick thought. *In a few days I'll be a soldier at last. Even though I'll be part-time, it means that I'll get free food and clothes and who knows, maybe even a roof over my head, too. I'll have to look out for myself until then.*

He touched the small leather pouch that dangled on a string under his shirt. At home, he had had to hand over every last cent of his wages. Pocket money had been out of the question. But those little jobs that he occasionally had gotten at the harbour had supplied him with a nice stack of pennies. He had secretly put aside these extra earnings for two whole years.

Clonmel was a town that had everything, including cheap lodgings above the many cafes. Yet Patrick chose the known over the unknown. He went out beyond the town, where the police didn't ask questions, and fell into conversation with a slightly drunk farm hand named Roy, who was returning from the market. They quickly reached an agreement over the price of lodging. Patrick got a spacious bedroom with a breathtaking view of the glowing valley, high and dry in a secluded barn. *What a bed,* he thought when he nestled in the hay. At home they all lay snoring together in one room. The barn was barely a ten-minute walk from the army barracks, straight across the fields and pastures. "You can wash up in the river below," Roy told him cheerfully "And one more thing: no smoking."

Patrick paid for three nights in advance, in case he failed the physical. To his great relief, the farm hand, according to their agreement, returned that evening with half a loaf of bread, some cheese, and a bottle of watery beer. What more could a young vagabond want?

The doctor, an army captain, found nothing wrong with Patrick's condition. On the contrary. Together with five other men—Patrick thought some were fairly old—he was thoroughly examined. The corporal from the previous day recorded all the personal information: height, weight, and hair and eye colour. Patrick then received a shot in his left arm.

"A bit thin, perhaps, for a seventeen-year-old boy," declared the doctor, and he winked. "But certainly fit enough for the Militia Battalion."

Patrick was floating. Imagine—the Militia Battalion! How his family would look up to him! Every Irishman knew about these militias. During the past three centuries, every powerful landowner had his own private army, manned by local inhabitants who worked part-time there. Meanwhile, those battalions made up a part of the regular British troops in Ireland. And he, Patrick Condon, had been inducted. Men from his neighbourhood would be green with jealousy when they found out. *The Militia Battalion!*

Patrick had trouble keeping up a tough appearance later that day. Three other recruits were going to the city to drink to their good outcome. Patrick didn't dare refuse when he was asked to join them. He was at least as excited as the other three put together, but he had no more experience with alcohol than most other twelve-year-old boys. After his fifth pint of dark stout, he'd had it, certainly when the others began standing in the doorway and calling out to anyone in a skirt—even calling out to old women of twenty-five years and up! Patrick staggered back to the farm. It took him a lot longer than ten minutes to reach the barn. Apparently the friendly farm hand had waited up for him, and he came knocking less than five minutes after Patrick's return, expecting to hear good news. And he had a well-filled hip flask with him.

Patrick himself couldn't say how the rest of the night turned out. The sun was already high in the sky when he awoke from his stupor. His breakfast went untouched that day.

What a Life!

Peas with bacon—mmm! Bacon with peas the next day. The day after that, the cook fell back to his first menu. Every once in a while, on days of great culinary inspiration, there was mutton stew on the table, and then Patrick felt as though he were back home again. But you never heard him complain about life in the barracks. Not at all!

He received intensive training for the first two

weeks. The drill sergeant was the same bully who had recruited him, but Patrick was actually glad to be in the command of such a howler. The boy enjoyed marching in rhythm among a troop of other puppets, who whirled and twirled wherever and whenever the lion tamer wished. As long as he dutifully did as he was told, the drillmaster's yelling didn't seem so offensive. Patrick liked being part of such a well-oiled military machine. After a couple of days, stepping from the barracks toward the drilling field to the cadence of "left-right-one-two" even gave him a pleasant tingling sensation in his belly. He belonged here—he had waited for this for such a very long time. As the youngest in the corps he was certainly the least important, but marching among the rows of recruits gave Patrick a completely new feeling of power.

Two weeks of being a full-time soldier in training couldn't stretch out long enough for him. Patrick liked target practice the best. It was a little game of dexterity and precision: ready your weapon, take aim at the target, hold your breath, pull the trigger ... and then feel the shock that jolted through your entire body. Even the smell of sulfur from the exploded cartridges gave him a buzz. They should have seen him here, those good-for-nothings in the streets of Ballybricken, who perhaps were now fighting over a pound of bruised apples or a young bird. He, Patrick Condon of Wheelbarrow Lane, alias John Condon, had a gun in his hand—a gun with real bullets! As a part-time soldier, he wouldn't often get a chance to use live ammunition. Therefore he enjoyed every shot he could fire under the approving eye of Sergeant Bully, who deeply appreciated Patrick's enthusiasm. The only activity that was somewhat unpleasant was bayonet practice. "But that's the last thing you'll ever have to use," the drillmaster assured them, and he kept the sessions brief.

It was truly a prince's life: playing soldier, three meals a day, free clothes—luckily not those modern, dirty khaki things—a bed, and a salary for all this, besides!

Patrick had chosen to live in the barracks during his training. Whoever lived nearby was allowed to sleep at home. He had talked to Roy about the possibility of returning to the farm after the two weeks, for he would then have to find a permanent roof over his head as well as a second part-time job.

The boy had just one worry: home. Sometimes the thought wakened him. It was high time he wrote to Waterford. Maybe everything would be all right when they heard that he was earning an honest living. But he wouldn't write just yet, for he was much too busy.

"Condon, eh?" asked the somewhat older man who was ladling the soup.

Patrick suddenly forgot to hold out his mess tin. He had a vague feeling that he'd met this man before, but with the white kitchen hat and spotless apron that blinded him in the midday June sun, the boy couldn't see his face very well. The fellow behind him poked him in the ribs.

"Uh, John, uh, Condon, that's right," he stammered in surprise. He was still getting used to his first name. "How did you know . . ."

"Hey!" a voice from the line interrupted impatiently. "Can't you choose between soup and soup?"

Patrick quickly put his tin forward.

"Tom," replied the server, and he nodded with a smile. He ladled deep into the kettle and treated

Patrick to a full portion of soup with lots of pieces of oxtail. "Pay no attention to those farm boys behind you," he said quietly. "Ranting like that won't get them their meal a minute sooner." He leaned forward. Patrick judged the cook's mate to be at least forty-five.

"You know where to find me if you need anything," Tom added, and he winked.

"Hey!" The voice from the back was louder now.

"All right, all right!" Tom answered.

Patrick quickly moved along with his overflowing soup tin. He sat down at one of the unoccupied tables in the courtyard. How did he know this Tom? Was it at the harbour in Waterford? The cattle market in Ballybricken, perhaps? He was searching his memory in vain, trying to place the kitchen worker's face. For a few seconds he feared that the man was among the dissatisfied customers from one of those countless jobs he'd had in the harbour. But no, this man's friendliness had appeared genuine.

Patrick slurped the delicious soup. Eating outside in this weather was wonderful, better than being in that stuffy soldiers' mess in the barracks. He concentrated on fishing out the last pieces of meat.

"The King's Arms," a deep voice called.

Patrick's spoon fell into the soup. He saw the cooking hat right in front of him.

"The cafe right here in Clonmel . . ."

It began to dawn on Patrick. He had forgotten the name of the pub, but of course *that* was it: last week, the fifth Guinness, which they had toasted to their success—this man had paid for that round.

"Tom! Of course!" exclaimed Patrick, a little too enthusiastically now. He couldn't have remembered the man's name for a million pounds.

"Weren't you having fun then?"

"Just give me a good bowl of soup," answered Patrick, and he laughed. He had no desire to talk about his hangover. "Do you work here in the kitchen, Tom?"

The man removed his hat. "Every now and then. It's a nice job, I tell you. Lots of variety. You get that after working here almost thirty years." He extended his hand. "Thomas Carthy, born and bred here in Clonmel."

"John Condon," said Patrick.

"Call me Tom or Tommy. Where are you from, John?"

"Waterford."

"Port Láirge!"

"Right. Do you know the area?" Patrick asked. To his surprise, he felt immediately at ease with this man. Was it Tom's gaze, so direct but so friendly, too? Was it his soothing voice?

"The pig market. I was there once or twice with my uncle, when I was a young chap."

"Ballybricken?" asked Patrick, wide-eyed.

"Yes! That's what it's called, now that you mention it."

"That's where I'm from!" said Patrick, but he quickly caught himself. "You don't know anyone there by chance, do you?"

"Have you something to hide, John Condon?" Tom teased.

"Of course not. Why?" Patrick was completely unsettled. "Why should I?" he added, trying to recover from his outburst.

"A bright little guy you are . . . for your age."

"Carthy! Come here!" A thickly whiskered man with a cooking hat that was clearly taller than Tom's shouted over the table in their direction.

"That's the chief-cook-sergeant. Keep your chin

49

up, John Condon!" Tom placed his white kitchen cap at an angle on his head and hurried back to the soup line.

TWO WEEKS LATER
20 June 1913
CLONMEL

Half Soldier

The heavy barracks door closed behind Patrick with a thud.

"See you soon, John!"

"See you later!"

The men's chattering to one another as they departed was turning into an unintelligible buzz.

"Get home safely!" a voice called cheerfully in the distance.

Wherever that *may be,* Patrick thought wistfully, even though the call hadn't been meant for him.

The gigantic bolt slid into the lock. The wooden bar moved into place with a dry cracking sound. The entrance to the army depot was closed for the night, sealed like a city gate in the Middle Ages—no one allowed in, no one allowed out.

"So, here you are, John," he said out loud to himself. "It's up to you now. If I can be you in the army, let's see if I can be you outside the army, too." He turned around and looked at the high wall of the barracks with deep respect. His training was over. *Part-time soldier, without a roof over my head,* he thought. *Half soldier and half good-for-nothing.* Seventeen years old to the outside world, much younger in his thoughts and in his heart.

As Patrick strolled toward the centre of the town, he wondered how he was going to fill his life and his wallet in the coming months. As soon as he turned eighteen, so to speak, he wanted to try his luck as a professional soldier. In the meantime, he had to be careful not to fall out of his role as a seventeen-year-old. His very first concerns now were to find a second job and decent shelter.

He had not left the military domain in two weeks. The barracks and grounds, the woods and stores, had become his new little world. The iron discipline and the harassing by the veteran soldiers had been tough to take. But he had been swept up by the genuine team spirit and unshakable enthusiasm of the recruits.

When Patrick saw the lights appear in the windows of the cafes, he realised that evening was fast approaching. He needed a place to sleep before dark. He hesitated. Should he go see Thomas Carthy, who perhaps could advise him? Or should he just rent a room in the town? Or simply return to that old, trusty barn, as he had planned? As he stared at the tips of his shoes, he noticed that shamrocks were blooming between the jagged cobblestones. He bent down and picked one. "A four-leaf clover," he called in surprise. *Summer begins tomorrow,* he realised. *A day to do something nice, a day to begin something new.*

He turned around. Fifteen minutes later, he lay stretched out in the straw. He had returned to the barn. No one would bother him there.

"Hey, soldier boy!" The voice sounded as if it were reverberating in the belly of a freighter.

Patrick rubbed the sleep from his eyes. *I didn't even take off my clothes or shoes,* he thought. *I must have fallen asleep right away.*

"It's afternoon, John," said the voice, which was nearby now. "The sun is already high in the sky. It's a shame to be sleeping in like this."

Startled, Patrick propped himself up on his elbows. A cone of glaring white light was coming straight through the open door and shining on his lower legs. He could see a silhouette in front of the door through his fluttering eyelashes.

"How about a hearty breakfast?"

"Roy, it's you!"

The farm hand threw a linen sack of provisions onto the straw next to the boy. "And here's a jug of fresh milk." He reached into a bin that stood outside the door.

"Thanks, Roy. This is fantastic. You haven't forgotten me," exclaimed Patrick, and lit into the food immediately. He was famished.

"Congratulations, little soldier! You withstood the test, I hear."

Patrick could only bring forth a few *mmm*s and nod with enthusiasm as he chewed and chewed. He realised that Roy must have contacts in the city or in the barracks. Patrick washed down the hunks of bread with a slug of lukewarm milk, then decided to ask his question straightaway. "Would you have a job for me?"

Roy didn't seem a bit surprised. "Who knows," he answered. "But how's this going to work?" He rubbed his thumb over his pointing finger. "Cash down."

"All right, Roy. I'll pay you. Tomorrow, after my first real day of service, I'll get my first wages. A full two weeks' wages, you understand!"

"Not bad. I'm counting on you, John Condon."

How on earth does he know my last name? I never told him, thought Patrick.

"Can you do some farming?"

"For the time being, yes."

"These are busy days here. Crops to be tended, and soon the harvest. And then the animals. All help would be welcome, I think."

"Fine. When do I begin?" Patrick asked, a little too eagerly.

"Just a minute. I'll have to ask Mr. McGuinness first. Can you drive a team of horses?"

"As well as the best of them," Patrick lied. "And I'm good with cows, too. I worked at the cattle market in Waterford, you see. Ballybricken."

"Ten percent for me," said Roy, very businesslike. "And that's not a bad deal. Let me work it out with the farmer. I know what you should charge; you don't." He winked and clapped Patrick on the shoulder.

The first workday in the barracks was like a dream. And it became more obvious with each task that this dream was real. Clonmel's reserve corps had recognised Patrick as a soldier—a part-time soldier, to be sure, not yet in the regular British Army. But still, he was a member of the military.

First they proceeded to the kitchen. Patrick and the five other recruits received their mess kits. The next stop was the tailor, who had worked very hard during the previous two weeks, making a gray-blue two-piece uniform for each man. Patrick couldn't tear his eyes away. He thought it was wonderful, especially with the shoulders that displayed the insignia CLONMEL—COUNTY WATERFORD. A gold harp, the symbol of Ireland, gleamed on each lapel.

"These are your summer uniforms," the tailor explained. "There's still time enough to make the winter version."

The last stop was the arsenal. The gunsmith was a tall, wiry fellow around fifty years old who smelled like lubricating oil. On the workbench behind him was a revolver that had been completely disassembled. "Don't touch it," he warned when he saw Patrick's admiring gaze.

Patrick wanted to ask if it was a Belgian FN, but he thought that would be a bit inappropriate on his first day.

"Get this into your head," said the gunsmith in a clear but friendly way. "You may never come to this locale alone or without permission." Slowly and carefully he allowed his gaze to pass along the six faces. "Anyway, it's always locked up tight, even when I'm here."

The recruits had already noticed the number of locks on the iron-fitted door and the grating in front of it.

"And your rifles are behind the screen."

Patrick watched in suspense as the man pulled on an iron roll-down shutter from above and revealed about thirty rifles. They were hanging neatly from a rack, and all were double-locked with a steel bar and a chain.

"Remember your number, and always set your weapon back in the same space." The chain jingled furiously as the gunsmith pulled it through the many rings, allowing it to fall in a heap next to his feet.

The recruits were each handed a rifle, one by one. Even though Patrick and his comrades had drilled with such a weapon dozens of times, this was completely new, for each of them now had his own rifle, his own personal weapon. Patrick was a real soldier now—or rather, a half soldier.

Half Farmer

Patrick had guard duty at the arsenal two, sometimes three, days a week, and he had the night watch every now and then. It wasn't really an exciting occupation, except for the time a stag got his antlers caught in the fence. It had been pitch-dark. The animal had created such a ruckus that Patrick and his mate were scared to death. They thought it was a burglar and even fired a warning shot. That shot elicited considerable moaning from the commander, and the soldiers joked about the incident for weeks. But Patrick loved this man's world, even though he had hoped for more action.

There was plenty of action on the farm during that summer of 1913. Roy arranged a sweet little deal between Patrick and Mr. McGuinness. Of course, he remembered to take his own cut, too. Patrick received room and board on the large farmstead. He set up a modest room next to Roy's, above the horse stalls. It was nice and warm at night and cozy, too, with the sounds of the animals below. However, it was a room that had quite a smell.

Paul McGuinness was an energetic, hard-working young man. Together with his wife, Sinead, they had taken over the farm from her uncle.

"Whoever is willing to roll up his sleeves is welcome, certainly in the summer," he said when Patrick had been introduced to him. "How old are you, John?"

"Seventeen, sir."

"Just call me Paul."

The farmer was a down-to-earth fellow. Patrick could see that Roy was crazy about him. "What a coincidence. My youngest brother, Brian, is also seventeen. He's in Dungarvan, down on the coast. That's where we're from."

"Oh, really?" said Patrick, somewhat carelessly.

"In what year were you born, John?"

"Nine . . ." Patrick faltered and felt the blood rush to his face. *Nineteen-oh-one,* he'd almost blurted out. He could tell that Paul had noticed his slip. "One . . . one of my brothers is named Brian, too," he lied as he managed a sick laugh.

"Another coincidence," said Paul, and he chuckled.

Paul McGuinness was very flexible. Patrick gave him his work schedule at the barracks and was allowed to help out on the farm as often as he wanted. He quickly felt at home there. *I'm more at ease here than I was on Wheelbarrow Lane,* he thought. He was a bit uneasy with this realization.

Trapped!

Plowing, harrowing, sowing, tending the animals. It seemed like a crash course in farming. Patrick helped out as much as he could and earned a substantial salary for his efforts. Usually he worked alongside Paul and Roy, who were diligent drudges but always good-humoured. The two of them laughed through the oppressive July and August heat that hung over South Ireland. Patrick rose to the challenge and plodded along, though it took effort to keep up with them.

Patrick appeared to have a remarkable way with animals. He could effortlessly harness the two horses in the morning and unhitch them in the evening. Paul quickly noticed this and sometimes let him drive the team, allowing him to take the fully loaded wagon from the field to the farm and sometimes even to nearby customers in Clonmel. Whenever Patrick had a free evening, he helped milk the cows or feed the pigs without being asked. Paul McGuinness and his young wife were delighted with him. Even though they hadn't expressed it in so many words, that was what Roy had told him.

Patrick Condon had found his niche on the farm in no time at all, though occasionally he yearned for freedom, for the luxury of doing absolutely nothing. Sometimes he even considered returning to Port Láirge, to the guttersnipes of Waterford, and to the little house at number two Wheelbarrow Lane. His thoughts often dwelled on his mother. *What would she be doing now? What would she be thinking?* he wondered.

The hardest thing for Patrick was being with

men and having to listen to their racy jokes and other crude talk, especially when girls were around. The language itself didn't bother him; in fact, he thought all that macho talk was cool. But he didn't always understand their slang when women were discussed. He hadn't learned anything from his sisters in that regard, especially at that low level. At the Waterford harbour, he had often had the feeling that the dockworkers were laughing twice: first at their own coarse jokes or dirty remarks, and then at him. He knew that his army comrades had chuckled more than once at his expense, but he had simply shrugged it off and tried to come back with a clever remark of his own.

The Letter

A yellowish light was flickering in the little room above the horse stall. It came from an oil lamp, which hung on a string that had been fastened to one of the roof ridges. Patrick was sitting on a milk stool, hunched over a small plank that rested on his knees. He lay his pen on the bed and read through the letter one last time.

Clonmel, 3 September 1913

Dear Father, Mother, Kate, Peter, Margaret,
and John,

This letter will certainly come as a
surprise. As you can see, I'm alive and well.
And I have good news. Maybe it will sound
unbelievable, but I've been a part-time
soldier for about two months now. What do
you think of that? I tried my luck at the
local county militia here in Clonmel. I had
to bluff my way through, because they
won't take boys my age (just like at the
harbour). But I had nothing to lose. If the
militia had turned me down, I'd have come
back to Port Láirge and spent my life at
the docks or at the brewery.

Oh, and I'm called John here, when you
write back to me.

Mother, I'm sorry if I hurt you. You
know me better than anyone—you know that
I've always wanted to be a soldier. And you
know that I'll be all right. I should have
told you goodbye, but I was afraid that
you'd all laugh at me for trying to join the
militia.

Father, I'm truly sorry. I hope I
can explain it to you again someday. But

remember, I'm earning more here than I did in Waterford. When I have time off, I work on a farm for people who are very good to me.

Father and Mother, if it's all right with you, I'll do my best to come home soon. By Christmas at the latest, if the commander lets me. What do you think? Anyhow, don't worry about me. I have lots to eat and good clothes. And if I come, I will bring along my savings, which is more money than I could have ever earned at home.

Tell everyone I said hello, including Mollie and the baby. And the priest and Mr. Baldwin, who will be reading this to you. Ask him to write back so that I'll know about coming for Christmas. I'll wait for your answer.

Your son,
Patrick

P.S. Again, please address your letter to JOHN Condon.

Patrick had swiped the sheets of paper from the guardroom of the barracks. At the newsagent, he had bought a postage stamp and two envelopes, one extra in case he made a mess of the first one. For weeks he had kept the writing paper under his pillow; his thoughts had needed time to ripen.

Patrick wasn't fluent with a pen. He had chosen his words very carefully, but he had particularly grave misgivings over the part about his false name. He was especially afraid that his parents would send someone to bring him home for good or even write a letter to the army commander.

Patrick held his breath as he slipped the letter into the post box. And for the first time since that five-pint drinking binge, he went to the King's Arms, to wash away his emotions.

Then he began to wait impatiently for a reply.

The Tension Grows—in Europe, Too

Days turned into weeks, and weeks into a month. Still there was no answer.

"No, boy, no post for you today," the corporal in the guardroom would say with a sigh when Patrick made his daily visit. He dropped by to check even when he was off duty.

"A girl in Waterford, eh?" the corporal had called

to him a couple of times with an amused wink. "Maybe you should go visit her!"

It's not a girl. It's my mother, Patrick would think.

October had arrived. It looked as though life had quieted down on the McGuinness farm. The weather was raw and chilly. Gradually all the chores were being done indoors. The animals were spending more and more time in their stalls, and most of the work went toward feeding and caring for them. Patrick was still welcome; he kept his room above the horses and felt at home there, but he really wasn't needed any longer. He helped out with the upkeep of the machinery and buildings every so often. He now took his meals in the barracks as frequently as he could, even though Paul and Mrs. McGuinness never charged him a cent for food.

In any case, Patrick greatly enjoyed army life. All part-time soldiers who were available were given the chance to rack up more service hours than usual. "It all has to do with the Home Rule Bill," the boy would hear. It was obvious that this new law was often discussed among his colleagues, but not when their superiors were around. Ever since the previous year, when the London Parliament had promised to give Ireland more independence, tensions had been surfacing all over the country. Public speeches were delivered in halls and squares. Supporters of an Irish Catholic republic were being confronted by Protestants who preferred to stay under British rule, especially in the north. Patrick was indifferent to politics, but the situation was favourable to him and his companions because it meant more work. Vigilance was markedly stepped up, even in the south. Guard duty took on a certain grimness; Patrick felt that it wasn't a game anymore.

At the same time, politicians and generals all over Europe were preparing for something much bigger. They were anxiously watching Germany as it became a military giant, ready to conquer the entire continent. Could war be avoided for much longer?

"There's something in the air," the oldest soldiers whispered, and Patrick understood that they were talking about more than just this Home Rule on which so many people had pinned their hopes.

"The old continent is stirring up a hornet's nest again," Thomas Carthy claimed when the boy went to see him. Patrick was visiting his pal more and more often now. Tom lived with his wife, Mary, in a stone cottage at 34 River Street. They had no children, even though Tom was forty-five years old.

"What?"

"The Kaiser," Tom began gravely. He moved his feet a little closer to the red-hot brazier of the peat stove. "I don't know anything about politics," he continued, "but it looks like the Germans need more room. Factories are springing up out of the ground like toadstools. They're rich but they want more land."

"Who says?" Patrick asked.

"Sooner or later those Fritzes will break loose, I tell you." Without commenting further, Tom waved a newspaper that had been lying behind him on an armchair.

Patrick shrugged. He had never held a newspaper before in his life.

"Lebensraum," Tom tried to pronounce in his best German. "The papers say that they want more living space."

"But Germany is a huge, huge place," Patrick suggested earnestly.

"Even though they're very rich, they're limping behind other countries," Tom explained like a seasoned schoolteacher. "If you calculate how spread out the French domain is, with all its colonies, and then there's the British Empire—"

"Where the sun never sets," Patrick solemnly chimed in.

"So big that those English even have to grab up Ireland," grumbled Tom's wife, who seldom spoke.

"No politics, woman!" Tom curtly reprimanded her.

And what are we talking about, then? Patrick wondered as he winked at Mrs. Carthy. Not wanting to add fuel to the fire, however, he kept that thought to himself. "Will we be called up more often now? Because of the Germans?" he asked.

"Of course. There's still the Home Rule, but those Fritzes, they play a part, too."

"Will there be a war?"

"Oh, it probably won't come to that. Let's hope."

"Well, I'd like to teach that Kaiser a lesson." Patrick raised his fist up into the air.

Tom and Mrs. Carthy burst out laughing.

TWO WEEKS LATER

October 1913

CLONMEL

A Rude Awakening

"I can't pass up this chance!" Patrick's eyes sparkled as he looked at Thomas Carthy.

"You've got to be at least eighteen," exclaimed his friend, and he winked. That gesture removed all doubt; Tom was on to him.

"Eighteen? That can be arranged, Tom," Patrick answered, laughing boldly. "My God! The Special Reserve! Not the real army, but almost!"

"You have a fair chance. There's a big demand for soldiers. They'll be recruiting in Waterford. You'll be able to go home again."

"Home, yes . . ." Patrick grew quiet all of a sudden. "They never did get in touch with me after I sent my letter."

Patrick didn't want to burn any bridges as he rushed away from Clonmel. He had just gotten settled in there.

"Whatever happens, you needn't feel ashamed to return," Tom said as they discussed the possibilities. "If your plans fall through, just come back to work here after your furlough. And if you're accepted into the Special Reserve, there's still a good chance you'll be stationed here in Clonmel. Thus we hold with the hare and run with the hounds."

Tom knew what to do and quickly arranged everything for Patrick. Because the boy had put in extra service hours, he had earned a week's leave. It was enough time to travel home and try his luck at recruitment into the Special Reserve. And he had time to hurry back to the army depot in Clonmel if need be. He wrote a letter of resignation in which he thanked everyone for the chances he'd been given. He was careful to stress the fact that he wasn't leaving the army; on the contrary, he wanted to advance in the military. Tom kept the letter and promised to make sure that the colonel would receive it if Patrick didn't return on the appointed day. If the boy failed to make the Special Reserve, he would simply come back after his week's leave.

"You're more than a second father to me," he whispered a bit shyly to Tom. "You're a true friend."

Immediately after his last evening on duty, Patrick went as planned to the Carthys at 34 River Street. He knocked twice. Then he knocked again. Tom opened the front door.

"Ah, finally," Patrick said curtly. The heat from the peat stove blasted him in the face.

"Did everything go all right?" Tom asked.

The boy nodded. "Is Mrs. Carthy here?"

"She's sleeping."

"Does she know anything?"

Tom shrugged. "What she doesn't know won't

hurt her. Come, let's quickly run through the plans again."

"Okay, but first this." Patrick reached into his pocket and pulled out an envelope. "For the McGuinnesses. Will you give it to them? They've done everything for me."

Tom took the letter hesitantly.

"And this is for Roy." Patrick gave Tom a bank note. "I owe him money. This should be enough. Tell him that I . . ." He felt a lump rising in his throat.

"You can count on me," said Tom.

"He wouldn't be able to read a letter anyway," said Patrick hoarsely.

Fifteen minutes later, a shadowy figure walked along the house façades and out of Clonmel. Patrick was somewhat conflicted. He could still feel his friend heartily embracing him when they'd said goodbye to each other, almost like a father would to a son.

He quickened his pace. He figured that he had at least a twelve-hour walk ahead of him. He needed to stop during the journey in order to grab a quick bite. He would be smarter this time, staying on the main roads and hitching as many rides off horse cars as possible. After all, Waterford was a long way, even for a trained soldier.

Just four short months ago, Patrick had travelled this same route in the opposite direction, with wild ideas and a head full of questions. Although different thoughts haunted him tonight, at least as many questions were running through his mind. How would the people of Waterford react to his visit? His friends, the street tramps, the stray dogs, but especially those at home . . .

A strong wind began to blow, dry and ice cold. *My leather cap,* he thought, shrugging his shoulders. He reached into his knapsack and took out a warm wool-lined hat. He pulled the earflaps down against the raised collar of his jacket. He put his everyday hat into his duffel bag and groped farther down to make sure his military cap wasn't getting wrinkled. *As long as the weather stays dry, I'll be content,* he thought. With a bowed head he walked briskly on toward home, his real home.

It was in the afternoon of the next day that Patrick looked across the wide, watery expanse of the Three Sisters and recognised the towers of Port Láirge in the distance. They had never looked so beautiful. The biting wind was blowing over the rivers and causing his lips to feel chapped. In spite of the discomfort, he stopped and stared, motionless, for many minutes. The harbour was surprisingly quiet on a Sunday; there were no trails of smoke or steam rising from the ships.

Patrick walked along the River Suir toward home. The clock tower of the Holy Trinity chimed once. The tower of Christ Church chimed immediately afterward, followed by the clocks of the smaller, more modest parish churches in the distance.

He turned away from the river and walked toward the centre of the town. The streets were deserted. Residents were eating a meal or taking a nap to get ready for a rough workweek. Even though he felt warm, Patrick kept his coat buttoned all the way up. He was approaching his neighbourhood now. His heart was beating in his throat.

"If that's not Patrick Condon, I'll eat my hat!" he heard someone call out far behind him. He turned around in surprise. Two familiar heads appeared from behind a fence about a hundred metres away.

"Rogers and O'Sullivan!" Patrick exclaimed unwittingly. *I couldn't stand them and here I am now, waving as if we were old friends,* he said to himself angrily.

"Damn, Condon, it's *really* you!" Rogers looked at him as if he were the Virgin Mary.

"Patrick!" cried O'Sullivan in an overly friendly manner. "We thought you'd disappeared from the face of the earth!"

"I've come straight from Clonmel. The whole way on foot," he said. His voice no doubt sounded deeper and more serious than before.

"You seem older, Patrick," exclaimed O'Sullivan, and he laughed. "Everyone thought you'd fallen into the water. *We* didn't believe it, of course." He nudged Patrick with a conspiring look.

"Why did you go to Clonmel?" Rogers wanted to know. "Wasn't Waterford good enough for you?"

Patrick gazed about and saw that the street was still deserted. Slowly he opened his overcoat, one button at a time. The two boys watched, puzzled. Then they saw the copper clasp of his broad coupling strap and the gold buttons down his middle glimmering in the afternoon light. He exposed the lapels of his collar and let the gilded Irish harps flicker in the weak autumn sun.

"Damn, Condon . . ." was all Rogers could manage to say.

O'Sullivan studied him from head to toe for a good ten seconds while no one said a word. Patrick hesitated a moment, then pulled his army cap from his duffel bag and set it on his head.

"Wow! *Wooow!*" the two boys cried in chorus.

Patrick couldn't let the pleasure end there. He decided to remove his overcoat. *I'll show them the shoulder insignias of Clonmel,* he thought.

A bit farther up, another five heads appeared over the fence.

Even though Patrick felt like quite the man amid the gazes of the street children, what he wanted most was to be completely alone when calling on his parents. He was constantly wondering how they would react. In the meantime, the number of children appearing from behind the fence was growing;

there must have been twenty-five, and more kept coming. It was impossible to shake them off as he headed toward Wheelbarrow Lane. The news of his return had spread like wildfire, for more and more people were clamouring up to him. Everyone had questions to ask, and the children tried to touch him. Although Patrick attempted to remain friendly, he strode resolutely along as he passed the cattle market and turned onto his street.

"Patrick!" a shrill voice cried out all of a sudden.

The sound of his name chilled the marrow of his bones.

"Patrick!" The voice was louder and more anxious now.

He stiffened. The crowd moved aside for him.

"Mother . . ." His knapsack fell to the ground. A weeping woman with two screaming girls at her heels rushed up to him. They fell into each other's arms. Kate, his older sister, grasped his shoulders. Margaret, the younger, grabbed at his hips. With his eyes shut tight, he pressed his mother to his chest and listened to her sobs.

There he was after all those months, at number two Wheelbarrow Lane, home again at last.

"Stupid boy . . ." His mother shook her head. "Stupid boy," she repeated again and again. "How could you do such a thing to us?"

Patrick looked at the floor and dared only to steal an occasional shy, quick glance at his mother and sisters, who sat staring at him with red, uncomprehending eyes. His mother held his hand. She kept sniffing and wiping her eyes on her sleeve. Her face was happy and angry at the same time.

"Tell me now, where have you been?"

"Didn't you get my letter?" he asked in surprise.

"We did. Father took it to Mr. Baldwin because none of your brothers and sisters were in. We had no idea who in God's name could have written a letter. The only letter we'd ever received was when Aunt Ella lay dying."

"And did the teacher read my letter to you?" Patrick pressed on impatiently.

"He read it to your father. I wasn't there . . ." She broke into sobs.

Patrick felt helpless.

"When he heard the teacher say that the letter

came from *you,* he tore it up immediately. He was furious—he scarcely wanted to know what was in it. He was going to kill you, he said! Your own father!"

Patrick cursed himself and wished that he had never returned. No, he wished that he had never run away from home in the first place.

"Where is Father now?" he suddenly called out in panic. "And John? And Peter?"

"Don't worry, they won't be coming home today," she assured him. "We wouldn't be sitting here if your father were around. Harsh words have been spoken about your possible visit."

"So you knew that I was coming after all?" he said, puzzled.

"Mr. Baldwin told me what was in the letter."

"But I didn't give the exact day of my arrival, did I?"

"No, but on Thursday evening we received your telegram."

"What telegram? I didn't send any—"

She held the message under his nose before he could finish.

```
Clonmel Post Office
Sender: John Condon, Militia
   Battalion of the City
Coming home Sunday./ STOP/
Everything's OK./ STOP/
Love/STOP
John, Tom, and Roy/STOP/
```

"The postman said that perhaps Tom and Roy were coming as well. Who are those two?" she asked.

Patrick stood as if he were nailed to the floor. At first he was speechless. "Tom and Roy?" he suddenly sputtered. "I'll have to tell you about them. Tom and Roy!" He burst out laughing. "Those devilish sneaks! And you specifically sent Father away because you knew I was coming?"

"I persuaded your father to go with your brothers to visit his family in Tramore for the weekend. Mollie and the baby have gone to her parents for a few days."

"If only I'd known about it before! All this worry . . ." That Thomas Carthy had made the plans with Roy, who therefore knew everything! The thought of the inevitable confrontation with his father had kept him up for hours these past three nights. Those two in Clonmel had grown to know him well—so well that they'd conspired to help him!

"Were you afraid that Father would hurt me?" Patrick was serious now.

She nodded wordlessly.

For the first time in years, ever since he was a sweet, naive little fellow, Patrick stared long and hard into his mother's eyes. Her face revealed the difficulties he had caused her, how torn she was in choosing between him and his father. She waited silently while he searched for words.

A Recruit Again . . . and a Step Up

He was back home, even if it might be for only a short time. Just being called "Patrick" again felt wonderful. Sometimes his false name hindered him like an overly tight jacket. He talked and talked about his new life in Clonmel that Sunday afternoon and through the entire evening. He noticed how quickly his mother perked up as he charmed her with his stories. He looked healthy and well dressed and he'd saved a pretty penny, besides. Perhaps the situation wasn't so bad after all. Father Condon would quickly come around, Patrick and his mother hoped, when he saw how much money his lost son had earned in such a short time. Patrick's dad had been out of work more often than ever during the past months, Patrick learned.

Father, Peter, and John were due home Monday afternoon. Over breakfast, Patrick arranged for his mother to speak privately with her husband as soon as he returned.

In the meantime, Patrick, using his alias, John Condon Jr., put on his civilian clothes and left for the city centre of Waterford. He planned to inform the personnel at the army recruiting office how and when he could report for duty. Just before he entered the office, he ran into Sergeant Bixby, an old comrade of his father's.

"Ah, the little Condon!" he exclaimed. "Back home again, so I hear?"

Even though Sergeant Bixby didn't live far away, it was obvious that the news was spreading very quickly. Yet he made no mention of Patrick's military adventures in Clonmel. The boy sensed that the man knew more than most, although he might not know about his name change.

"So you want to be a recruit in the Special Reserve?" Sergeant Bixby asked in a stern voice. "A bit early, eh, fellow?"

Patrick felt himself blush. Was his entire plan going to fall through?

"Or rather," the sergeant continued, "a bit late. They begin here at nine o'clock. Come back tomorrow . . . when you're eighteen."

He clapped him on the shoulder and walked on, leaving Patrick speechless.

There was little time for bickering in the Condon house later that day. Father and son barely exchanged words. The man had never been much of a gabber, but his silence hurt. Embarrassed, Patrick tried to start with "Sorry, Father," but was unable to say more. His father acted as if he hadn't heard him. The tension in the air could have been cut with a knife. His mother followed the two with eagle eyes but was more than satisfied that everyone in the house was at least keeping quiet.

After four o'clock, Father put his coat on "to see if there is work to be had in the city tomorrow." He disappeared for the rest of the day.

Patrick and his brother John grabbed the chance to talk freely about their adventures of the past months. Kate and Margaret hung on every word. Mother listened quietly as she folded the washing and prepared Patrick's favourite mutton stew.

24 OCTOBER 1913
RECRUITING OFFICE, SPECIAL ARMY RESERVE
WATERFORD

The Big Test

The preliminaries went faster than Patrick had feared. When asked his occupation, he wrote "bottler," a job that could be verified at Sullivan's Brewery. It was probably better not to put down "dockworker" because of that little incident with Fatso, even though it had been months before. As for "cow watcher," that was something he'd been only sporadically at the cattle market. "Soldier" seemed totally dangerous, for imagine if they were to sift through his file in Clonmel. In the space marked "age," he had confidently marked "eighteen," a year older than what he had reported to the militia in June.

Obviously there was a great need for reservists. A tall boy who was turning eighteen in December got a second chance and a new application form with the comment that it would be better not to report an exact date of birth. Two old men and a slovenly fellow who reeked of gin a bit too early in the day were taken aside and whisked back to the street a few minutes later.

The names of the candidates were now called up one by one: "Adams, Condon, Connolly, Dempsey . . ." Patrick was the second to be examined by Major-Doctor Power. *Back to square one,* he thought as he stood there naked. *I've already played this little game.*

He was weighed and measured; his eyes were examined and he had to take some deep breaths. The doctor's only question concerned the scars on one leg—a souvenir from Clonmel, when Roy had been gathering hay and had torn Patrick's pants to shreds with his pitchfork.

The information for his medical file was notated in thick black pen strokes:

Stated age: 18 years

Occupation: bottler

Religion: Roman Catholic

Height: 5 feet 4 inches

Weight: 118 lbs.

Hair: brown

Eyes: brown

Vision: L & R, 6 on 6

Vaccinations: right 1, left 2 (infirmary)

Outstanding characteristics: 3 scars left thigh, outer side

"No problem, not for me," said the friendly major-doctor. "Next!"

An hour later, Patrick stood facing the recruiting officer, Captain J. P. T. Mackesey. The man went over a number of personal questions out loud while Corporal Conway steadily dipped his pen into the ink pot and scratched away, filling an entire sheet of paper. It went quickly, except when Patrick hesitated a moment after he was asked, "Have you ever served in the Royal Navy, the Militia, the Volunteers, etc.?"

Actually, my experience would be an advantage, he suddenly thought.

"Have you ever been in the army?" inquired the captain, scarcely looking up.

"No," Patrick answered reluctantly.

"Put your hand on the Bible," the corporal commanded.

"Repeat after me," began Captain Mackesey. His voice was solemn. "I, John Condon, son of John Condon of Waterford, pledge my allegiance to His Majesty King George the Fifth, to his heirs or successors, and to the generals and officers of his armies."

Totally bewildered, Patrick then had to put his signature down in a space next to his filled-in name. His scribbling looked pitiful in contrast to the graceful letters of the military.

"Of course, there will be a brief examination of possible acquaintances whom we trust," said the captain without looking up. "If no objections arise, you'll be accepted. Soldier six-three-two-two, Private John Condon, congratulations and welcome into the Special Reserve of the Royal Irish Regiment."

"Thank you, sir," said Patrick. He jumped to attention, but the captain and corporal already had their eyes on the doorway.

"Next!"

A Raw Recruit

Patrick succeeded in exchanging a few words with his father that evening after all. When he said that the recruitment process had gone quickly, the man growled an indifferent "I see" to himself. "There never was any real work in soldiering anyhow," he remarked spitefully a bit later.

It grew quieter in the living room. Father spoke to his wife, but his words were meant for his son.

"And that pay—it's for us. Understood? The army covers his room and board. Drinking money and other expenses he can scrape together himself. He's cunning enough to do it."

It's one positive note, anyway, Patrick thought. He kept his mouth shut.

Training began in earnest the next day. The scores of recruits who had reported during the past weeks were arranged in long rows in the courtyard of the barracks and put through their first marching paces. It was a ludicrous sight, a disarray of large and small, colourful and gray, hats and caps, long coats and short jackets.

The big difference between this arsenal and the one in Clonmel was the cold, rigid manner of the noncommissioned officers here, to say nothing of the arrogant officers who were totally unapproachable to boys like Patrick. "John" Condon was merely soldier 6322 of the Third Battalion of the Royal Irish Regiment. Period.

For hours at a time, they were shouted at and scolded by tireless drillmasters. If the men made too many mistakes or if their training in marching, saluting, and turning didn't progress quickly enough, the sergeant ordered them to stand at attention, in the rain and the wind, for half the day if need be. Patrick was barely allowed to go home in the first weeks. His only protection against the raging officers was his experience. He never made mistakes, and he let the verbal abuse pass over him like water off a duck's back.

Recruit Condon led a true double life in those days. At the barracks he was "Little John" and eighteen. At home or with friends he was Patrick, a strapping lad of twelve. Only in a big city such as Waterford, or well away from this area, could he keep playing those two roles at the same time.

Occasionally Patrick was allowed to go home for a couple of days, such as at Christmastime and New Year's. Patrick realised that sooner rather than later he'd be sent to a different barracks, far from friends and acquaintances; therefore, he enjoyed every hour at home, where no one asked difficult questions. His relationship with Father remained awkward, but the man spent more time outside the house than inside. Patrick especially found his sister-in-law, Mollie, to be a breath of fresh air. She was much more cheerful and spontaneous than Kate and Margaret, though he had to admit that his sisters relied entirely on Mollie and were slowly blossoming because of her presence. Peter and Mollie's cute little toddler brought a great deal of liveliness to the household and had completely won over the girls—and him. Or was Patrick looking at women and families differently than he used to? His thoughts returned to Thomas Carthy and his wife, Mary. And to Roy and the McGuinnesses. How were they doing? He would have to send them all a Christmas card right away.

The World on Fire

Patrick's training in the Special Reserve lasted exactly four months. It was too long for his liking. He could barely wait to be treated as a real military man. And at the end of February 1914, the time had come; his efforts were rewarded and he was placed in the regular army. Soldier 6322, J. Condon, truly belonged to the Third Battalion of the Royal Irish Regiment now. The drillmaster didn't prolong the ceremony in the courtyard any longer than necessary, after which he informed the successful recruits that they would be sent immediately to Clonmel, where the battalion was headquartered. Patrick was looking forward to going. He craved the real soldier's life and longed to see his old friends again. And home? Now that the coziness of the Christmas holidays was past, the house on Wheelbarrow Lane suddenly seemed too small and too snug. He wanted space, an actual life, a return to freedom, which he'd already tasted for a bit. Therefore, saying goodbye to his family wasn't difficult in the least. And although his mother and sisters cried, Father was unflinching.

"At last, Tom!" Patrick lowered his rifle and threw his free arm around Tom's shoulder. "I'm finally back in Clonmel, happy to see you again." He sighed and wrested his arms from the straps of his knapsack, which Tom then took from him.

"Is everything all right with your wife, Tom? Will you give Mrs. Carthy my very best?"

"Everything's okay, thank you. And congratulations, eh? A soldier at last!"

Patrick led his friend aside. "There was no trouble

with my unexpected departure from the militia, was there?" he asked anxiously.

"I made sure of that, didn't I? Your resignation was no disaster for Clonmel. And I arranged for your personal items with the quartermaster and the men of the magazine. Just be matter-of-fact about it, and then no one will ask questions. In any case, we have a new colonel and he has other things on his mind besides wanting to shear a runaway sheep."

Tom was right. Old acquaintances in the barracks thought it was fine that Little John had climbed up to the regular troops. No questions were asked; he was accepted. Patrick Condon of Waterford had a new start. He put his past—his boyhood years, his double life— behind him. The world lay open before him. And his permanent name was John Condon now.

AUSTRIAN CROWN PRINCE AND PRINCESS MURDURED

From our correspondent in Sarajevo

Yesterday, 28 June 1914, while visiting the Bosnian capital of Sarajevo, the Austrian crown prince Franz Ferdinand and his consort, Sophie, were shot and killed by a Bosnian nationalist. Earlier that day, the royal couple barely escaped a bomb attack. Their chauffeur was able to accelerate just as the explosive rolled over the roadway, but three people in the following auto were injured. Seven spectators were hurt as well. As they were returning from the hospital, where the prince was visiting the victims, a certain Gavrilo Princip jumped onto the running board of the royal auto and at close range shot His Royal Highness Franz Ferdinand of Austria in the neck. Princess Sophie was struck in the lower belly. Both died at the scene. The perpetrator was immediately overpowered . . .

Thomas Carthy, frowning, folded up the evening paper. "I'm just an ordinary soldier who doesn't know much about politics, but this could well have set off a powder keg."

"You mean war?" asked John Condon, who was next to him on the bench. They were sitting in Tom's garden, enjoying the evening sun with a glass of beer in hand.

Tom didn't answer.

"Sarajevo isn't exactly in our backyard," said John. "Why are you worrying about it?"

"Austria is a good chum of the German Kaiser," replied Tom. "Europe will be too small if those Germans break loose. And don't think that war is a lark. Anyway, it hasn't yet come to that. Besides, you have to be nineteen to go to the front, soldier boy!"

"One more year!"

"Rookie," said Tom with a laugh.

A month later, on 4 August 1914, Germany invades Belgium. The Germans had figured on a free thoroughfare for attacking France, but it has turned out differently. "Poor little Belgium" is being crushed by "the Hun"—their women are being assaulted, their children murdered. That's what the London politicians and British newspapers are saying about the Germans. Little Belgium must be rescued. Great Britain immediately declares war on Germany. The entire British nation is turned upside down. Because the regular army numbers only 750,000 men, the minister of war, Field Marshal Lord Kitchener, seeks volunteers. He starts a media campaign and has posters created with life-size pictures of himself printed upon them. With his military mustache and military dress, Lord Kitchener addresses each British man threateningly, telling him to do his patriotic duty. "BRITONS, JOIN YOUR COUNTRY'S ARMY." And the minister in the poster points his finger at the reader: "KITCHENER WANTS YOU" or "REMEMBER BELGIUM." Hundreds of thousands of men let themselves be hustled by writers, journalists, schoolteachers, and hired speakers, all of whom urge the masses to join the war effort. Many Irishmen even believe that the English king will grant them true independence after the war if they report in droves to the front. It seems like a romantic adventure, a chance of a lifetime for real fellows, a great picnic for men among men. "*We'll be home for Christmas*" resounds in all of the English-speaking countries of the world. A healthy man must come up with good reasons not to participate. Besides, the minister has guaranteed each soldier a minimum weekly salary of seven shillings for as long as the war lasts. Many teenagers let themselves be dragged into the fray, too. You must be nineteen to go to the front, but most lie about their age. The recruiting agents merely look the other way.

For John Condon—Patrick, that is—the age problem was solved long ago. He is in the regular army now and is mobilised on 7 August 1914. And just like his oldest army friend, Thomas Carthy, and the rest of the Third Battalion, he would be put through a crash course in preparation for the real fight.

In Dublin's Fair City . . .

The usually quiet army post in the southern Irish town of Clonmel turns into an ants' nest. The barracks looks like a fortress of men who are armed to the teeth. Recruits come flocking in without stop, causing the buildings to nearly burst at the seams. Everyone is wound up, as if the enemy were to appear at the gate on that very day. Reports from Belgium and France seep in through the newspapers and are laid on thick. The First Battalion, which conscripted a lot of John and Tom's comrades, is the first to leave. No one knows where it is going. Later they hear that the battalion is fighting with the Tenth Division in Egypt and Palestine.

It's not long before the Third Battalion leaves by train and heads north. John Condon ends up in the vicinity of Dublin, where the Royal Irish Regiment stays in the countless barracks around the capital.

The men receive rigorous training in Dublin. Even so, John has a wonderful time: endless shooting practice in the freezing cold, marching with full packs for hours and hours, man-to-man combat, bayonet practice in which they attack huge straw dummies and heavy jute sacks that are swishing all around . . .

"Look, you have to turn the bayonet around in the damned Hun," says John as he demonstrates to Tom. "Then the wound won't heal." John learned about that from his old drill sergeant.

It's a game for young John as long as sand is spilled, not blood, Thomas Carthy thinks. The forty-six-year-old

Irishman secretly hopes that it will remain a game. But such a thought is better kept to oneself.

The British Army hauls the newest weapons out of the closet. John can't take his eyes off them. Biplanes and triplanes stretch in formation flight above the glowing rocky practice fields and are applauded by the foot soldiers. The pilots, clad in leather caps and goggles, wave to the men on the ground and disappear in their crafts behind the hills surrounding the city.

The regiment receives a demonstration of a gigantic Vickers machine gun. No one has ever seen the likes of it: a fire-spewing monster on a tripod and a water-cooling system to go with it.

"I could win the war all by myself with that," John crows.

Tom shrugs. "You need a whole platoon just to lug that thing along. Besides, *they* have those machine guns, too."

John throws his first grenade into a practice trench. *Get down to the ground, cover your ears, there's a dull bang, the earth shakes . . .* What an experience!

The captain walks approvingly among the crawling troops. Using his cane, he urges those lagging behind to move closer. A strange apparatus is being dragged over the field. The soldiers must come see this new gadget: a grenade launcher. Everyone admires this little machine. It looks like a portable mini cannon without a barrel. The captain inserts a blank cartridge, slips a whopper of a shell into the holder, and fires. The officer is applauded when the projectile is hurled effortlessly a hundred yards into the air.

"Those Fritzes don't stand a ghost of a chance, Tom!"

"The Germans weren't born yesterday. Their steel factories have been going at full speed in preparation for war," Tom says grimly.

In spite of the difficult military maneuvers, there is time for other activities, such as the compulsory afternoon review of troops for all those who don't have to crawl over the rocky practice fields of Dublin. It's a matter of hammering in the right spirit and discipline. Lieutenant Edmunds conducts his inspection and remains standing by John.

"Name?"

"Soldier Condon, John, number six-three-two-two, *sir!*"

"Sergeant-Major Lewis, make sure that this dirty sod gets his just punishment. Face isn't washed, hands are dirty, shoes are filthy."

John receives four days' confinement to his quarters. He must remain in the barracks during his free time. It's quite a blow, certainly now that groups of soldiers are allowed to spend an afternoon in the city.

"In Dublin's fair city, where girls are so pretty, I first set my eyes on sweet Molly Malone ..." All the men are singing and laughing at him as they leave the barracks. Disillusioned, John remains behind. He has lots of cleaning up to do.

When the sergeant-major conducts his inspection rounds an hour later, he finds that soldier 6322 is not in his room in the barracks. After two hours, John is back again. Lieutenant-Colonel Kavenagh gives him a proper dressing-down. "Where have you been? Taking a walk, perhaps? Condon, do you realise what you're risking? Desertion! And that carries the death penalty! This is war, man!"

"I'm sorry, sir," John says, trying to excuse himself. He comes off with a doubling of his punishment.

Just before dusk, his comrades return from Dublin. He can hear them singing in the distance: ". . . through the streets broad and narrow, singing cockles and mussels alive, alive-oh!"

That same month, November 1914, a few hundred men of the Second Battalion leave for an unknown destination. The excitement in the camps is great. Of course everyone knows that they'll be sent to the front in France. Most likely everyone has heard, too, that this same battalion was as good as annihilated during the very first battles, when the advancing Germans flattened "poor little Belgium." No one really wants to listen to those stories of their predecessors. Intensely jealous, John walks among the men of the Second Battalion and tastes the excitement that rises above their conversations.

"Are you coming with us, boy?" they shout, half drunk.

"I would if I could, and right away!"

There is promising news on 16 December. John and Tom's platoon is transferred from the Third Battalion to the Second. For the first time in months, John spends his evening drinking a couple of bottles of beer.

To his surprise, he meets his former neighbour from Waterford, Michael Mahoney, who has just arrived. He's in the Second Battalion, too.

"Hey, Patrick!" Mahoney calls. "So here you are, you brat!"

John gestures for him to be quiet.

Mahoney chuckles. "Sorry. 'John' is what I should say. You don't have to explain to me, lad. Our whole street knows about it anyway. And I can keep a secret."

It is already late in the evening. John is searching for his bed, his mind a blur after all the beer. "We're finally moving up, Tom." He is rattling on like a crazy alarm clock to his mate. "When the Royal Irish Regiment sends troops again, they'll almost certainly come from the Second Battalion! It'll be our turn then."

Thomas Carthy knows all too well why the Second Battalion needs fresh troops. At the front they are dying at an alarming rate. He grabs John just before he tumbles out of his bed.

The Last Christmas

The Second Battalion is clearly under the war's spell. The practice fights are harder and fiercer. Everyone in Dublin is trained and motivated and looking forward to the real confrontation with the enemy. The men expect each day to be *the* day, but they are kept hanging in the air. In their euphoric moments they show off for one another and say how much they would like to run a bayonet through a Fritz. When the battalion unexpectedly returns to Clonmel right before Christmas, the reactions are mixed. There is disillusionment, but relief too. A break is welcome.

Whoever lives nearby is allowed to leave the ever-crowded barracks. Tom has his wife and tiny cottage. John has his second home and his horses at the farm. He can't return to Waterford because it's too far. For the first time, he spends Christmas Eve without his family. Never before has he so missed the people of Wheelbarrow Lane. The holiday always used to be something special. Usually they stayed up extra late at home, drank a glass of whiskey, then left together to celebrate midnight mass at the parish church of St. Patrick of the Holy Trinity Without. John even misses his friends tonight. He doesn't want to bother Thomas Carthy and his wife, and the McGuinnesses are having their family over at the farm. Even Roy has gone out. Although John isn't on duty, he hangs around in the barracks for a while, chatting with the unlucky soldiers who must keep watch. He finally kills time in his room with a book of maps. The ticking of the clock on the wall is exasperatingly noisy and slow. At half past eleven he takes his jacket and cap from the clothes peg and heads for the church. He is one of the first to arrive, but by midnight the nave is full. All the faces are those of strangers. He thinks about what is to come—the front, the trenches that the men have been talking about every now and then. John is longing to go. He sees his frozen breath evaporating in the weak gaslight. The church radiates something very special: the living crib, the smell of the ox and the donkey, the thin voices of angels that reverberate high against the rafters, the centuries-old Celtic songs, and especially the darkness, the mystique of this nighttime service.

John can't take his eyes off the living figure of Mary. Is it his imagination? An omen? She looks exactly like his mother. Most people call her Mary, too, even though her real name is Catherine.

John goes calling on the Carthys on Christmas Day. Mary answers the door.

"Ah, the young Condon!" she exclaims. The

reunion is cordial, but John immediately notices that the woman is trying to hide her anxiety.

"I've come to get Tom. We have to be back at the barracks in an hour."

She nods and lets him in. "We have a visitor," she says. "He's just returned from the front." She points to a tall, thin soldier at the table. He is sitting with his back toward John.

"Jim, this is the boy I was talking about," Tom says. He motions for John to take a seat.

"My cousin Jim was wounded in Belgium," Tom continues. "He's in the Second Battalion."

John feels his heart begin to beat faster. A real soldier at the front, someone who has seen the war! *Really?* he almost calls out.

The man remains motionless. John would like to shake his hand, but stiffens when the stranger finally turns around. His right eye has been crudely sewn shut. Pink babylike skin is stretched over the area that was once his cheek. It's full of little wrinkles.

"Hi, John," says the man, breaking the silence. He raises his right arm, which is half gone. "Sorry, the rest of it is in Belgium." He extends his left hand now.

John stares at the deformed face in shocked

silence. This is not at all what a war hero should look like . . .

The humming of the stove fills the quiet room.

"He was allowed to leave the hospital for a little bit because it's Christmas," says Tom, trying to keep the conversation going.

"Do take a seat," Mrs. Carthy says to John. She sniffles.

A bottle of whiskey is on the table. Cousin Jim refills his glass and tells how they eagerly set foot in the French harbour city of Boulogne in August. Together with the BEF—British Expeditionary Force—they were the first to enter Belgium. Near Mons, their battalion was wiped off the map just as quickly as the Belgian troops were.

"It was terrible," Jim continues. "Those first deaths don't seem real. You can't believe it. Until you search for your best friends and find them without arms or legs or even heads." He gulps down his whiskey and gropes awkwardly for a handkerchief.

"Quiet, Jim," says Mrs. Carthy, trying to soothe him. "You don't have to talk about all this."

"I've got to," he answers aggressively. "Otherwise . . . otherwise . . ."

"Was that your last battle?" asks John. The others are startled, because the boy hasn't spoken until now.

"My last was a few weeks afterward, at Le Pilly."

Jim searches for words. In fits and starts, he tells how the Second Battalion, to which John and Tom now belong, had to compete against the superior strength of German cannons and infantry. It was pure suicide. Major Daniell led a greatly depleted battalion of 17 officers and 561 Irish boys. After the last, useless bayonet attack, with Daniell at the head, half the men lay dead and the other half were taken prisoner. Most were seriously wounded. Only thirty boys got away. Everyone thought that Jim was dead, but he ended up in a field hospital. That's where his eye was removed. His arm had to be amputated two days later.

"Home before Christmas!" Jim mutters cynically. He's a bit drunk. "Somehow I had imagined that this Great Picnic would be different."

Away at Last

John is not allowed to leave the barracks once the news of their departure is confirmed. Tom enters the room, where everyone is busy packing. He looks as though he has aged five years. John doesn't dare ask what saying farewell to Mrs. Carthy was like.

As they march out of the barracks a few hours later, a mass of spectators is standing at the gate. The military police do almost nothing to separate the throng from the soldiers.

"John! Tom!" A faraway voice rises above the turmoil.

"Over there." Tom points with little enthusiasm. He forces a smile.

"Hey, Roy!" John notices the farm hand, who pushes his way forward.

Roy hands John a small linen sack. "Blood pudding for your journey!" he calls excitedly. A burly MP grabs him by the collar.

"The others have come, too! Over there!" Roy adds. He is shoved back.

A little farther, in the third and fourth rows of people, John can just catch a glimpse of Paul and Sinead McGuinness waving and shouting enthusiastically.

"We'll get those Krauts!" John shouts. His voice is cracking, but no one can hear it above the noise.

John would like to forget the boat trip to France as quickly as possible. If the rocking and rolling doesn't do you in, you might well be sick as a dog from the stink of vomit in the overcrowded hold. Getting a bit of fresh air up on deck is no comfort, for there is always someone retching over the rails. John feels his best when he's with the horses. There must be a hundred of them stabled in the forecastle: splendid mounts as well as hefty farm animals, all requisitioned by the army, all taken from their quiet villages in Great Britain and lugged over the Channel to the front.

The battalion moves in long rows through the busy harbour of Boulogne-sur-Mer. The men march to the singsong music of three flutes and a couple of drums as they proceed in the direction of the station. John can see a terrified stallion being lifted onto the wharf by an enormous crane. His attention quickly shifts to the green banners that stand out above the bobbing of military caps. Here come the Irish, and those French "Frogs" and English "Tommies" need to know about it. John, who for many is the mascot of the Second Battalion, is handed a green-coloured banner, too. He has yet to receive his baptism by fire, but already he feels like a true hero now.

"The ragamuffins of Ballybricken should see me here, Mike!" he cries to Michael Mahoney, his former neighbour on Wheelbarrow Lane.

"Condon! Keep your pace!" a sergeant admonishes him.

John does a one-two skip and falls back in cadence. Way in the distance, he can see the battalion commander, Colonel Moriarty, leading the procession on horseback.

An unbelievably long train takes them eastward into France, almost to the Belgian border. For the time being, they end up in Rue de Bois, a little place in northern France, where they pitch their tents. It is teeming with green banners and ribbons, for other Irish newcomers have arrived. The Second Battalion Royal Munster Fusiliers are billeted here, too. Before they have fired a single shot, John, Tom, and their mates spend an evening of uproarious fraternising. They are treated to strong drink, stronger stories, lewd songs, and even a little concert.

"This war isn't half bad!" John screams above the

noise to Tom. "Here, this rum is for you. Much too strong for me!"

"Cheers!" Tom answers. "Santé, mademoiselle!" He has already had enough to drink. He laughs himself silly as he watches the sketches of the men dressed in women's clothes on the improvised podium.

"Do all women have those mustaches here?" a jokester asks during a momentary lull. Laughter erupts once more, and the veteran soldiers begin to sing again:

If the sergeant steals your rum, never mind.
If the sergeant steals your rum, never mind.
Know he's just a bloody sot;
Let him take the bleeding lot.
If the sergeant steals your rum, never mind.

A hundred men join in with each "never mind." Their shouts fill the tent. And the text grows lewder by the stanza.

The next day, reports are seeping through that units of the British Expeditionary Force have been ground into mincemeat at Neuve-Chapelle. John listens in surprise to the gruesome testimonies about the German barbed wire in northern France. He hears about the wounded boys, entangled for days, who were finally finished off. The British professional army was already greatly depleted six months ago at the Battle of Ypres. Now there is hardly anyone left.

John doesn't let himself become discouraged, however. *They won't trifle with us,* he thinks. Instead, he lets himself be carried away by those crazy marching songs as they stride toward the Belgian border. Only the men who have already been to the front know that they are singing in order to forget.

> *Mademoiselle from Armenteers, parlez-vous.*
> *Your pommes de terre frites*
> *They give us the squits.*
> *Inky pinky parlez-vous . . .*

A few hours later, these same men who were trying to outdo one another with their most vulgar of verses are on their knees in prayer. They're Irish soldiers, all of them, from different battalions. Green pennants are fluttering everywhere, for the men are proud of their heritage. There is talk again about Irish independence. "We can finally fight for it here," John hears someone say. "We'll let the English king see what we're worth."

The men are quiet as mice when Father Gleeson, the padre of the regiment, presides over the hundreds of bowed, bared heads. From high on horseback he offers his blessings and forgives each man his sins. Afterward, a resounding hymn rises to the sky: "Hail, Queen of Heaven!" The Virgin Mary effortlessly takes the spotlight from the Mademoiselle of Armenteers. Here and there a soldier brushes away a tear.

After prayers, the men swarm back to the encampment. Their voices are subdued. There is high tension in the air, an indescribable feeling of solidarity. Thomas Carthy is daydreaming, staring in the direction of the chaplain. The padre is folding up his portable altar and lashing it to his horse.

"Tom! Are you coming?" John calls.

His friend doesn't answer; he is lost in thought. John goes over and pulls on his sleeve.

"Oh," Tom says, startled. "Just a moment."

"Is something wrong?" John asks.

Tom shrugs. He has a faraway look in his eyes. "I think things will soon be getting serious here, John."

"Yes, I hope so, too."

Tom looks at his young friend and shakes his head. "You go ahead. I'll be along shortly."

John walks toward the camp. When he looks back, he sees his friend talking to Father Gleeson.

Soldiers in All Colours

Their battalion approaches the French-Belgian border. The soldiers spend the nights on farms; the first winter months of 1915 are cold and harsh. In the lost hours, John's comrades take silly pleasure in a pocket book called *French Lessons*. Reading does nothing for John. His head is full of anticipation of the war. Most of the men have other adventures on their minds—perhaps they can nab a French girl!

"Bone-jure, mademwezel. Como tolly voo?"

But when the farmer's daughter pokes her head around the barn door a little later, no one can utter a single word.

John has absolutely no knowledge of this area. He's aware that he's in France, of course, but France is a big country. They spend two days near the Katsberg, in a little place called Godewaersvelde. Because the British are unable to pronounce the name, they say "Gertie wears velvet." *It's such a pretty name for a French town—I'll have to remember it,* John thinks.

The battalion marches into Belgium that same week. They continue to proceed to Poperinge, a garrison city behind the frontlines. All soldiers are sent to the battlefield from "Pops"—first to Ypres, from where they will spread out over the surrounding villages and glowing landscape and take their positions. If they're lucky, they will return via Ypres to Poperinge.

The front has remained stationary these past few months. All the troops have dug themselves into trenches that stretch for kilometres. Some are only a few dozen metres from the enemy. A stubborn battle is being waged around Ypres. The Germans have moved their artillery to the tops of hills surrounding the city and beyond, where they can easily keep the French and British positions in range of their cannons and howitzers. The frontline runs diagonally across the map of Europe, from the north at Nieuwpoort by the North Sea down to Switzerland in the southeast. The line makes a marked bulge in the vicinity of Ypres; the British call this the "Ypres Salient." It is here in the thick clay that the horrifying history of the war is being written with the blood of hundreds of thousands of young men.

The icy wind rips into John's face. He pushes his cap farther down over his dark hair. The straps of the leaden rucksack dig into his shoulders. He must support his rifle with both hands. The hilly country roads, with their dangerously slick cobblestones, make marching difficult. All the men are complaining about their aching feet. John can see Poperinge in the distance. Just before they approach the first houses, they pass a farm with enormous Red Cross tents everywhere. Even though it's freezing, scores of soldiers are lying on stretchers outside. It slowly occurs to John that these are fresh corpses. This realization of death casts a shadow over the battalion as it marches by. The buzzing of voices stops; there is only the stark cadence of hundreds of boots on the cobblestones. Nurses walk in and out of the tents in silence. John sees two doctors in a heated discussion as they walk across the grounds to the field hospital. He hears fragments of English. Their white aprons are covered with blood. A long, piercing scream is coming from a hospital tent. John and his mates look around. The doctors don't react; they are lighting cigars.

A half hour later, the Second Battalion Royal Irish Regiment marches between the tall terraced houses of the Gasthuisstraat. Cafes and driveways are everywhere, and the local citizens and military personnel go in and out of them like bees swarming around a hive. The Irish turn up at the Grote Markt. It looks like a carnival. When the long rows of steaming bodies finally come to a halt, John hears a buzzing among the masses of spectators, who are curious about the new arrivals. Everyone calls out to John and his buddies; perhaps they have news from the motherland.

The men begin to joke with a group of Scottish soldiers. "It's some weather for a kilt, eh, Mac?" Michael Mahoney shouts.

"It's a good thing there's whiskey to warm you up," another Irishman adds with a laugh.

"But where would he keep his flask?" yells another.

One Scot takes off his plaid cap and raises his fists. His comrades calm him down and lead him away. As they depart, another Scot lifts his kilt defiantly and moons the Irish company. All the soldiers go crazy now and roar with laughter. The highlander is treated to catcalls.

"Look there," Thomas Carthy says a bit later. He points.

Everyone looks around. "Blacks!" they shout together.

A group of Senegalese soldiers in black-blue uniforms are shivering in the cold and watch the

Irish from a distance. They have bright red fezzes on their heads.

"What are those fellows doing here?" John asks his friend. He has never seen a black man before, like most Irishmen.

"They're West African troops from the French colonies. Troops from our colonies are here, too."

A few hours later, after everyone has found a place to sleep in an old factory, John and Tom go into the city. There are drinking houses galore, one smoky cafe after another. The citizens of Poperinge are earning good money from the war. There's no shortage of women, either. John stares in disbelief at mothers who turn a blind eye and allow their young daughters to be manhandled by grabby Tommies.

"As long as the soldiers pay," Tom says grumpily from his chair in a cafe. "In cash!"

Africans pass by the cafe without entering. John gazes at them through the window.

Money is spent freely indeed. Tom and John fall into conversation with a very tipsy Welshman. He drivels on about life and death in garbled English.

"Tomorrow could well be the end. Have a drink on me, Irishmen."

Tom begins to rise, but the man pushes him back into his chair.

"Wait a minute," John presses on. "I want to hear about Ypres."

"Ypres? Pretty town!" the man says, slurring his words. "Walls weren't enough for them. Now they have trenches, too, and they let them fill up with blood. *Our* blood!"

Both the Welshman and the men of the Second Battalion will be moving to the front tomorrow. The drunken soldier has obviously not spent all his money. He raises three fingers and motions to the hostess at the bar. She worms her way through the packed house and sets three bottles down on the table. The Welshman hands her money and lets her keep the change—for a kiss, of course.

Tom and John quickly drink their beer and rid themselves of the man. They walk through the town. Glowing cigarette tips dance like fireflies in the evening. Soldiers are standing around in the streets, waiting to shuffle into the half-darkened pubs. The officers slip in through their own entrances. Each uniformed man is living in the whirl of his very last evening, the night before Judgment Day.

"Those men are from *our* colonies," Tom whispers.

"Turbans!"

"Shh!"

John puts his hand over his mouth. What a fascinating city Poperinge is for a thirteen-year-old street kid! A group of five Sikhs from British India walks past. They have dark skin and enormous beards. John steps back to get a better look.

Queue to the Front

Spirits are high as the Second Battalion Royal Irish Regiment travels by train via Vlamertinge to Ypres. It feels like they're going at a snail's pace, for John, Tom, and their company are standing shoulder to shoulder in open cars and it's freezing cold. They wave with their caps and call to the passersby. The French troops, clad in red knickers and tall, round caps, are attracting attention in the distance. The

French lessons from the communal book come in handy again for the Irish, for they help maintain the atmosphere during the trip.

The train comes to a halt at the western edge of Ypres. Everyone gets off and lines up for inspection of the new khaki uniform. Each has black shoes, green puttees that reach to just below the knee, and a thick winter coat. On top of the coat is a leather harness consisting of a pistol belt around the middle, with two bands rising straight over the shoulders. On the back is a flat rucksack; on the left hip, a pouch and a bayonet in its scabbard. The corporals and sergeants distribute the personal ammunition. On each side of the breast pocket are five leather cartridge holders mounted on the belts. The ten little bags are filled with bullets. There is one last inspection of the rifle. Everyone is ready now. Ready for what? No one knows.

They march across the city wall and enter the centre of Ypres through the Lille Gate. Now and then a cannon rumbles in the distance. After almost six months of war, the medieval centre bears grievous traces of the German artillery. To the left and right are big gaping holes in the rows of houses.

"It's such a shame," Tom says with a sigh when they make a right turn toward the market.

"Wow! What a town hall!" John calls. He points to a tall building on his left. It is one hundred fifty metres long. The roof and entire pieces of the impressive façade have been blown to bits.

"That must be the Cloth Hall," says Tom. He knows all about this building and its fate because back in Ireland he faithfully read the reports from the front in his newspaper. "Look there—the Bell Tower. God, what destruction. Centuries of history in ruins!"

"Over there you can see a church through the rubble." John points excitedly to the cathedral behind the Bell Tower, next to the Cloth Hall. He feels that the real war, the adventure that he has anticipated for such a long time, is no longer far away. What he doesn't realise is that just four or five kilometres from the Grote Markt are the British and French trenches. They form a crescent-shaped frontline encompassing the eastern edge of Ypres. A few dozen metres farther—and sometimes just a few metres farther—are the Germans, positioned and waiting to capture the city.

At about five o'clock, the winter sun begins to sink behind the Cloth Hall. The battalion prepares to move through the Menin Gate to the trenches. The market square is teeming with soldiers; some are waiting impatiently while others are marching by. Before departing, Colonel Moriarty inspects his troops once again. He boosts their morale in a short, moving speech. It is obvious that he too is nervous, and curious about what awaits them. When he walks past John, who is a bit smaller than most of the others, he pats him approvingly on the back and straightens one of his shoulder bands. John turns all warm inside. He can see that parade on the wharf at Boulogne again and the image of the colonel triumphantly leading his troops on horseback. *I'll go through hell for this man,* he thinks.

The Menin Gate appears to be a gap in the old star-shaped walls of defense that Vauban, Louis XIV's architect, once had erected around Ypres. The road that begins just beyond the city wall—Menin Road—is wide and quite busy. Citizens and soldiers enter and exit the city in carts and on horseback.

Troops from all corners of the earth come and go. And according to tradition, there is always a group of British spectators calling to the departing soldiers, "Will the last person to leave shut the gate?"

After two hundred and fifty metres, the Menin Road turns sharply to the right. It is here that the route to the front truly begins. The battalion ends up in a queue. The hundreds of Irish shuffle forward inch by inch. In the meantime, it is growing pitch-dark. A few men light lanterns. They wait, smoke, and grumble because their progress is so slow. Suddenly the traffic from the other direction is noticeably busier.

"Where are they all coming from?" John wonders aloud.

"Where do you think?" Tom replies. "From the trenches, of course. They had to wait until dark before returning."

In the dim lamplight, the Irish get a better look at the weary faces of these approaching soldiers. The first march past silently in their platoons. They are followed—much more slowly—by ragtag groups of four or five men. Some walk all alone. No one reacts to the questions asked by the fresh troops. Drivers shout "Move aside!" and maneuver their horse carts with ghastly precision over the heavily travelled Menin Road.

"Poor sods," whisper a few men behind John and Tom.

"What do you mean?" John asks.

"Didn't you just see that, little man?" says Michael Mahoney. "Let's hope they won't be sending *you* back like that tomorrow, Condon."

"Dead bodies were in those carts," says Sergeant Kelly, who is passing them as he walks to the front of the line. His voice is shaky and hoarse.

John and Tom are about to reply when a motorised ambulance with its lights off emerges from the darkness. Furious shouting and a heart-rending call for help rise above the noise of the vehicle.

"Some wish that they were dead, too," growls an MP—a military police officer—who is standing nearby and directing traffic. "But you don't have a choice out there. An arm, a leg . . . you can't place your order with the Fritzes." He pushes the Irish to the side. "Look out, here comes another ambulance. Out of the way!" he calls, waving a lamp.

The soldiers keep coming. Some are limping

along, supported by their comrades. Others are wrapped in bandages. They all appear equally filthy and bedraggled.

Suddenly there seem to be many more MPs on the scene. "From here on, all lights and lanterns must be put out!" shouts one in a gruff and commanding voice.

Everyone is startled by the unexpected order, but within two seconds the entire battalion is engulfed in silence and darkness. Each person holds his tongue and waits.

"You might well ask why *I'm* not putting out my lantern," the raspy voice continues. "That's because we're still standing between houses. A little farther up there's nothing more, not even a tree to pee against, because most have already been destroyed."

"What an animal," John whispers to Tom.

"A blessing for his wife that there's a war on," Michael Mahoney adds scornfully.

The blunt MP comes forward and stops in front of Michael. "Can *you* explain it better than I?" he snaps. "No? Move along, then!"

John holds his breath. Michael looks down at his toes. The storm blew over.

"If you want the Krauts to aim a shell between your legs, put your light back on," the MP continues. "Or do you want to lose the tip of your nose? Then light a cigarette."

"So no smoking?" Sergeant Kelly asks.

"Right, Sergeant! Lights out, cigarettes away. Whoever doesn't want to obey my command will soon suffer the consequences. We don't want the whole battalion blown into the air before you've seen the front. It would be a terrible waste of your travel expenses. Orders to cross at Hellfire Corner will be given by our officers immediately."

Hellfire Corner: Green Light for Screaming Horses

Hellfire Corner is one and a half kilometres from the Menin Gate, yet Colonel Moriarty's Irish battalion takes hours to reach it. For John, Tom, and their comrades, it means waiting in line amid the other troops and dozens of carts and horses. Crossing this junction is something else again, however, for Hellfire Corner is generally considered to be the most dangerous place on earth. The front is just straight up ahead along the road to Menin—not even a five-minute walk to the first trench. But the railway to Zonnebeke and Roeselare cuts diagonally across the way here, and the cobblestone road to Zillebeke traverses this point, too. From on top of the Frezenberg and the Bellewaarde Ridge, the Germans follow every movement with eagle eyes. The far-off hills and windmills serve as observation posts as well. Almost all British and French troops must be funnelled through this dreaded intersection to the front, and if they survive, they must return along the same route.

In addition to watching the movements of the troops here, the Germans also keep an eye on the railway traffic. In clear weather they monitor the surroundings from small anchored zeppelins. The crucial delivery of ammunition and food for the many thousands of soldiers in the trenches must cross Hellfire Corner, too. At first these supplies are shipped by night trains, then by horse and cart because it is safer. Intersections like Hellfire Corner are notated on every topographic map, including German ones. Poor visibility or darkness of night are not problems for the German gunners; they are true wizards at geometry, and though they might have to move their artillery every now and then, they can easily land their shellfire in the area of the pitch-dark traffic junction.

"You're in luck tonight. It hasn't been this quiet in weeks," calls an unfamiliar officer who has come to brief the Irish.

"Downright quiet—you can say that again." John snickers as he looks at the swarms of people, horses, and carts.

"From here you must manage to reach the following intersection, Birr Crossroads. There you'll duck down into the trenches, which will be on your left and right. These are your frontline positions. Birr Crossroads is no farther than one hundred fifty yards from here."

"Simple—a stone's throw away," John mutters to Tom.

"Be quiet!" Tom hisses.

"*But!*" the officer continues. He seems to be enjoying the anxiety displayed by the newcomers, and pauses carefully to add weight to his words. "But . . . these one hundred fifty yards could also be your last. When the red lanterns are extinguished, sit as quiet as mice. Then wait for the green light, and be ready for the race of your life. In total darkness. The only things you'll see are our signalers, unless a shell comes overhead. These signalers are situated on both sides of this part of the road, deep down in the ditches, with their backs to the east, to the enemy. And remember: keep to the left, for there could be traffic coming from the other direction."

The instructor has barely finished his sentence when there are frantic cries of "Down! Shellfire!"

Everyone plops face-down, just as the troops so often did in their practice drills. With his nose to the ground and his ears pricked, John can hear the fear spreading over the road. Horses are neighing in front of and behind him, as drivers swear at the snorting animals. Farther away, somewhere above the dreaded one hundred fifty yards, three or four whistling shells skim overhead. The whizzbangs come buzzing down into the fields next to the road. Mules balk in terror, and the horses seem to be screaming. John looks in the direction of the explosions. The half-frozen ground shakes under his pounding heart. When the explosives land, they act as spotlights. He finds it exciting to see clumps of earth flung up high in the flashing light. A horse bolts next to the road, dragging its harness as it runs into the fields. It is only now that John can get a picture of what this intersection actually looks like. The chaos and the masses of people and animals surprise him more than anything else.

When it's far into the night, the battalion readies itself for the big leap. First the men wait for the Royal Engineers, who have to repair the railway line that's been damaged by German shells. They fill in a small hole next to the tracks, then replace a few splintered ties and a bent rail—not more than an hour and a half of work. In the meantime, the Irish make way for a sea of soldiers returning from the trenches. John and Tom are now standing in the front of the line. Even after hours of waiting, their eyes are not used to the pitch-dark. The only points of light are the first covered red lanterns of the signalers. Their company is lined up behind a transport unit. The convoy consists of about five pairs of horses; one pair is pulling a hooded cart, and the others are hitched to flat wagons. John noticed this when the last shell struck. Each team of horses has one driver, who sits astride one animal while holding the reins of the other. The horses snort restlessly. Everyone's patience is being tested—the animals' patience, too.

Suddenly it is quiet. John turns around and looks for the lights. They are gone.

"The time has come," Tom says, and he sighs.

"Ready for the green light?" calls a grim voice somewhere in front of them.

Nothing happens. John makes sure his shoulder bands are in place and pushes his cap way down over his ears. And waits . . .

Green light. "Go! Go, go, go!" Sergeant Kelly shouts. "Yeah! Come on!" the teamsters yell, and they dig their heels into the horses' flanks. The animals rear up and whinny. The carts rattle and creak as they lunge forward. Slowly they gain speed. At first, John and his friends run effortlessly along with one hand on a tailgate. They must let go of the wagon ten seconds later, for the convoy starts moving much too fast for them now. The iron wheels clang over the sloping train tracks and ties in the middle of Hellfire Corner. John follows on the far left of the road and passes four or five signalers hunkered down along the side. Then he himself can feel the slippery sleepers and tracks of the level crossing. He knows that Tom is somewhere next to him. Three lights further, there is a resounding boom; it sounds as though lightning has struck right next to John. For two seconds the junction is engulfed in a glaring light. He is hurled to the ground. There is a second flash and a third. John can't hear anything now. A horse lies in front of him; its hind legs are shattered and its intestines are spilling out of its belly. The animal is trying to scramble to its feet. Two boots protrude from under its body. A wheel dances over the road. At that moment, ten men or more jump out of a ditch and drag away the wreckage—cadavers, wounded men, and injured horses. The road must be kept open and clear. John stumbles ahead as fast as he can. His ears are buzzing now; he can hear all the racket again and he can hear voices, including Tom's. He is driven along with the others to Birr Crossroads. Two minutes later, he's catching his breath in a long trench. This is the front. This is the war.

War Is a Frightful Routine

All the Irish have survived the first trip to the front.

"A lucky coincidence," say those in the First Battalion King's Own, who are catching their breath behind the weakly lit rampart at Birr Crossroads before making the perilous journey back to Ypres.

"Just call it a big fluke. I've already seen hundreds of bleeding boys being carried away," one signaler says. "I didn't believe hell existed until I arrived on this spot, but I know where to find it now. From here to Hellfire Corner . . ."

John Condon's group leaves via the trenches in the back line of defense to the north of the front bow. Over a maze of small, deeply dug paths, they walk a few kilometres along the Salient, the defense bow around Ypres. Gradually they move over to the right to the dangerous exterior, where the front trenches form the winding frontline. Long silences are broken by nasty machine-gun fire. Sometimes the guns are far away and at other times perplexingly close. The jet-black sky is regularly illuminated by exploding shells. Iron splinters whiz through the air.

They come across other army units on their grim walk. Some have been there for days and are stiff from the cold. Most of the men are silent. Others sullenly shoot a few bullets over the parapet or between the sandbags. Twice John and his mates have to leave the trench to move faster to the front positions. Shots are fired; John and Tom don't know who is doing the shooting. Scared to death, they hunker down and follow the little white ribbons that point the way.

Thanks to an experienced guide, they find the

holes in the barbed wire, which is everywhere to be seen.

At daybreak, they learn that they are now in the area of Het Wieltje. The sergeants are taken aside and given orders from the officers. John can't take his eyes off Colonel Moriarty. The man truly radiates charm and charisma! Tom thinks that the colonel cuts an unusually fine figure for an officer as well.

They spend the first day settling in. The greatest enemy seems to be the winter cold. John is swathed in thick clothing, but it's a struggle to keep the feet warm on the duckboards. Whoever continues to walk on the sticky clay makes a filthy mess indeed.

"Above all, keep your feet dry," the sergeant warns.

Each soldier in John's group is given a little jar of grease. "It's made from whale oil," the sergeant adds.

"What are we supposed to do with this, Sergeant?" Michael Mahoney asks.

"Smear it on your feet, honey, all the way up past your shoes," says the man, and he snickers.

John opens his jar and sniffs. "Ugh! That's worse than cod-liver oil!"

"It'll keep you dry. According to the colonel, the army is losing too many men to frostbitten toes."

The Irish take turns watching for the enemy. In the meantime, those not on lookout duty play cards, smoke, drink rum, and tell jokes. A shot rings out only every now and then. Usually someone shoots back. They are so close to the enemy that sometimes they hear German songs. The war seems like a game on that first morning. But before the day is over, John knows that he is horribly mistaken.

"Is there something to see across the way, Murph?" Tom asks.

Murphy, who is on lookout duty, doesn't answer. When Tom nudges him and asks the same question two minutes later, Murphy collapses, falling backwards. He lies next to John's feet and stares at the gray snow clouds, not saying a word. Dark red blood oozes out of his nose and mouth. There is a small hole above one of his eyebrows.

They quickly send for Lieutenant Fottrell. "Sniper," he says when he arrives, and he sighs.

"That fellow never did anyone any harm," John says to himself, dazed.

"Damned snipers," the officer hisses. "Men, don't stick your head over the wall unnecessarily."

"But . . . he had to, didn't he . . . ?" Tom says hesitantly.

"Sergeant!" Lieutenant Fottrell calls. "Have the poor sod removed. Has anyone taken his place yet?"

A second victim falls fifteen minutes later. A jolly platoon that John and his buddies have come to relieve is returning from the field kitchen. The men know nothing about the shooting. A tall soldier named Dobson is clowning around as always. Everyone laughs when he sinks to his knees, until they notice that he is taking a very, very long time to get up, He's been shot through his cap.

From that day on, the fear of snipers holds everyone in its grip. It will remain a burden in the coming weeks and months as well. Every move the soldiers make in the narrow trench weighs on them like a rucksack full of bricks.

The two unlucky soldiers are buried that same afternoon. Nearby is a small snow-covered lot, where already about a hundred wooden crosses are standing. Father Gleeson's brief service makes a deep impression on John and the platoon to which the fallen soldiers belonged. Black spots indicate where the fresh graves lie.

A little later, John and Tom are sent with about ten others three kilometres farther up, along the road from Ypres to Pilkem, to fetch sacks of coal. Not only are the lumps of coal used for cooking; they are especially needed to fill the scuttles that help keep the men warm. On the way back, John notices more patches of ground covered with crosses. One plot contains large holes from a recent shelling. Two men silently drag a uniformed torso and return the legless body to its grave, which is now a crater. In the hole lies another body, half naked, half buried.

John sets down his sack of coal.

"Is something wrong?" Tom asks.

"That . . . that was a lieutenant," John stammers. "There was a gold star on his epaulet."

Then he vomits.

❧

The Second Battalion Royal Irish Regiment sets up camp in the area of De Brieke, a hamlet a bit north of Ypres. Just as on typical days in the trenches, not much is happening there. The brick buildings that are still standing have been deserted. Officers take over the best lodgings in safe cellars; then the non-commissioned officers choose their spots. Corporals get the ramshackle remains. Ordinary boys like John must try to keep warm and dry in drafty sheds, barracks, and army tents, where they spread out their bedding on some straw.

Every four days, John and his platoon are sent to the frontline. They remain there for four days and nights before returning to De Brieke, where they spend their time resting and doing odd jobs. And so it goes, week after week.

"Why did we train so hard in Ireland?" John wonders aloud. "Nothing is happening."

Tom puts a pipe in his mouth and checks to see if any of his superiors are around the corner of the trench. "To be honest, lad, I hope it stays that way," he says.

Michael Mahoney leans against the sandbags and looks out through a split every so often. "John is right. The place is dead, Tom. If it were summer, we could be lying in the sun now!"

"I'm afraid this isn't going to be a picnic, Michael."

"I thought we were going to teach those Huns a lesson," John complains.

"Teach them a lesson?" Tom snickers. "Remember my cousin Jim?"

"Christmas at your house," John recalls. "Poor man."

"What about him?" Michael wants to know.

"Oh, you're aware of those gruesome stories that Kinsella and Driscoll tell, aren't you?" Tom says with distaste. "It was really one of the first battles the British troops were involved with in this war. Most of them were ground into mincemeat by the Germans." Michael listens and nods.

"Yup," Tom says with a frown as he puffs away on his pipe. "That was last year, when they were the first to be sent to France and Belgium."

"Do you mean we can't beat those Fritzes?" John calls. He looks rather silly as he jumps up and grabs his rifle.

"You need a fresh nappy?" Michael Mahoney says, laughing as he remembers when John was a toddler and still called Patrick.

"The front isn't moving and we're shooting a few bullets back and forth, but who is going to teach whom a lesson when all hell truly breaks loose here?" Tom asks.

The days and nights in the trenches are long and cold, with little movement at the front. Officers and sergeants make up all sorts of odd jobs to keep their men busy: polish shoes, weapons, and all the equipment; fill sandbags; keep the trenches in good repair; bring in supplies; help out in the field kitchen; even hold small drill practices. The most bizarre activity is catching rats. On some days, the area is crawling with them. They are as big as rabbits and so bold that they scurry across the backs of the men who are on guard duty. Rat catching becomes a game in which the men keep track of how many they catch. John is one of the favourite players; he spears the animals with his bayonet and grabs them with his bare hands when need be.

Yet the war remains a dirty business, with machine-gun fire and snipers who patiently lie in wait for their enemies. Each week there is usually someone who, because of the tedium and boredom, falls victim to his own absent-mindedness. And the frontline is long. Snipers weigh heavily on the morale of the troops. Even if it's relatively quiet, a small team must always be on the lookout, with weapons in hand. And a few shells land in their area nearly every day.

Suddenly gunshots are ringing out. John can hear the plop of their impact.

"Help, Mother! They got me!" he shouts from his post. Panicked, he feels the warm blood running over his face and down his neck. Thick red drops pour from his hands.

Everyone gets up and rushes toward him. Horrified, the men stay a couple of metres away.

"We were just talking, Walsh and I," John cries hysterically to the gathering soldiers, "about his girl who often writes to him . . ." He stares vacantly at the silent faces.

"My God! Didn't you hear that whizzbang coming?" Sergeant Kelly asks worriedly.

"We did," John sobs as he shakes the dark brown mud from his right sleeve. "Walsh pushed me against the wall for protection."

"Nasty shrapnel, Sergeant," mutters a corporal, squatting down to look.

John is just beginning to see the bloody torso lying at his feet. The head and arms are gone; Walsh is merely a lump of quivering, steaming flesh.

Everything is slowly spinning around John now. He sees a cap on the ground and the photo of the girl next to it. Thomas Carthy's voice sounds closer. Then John faints.

John and Tom talk about the incident during the following weeks. What is worse? To be hit by a piece of shrapnel that tears off a limb and rips open your belly? Or to be killed right away?

Most soldiers write letters during the four days of rest in De Brieke. Thomas Carthy seems like a true professional writer. Sometimes he scribbles ten letters a day for the dozens of illiterate men in the battalion.

"Oh, I could curse this war," Michael Mahoney exclaims. "Two whole weeks without a single letter from home!"

If the mail doesn't arrive on time, the Ypres Salient is full of soldiers with long faces and dragging feet.

"It's the postmen who will win the war," Tom declares, and he laughs.

"Then they should go on the offensive right away," Michael says earnestly.

"Shall I send something to Waterford for you, John?" Tom asks.

"No, not right now, Tom. Thanks."

"That's what you always say."

"*I* will send greetings to Thomas's Avenue. All right?" Michael volunteers.

"I'd rather you didn't, Mike."

"Greetings from the one true *John* Condon, the hero of Wheelbarrow Lane," Michael teases.

"*No.* Lay off, I tell you!"

"Ohh! We'd best leave the children alone," Michael states. He is grumpy now as well.

John storms out the door. Tom approaches him a bit later.

"It would do you good to get a letter from home sometime, don't you think?" he begins. "Look . . ." He pulls an envelope from his breast pocket. "A photo of Mary in front of our cottage. *She* sends her greetings, at any rate."

"Thanks, Tom. It's sweet of her to think of me. Tell Mrs. Carthy I say hello to her, too."

"And Waterford—your mother, your sisters?"

John shrugs and turns his back to his friend.

"Do they have *any* idea at all that you're at the front, John?"

John clenches his teeth and runs away behind a shed where no one can see him.

APRIL 1915
BERLIN, GERMANY

Herr Doctor Haber and His Silent Killer

At the Kaiser Wilhelm Institute, the forty-seven-year-old director, Fritz Haber, bites his nails as he waits for news—a single telephone call that could change his life. Day and night he has toiled, not without danger, to write about the effects of new gas compounds. He has spent the best years of his life in the laboratory, spreading the renown of his scientific institute over Germany and the wide world. And spreading his own reputation, too, he must admit. *Surely those clever fellows on the Nobel Prize committee are acquainted with my work as a chemist, aren't they? Who knows, maybe someday . . . ?* Professor Haber muses. Because he is a true *"Herr,"* a bit of vanity is not alien to him.

Those sixty-three thousand kilograms of gas-filled shells used against the Russians last winter were a fly in the ointment. His chemical gas compound appeared to be useless in the freezing cold. Those Cossacks had certainly inhaled it, but they unfortunately had lived to tell about it. An earlier attempt, in which the Germans used a kind of tear gas against the French and British in northern France, also fizzled out. That was in October. Those Frogs didn't even notice the gas, the swine!

It must *work this time,* Herr Haber frets. He is still fascinated by the first test, which he conducted safely behind glass. He recalls how that dirty brown stuff suddenly began to swirl when he broke open the ampoule—the hissing, effervescent dark green cloud; those thick chlorine fumes that remained suspended at a knee-high level above the floor in the test area. He remembers the dogs as they fell on their backs, howling in agony. The monkeys were like rubber balls bouncing against the ceiling. He *did* feel a little sorry for the horse. *But ach, so it goes in science,* the professor thinks, mollified. That old nag had already been blind from the previous chlorine gas test. At first the mare didn't react at all, because the cloud hovered under its belly.

"We need a bit of a draft," he had said to his assistant. "Just a light one."

"Shall I turn on the ventilator?" the fellow had suggested. "The exhaust system, perhaps?"

Fritz Haber can still picture the fumes spiraling up high. He sees the horse pull loose in panic, snort, cry, stretch its neck and cough, vomit, and finally spit blood until it falls over with a groan. The convulsions had lasted only three minutes. The test was a success.

The telephone on the desk rings.

"Hello? *Nein,* Schmidt. *Jetzt nicht.* This line must be kept open. I can't talk now. *Verstanden?*"

He puts the telephone receiver back and begins to pace up and down the dimly lit room. They *did* do everything properly, didn't they? Step by step, he walks through the drill practices, the same ones he had gone over countless times with the *Gaspioniers,* a secret army unit.

Dr. Haber hisses through his clenched teeth. *If all goes well,* he thinks . . .

APRIL 1915

Wieltje, Belgium (near Ypres)

Pee on Your Handkerchief

John and Tom roll up their thick winter jackets to the size of pillows.

"We can best put these warm things away until this evening, Tom."

"That bit of spring sun is wonderful. If the Fritzes were like us and wanted to enjoy some warmth, then maybe this war would be different," Tom says with a sigh. He looks for a dry spot on the long footboard that soldiers step up on as they emerge from the trench and run to the battlefield.

"Nothing to see across the way as usual, Mike?" John asks. His eyes are closed.

"Enjoy your rest," Michael Mahoney answers. "The Huns are sleeping."

"Tom, have you noticed those bright red buds? A few have already opened. Pretty, aren't they?" says John.

"They're poppies," Tom replies. "Soon you'll find them everywhere. Those little flowers are even blooming between the crosses of our comrades back there."

Generals are usually oblivious to poppies. John and Tom don't know that their relatively calm life at the front during the spring of 1915 is about to be disrupted by the plans of the German army command.

"We've sat in those trenches long enough," Commander-in-Chief Erich von Falkenhayn roars. "It is high time we reached the French harbours on the English Channel."

"Ypres must fall into our hands first," one of his stooges remarks dryly.

The other generals gathered around the table are silent. They know that capturing Ypres will be a bloodbath.

"Our new weapon, perhaps?" the same fawning voice asks.

The commander nods coolly. His lackey has played his role well. "*Meine Herren,* this is my proposal ..."

His proposition almost sounds like a friendly question. But who would dare offend this top general by objecting to his plan?

At night, when French and British pilots are unable to spy, the Germans quietly work long and hard on their gruesome plan for Ypres. Special troops put five to six thousand steel canisters under the ground in the trenches. Each cylinder contains twenty to forty kilogrammes of compressed chlorine gas. The largest ones are two metres tall. Only the valves are visible above the clay. There is a rubber tube on each gas valve, ready to be laid over the parapet. The burrows in the earth will last more than a month. It's now just a matter of waiting for a light breeze from the right direction.

Early in the morning of 22 April 1915, the German cannons bombard the French and British-Canadian positions north of Ypres. Tom and John don't understand what has come over the enemy all of a sudden. They lie with their Irish battalion about two kilometres to the south on the defense bow. Shells and shrapnel keep raining down on them. The whole day they hear the booming of artillery and see smoke from the explosions rise up above the northern part of the Salient. Around five o'clock, it suddenly becomes dead still.

"Finally," Michael Mahoney pants.

"A person could get tired from all this," John says with a laugh.

"It's strange, though, that it's *so* quiet all of a sudden." Tom doesn't trust this entire business.

"There's nothing to see, just as always," Michael reports. "Maybe they've run out of shells!"

"Hey, Tom, Michael! Do you smell that?"

"Ugh ... Bleach!" Michael calls.

"Are the Fritzes beginning their spring cleaning?" John jokes.

Tom doesn't understand what is happening, either.

"Shh. Be quiet," John demands. "Do you hear those voices?"

"It's the French," says Michael. "They're far away, but I can hear them shouting."

"It's coming from the Zouaves, if you ask me," Tom states.

"The Africans with their wide trousers and those flowerpots on their heads?" asks John.

"They're French colonial troops from Senegal," Tom explains.

"God, what could be the matter over there?" John wonders out loud.

"The shouts are coming from nearby now. From the Canadians, I think," Michael exclaims. "There's Sergeant Kelly."

"Something is going on with our neighbours, eh, Sergeant?" says Tom, the oldest in the group.

"I can't make much sense out of this, boys. The lieutenant with his periscope even less, for that matter. In the meantime, get ready. I've heard that reinforcements are coming."

For the first time in weeks, the men of the Second Battalion Royal Irish Regiment are lined up in row after row, ready to go over the top once again. John, Tom, Michael, and hundreds of others lean against the sandbags with their bayonets on their rifles and wait for the command to jump over the parapet.

"Now or never, Michael!" John says excitedly to his neighbour from Wheelbarrow Lane. They are standing way up in the first row.

Michael turns around to face Tom. "You look so pale," he says.

Tom is standing down on the foot plank in the overcrowded trench. Amid the jostling of elbows and shoulders, rifles and bags, he holds his cap in the air and wipes the beads of sweat from his forehead with his sleeve.

"Are you all right, Tom?" John asks, and he winks at Michael.

"It must be his age catching up with him, don't you think?" Michael whispers without looking back. "How old is our daddy, anyway?"

"Forty-seven. That makes a difference, eh? And how old are you? Nineteen, like my brother?"

"So we're the same age, eh, little one," Michael chuckles, and he winks.

"God, if those little boys in Ballybricken saw us now, how jealous they would be." John sighs.

"You mean your old friends?"

"Oh, O'Sullivan, Rogers, and that group of schoolgirls," he explains jokingly.

"Just listen to him," Michael says with a laugh. "Who's the schoolgirl here, Condon? I know O'Sullivan, at any rate. His older brother was in my class."

"School—Jesus, don't remind me!" John crows, and he suppresses a laugh. "Imagine, Mr. Baldwin here in Ypres!"

They burst out laughing. The men next to them can't understand why they're so cheerful. Their own nerves have reached the breaking point.

The big attack seems to have been cancelled for that day. John and Michael are disappointed. Tom heaves a sigh of relief.

Little by little the next day, they hear about the unspeakable drama that played out for just a few short moments in the trenches a few kilometres farther up. From Steenstrate, the front lay open for hours over a breadth of six kilometres. African soldiers from the French colonies and *les pépères,* a division of older military men from Bretagne, didn't know what had hit them when the deadly chlorine gas cloud descended. Hundreds suffocated on the spot and died a silent, lonely death. More men fell dead in the skirmish immediately after the gas attack in hand-to-hand combat with the bayonets on their rifles. Whoever was still able to move fled to the bridge across the Canal Ypres-Yzer in Boezinge. Some didn't get that far—with burning lungs they jumped into the water. There were soldiers who remained on the ground for hours, spitting up blood. No one could help them.

The Germans seemed just as surprised by the effect of their new weapon. Only then did they realise that the way to Ypres was completely open and that the city was theirs for the taking. But there were no reserve troops to make the leap. When the Canadians launched a massive bloody counterattack in which they sacrificed hundreds of lives, the Germans succeeded in closing the breach. But by that time, it was too late for them to claim victory.

Less than a day later, at the crack of dawn on 24 April, thousands of Canadians died near Sint-Juliaan in a second gas attack. Just as many would suffer permanent lung damage.

"What? Pee on our handkerchief?" each man asks himself out loud.

There is much laughter on the practice square in De Brieke.

Tom scratches under his cap. "Ever hear of such a thing?" he asks John and Michael.

"Could I use an old sock instead?" John inquires.

"*That* already stinks," Michael snorts.

"You can't hold *two* weapons at the same time and a handkerchief, too!" yells someone in a back row.

"Silence!" Sergeant-Major Larkin roars. He is the highest ranking noncommissioned officer of the company, and somewhat of a father figure to the battalion.

The other sergeants turn around and shout commands to their platoons. The men grow quiet.

"I repeat: pee on your handkerchief and hold it over your mouth. It's the only thing you can do to protect yourself against that goddamned gas when you're in the trench," Sergeant-Major Larkin calls sternly. "Colonel Moriarty has urgently asked headquarters to send us real gas masks."

Various gas attacks follow during the next two weeks. John and his mates receive primitive masks for protection—cloths that have been saturated with a special liquid. When the men put these damp rags over their mouths and secure them with ribbon, they are scarcely able to breathe. The real gas masks are on the way, promises the colonel. Life in the trenches becomes depressing and grim. After all, you can't fight a gas cloud.

9 MAY 1915
SINT-JULIAAN, BELGIUM (NEAR YPRES)

In the Mousetrap

At the beginning of May, the Second Battalion Royal Irish Regiment is finally ready to go over the top once again. The Irish occupy the first trench between the hamlet of Het Wieltje and the town of Sint-Juliaan. Next to them are the Royal Northumberland Fusiliers, the Fifth Battalion South Lancashire, the First King's Own, Second Essex, Second Royal Dublin Fusiliers, and on down the line.

"We must secure Mousetrap Farm and occupy it," Sergeant Kelly informs them.

"He means 'Shell Trap Farm,'" Tom whispers to John.

Everyone knows about the walled manor farm. It is a true magnet for shelling attacks because it is notated on every topographical map. Naturally, no one is going to be chomping at the bit to attack a farm called "Shell Trap." Therefore the place was renamed "Mousetrap," by orders from headquarters.

From the second firing line, the British continually lob shells over the ruins of the farm in the direction of Mauser Ridge, which lies behind it. Suddenly the field telephone rings a few steps from John. Michael nudges him.

"Here it comes," says John.

"Don't try to play the hero," Tom warns.

"You're nervous, aren't you?" John says with a laugh.

Tom is silent. The three watch Sergeant Kelly as he hands the receiver to Lieutenant Fottrell.

"Right, sir!" Fottrell exclaims curtly. He nods resolutely to Sergeant Kelly and looks at his wristwatch. No one has ever seen the lieutenant take his gun from the holster. The tension is nearly unbearable. The officer checks the little green cord dangling from his neck, which is attached to the butt of his revolver.

"Ready for attack, Sergeant?" he asks in a clear voice now. A forest of upright bayonets begins to move uneasily.

"Ready for attack!" Sergeant Kelly shouts through the passageway. His command is echoed by other sergeants farther up the trench. A red flare is fired above Mousetrap Farm. Someone blows a whistle in the distance.

"Go! Go! Go!" is resounding from all sides now. Before he realises it, John is running amid a mass of shouting soldiers. A thick curtain of sulfur smoke reduces his visibility to just a couple of metres. He slows down and tries to get his bearings. The earsplitting explosions from shells drown out the clamouring of his comrades. With his head bowed and bayonet thrust forward, he walks between the bullets that are whistling past him. Nasty machine-gun fire is coming from the left. *The farm must be over there,* he thinks. At that moment there is a gigantic explosion. A sea of earth knocks him to the ground like a sledgehammer.

"Where am I?" John wipes the dust from his eyes and blinks in confusion at the bright blue sky above him.

"Quiet, John. Stay down," a familiar voice whispers.

But John struggles to sit up. Dazed, he finds himself on a pile of sandbags in the corner of a zigzagging trench. Filthy, mud-covered men walk back and forth as they drag limp bodies through the passageway. The sound of wailing is everywhere.

"Tom! What's happening?" John shakes the clay from his uniform. "Where is everyone?"

"Shh. We're safe here," Tom replies soothingly. "Our trench is just a little farther up—on that side, I think."

"Hey! Where's my rifle? And my cap?" John jumps up and looks around anxiously.

"I didn't look for them in all that mess on the battlefield." Tom sighs. "When I found you, I thought at first that you were dead as a doornail. There are *so* many wounded boys back there who were finished off with a bayonet. God, how frightened I was," he adds in a trembling voice. His head is between his knees.

"Did *you* bring me here?" John asks warily.

"Drag you here. Yes."

"And Mousetrap Farm? Did we take it?"

"John Condon!" Tom shouts angrily. "What the hell do I care if we captured that pile of bricks? Today it's ours, tomorrow the Germans'. In God's name!" He storms around the corner.

"Tom! Tom, I'm sorry!" John calls, and follows him. His body feels completely knocked around. He finds Tom and stands with him.

"Stay calm," Tom orders in a fatherly way. "You've had darned good luck."

"Are we going to look for the others?"

"The others?"

"Yes. I want to know what Michael Mahoney thought of the attack."

Tom chooses his words carefully. "I'm afraid I haven't gotten through to you, John. Michael isn't the only one who fell today."

"Is he . . . ?"

Tom nods.

"How?"

"You don't want to know, John."

Michael Mahoney, John's neighbour from the

same little alley in Waterford, is dead. No one will ever hear from him again. During these days, hundreds of nameless fellows disappear under the clay soil at Ypres, thousands of kilometres from home. Or they are smashed to a pulp by one of the countless shells.

At midnight on that same day, 9 May 1915, the German boys of the 234th Regiment are finally relieved after nineteen days and nights at the firing line. They have lost 1,463 men and 34 officers since the first gas attack on 22 April. Their ranks have been depleted by two thirds.

During April and May 1915, the Second Battle of Ypres cost over 100,000 lives, on both sides. John Condon's battalion, the Second Battalion Royal Irish Regiment, which totaled about 800 men, was virtually wiped out. It was not the only Irish battalion in that campaign to suffer a great deal.

WHIT MONDAY
24 May 1915
WIELTJE, BELGIUM

The Last Day

Midnight. The sky is full of stars. A forgotten church tower chimes in the distance.

"Father Gleeson's service was beautiful yesterday," Tom comments. "And on such a sunny Whit Sunday ..."

They are silent. Tom and John are thinking about the same thing: the reading of names during the chaplain's sermon, the unbelievably long list of friends who are no longer with them.

"Masks on!" one man after another calls out through the trenches. Yesterday, each soldier was given a pair of goggles as well as a mask for use against tear gas and chlorine gas.

At around one o'clock, Colonel Moriarty himself comes to warn his men. The troops who have just been relieved have smelled gas. It's likely due to technical problems of the German *Gaspioniers*. Each person puts on his primitive gas mask, a dirty, damp wad of cloth that fits over the mouth.

The machine gunners must wear their newly delivered hypo-helmets. The men look like ghosts in these thick flannel hoods with large mica windows. If a gas cloud comes, *they* certainly must hold their ground.

After the colonel and his entourage have left, most of the men remove their masks.

Three o'clock in the morning. The Germans launch three red flares into the sky from a hot-air balloon. For five seconds, the black, star-filled sky above the village of Poelkapelle turns into a bright red poppy. Then the heavens close up again, and the front is pitch-dark. John and his battalion are in the trenches near Wieltje, only two miles from Poelkapelle.

"In the name of God, what is happening now?" Tom whispers.

"Shh. Do you hear that?" says John.

The German trench that is closest to Mousetrap Farm is only 150 metres away. The hissing of hundreds of gas valves is very clear now.

"Gas!" ten voices call out at the same time, but the thick, poisonous clouds are already clinging to the ground nearby and rolling over the sandbag parapets. The first chlorine fumes wind their way into the British trenches. Men swear and walk over one another, tumbling over the footboard and kicking and thrashing in every direction. Helplessly they scratch their faces and necks to ribbons and purse their lips in search of air. Their death rattles are drowned out by the noise of the Irish machine-gun nests, which aim straight across the dark, swirling gas.

John feels his eyes starting to water. He squeezes them shut. His mouth mask is working fairly well. Tom is also withstanding the attack.

Glowing projectiles make a whining noise as they fly through the air and land several metres behind the men. Luckily the Irish are sitting deep in their trenches.

John and Tom shoot a few bullets in the direction of the invisible enemy every now and then. The machine gunners receive the command to hold their fire. Rifle fire stops, as well. The sky gradually turns pale beyond the distant horizon. Everyone must now help lift the dead out of the passageways and roll them behind the trench. It is impossible to talk and complain through the masks. John's stomach lurches as he looks at all the contorted faces and ruptured eyeballs. He knows these dead soldiers very well, each and every one.

The wind picks up. The thick poison clouds have disappeared. More and more boys let their gas masks dangle around their necks. Suddenly they hear smaller explosions directly in front and up ahead to the right.

"Damn," Tom curses. "Those are hand grenades."

"Correct." A deep voice sighs behind them. It is Colonel Moriarty.

Soon it becomes dead still again. Then they hear clicking. John peeks through the top sandbags.

"There!" he whispers. "Colonel, sir, they're

sneaking up on us." He is shocked by his own behavior, for ordinary soldiers are not allowed to speak to officers.

The battalion commander peers through the opening. "They're cutting through the barbed wire," he mutters.

"Do they think that we ran away because of the gas?" John asks Tom quietly.

"Or they think we've all suffocated," Tom mumbles back.

"Lieutenant!" It is the muffled voice of the colonel. "Hold your fire! Stay quiet—no one shoot."

The instructions are passed on immediately.

The shadows move closer at a slow, agonising pace. The Irish wait anxiously for a command. Will they have to shoot or jump out of the trench? The mouse-gray uniforms of the German infantrymen now appear razor sharp in view. John notices the uncertain looks on their faces. *Ordinary boys, just like us,* he thinks. *They don't know what's in store . . .*

The Irish machine guns rip through the silence with a devilish rattle. The gray jackets become splattered with bright red blood. A large fellow jumps up and tries to throw a hand grenade but is riddled with bullets. Two seconds later, the grenade goes off with a dull crack, blowing him apart. The machine guns stop firing. A whistle shrieks through the passageway.

"Go, go! Go!" the sergeants yell.

John rushes forward with Tom behind him. The British storm ahead in broad rows, roaring like wild animals as they run toward the German side, where at least as many enemy soldiers are now brandishing their bayonets and yelling and shooting. Men to the right and left are falling down next to John, mortally wounded. It's impossible to recognise them in the turmoil. He fires again and again. Men are dropping in front of him, too. Dozens of Germans are lying in the barbed wire now.

John tries to find a hole in the barrier. "Colonel Moriarty!" he cries, startled to run into his leader.

With his pistol drawn, the high officer ducks through a narrow opening in the barricade and sinks to his knees. There is a large, round bloodstain on his back.

John hesitates.

"Leave him!" Tom shouts above the hellish din. "He's not going to make it."

The German voices that ring out are nearby and crystal clear. Suddenly, Tom and John are standing head to head with a small boy. The little German thrusts his bayonet forward and jumps. John fires. Everything is turning black . . .

Dead and (Twice) Buried

The sun is already shining high in the sky when John awakens, wide-eyed and frightened.

"Air . . . God, air! My throat is on fire. Aachh! Tom! I'm suffocating, Tom! Where are you? Bloody hell, answer me."

The clay earth and the thin, sparse grass surrounding his head have a pungent odor. He tries to turn on his side. "Aachh, my lungs are bursting . . . I'm going to puke . . . Gas, *gasss* . . . I've got to get away from here."

Screeching shells fly across the battlefield. John gasps for air. He tries to remember exactly what has happened. *But first open this jacket and breathe,* he thinks. *The collar is pinching me.*

His fingers are sticky from the clay. He struggles with the buttons. "Mama, help me!" he begins to whine in a high voice. "Mother! They got me, those Fritzes."

Big tears roll down his cheeks. Wheelbarrow Lane, Ballybricken, St. Patrick of the Holy Trinity Without, Rogers and O'Sullivan, Mollie and the baby, Fatso, his father . . . Everyone and everything flashes through his head.

John finally opens the top button. Then another. He clutches his chest. His shirt is clammy. He wrinkles his nose and looks at his fingers through half-closed eyes. "Bwaaah!" he cries. "All this blood is under my clothes! Tom! Help me, damn it."

Suddenly he opens his eyes wide and mumbles, "Holy Mary, what is that? My crotch is warm and wet. No . . . Have I peed in my pants? Air, fresh air—I can't breathe . . ."

He loses consciousness again.

John awakens, crying softly. He wants to get up, but his muscles refuse to move. He is unable to speak. It's dusky and cold. Someone has moved him. An unknown face studies him for a long time. John is turned on his side. Grass brushes against his feverish cheek. Someone is lying next to him. He feels a shoulder and sees a face nearby.

"Tom! T-T-Thomas Carthy!" he stammers. "Is . . . is that you, Tom?" He wants to talk, but his strength is gone. He shivers uncontrollably.

Why are you staring at the dark sky, Tom? he asks to himself wearily. *Answer me!*

"That boy wants to tell us something," says an unfamiliar voice high above him.

A man puts his ear to John's face. "Nineteen? Yes, that's it," he calls to someone far in the distance.

"No!" John groans angrily. He feels himself slipping away but wants to remain awake. He digs his nails into the grass.

"'Fourteen next month.' *That* is what he's saying!" the man calls out again.

John feels the ear brush against his dry lips.

"Fourteen. Not nineteen. Lies. Is that what he said?"

John is running through a long dark corridor. His feet are not touching the ground. Someone is standing in the white light far away, friendly and beckoning . . . At last.

ONE DAY LATER
25 May 1915
GERMAN MILITARY HEADQUARTERS
BERLIN, GERMANY

New Strategies

The German chief of staff Erich von Falkenhayn is in a foul mood. The generals sitting around the table are curling their toes. Who will be the scapegoat today?

"*Meine Herren*, I've decided to call off the attack on Ypres for now."

The arrogant strategist nervously twirls the tips of his mustache. "On twenty-second April, our

Gaspioniers surprised the enemy. The experiment was a success."

There are sighs of relief. But the tall, blond von Falkenhayn stands up and continues in a trembling voice. "Alas, our officers missed their opportunity!" He examines the generals one by one.

"What has this Second Battle at Ypres procured? A few dozen square kilometres of ground! Nothing more. But yet . . ." he continues more quietly, "in one month at Ypres, we've knocked out an estimated sixty thousand of the enemy. British, Canadian, French, and Belgian troops, dead or wounded."

The generals nod approvingly.

"Alas," the commander says in a cold, careful voice, "we mourn the loss of thirty-five thousand of our own soldiers and officers. So it goes in war . . . They gave their lives *für Gott und Vaterland*."

Each man looks at the table in silence.

"For the time being, we'll hold our positions around Ypres just as they are. No more than that. We'll shift our offense to other fronts."

The commander takes his pointer and steps toward the map on the wall.

EIGHT YEARS LATER

25 July 1923

Office of the Imperial War Graves Commission

Ypres, Belgium

Ten in a Row

"Ten British soldiers, you say? Buried in a row? No false alarms, then?"

The old British serviceman Cleeve has the telephone pressed against his ear as he speaks to his assistant. "Tell me, Harris. I'll make a note of it."

There is crackling on the line. Cleeve scribbles down the message on a designated form. "So, along the Ypres-Zonnebeke railway," he repeats, "one kilometre from Hellfire Corner? What? Yes, I know it well. By the level crossing. Railway Wood is on the right. Take a left, toward Potijze. The mass grave lies just left of the road, a few metres from the railway bedding. Right by the monument of Captain Bowlby."

A half hour later, Cleeve parks his motorcycle with sidecar at the crossing. He stands straight as an arrow, as befitting a retired officer, and walks toward Harris and his two helpers. He greets them in his stuffy manner, well aware of his rank and class. "Good maawning!"

The gravediggers mumble something back while each quickly but politely grasps the visor of his cap with his thumb and finger. Cleeve begins to walk in a bow around the grave but doesn't get farther than halfway.

"Right." He nods curtly and reaches instinctively into his pocket, takes out a snow-white handkerchief and holds it over his nose. The gravediggers exchange amused glances.

"If you want to avoid the smell, it's better not

to walk on that side, sir," Harris says, intentionally delaying this information. "The wind is coming from here, you see."

"Ten in a row," Cleeve exclaims with a stiff upper lip. He sighs, then walks back around the long pit and stands next to Harris.

"And reasonably well preserved, too, sir," his assistant adds.

"Most have been wrapped in a blanket, that's why," Cleeve mutters. "And then the clay, of course."

"Although they *are* beginning to stink rather awfully," Harris says, stating the obvious. "The sun and fresh air, you understand."

"Any identification possible, Harris?"

"I believe so, sir." He snickers, thinking about the mound of paperwork that awaits his boss.

"Numbers seven and eight seem a bit unusual," Harris continues. He jumps into the pit, straddles the seventh corpse, and unfolds the blankets around the two bodies.

"Two soldiers from the Royal Irish Regiment, sir. The uniforms are still easily recognizable. Besides, their chest straps are marked." He takes the belt from number seven, turns it over, and calls, "Soldier six-five-six-six!"

Cleeve begins to write diligently in his notebook. "We can identify him right away. And the other one?"

"Yes—the number is on his belt as well. It's even on one of his shoes. Number six-three-two-two."

"So, number eight in the row, soldier six-three-two-two," Cleeve says aloud, writing it down.

"Sir? You noticed, as well?" Harris asks a bit hesitantly. "You noticed that they're lying very close to each other?"

"This one was very young." Cleeve points to number eight. "No longer a child, but . . ."

"Not yet a man, eh?"

Cleeve nods.

"And the other one could have been his father." Harris sighs.

Three days later, Cleeve signs the last exhumation report with a flourish. *Two weeks' vacation at last*, he thinks. *Tomorrow morning I'm on the first train out of*

Ypres, and then I'll catch the ferry from Oostende to Dover and spend a few days with the family.

He licks the brown envelope closed and files the duplicate copies in a thick ring binder. His eyes focus on the top sheet. *Private 6566 T. Carthy, 47y., Clonmel (Ire.), and Private 6322 J. Condon, presumed 14y., Waterford (Ire.). Both 2BnRIR. Both missing (dead) since 5/24/1915. Now buried next to each other in plot LVI, row F, Poelkapelle, British Cemetery, in Flanders, Belgium.*

"A rather strange case," he mumbles to himself. He closes the binder and sets it in on the rack. He glances at the clock. Five minutes to six.

"I have a few moments yet." Cleeve sighs. An English newspaper is spread open on the large table. He decides to kill time by reading for a bit. A small article catches his attention: *Nobel Prize winner Doctor Fritz Haber to be the guest . . .*

SOME WORDS FROM THE AUTHOR

Who was Fritz Haber?

Fritz Haber (1868–1934) was a German chemist who developed chlorine gas (1915) and mustard gas (1917) for use in warfare. In 1918, Haber received the Nobel Prize in chemistry, not for creating these deadly gases but for other work, primarily for what became known as "the Haber-Bosch process," in which nitrogen and hydrogen are combined to form ammonia. This method is critical for the manufacturing of artificial fertiliser, and was responsible for vastly improving agriculture all over the world. Because nitrates are a key component in explosives, the process also boosted Germany's munitions production during World War I.

Haber's wife, a brilliant chemist in her own right, was horrified by her husband's work with poison gas. She committed suicide while Haber was supervising the first gas attack at Ypres. Apparently he put the war before his family, for he did not even attend her funeral.

Haber felt a great sense of patriotism toward his country. When the war ended and Germany was forced to pay huge reparations, he wanted to contribute to the costs. For years he tried to extract gold from seawater, but his efforts were to no avail.

Was John Condon really fourteen years old?

Yes, I strongly believe that John Condon was, at the time of his death, fourteen years old. You can find the Condon family of Thomas's Avenue, Waterford, Ireland, in the 1901 and 1911 censuses. If you presume that the brothers Patrick and John made a deal and swapped their names, then "age fourteen" matches. These documents may not always have been filled in with 100 percent accuracy by the local policemen.

How can nonbelievers explain that this story of John's being fourteen was so well known shortly after the war? That the Waterford boy was the talk of the town for many years? Why did newspapers go on repeating this story after World War I? The fact that he was eighteen on his enlistment, which can be found in the army archives, does not prove his real age. Of course he had to pretend he was old enough to enlist.

There is also a document stating that Patrick Condon died in 1940. Someone changed his age there: forty-two was crossed out, and replaced by thirty-nine. There must have been some confusion there. Were they still afraid to reveal his real age, maybe fearing the loss of a pension or other consequences?

There are still some loose ends to the John and Patrick Condon story. There are strong indications that Patrick Condon, using his older brother John's name, ran away from his Irish hometown of Waterford to Liverpool, England, before he went to the front. I did not know these facts when I wrote the original novel (in Dutch, published in Belgium). On 7 July 1938, the *Waterford News* published an article entitled "Ran Away to Great War. Waterford Youth Who Was Killed at Age of Fourteen. Boyish Adventure. Hid in Ship, Pretended He Was Eighteen." The author interviewed Nicholas Condon, Patrick's cousin and inseparable playmate. They were so attached that they were called the Condon twins. Nicholas shares the following: "Patrick was thirteen at the end of 1914. I was a few years older. On a sudden impulse we got on board of the *Clodagh*, a small steamer which plied between Waterford and Liverpool." The two stowaways arrived at their uncle's in Salford. The uncle offered to help them find work, but there were so many young men in uniform passing to and fro that they joined the army. Nicholas says they both enlisted with the Lancashire Fusiliers, later to be posted with the East Lancashires: "Patrick was a strapping lad for his age. They asked no questions when he said he was eighteen. But my cousin wasn't satisfied. He wanted to join the Royal Irish Regiment. This was our first and last separation. We never saw each other again. I came through the war all right. But my cousin was killed by a bursting shell. He could only have seen a few months' fighting."

A few years ago, in 2003, I met John Condon, son of Patrick. He was an elderly man, and together with his cousin Sonny he visited the grave of his uncle "John" in Belgium. They were the first of the Waterford Condons ever to visit the grave of their relative John Condon, who died in 1915. Talking to them reassured me that "John" really was a kid when he was killed in Flanders Fields. They were very convinced. And did they know anything about the identity swap? No challenge arose at all when I gave them my interpretation of "John" being in fact his younger brother Patrick. But they also preferred not to elaborate on that issue. Does it still remain a half secret among the family members?

Is it John Condon's grave?

Some say that the body in John Condon's grave is not his but that of the rifleman Patrick Fitzsimmons, and that there has been a misidentification. John Condon and Patrick Fitzsimmons had the same service number: 6322. John belonged to the Second Battalion Royal Irish Regiment (RIR), while Patrick was one of the Second Battalion Royal Irish

Rifles (also RIR). No one can exclude a misidentification, and only a DNA test would prove the truth.

But no one can doubt that there once was a Waterford boy who dreamed of adventure and glory. There was nothing he wanted more than to become a soldier. He went off to war in France and Belgium, but he never returned to Ireland. His body rests under a headstone somewhere in Flanders Fields.

This novel is not just a true story about a boy soldier who lived almost a century ago. Let's not forget that UNICEF estimates that there are some 250,000 child soldiers in the world now, mainly in Africa.

The

DEADLY
TOUCH
of the # TIGRESS

IAN HAMILTON

sphere

SPHERE

First published in Canada in 2011 by House of Anasi Press Inc.
First published in Great Britain in 2011 by Sphere
This edition published in 2012 by Sphere

A CIP catalogue record for this book
is available from the British Library.

ISBN 978-0-7515-4796-2

Typeset in Minion by M Rules
Printed and bound in Great Britain by
Clays Ltd, St Ives plc

Papers used by Sphere are from well-managed forests
and other responsible sources.

MIX

For La

1

When the phone rang, Ava woke with a start. She looked at the bedside clock. It was just past 3 a.m. 'Shit,' she said softly. She checked the incoming number. It was blocked. Hong Kong? Shenzhen? Shanghai? Or maybe even Manila or Jakarta, where the Chinese hid behind local names and were often all the more Chinese because of it. Wherever the call originated, Ava was sure it was somewhere in Asia, the caller ignorant about the time difference or just too desperate to care.

'*Wei*, Ava Lee,' a male voice said in Cantonese. It was a voice she didn't recognize.

'Who is calling?' she said in his dialect.

'Andrew Tam.'

It took a second for the name to register. 'Can you speak English?'

'Yes, I can,' he said, switching. 'I went to school in Canada.'

'Then you should know what time it is here,' she said.

'I'm sorry. Mr Chow gave your name and number to my uncle and told him I could call you anytime. He also said you speak Mandarin and Cantonese.'

Ava rolled onto her back. 'I do, but when it comes to business, I prefer English. There's less chance of confusion, of misunderstanding from my end.'

'We have a job for you,' Tam said abruptly.

'We?'

'My company. Mr Chow told my uncle he was going to discuss it with you.' Tam paused. 'You are a forensic accountant, I'm told.'

'I am.'

'According to what Mr Chow told my uncle, you have an amazing talent for finding people and money. Well, my money is missing and the person who took it has disappeared.'

'That is rarely a coincidence,' Ava said, letting the compliment slide.

'Ms Lee, I really need your help,' Tam said, his voice breaking.

'I need more information before I can say yes. I don't even know where or what the job is.'

'It's a bit of a moving target. We're based in Hong Kong and we were financing a company owned by a Chinese, which has offices in Hong Kong and Seattle and was doing production in Thailand for a US food retailer.'

'That isn't very helpful.'

'Sorry, I don't mean to be so vague. I'm actually better organized than I sound; it's just that the stress right now is—'

'I understand about the stress,' Ava said.

Tam drew a deep breath. 'After talking to my uncle about your company yesterday, I forwarded a complete package of information to a family member who lives in Toronto. Could you free yourself later today to meet?'

'In Toronto?' It was an oddity for her work to involve her home country, let alone city.

2

'Of course.'

'When?'

'How about dinner in Chinatown?'

'I would prefer something earlier. Dim sum, maybe.'

'All right, I'm sure dim sum will be fine.'

'And not in the old Chinatown downtown. I'd rather go to Richmond Hill. There's a restaurant, Lucky Season, in the Times Square Mall, just west of Leslie Street on Highway 7. Do you know the area?'

'Yes, I do, generally speaking.'

'Tell them to meet me there at one.'

'How will they recognize you?'

'I will recognize them. Tell them to wear something red – a shirt or sweater – and to carry a copy of *Sing Tao*.'

'Okay.'

'Man or woman?'

'A woman, actually.'

'That's unusual.'

He hesitated. She sensed that he was about to launch into another explanation, and she was about to cut him off when he said, 'My uncle tells me that Mr Chow is your uncle.'

'We're not blood relatives,' Ava said. 'I was raised tradition-ally. My mother insisted that we respect our elders, so it's natural for me to call our older family friends Uncle and Auntie. Uncle isn't a family friend, but from the very first time I met him it seemed appropriate. Even as my business partner he is still Uncle.'

'He's a man whom very many people call Uncle.'

Ava knew where Tam was headed and decided to cut him

3

off. 'Look, I'll meet with your contact later today. If I'm happy with the information she brings and I think the job is doable, then I'll call my uncle and we'll confirm that we're taking the job. If I'm not happy, then you won't hear from me again. *Bai, bai*,' she said, putting down the phone.

She struggled to find sleep again as Tam's voice, with its too familiar sound of desperation, lingered in her ears. She pushed it aside. Until she took possession of his problem, that's all it was: his problem.

2

Ava woke at seven, said her prayers, stretched for ten minutes, and then went to the kitchen to make a cup of instant coffee, using hot water from the Thermos. She considered herself to be Canadian, but she still clung to habits engrained by her mother, such as an always-full rice steamer and a hot-water Thermos in the kitchen. Her friends made fun of her taste in coffee. She didn't care. She didn't have the patience to wait for it to brew and she hated waste; anyway, her taste buds were strictly attuned to instant.

She emptied a sachet of Starbucks VIA Ready Brew into her cup, poured in the water, and went to fetch the *Globe and Mail* at the door. She brought it in and settled onto the couch, turning on the television to a local Chinese channel, WOW TV, that had a current affairs show in Cantonese. There were two hosts: a former Hong Kong comedian who was trying to extend his best-before date in the boondocks, and a pretty young woman without any showbiz pedigree. She was low-key and seemed intelligent and classy – not a usual combination for women on Chinese television. Ava had developed a slight crush on her.

When the show broke at eight for a news summary, Ava dialled Uncle's cellphone number. It was early evening in Hong

Kong. He would have left the office by now, maybe had had a massage, and would be sitting down to dinner at one of the high-end hotpot restaurants in Kowloon, probably the one near the Peninsula Hotel.

He answered on the second ring. 'Uncle,' she said.

'Ava, you caught me at a good time.'

'Andrew Tam called me.'

'How did you find him?'

'He speaks English very well. He was polite.'

'How did you leave it?'

'I'm meeting with someone today who has details about the lost funds. I told Tam I'd talk to you after I had the information and then we'd decide what to do.'

Uncle hesitated. 'It isn't so straightforward from my end. I'd like you to make the decision about whether or not we take on the job.'

Ava tried to think of some other time when she'd been the sole decision maker on a job. She couldn't. 'Why leave this up to me?' she asked.

'Tam is the nephew of a friend, an old and very close friend. We grew up together near Wuhan, and he was one of the men who swam here from China with me.'

She had heard the tale of the swim many times. Over the years the danger that Uncle and his friends encountered during those eight hours in the South China Sea, escaping the Communist regime, had become a distant memory, but the brotherhood they had forged remained all-important. 'So it is that personal?'

'Yes. I knew it would be hard for me to be objective, so I

6

thought it would be best for the nephew to tell you what happened, and then you can decide if the job is worth taking on its own merits. And Ava – don't agree to do it if it doesn't have merit.'

'What about our rate?' she asked. It was usually thirty percent of what they recovered, split evenly between them.

'For you, yes, but for me … I can't take my share. He's too close.'

She wished he hadn't said that. It made it even more personal, and they tried to keep the personal out of their business.

'Call me when the meeting is over,' Uncle said.

Ava hung up and puttered around the apartment, answering emails, catching up with bills, looking into winter holiday packages. She debated what to wear to the meeting. Since she didn't need to impress anyone, she decided on a black Giordano T-shirt and black Adidas training pants. No makeup, no jewellery.

She looked at herself in the mirror. She was five foot three and her weight hovered around 115 pounds. She was slim but not skinny, and her running and bak mei workouts had given her legs and butt nice definition. She had large breasts for a Chinese woman, large enough that she didn't need a padded bra for them to get noticed. In the T-shirt and training pants her shape got lost; the outfit made her look smaller and younger. There were times when looking young worked to her advantage. There were also times when a different look was needed, so she had a wardrobe of black form-fitting linen and cotton slacks, knee-length pencil skirts, and an array of Brooks Brothers shirts in various colours and styles that showed off her chest. The slacks and shirts, worn with makeup and jewellery, were her professional look: attractive, classy, capable.

At eleven she called downstairs and asked to have her car brought up from the garage.

Ava's condo was in Yorkville, in the heart of downtown Toronto. Like the properties around Central Park in New York, Belgravia in London, and Victoria Peak in Hong Kong, it boasted the city's most expensive real estate. She had paid more than a million dollars for the condo – in cash. Her mother, Jennie Lee, had been pleased by her choice of location, and was even prouder that her daughter wasn't carrying a mortgage. The condo came with a parking spot in which she had deposited an Audi A6. It was a waste of money, that car. Most everything she needed was within walking distance or, at worst, a five-minute subway ride. The only time she used the car was to visit her mother in Richmond Hill.

At ten after eleven the concierge called to say that her car was available. As Ava drove east along Bloor Street, she passed five-star hotels, innumerable restaurants, antique dealers and art galleries, and high-end retailers such as Chanel, Tiffany, Holt Renfrew, and Louis Vuitton – stores she rarely ventured into. She knew that if she did, any mention of her mother's name would set off a serious round of kowtowing.

She took the Don Valley Parkway north towards Richmond Hill, and for once the traffic was flowing smoothly. She got to Times Square half an hour early. The mall was named and modelled after one in Hong Kong; its main building, fronting Highway 7, was three storeys high. The parking lot in the back was encircled by stores selling Chinese herbs, DVDs, and baked goods, and by restaurants serving every type of Asian cuisine.

Toronto has a huge Chinese population – half a million or more – and Richmond Hill is its epicentre. About twenty kilometres north of downtown, Richmond Hill is a sprawling expanse of suburban tract housing and malls. East and west along Highway 7, the malls are almost exclusively Chinese. Once a traditional European-Canadian suburb, Richmond Hill is a place where English isn't needed any more. There isn't a service or commodity that can't be acquired in Cantonese.

It wasn't always this way. Ava could remember when there was only the old Chinatown downtown on Dundas Street, just south of where she lived now. In those days her mother had been a bit of a pioneer, one of the first Chinese people to settle in Richmond Hill. Every Saturday she still had to drive Ava and her sister, Marian, into Toronto for their Mandarin and abacus lessons. While the girls studied, she shopped for the Chinese vegetables, fruit, fish, sauces, spices, and ten-kilo bags of fragrant Thai rice that made up their diet.

All of that had changed when Hong Kong began to prepare for the end of British colonial rule in 1997. The uncertainty of life under Communist China hadn't exactly caused panic, but many felt it would be prudent to have other options, and Canada made it easy for those with money to establish a second home. Toronto's downtown area couldn't accommodate the influx of new Chinese immigrants, so Richmond Hill became the next best landing spot – and why it was chosen was simple.

For years, Vancouver, British Columbia – more specifically,

the nearby suburban city of Richmond – had been the most desired location for Chinese immigrants coming to Canada. Its name evoked wealth and was therefore considered auspicious. Ava's mother was no exception; she had lived in Richmond during her first two years in the country. When Toronto began to supplant Vancouver as the economic hub of Canada, western Chinese-Canadians migrated to Richmond Hill because they assumed it would be like Richmond, BC – that is, Chinese. Eventually, as always with the Chinese, more begot more, until you could walk into nearby Markham's Pacific Mall and believe you were in Hong Kong.

Ava had to circle the Times Square parking lot twice before she found a spot. The Lucky Season was full, and she had to wait ten minutes before getting a table. Her mother had introduced her to the restaurant, which on weekdays offered every dim sum dish for $2.20. A party of four could drink all the tea they wanted, stuff themselves for an hour, and still spend less than thirty dollars on a meal. It was remarkable, Ava thought, and all the more remarkable because the food was excellent and the portions traditional dim sum size.

Her mother ate there two or three times a week, but this was Tuesday, and Ava knew she had an appointment with her herbalist, followed by her weekly session with the manicurist. Still, she did a quick scan of the room just in case.

Ava sat at a table facing the front door. There was a steady stream of people, none of them too rich or too poor to pass up two-dollar dim sum. It amazed her to what lengths the Chinese would go to for perceived value. You could put four restaurants serving almost identical food beside each other, and for reasons that seemed beyond logic, one of them would develop a reputation for being the best. That restaurant would be besieged by long lines, creating endless waits, while the others would be almost blissfully empty. Her mother epitomized that mentality.

Jennie Lee was a constant presence in Ava's life. It was something she had grown to accept, although her sister had problems with it, mainly because she was married to a *gweilo* – a Caucasian with British roots – and he couldn't understand their mother's need to maintain such close contact with her daughters. He didn't have any concept of family Chinese-style: the constant intrusions, being joined at the hip for life, the obligations children had to their parents. He also couldn't fathom the life that had brought their mother and them to Canada.

Their mother had been born in Shanghai and, though raised in Hong Kong, considered herself to be a true Shanghainese – which is to say strong-willed, opinionated, and loud when required, but never rude, never tacky, and never pushy, like Hong Kongers. She had met their father, Marcus Lee, when she worked in the office of a company he owned. He was from Shanghai too. She became his second wife in the old style, which is to say he never left or divorced the first. Ava and Marian became his second family, acknowledged and cared for but with no hope of inheriting anything more than their names and whatever their mother could put aside for them.

When Ava was two and Marian four, their mother and father had become embroiled in a dispute, and Jennie's presence in Hong Kong became too much of a burden. Ava learned later that a third wife had emerged, and though her mother accepted subservience to wife number one, she wasn't about to play second fiddle to a newcomer. In any event, their father decided that the farther away they were, the happier his life would be. He relocated them initially in Vancouver, a direct flight from Hong Kong if he wanted to visit but far enough away for them not to be a nuisance. But her mother hated Vancouver; it was too wet, too dreary, too much a reminder of Hong Kong. She moved the girls to Toronto, and there were no objections from the Hong Kong side.

They saw their father maybe once or twice a year, and always in Toronto. He had bought their mother a house, had given her a generous allowance, and looked after any special needs. When he did come to visit, the girls called him Daddy. Their mother referred to him as her husband. For one or two weeks they would lead a 'normal' family life. Then he was gone, and the couple's contact would be reduced to a daily phone call.

It was, Ava realized later, a businesslike relationship. Their father had got what he wanted when he wanted it, and her mother had the two girls and a notional husband. He would never deny her or the family, and her mother knew that; so she deliberately set about squeezing him for every dollar's worth of security she could get. He must have known what she was doing, but as long as she played by the rules, he was okay with it. So she had the house, she had a new car every two years, and she was the beneficiary of a life insurance policy that would replace her monthly allowance (and then some) if anything happened to him. He paid all the school fees, and she made sure the girls went to the most expensive and prestigious schools she could get them into. He paid separately for family vacations, dental work, summer camps, and special tutoring. He bought each of the girls their first car.

Marcus Lee had four children by his first wife, two with Jennie, and another two with wife number three. His third wife and their two children lived in Australia now, and Ava was sure that he loved and looked after them as much as he did the other children and wives. It was – at least to Westerners – a rather strange way to live. But in Chinese eyes it was traditional and acceptable, and Marcus Lee was respected for the manner in which he discharged his responsibilities. It wasn't a lifestyle for a man without wealth. Marcus had been fortunate in that regard, making his first serious money in textiles before manufacturing went offshore to places such as Indonesia and Thailand. He made a successful transition into toys and again showed foresight by exiting before Vietnam and China became major players. Now most of the family's capital was tied up in real estate in the New Territories and in the Shenzhen economic zone; by all accounts it was delivering a steady revenue stream and building value.

Jennie never worked again after Marian was born. Her life was devoted to being a second wife and to raising her two girls. Given her husband's absence, her life's focus had narrowed down to the girls. Not that their mother didn't have other interests. She played mah-jong a couple of times a week, and once a week she took the Taipan bus north to Casino Rama for a day of baccarat. She had also made a semi-career out of shopping. Everything she bought had to be the best. She had a complete aversion to knockoffs; if she wanted a Gucci bag, it had to be a real Gucci bag.

Jennie Lee was well past fifty, but she didn't look it and didn't want to acknowledge it. She loved nothing better than being mistaken for her daughters' older sister. And she spent money on maintaining that look: creams, lotions, herbs, hair-styling, clothes. Marian had two children of her own, but since they were being raised in Ottawa with their *gweilo* father, their Chinese was scant. They knew that *gweilo* means 'grey ghost' in Cantonese. The other word they knew was *langlei*, which means 'beautiful one.' That was how they referred to their grandmother. Calling her anything else – such as Grandma – was a no-no.

In many ways Ava's mother was a princess, spoiled and self-indulgent. But then again, so many Chinese women were. They made the 'Jewish princesses' Ava had known in univer-sity look like amateurs. And that thought crossed her mind once more when she saw a woman in a red silk blouse with a copy of *Sing Tao* tucked under her arm walk into Lucky Season and survey the room.

She was tall for a Chinese woman, and made taller still by stiletto heels that looked as if they were made from the finest, most supple red leather. The silk blouse was worn with a pair of black linen slacks and a gold belt with the Chanel logo on the buckle. Her eyebrows were plucked into two thin lines and her face was caked with makeup. And even from a distance Ava could see the jewellery: enormous diamond stud earrings, two rings – one looked like a three-carat diamond, the other was carved green jade surrounded by rubies – and a crucifix encrusted with diamonds and emeralds. The only thing that marred the picture of a perfect Hong Kong princess was her hair, which was pulled back and secured demurely at the nape of her neck with a plain black elastic band.

Ava stood and waved in her direction. The woman's eyes settled on her, and in them Ava read – what? Disappointment? Recognition? Maybe she hadn't been expecting a woman. Maybe she hadn't been expecting one dressed in a black Giordano T-shirt and Adidas track pants.

They greeted each other in Cantonese, and then Ava said, 'I do prefer English.'

'Me too,' she said. 'My name is Alice.'

'Ava.'

'I know.'

They perused the dim sum menu, finally ticking off six boxes. When the waiter took their sheet away, Ava said, 'I know this place seems ridiculously cheap, but the food is very good.'

'I've eaten here before,' Alice said.

'So, Alice, how do you know Andrew?'

'He's my brother.'

'Ah.'

'That's why I'm here. Andrew's trying to keep this problem quiet. He doesn't want to unnecessarily alarm other members of the family.'

'Someone else already knows – your relative in Hong Kong who went to my uncle.'

'He is my mother's brother, our oldest uncle, and he is very discreet. But even then he doesn't know that much, only that Andrew needs help collecting some money that is owed.'

'Three million dollars.'

'Actually, a bit more than that. Maybe closer to five million when all is said and done.'

'Is this one of those Chinese deals?' Ava asked.

Alice looked confused.

'You know,' Ava continued, 'one of those deals where someone needs some money and can't get it from a bank or other normal sources, so they go to their family, but if the family can't come up with enough money they go to a friend of the family, or maybe he has a friend, an uncle, and the money finds its way to the person who needs it and there are handshakes all around – not a shred of paper – and everyone in the chain, all the family members and friends, has a share in the responsibility for making sure the money is repaid.'

'No, it wasn't like that at all,' Alice said. She pulled a fat manila envelope from inside the *Sing Tao*. 'Everything is in here. There's a letter from my brother explaining how the deal was structured and how it progressed until it went off the rails. There's all kinds of backup documentation: the original lending contract, purchase orders, letters of credit, invoices, emails. My brother is quite thorough.'

'That's a welcome change,' Ava said.

The first of the dim sum arrived: chicken feet in *chu hon* sauce and crescent-shaped chive-and-shrimp dumplings. They both reached for the chicken feet, and the conversation waned as they sucked skin and meat from bone. Then came *har gow*, spicy salted squid, shrimp and meat wrapped in steamed bean curd, and radish cake. Alice kept Ava's teacup full, and Ava tapped her finger on the table in a silent thank-you each time the other poured.

'Are you involved in the business?' Ava asked.

'No, I have nothing to do with it, but my brother and I are very close.'

'What kind of business is it?'

'It's a company that specializes in financing purchase orders and letters of credit. You know how it is these days. Companies get big orders and may not have the money to finance production. Even if they have letters of credit, the banks can be very sticky. And even if the banks do help, it's never for the whole amount. So my brother's company fills in the gaps. It advances the company money for production – at very high interest rates, of course, but the companies know that upfront and build it into their margins.'

'How high?'

'Minimum two percent a month, normally three.'

'Nice.'

'They're filling a gap.'

'I wasn't being critical.'

'Anyway, once in a while they have a problem. Normally, because of the amount of due diligence they do – and because they don't finance anything that seems risky and the purchase orders and letters of credit are typically from blue-chip companies – those problems have been small and infrequent.'

'Until now.'

'Yes.'

'What was the blue-chip company, or is this an exception?'

'Major Supermarkets.'

Ava was caught off guard. 'That's the largest food retailer in North America.'

'Yes.'

'So what went wrong?'

Alice started to reply and then caught herself. 'I think it's better if you read the contents of the envelope. If you need more information or any clarification, you should call my brother directly. His cellphone number and private home number are in the envelope. He doesn't want you to email him or call him at the office. He also said you could call him any time, night or day. He hasn't been sleeping much.'

'All right, I'll read the documents.'

'This is very difficult for him,' she said slowly. 'He prides himself on being cautious and always acting with integrity. He's having trouble accepting that this is actually happening to him.'

'Stuff happens,' Ava said.

Alice fingered the crucifix around her neck, her eyes taking in the simpler one that Ava wore.

'You're Catholic?' Ava asked.

'Yes.'

'Me too.'

'You live here in Toronto?'

'Yes, I'm the only one. The rest of the family is in Hong Kong.'

'What do you do?'

'We're in the clothing business, my husband and I. He is Chinese too – mainland – and we have factories there and in Malaysia and Indonesia.'

18

'Tough business. My father was in it for a while,' Ava said.

'We've been lucky. My husband decided years ago that the only way to survive was to move into private-label lines. So that's all we do now.'

'Are you involved in the day-to-day activities?'

The woman looked across the table, her eyes suddenly curious. Ava wondered if her question had hit a sore spot. 'I don't mean to pry,' she said quickly.

'*Momentai*,' Alice said. 'I have two sons now, so I spend most of my time raising them and looking after our home. My husband keeps me up to date on most things, and I still have to suck up to the wives of the buyers, but no, I'm not that involved.'

Ava reached for the dim sum list but Alice beat her to it. 'I'll pay,' she said.

'Thanks.'

Ava's Adidas jacket was draped over the back of her chair. As she turned to get it, she saw Alice's eyes lock onto her again. 'Have I said or done something wrong?' she asked.

'No, not at all. It's just that you look familiar to me. Where did you go to school?'

'York University here, and then Babson College, near Boston.'

'No, before that. I mean high school.'

'I went to Havergal College.'

'I did too,' Alice said.

'I don't remember you.'

'Do you have an older sister named Marian?'

'Yes.'

'I was in the same class as her. We were part of the first big wave of Chinese students and we hung around together. You would have been, what, two or three years behind us?'

'Two.'

'I remember seeing you with Marian.'

Ava searched her memory and came up dry, but then Marian had hung out with a gaggle of Chinese girls that reached double figures. 'She's married now and has two daughters and a husband who is a rising star in the Canadian public service.'

'Is he Chinese?'

'No, Canadian.'

'That's Havergal Old girls for you: they know how to marry well,' Alice said, and then glanced at Ava's ring hand. 'You aren't married?'

'No,' Ava said.

'A working girl.'

Alice held up the dim sum list for a server to collect and take to the cashier. When it was gone, she folded her hands neatly in front of her, and again looked intently at Ava. 'How did you get into this kind of work? I mean, it is a bit unusual. My brother told me what it is your company does, and when I was told I was meeting a woman, my imagination certainly didn't conjure you up. In fact, I assumed the woman would be more of a go-between than an active participant in the business. You are active, aren't you?'

'I am.'

'I thought so ... I wasn't being condescending. My husband has had to employ companies like yours in the past, so I know something about how they operate and the kind of people

who work in them. That's why I didn't expect to meet someone quite so young.'

'And on top of that, I'm a woman,' Ava said with a little smile.

'Yes, that too. So how did you get into this?'

The question had caught Ava off guard. She was more used
to asking questions than being asked, and she hesitated. 'It's
boring,' she said.

'Please,' Alice insisted.

Ava poured tea for them both, Alice tapping her finger on
the table in thanks. 'It really is boring.'

'I'm not sure I believe you.'

Ava shrugged. 'When I got out of school, I went to work for
one of the big accounting firms in Toronto, and I quickly
found out it wasn't for me. I was a crummy employee, really.
I found it difficult being part of a big bureaucracy, doing what
you're told without being able to question the effectiveness or
efficiency of it. Looking back, I was probably quite arrogant,
a bit of a know-it-all, always ready to argue with my bosses. I
lasted six months before packing it in. I think they were as
glad to see me go as I was to leave.

'I decided to open my own little firm, so I took an office up
here – two buildings over, actually – and began doing basic
accounting for friends of my mother and some small businesses and the like. One of them, a clothing importer, believe
it or not, ran into a problem with a supplier in Shenzhen.
When he couldn't collect his money, I asked him to let me try,
for a percentage of whatever I could recover.'

'What made you think you could do that?'

'I've always been persuasive.'

'And you actually went to Shenzhen to do this?'

'Yes, but when I got there, I found that the supplier had been screwing over more than one customer, and there was a lineup waiting to go after him. Except, of course, he was nowhere to be found. He'd taken off with whatever money he had left. In the course of nosing about, I discovered there was another company trying to do what I was doing. I figured it would be counterproductive to compete against them, so I suggested we join forces. That's when I met Uncle.'

'Yes,' Alice said, her eyes averted. 'Andrew mentioned Mr Chow. He has his reputation, of course, and who knows really what's true or not . . . So he's not a blood relative, then?'

The same question her brother had asked. 'No, he's a Chinese uncle in the best sense of the word,' Ava said.

'I see.'

She wants to ask me about him, Ava thought, and then quickly moved on. 'I didn't deal with him directly at first. He had some people working for him who were, frankly, a bit rough around the edges – the kind you'd expect to encounter in a business like that. They agreed to work with me, although I think, looking back, they were probably humouring me, or maybe they thought it was a way to get me into bed. Anyway, Uncle had a great network of contacts and we tracked down the guy in no time. But when it came to collecting, Uncle's people had no finesse whatsoever. The guy would have talked his way out of returning about two-thirds of the money he owed if I hadn't gotten involved and done a little forensic accounting work.

'Word got back to Uncle about what I had done, and he asked me to come and work with him. I said I wasn't thrilled about his other employees. He told me he'd phase them out, that he thought my style and his were compatible. That was ten years ago, and the business has been just Uncle and me for most of that time.'

'And you've obviously been successful.'

'We've done well enough.'

The bill came to the table and Alice put twenty dollars on the tray. 'Ava, did my brother sound desperate to you?'

Ava slipped on her jacket. 'Not any more than most of our clients do.'

'Well, let me tell you, he is desperate. That five million dollars represents nearly all the capital our family has accumulated over the past two generations.' She reached across the table, grabbing Ava's hand and squeezing. 'Please do everything you can to help.'

It was almost four o'clock when Ava pulled up in front of her condo, tossed her car keys to the concierge, and went upstairs, the manila envelope, still unopened, tucked under her arm.

She opened a bag of sour candy, made herself a coffee, and sat at the kitchen table. Her mind wandered. It had been a long time since she had thought about, let alone discussed, how she and Uncle had gotten together and built their business. She had told Alice Tam the truth, but it was the bare-bones truth. When she thought about how naive she had been when she started and what she was now able to handle, it was as if she were looking at two different people.

In the beginning she'd been adept enough at the financial side of things, her curiosity, imagination, and training helping her track and find money in places where the thieves had thought it untraceable. And at first that was her main focus. Only gradually did she take on the collection role. She began by working on targets as the soft opener – she had a knack for getting people to talk, especially men, who saw her as a soft-spoken, polite, exotic young thing who needn't be taken too seriously. By the time they realized the opposite was true, it was usually too late.

Ava didn't start closing accounts until she saw the muscle

Uncle was using botch projects by going too far. There's a fine line between instilling enough fear to get someone to do what you want and applying so much pressure that the target figures he's toast no matter what he does, so he might as well try to hang on to the money. Ava had a talent for finding the tipping point. Uncle would say, 'People always do the right thing for the wrong reason.' Ava made that her mantra, striving to pinpoint the core self-interest in her targets, the one thing that was more important to them than hanging on to stolen money.

Uncle also said, 'Once they have the money they forget where it came from, how they acquired it. In their minds, it is theirs. You need to remind them that it has a rightful owner and that the only thing open for discussion is how they are going to return it.'

Not that they didn't try to hang on to it anyway. Being yelled at, cursed, and threatened was just part of the job. Knives, guns, and fists weren't uncommon either, and that's why Uncle said he used muscle. If there was going to be intimidation and violence, he wanted to have the most firepower. The problem, in Ava's mind, was that the muscle invited a negative reaction. One look at Uncle's original crew and the targets would gear up for the inevitable conflict. The violence clouded the process, made the money almost a secondary objective.

Ava urged Uncle to let the enforcers go, using them only on a must-need basis. His only concern was the potential for physical danger the targets posed. 'I can look after myself,' Ava said. And the truth was, she could.

She had started taking martial arts when she was twelve and had almost immediately shown ability. She was quick, agile, and fearless. In a matter of months she was so far ahead of everyone else in her class that the teacher moved her up to train with the teens; a year later he moved her again, to work out with the adults. By the time she was fifteen, Ava's skill paralleled his. That was when he took her aside and asked if she was interested in learning bak mei. It was an ancient form, he explained, reserved for the most gifted. It was taught only one-on-one, traditionally passed down from father to son but now also from mentor to student. There was one teacher in Toronto, Grandmaster Tang. Ava met with him several times before he agreed to accept her as a student. She was his second pupil; another teenager, Derek Liang, was the first, and though he and Ava never learned or practised together, over the years they had become friends.

From time to time Ava had called upon Derek to help her with collection. It was something they never discussed with their other friends, none of whom knew about her job. They had simply come to accept that once in a while Ava would leave the city on business for a few days or even weeks. She doubted they even noticed she was gone.

Ava thought that bak mei was the perfect martial art for a woman. The hand movements were quick, light, and short; they snapped with tension to their fullest extent, where the energy was released. It didn't take a lot of physical strength to be effective. Bak mei attacks were meant to cause damage, directed as they were at the most sensitive parts of the body, such as the ears, eyes, throat, underarms, sides, stomach, and, of course, groin. Kicks were hardly ever aimed above the waist. Bak mei hadn't come naturally to Ava. She had to learn to overcome her lack of power – at least, compared to Derek and Master Tang – and to exploit her strengths: her lightning-quick reflexes and her uncanny accuracy.

And learn she did. 'I can look after myself,' she had told Uncle. And in all the years they'd been working together, she'd never given him any reason to doubt her.

They had been profitable years, with Ava earning enough money for the condo and the car and an impressive investment portfolio. But the best thing about the jobs she and Uncle did was that when they were successful, the income was only part of the satisfaction. First there was the ride getting to the money – it was never the same twice, and though it taxed her emotionally, it also forced her to expand her senses and her thought processes. Then there were the clients. Although she complained about them sometimes, especially those who in utter desperation were far too clinging and demanding, she also accepted Uncle's conviction that they were simply lost souls looking for redemption. 'When we get them their money back, what we are really doing is saving their lives,' he would say. Ava believed that too.

Ava reached for a black Moleskine notebook resting on the corner of the table, opened it to the first page, and wrote *Andrew Tam* across the top of the lined page. Every job she had ever done had its own notebook, a meticulous day-by-day record of everything she deemed relevant. The completed notebooks sat in a safety deposit box at the Toronto-Dominion Bank two blocks from her condo.

The manila envelope was stuffed with paper, and she quietly groaned at the prospect of wading through it all. However, a quick scan soon brought a smile to her face. The paperwork was beautifully organized, a complete chronological record of Andrew Tam's dealings with a company called Seafood Partners, starting with a letter from him summarizing the events from start to finish. The letter even referred to appendices that were attached and neatly numbered. Ava admired his thoroughness. Then she wondered what moment of madness had caused him to go into business with a seafood company.

Of all the characters she had dealt with in the past, the seafood guys were the worst. It was as if they were programmed to steal, and once they had your money, getting it back was harder than pulling teeth with your fingers. One of her clients in Vancouver had bought two forty-foot containers of Chinese scallops; when the product arrived in Canada, he found that the boxes – clearly marked SCALLOPS – were filled with freezer-burned mackerel. It had taken her close to two weeks' trekking around seafood plants in dusty, dirty Dalian in northeast China, on the Yellow Sea near the Korean border, before she caught up with the packer. It took another week before she got the money back. Even then the job wouldn't have wrapped up so quickly if Uncle hadn't put her in touch with a high-ranking general. They had to split their recovery fee with him (and probably the rest of his unit), but without his influence she might have been there for several weeks more.

Tam's company was called Dynamic Financial Services. It was on Des Voeux Road, almost next door to the headquarters of the Hong Kong Shanghai Bank, on Queen's Road in

Central, the very heart of Hong Kong's financial district. About a year before, Seafood Partners had come to Dynamic Financial Services with a master purchase order from Major Supermarkets for six million pounds of Thai shrimp, cooked, peeled, and deveined, with the tail on.

Ava made her first note: *Who introduced Dynamic to Seafood Partners?*

The purchase order was of twelve months' duration, and the selling price was locked in for the entire period.

Note 2: *Isn't shrimp a commodity? Don't prices fluctuate? How could Seafood Partners commit to Major Supermarkets for a year?*

The product was to be packed under Major Supermarkets' own label, and Tam had affixed a copy of their specifications. They didn't seem particularly onerous. There had to be an average of thirty-seven to thirty-nine shrimp in every bag. Each bag had to have a true net weight of one pound, true net weight being the weight after the shrimp had thawed. The tails were to be a uniform red colour, with no black tails allowed. Tripolyphosphates and/or salt were permitted up to a residual level of two percent. The shrimp had to be processed from fresh and frozen only once. On the specification sheet Tam had highlighted in yellow the net weight requirement and the tripolyphosphates level.

It was anticipated that Major Supermarkets would need about 500,000 pounds of shrimp a month. In order to manage that level of business, Seafood Partners would need to have 1.5 million pounds of shrimp in their system at any one time – an on-hand inventory of 500,000 pounds, another

500,000 pounds in transit to the US from Thailand, and another 500,000 pounds being processed. Seafood Partners was buying the shrimp at $4.10 a pound and selling to Major Supermarkets at $4.80 a pound.

Note 3: *Given what was essentially 90 days' financing at 2 to 3 percent a month, and given customs, storage, trucking, and distribution charges, how the hell did Seafood Partners expect to make money?*

The master purchase order was from Major Supermarkets to Seafood Partners. Seafood Partners assigned the purchase order to Dynamic Financial Services, and Dynamic issued letters of credit to the Thai packer and imported the product into the US. Major Supermarkets had six distributors that drew up weekly purchase orders for shrimp; Seafood Partners and Dynamic Financial Services were copied on those purchase orders. Seafood Partners released the product from inventory and Dynamic Financial Services sent an invoice for the product directly to Major Supermarkets. The cheques went to Dynamic, which took its money and interest off the top and then sent the balance of the funds to Seafood Partners.

Note 4: *Why didn't Dynamic retain complete control of the inventory? Why did they allow Seafood Partners to release product?*

After five months, relations between Major Supermarkets and Seafood Partners began to go sour. Shrimp sales were not meeting expectations, and the buyer at Major Supermarkets was having second thoughts about the length and volume of his commitment. The documentation included copies of emails that had gone back and forth, and in many of them the buyer was looking for price relief. He claimed that the market had tanked and that he could buy the same shrimp more cheaply almost anywhere. He needed help to remain competitive.

At first Seafood Partners refused. A deal was a deal, they repeated. The buyer kept at them to reduce their prices, making (not very subtle) threats to go elsewhere to average down the cost of Seafood Partners' product. Finally Seafood Partners relented and dropped their selling price to $4.40.

Note 5: *Didn't Dynamic Financial Services ask if dropping the selling price of the shrimp was even remotely possible?*

As Ava read on, she could see the train wreck coming. She didn't know what form it was going to take, but Tam's yellow highlighting of the net weights and chemical levels offered a clue.

There are several ways to make more money on a basic food commodity than the market warrants. Cheating on weights is perhaps the simplest. Put a label weight of one pound on a bag and then put 15 ounces of product in it, and you can increase your profit by seven percent. If someone actually weighs the bag, the packer has a problem. But the weight of shrimp is easier to manipulate than most other seafood products, since you have to add an ice glaze to protect the flesh. Under normal circumstances a five percent glaze is added, meaning that a one-pound bag's gross weight becomes 16.8 ounces. If Seafood Partners put a twelve percent glaze on the shrimp, the bag would still have a gross weight of 16.8 ounces, but 1.8 ounces would be ice, leaving only 15 ounces of shrimp. The product would pass any rudimentary inspection.

Another common trick is to 'pump' the product, to add moisture to it. Ava didn't know who had discovered this technique, but she knew that just about every protein sector – including beef and chicken producers – did it. With shrimp it's very simple: all you have to do is soak them in a chemical solution, typically a tripolyphosphate. The longer you soak the shrimp and the more potent the solution, the more moisture the shrimp absorbs. The moisture adds weight – artificial weight.

The economic impact of adding weight goes beyond the extra weight itself. Shrimp are sold by size: the larger the size, the higher the price. Shrimp that come to between 31 and 40 pieces per pound sell for more than smaller shrimp that count between 41 and 50 pieces per pound. So if Seafood Partners added enough weight chemically to change a 41–50 count into a 31–40 count, they would make more on a per pound basis.

How many stunts had Seafood Partners tried? As it turned out, all of them. Ava could hardly believe it. Cheating using one method was risky enough. Trying two was begging for trouble. Doing all three? Craziness – or complete desperation.

And Major Supermarkets had caught them out. Actually, the US Food and Drug Administration caught them first, in a random inspection, which was when the weight discrepancy was identified. The FDA turned the problem over to Major Supermarkets' in-house quality-control team, which bored in and exposed the whole mess. It was the excuse the buyer needed to get out of the twelve-month contract. The day after the internal inspection results, Seafood Partners were informed that they had been delisted. The product already in stores was to be picked up, the master purchase order was cancelled, inventory in the US and on the water was now their problem, and none of the outstanding invoices would be paid.

Seafood Partners did not tell Dynamic Financial Services about the fiasco. It was not until Dynamic called Major Supermarkets about the outstanding invoices that they were told what was up. In the meantime, Seafood Partners had moved the inventory and Dynamic had no idea where it was. More than a million pounds of shrimp had gone missing. Add close to a million dollars in unpaid invoices, and Dynamic was out of pocket at least five million dollars.

Andrew Tam had done a good job of piecing it all together. There were copies of the financing agreement, the master purchase order, the letters of credit Dynamic had issued, and examples of Major Supermarkets' purchase orders. He had also attached the FDA inspection report and Major Supermarkets' quality-control team reports, and he had somehow accessed a series of emails from Seafood Partners to the packer that outlined, in bold terms, what they wanted him to do.

Note 6: *Has Tam spoken to the packer? Does the packer have any liability?*

Ava checked her watch; it was 4 a.m. in Hong Kong. She dialled Tam's cellphone number. To her surprise he answered. 'I was hoping you'd call,' he said.

'I've just finished going through your paperwork. What a mess.'

There was silence from the other end, and Ava wondered if she had insulted him. Then he said, 'Tell me about it.'

She looked at her notes. 'I see two signatures on the financing agreement on behalf of Seafood Partners. How many partners are there?'

'Those are them: George Antonelli and Jackson Seto. Antonelli lives in Bangkok. He handles production and the technical side of things.'

'Like short weights?'

'I guess. Seto kind of floats between Seattle and Hong Kong. He seems to have residences in both places. He is the marketer and the money guy.'

'I take it you've spoken to them about this problem?'

'I've tried to.'

'And?'

'They initially tried to pin it on the buyer for Major Supermarkets, saying that he was just looking for a way to get rid of them and buy some cheaper product. But after I got hold of the FDA's and Major's inspection reports, they switched gears and told me I should be going after the packer, that he had screwed up the specifications and was liable for any loss. The packer was the one who supplied me with the emails from Antonelli instructing him to change the specs. The emails were very specific.'

'And then what?'

He paused. 'And then they stopped answering my emails and taking my phone calls,' he said.

'Where is the company registered?'

'Hong Kong.'

'Bank account?'

'Also in Hong Kong, and it has nothing in it.'

'Is that the account you sent money to?'

'Yes.'

'Always to Hong Kong?'

'Yes.'

'They could have an offshore account.'

'I wouldn't know.'

She chewed on a sour candy. 'Tell me, Andrew, who made the introduction? Who brought you together?'

'An old schoolmate of mine. He met Seto in Hong Kong through another friend of his. Seto mentioned that he was looking for purchase-order financing and the schoolmate put him on to me. I don't think he knew Seto very well.'

'I've looked at the numbers, and the profit margins look thin. That didn't concern you?'

'Seto told me they're standard for the industry, and then he implied – actually, more than implied – that they were getting back-ended by the packer.'

'How about when the selling price to Major Supermarkets was reduced – still no concern?'

'Quite a bit, really. But I still had all my costs and interest covered, and Seto told me they would get what they needed from the packer.'

'You did the invoicing?'

'Yes, it wasn't onerous. Usually about six invoices a week, and with net thirty-day payment terms, we had only twenty-four to thirty invoices outstanding at any time.'

'Why didn't you retain ownership of the inventory?'

'We did.'

'Then how come your inventory disappeared on you?'

'Seafood Partners was authorized to do releases. We aren't equipped to deal with warehouses and truckers and the like. I mean, there's a twelve-hour time difference between here and most of Major Supermarkets' distribution centres, and sometimes they wanted product on very short notice. I don't have the staff to handle logistics.'

Ava walked over to her window. It was late afternoon and winter's darkness was settling in. Below her the traffic crawled bumper to bumper up Avenue Road. It would be that way till past six o'clock. 'Do you have any idea where the inventory is?'

'No. I talked to the warehouse and they gave me the name of the trucking firm that did most of the pickups. They wouldn't give me any information. They said their customer was Seafood Partners, and unless Partners authorized it they weren't in a position to release any information to me.'

'Are their names in the file Alice gave me?'

'Not all of them.'

'Can you email them to me?' she said.

'I'll do it when I get to the office.'

'What else have you done to recover your money and your shrimp?'

'I hired collection agencies.'

'Agencies?'

'One in Bangkok, one in Seattle, and one in Hong Kong.'

'Regular firms?'

'What do you mean?'

'I mean they don't use machetes.'

'Ms Lee, we are a reputable financing firm.'

36

'That doesn't answer my question.'

'I used collection agencies that were recommended to me by various friends. They are – were – very professional. They just weren't effective.'

'So you went to your uncle.'

'I had to talk to someone, and he has been through a hell of a lot.'

'Including swimming from China.'

'Yes, that's true. With your uncle.'

'That is the story,' she said.

'And now they've brought us together,' he replied.

She picked up the sheaf of documents he had provided and leafed through them, looking for personal information on Seto and Antonelli. When she couldn't find any, she asked Tam what he had.

'I have phone numbers and some addresses.'

'No passport copies, Hong Kong ID card, driver's licences, photos?'

'No.'

'Email me what you do have. Also, send me the name and phone number of the guy who hooked you up with Seto.'

He paused again. In her mind's eye she could see him sitting in the dark in some apartment in Hong Kong, the mid-levels probably, a nice middle-class 110-square-metre apartment that would have cost more than a million dollars and still didn't offer a view of the waterfront beyond the wall of skyscrapers that lined Victoria Harbour. You had to be higher – in the upper levels, on the Peak – and have a net worth of a lot more than five million dollars to be able to afford that view. The Peak was the top of Victoria Mountain, the highest elevation in Hong Kong. The mountain ran straight up from the harbour, through the financial district, and past a host of five-star hotels, shops, and restaurants, the land costs rising with every yard.

'Ms Lee,' he asked quietly, 'does this mean you're taking the job?'

'Yes, we're taking the case,' she said.

'How long do you think it's going to take?'

'I have no idea, and please call me Ava.'

'Ava—'

'Really, I have no idea, and not just about the time. I also have no idea if I'm going to be successful or not. And I mean that – we make no promises. We do the best we can and sometimes it's good enough. I'm sure my uncle explained that to your uncle.'

'He said you're remarkably good at what you do.'

'That doesn't mean it always works.'

'Do we need to talk about your fee?' he asked.

'Did your uncle explain how it operates?'

'He said you keep one-third of everything you collect.'

'We do. It seems like a lot, but we don't ask for anything upfront, we pay all our own expenses, and if we don't collect, then not only do we not get paid, we are also out of pocket for the money we've spent.'

'Yes, he said that too.'

'Good. Andrew, send me the information I requested, and be available if I need to talk to you. If you don't hear from me for a while, don't sweat it. I'm not going to call you with regular updates.'

She hung up and walked back to the window. It was snowing, and the long-range forecast called for more of the same. A week or two in Hong Kong and Bangkok didn't seem like such a bad idea.

4

Ava slept well and woke with a sense of purpose, but she didn't hurry her morning routine of prayer, stretching, coffee, *Globe and Mail*, and TV. It was nine o'clock before she called Uncle. From the background noise she could tell he was in a restaurant. She explained to him in detail what had happened to Tam.

'Stupid,' Uncle said.

'We've seen worse.'

'He is supposed to be a professional.'

'He finances purchase orders. Who is more credit-worthy than Major Supermarkets?'

'True. What will you do?'

'I'll start off by finding the shrimp and/or the money.'

'Will that be hard?'

'No, I should get it done this morning.'

'And then?'

'I'll have to find Seto and Antonelli.'

'That's an unusual combination for partners: a Chinese and an Italian. They usually like to stick to their own.'

Ava hadn't thought about it, but it was true. 'I might have to come to Hong Kong and I'll probably have to go to Bangkok.'

'When?'

'In a day or two.'

'Let me know your schedule. I'll meet you at Chek Lap Kok.'

'Uncle, I may need some help in Bangkok.'

'I'll call our friends.'

'If I go, I'd like a car and a driver who can speak English and handle himself, and I'll need some of the usual odds and ends.'

'It will be a cop. That is who we are connected to. It has to be either the police or the army, and since we don't smuggle drugs or sell rocket launchers, the cops are the best choice.'

'That's fine. As soon as my schedule is set, I'll send it to you.'

She had called Uncle from her land line. She put down that phone and pulled out her cell, opened the back, and took out her local SIM card. From a drawer in her desk she pulled out a business card organizer, but there were no business cards in the clear plastic sleeves. Instead there were about forty SIM cards, each neatly identified by city and country; in the back were prepaid phone cards. She found the SIM card she wanted and slid it into her cell. When the phone was turned on, it read WELCOME TO AT&T 202-818-6666 – a Washington, DC number.

The Andrew Tam file was open in front of her. She found the phone number for the trucking firm that moved most of the shrimp and punched it in.

'Collins Transport,' a woman said.

'This is Carla Robertson from the Food and Drug Administration,' Ava said. 'I need to speak to the person who runs this business.'

There was a pause. Any mention of the FDA always caused a pause. 'That would be Mr Collins.'

'Then put me through.'

Another pause. 'I'm afraid he's in a meeting.'

'Ma'am, I don't care if he's in a meeting. It's imperative that I speak to him. Please interrupt whatever he's doing and put him on the line.'

'Let me see what I can do.'

'Thank you.'

It was a few minutes before Collins picked up the line. Ava guessed that he really had been in a meeting. 'Hello,' he said, 'this is Bob Collins.'

'Mr Collins, good morning. My name is Carla Robertson and I'm a senior inspector with the FDA here in Washington.'

'Yes, Ms Robertson, what can I do for you?'

'Mr Collins, about eight weeks ago your firm picked up multiple truckloads of shrimp from the Evans Cold Storage Warehouse in Landover, Maryland.'

'We did.'

'That shrimp, Mr Collins, had been inspected by us and found to violate several FDA regulations. It was our intent to put it on formal hold, but before the paperwork could be processed the product was moved by your trucking firm.'

'Ms Robertson, we had no idea about any FDA involvement,' he said quickly. 'We were given the business and treated it like we would any other. The cold storage facility would never have released the order if it was on hold.'

'As I said, we were slow to act, but the product should not have been moved. Who authorized it?'

'A company called Seafood Partners.'

'Have you done business with them before?'

'Actually, no. We got the business through a freight broker. We never talked to them.'

'Where did the product go?'

'Biloxi, Mississippi,' he said.

'Where in Biloxi?'

'The Garcia Shrimp Company.'

'I would like an address, phone number, and contact name for that firm.'

'I don't have it at my fingertips. Can I email it to you later?'

'No, I'll wait.'

She heard him mutter and then put the phone down. The next voice she heard was that of the receptionist, who gave Ava the information she wanted. Their contact at the Garcia Shrimp Company was a man named Barry Ho. What was a Chinese guy doing running a shrimp company with a Mexican name in Mississippi?

She dialled the Biloxi number Collins's receptionist had given her. The phone went directly to voicemail. She debated about leaving a message, but in the end she did, emphasizing how important it was for someone to get back to her.

Twenty minutes later her cellphone rang. 'Carla Robertson, FDA.'

'This is Barry Ho.'

'Thanks for returning my call so promptly.'

'When it comes to the FDA, we take things very seriously,' he said, with a slight trace of a Chinese accent and a stronger trace of stress.

'We appreciate that. It makes our job a lot easier when we get cooperation.'

'So what can I do for you? Your message said it was important.'

'Do you do business with a company called Seafood Partners?'

Ho hesitated, and Ava swore she could hear him wondering whether he should try to bullshit her or not. 'Yeah, I do. Not that often.'

'According to our sources, they trucked a substantial amount of shrimp to your plant about eight weeks ago.'

'That's right.'

'Why did they ship it to you?'

'They needed it repacked. That's our specialty – repacking.'

'Repacked how?'

'They had a couple of problems.'

'Such as?'

'Ms Robertson, I'm not sure I should be talking to you without their permission.'

'Mr Ho, we inspected this product just before they moved it. We were about to put it all on hold, but they beat us to the punch. Now, there's no way you could have known that, and we're not going to hold you responsible for acting as if everything was above board. But let me assure you, it would be beneficial for you to tell me what you know.'

Ho sighed. There was no upside to refusing her. 'Well, the product was packed in retail bags for sale at Major Supermarkets, and it was short weight. We repacked a lot of it for another retail chain, and the rest we put up in a Seafood Partners bag.'

'With the correct weights?'

'Of course, and it wasn't easy. Usually we need to overpack by about five percent to make up for glaze. This time we were at ten percent and more.'

'Who was the retailer?'

'G. B. Flatt.'

'In their bags?'

'Yeah.'

'How much product?'

'Twenty truckloads.'

'Do you still have any of the product?'

'No, no, we shipped it out as soon it was repacked.'

'Where did the G. B. Flatt product go?'

'To their central distribution centre in Houston.'

'And the balance?'

'To a warehouse in Seattle.'

'Which one?'

'Continental. They only have the one freezer.'

'Care of?'

'Seafood Partners.'

'Have you been paid?'

'We wouldn't let product leave our warehouse unless we were paid.'

'By cheque?'

'Yeah.'

'From Seafood Partners?'

'Yeah.'

'You wouldn't have a copy of that cheque handy, would you?'

'Sure.'

'Please get it for me.'

She heard a filing cabinet opening and closing, paper rustling.

'I have copy in front of me,' he said.

'Give me the particulars,' she said.

It was from Northwest Bank, a major financial institution headquartered in Seattle. Seafood Partners had an account at a branch near Sea-Tac Airport. Ho provided the address, phone number, and account number.

'Who did you deal with at Seafood Partners?'

'Jackson Seto.'

'Just him?'

'No one else.'

'Did you ever meet his partner, George Antonelli?'

'No, and I never really met Seto. We did business over the phone.'

'When was the last time you heard from him?'

'I called him about four or five weeks ago, when the last of the product was repacked.'

'What phone number did you call?'

He gave her the same cellphone number that Andrew Tam had provided.

'Tell me, Mr Ho, how did Jackson Seto find you?'

He laughed. 'In this business, sooner or later everyone in the US needs to find me. That's all I do – fix other people's problems.'

'Well, this is one problem I would appreciate your not discussing any further with Seto. There is no reason for you to call him, and if by chance he calls you, I would not mention this conversation.'

'He's all yours.'

'Thanks.'

'But I'd be happy if you could make a note in the report you're going to write that I was cooperative.'

'Consider it done, Mr Ho,' she said.

Ava did a search on the internet to find G. B. Flatt. It was the largest retail food chain in Texas, with more than three hundred stores. She trolled through the various departments until she found the seafood director in a sub-listing in the perishables department. The name was J. K. Tran – Vietnamese for sure. Man or woman? Not so certain.

She debated whether or not to maintain the FDA persona. *It's working well enough*, she thought. Carla was on a roll.

J. K. Tran wasn't happy to hear from her. 'We've done nothing wrong,' he said the instant she mentioned the FDA and Seafood Partners.

Why is he so defensive? she wondered. *Is he on the take? Did Seto pay him off to take in the product?*

'Mr Tran,' she said slowly, 'our interest is solely in Seafood Partners. We have already talked to Barry Ho at Garcia Shrimp, and he swears that the product is now entirely within regulations. My problem is that we told Mr Seto the product was not to be moved. I just need to confirm that you have that product. We have no, I repeat, no axe to grind with G. B. Flatt. You can keep the product. I just need you to confirm who you bought it from.'

'Seafood Partners.'

'Jackson Seto?'

'Yes.'

'How much did you pay?'

'Why do you need to know that?'

Tran's not slow, she thought. 'There's going to be a fine. It will be based on the value of the goods sold.'

That must have sounded plausible, because Tran said, 'I paid four dollars a pound.'

'For how many pounds?'

'Just over 900,000.'

'And how were they paid?'

'We sent them a wire.'

'Is that usual?'

'It was a one-of-a-kind deal. The price was exceptional, so we didn't mind the terms.'

'Where was the wire sent?'

'I don't know.'

'Who does know?'

'Accounts payable.'

'Who should I speak to there?'

'Rosemary Shields.'

'Mr Tran, could you do me a favour? Put me on hold, call Rosemary, and tell her to give me the wire information. I will make sure that you, she, and G. B. Flatt are kept out of this mess as we go forward.'

'Wait,' he said.

The line went dead for close to five minutes, and Ava began to think she had been cut off. She was just about to hang up and redial when Tran came back to the phone. 'The wire was sent two weeks ago. It went to Dallas First National Bank, 486 Sam Rayburn Drive, Dallas, Texas.'

'Whose bank account?'

'Seafood Partners, who else?'

'Do you have a contact at the bank?'

'No.'

'Phone number?'

'None.'

'Well, thanks for this. I'll follow up with the bank.'

Ava hung up and went back to her computer. Dallas First National was a two-branch bank, and the main branch, on Sam Rayburn Drive, was located in a strip mall. Jeff Goldman was the chairman, president, and CEO. *Busy man*, she thought.

The FDA cover wasn't necessarily going to have an impact on Goldman. It was time to bring Rebecca Cohen out of the drawer.

She called the general phone number provided on the website. For close to a minute she listened to a Texas drawl extolling the virtues of hometown banking and personal service, and then she was transferred to voicemail. Again she debated about leaving a message. In the end she felt she had no choice, and added that the number she was giving was her direct personal line.

Goldman didn't call her back until mid-afternoon. In the meantime Ava had convinced herself that he had checked her out and was never going to call, so it was with some relief that she saw the 214 area code appear on her screen.

'This is the Treasury Department, Rebecca Cohen,' she said.

'Ms Cohen, I'm Jeff Goldman, Dallas First National Bank. You called me earlier today.'

The accent was hardly Texan; he sounded more like a New Yorker. 'Yes, I did, and thank you for returning my call.'

'Ms Cohen, exactly what part of the Treasury Department are you with?'

'Internal Revenue.'

'That's still pretty vague.'

'My section specializes in money laundering,' she said.

'So why in hell are you calling me? We're a local bank, a mom-and-pop shop.'

She waited for him to consider some possibilities, then asked, 'Do you have a customer called Seafood Partners?'

She heard his fist banging on the desk. 'Shit,' he said.

'How long have they been a customer?'

'Shit, shit, shit.'

'Mr Goldman,' she prodded, 'how long have they been a customer? Not very long, I would wager.'

'About three weeks,' he said, his voice pinched.

'Who opened the account?'

'A Chinese guy named Seto.'

'How much did he put in the account?'

'A thousand dollars.'

'Did he do it in person? Did he come into your branch?'

'That's the only way we do business.'

'So you met him?'

'No, one of my account officers handled it. I mean, it was a business account with a thousand-dollar deposit. I saw the guy, though. Tall, real skinny, scrawny moustache.'

'And then about two weeks ago the account received a wire transfer from G. B. Flatt in Houston for close to four million dollars. You saw that, I bet.'

'I sure did.'

'You didn't find that a bit strange?'

'No, why would I? We're a small bank, but this is Texas, this is Dallas, and million-dollar transactions are common enough.'

'Still, one of your staff brought it to your attention.'

'We had to make sure it was legit.'

'How did you do that?'

'We called the issuing bank, and then to make doubly sure, we called the accounts department at G. B. Flatt.'

'And?'

'Flatt said they had bought a lot of shrimp from them. It made sense.'

It was time to back up, she thought, not to press too hard too quickly. 'This Seto – what kind of information did he provide on his company?'

'They're registered in Washington state, with a Seattle address.'

'So why use a Dallas bank?'

'He told my girl they were thinking of relocating to Texas. Looking at the deal they did with Flatt and knowing how big the shrimp business is in places like Brownsville, it was kind of logical.'

'So they didn't have a Dallas address or phone number?'

'No, everything was Seattle.'

'Can you give me that information, please?'

'It'll take a minute.'

'I'll wait.'

The address and phone numbers were the same ones she had gotten from Andrew Tam and Barry Ho.

'Now, Mr Goldman, that money from G. B. Flatt, is it still in their account at your bank?'

'Some of it is,' he said carefully.

'How much?'

'About ten thousand.'

'Are you joking?'

'No, and the way this conversation is going, I wish I was.'

'Mr Goldman, don't fret,' she said. 'This happens all the time. A bank, a good honest bank, opens an account for a customer who seems entirely above board, takes in deposits for genuine commercial transactions, and then at the customer's request transfers that money elsewhere for what are thought to be other real commercial transactions. That's just about what happened, isn't it?'

'You got it.'

'So where did the money go?'

'The British Virgin Islands,' he said.

'I could have guessed,' she said.

'How's that?'

'Mr Goldman, the BVI are the world's tax haven. There are more than half a million offshore companies registered there – that's about half the world total.'

'I run a small local bank, that's all,' he said.

'I understand, I understand. Now, to which company was the money sent?'

'S&A Investments.'

'Address?'

'I have a copy of our wire in front of me. It was sent six days ago to S&A Investments, P.O. Box 718, Simon House, Road Town, Tortola, British Virgin Islands.'

'Care of which bank?'

'Barrett's.'

'Account?'

'Account number 055-439-4656.'

'Great,' she said. 'You've been just great.'

'We don't like to get mixed up in things like this,' he said.

'I know, but sometimes it's difficult to avoid people like Seto.'

'Never again. I'm closing his account as soon as I get off the phone with you.'

'Oh no, don't do that,' she said quickly. 'Please leave it alone. I need you to call me at once if Seto comes back to the bank or contacts you in any way.'

'Ms Cohen, you do know there was a second wire as well?'

Ava couldn't help being surprised. 'No, I didn't.'

'Yeah, for just over a million dollars, from Safeguard, a retail food chain in Portland, Oregon. We sent it to the same account in the British Virgin Islands.'

'When?'

'Two days ago.'

It looked as if Seto had cleared out the inventory. That was a good thing. Money was easier to repossess than goods, and she wouldn't have to worry about selling it if she got her hands on it.

'You've been terrific, Mr Goldman. Let's hope I don't have talk to you again.'

It was just past two o'clock and Ava hadn't eaten anything all day except a bowl of congee for breakfast. There was a Chinese restaurant on Bloor Street that served dim sum till three. She looked out her window at the street below. It wasn't snowing but it was cold and blustery, and the few pedestrians who had ventured out were wrapped up tightly and walking as quickly as they could, chins buried in their chests. She called the Italian restaurant where she had eaten the night before and ordered a pizza for delivery.

Then she called the travel agent she always used to book her trips. Most of her friends booked online, but she preferred having a buffer between herself and the airlines in case she had to make schedule changes, which she often did. She told the agent to book her on a flight to Seattle and to reserve a seat from there to Hong Kong and then on to Thailand.

Ava called her mother and her best friend, Mimi, to let them know she was getting out of town. The winter was wearing her down, she said, and she was heading to Thailand for ten days or so of fun and sun.

'Are you going through Hong Kong?' her mother asked.

'Yes.'

'Will you call your father?'

'No.'

She heard disappointment in her mother's voice. 'So, you are just seeing Uncle?'

'Mum, I'll be in transit in Hong Kong. I probably won't see anyone.'

Ava travelled light. It took her less than half an hour to pack her Louis Vuitton monogrammed suitcase and her Shanghai Tang 'Double Happiness' bag. The suitcase was where she packed her business look: black linen slacks, a pencil skirt, Cole Hahn black leather pumps, two sets of black bras and panties, and three Brooks Brothers shirts in powder blue, pink, and white – one with a button-down collar, the other two with modified Italian collars, and all of them with French cuffs. She chose a small jewellery case to hold her Cartier Tank Française watch, a set of green jade cufflinks, and a simple gold crucifix. She then went through the leather pouch that held her collection of clasps, pins, barrettes, headbands, and combs and took out an ivory chignon pin she especially loved, adding it to the jewellery case. Ava wore her hair up nearly all the time and liked to accentuate it. Nothing did so better than the chignon pin.

Her toilet kit was always packed and ready to go: toothbrush, toothpaste, hairbrush, deodorant, shampoo, Annick Goutal perfume, one lipstick, and mascara. The shampoo was in a hundred-millilitre bottle, as required by airport security. She had four such bottles neatly packed in the plastic bag that was also required. Only one of the bottles held shampoo; the other three contained chloral hydrate.

The contents of the Shanghai Tang bag were more eclectic: the Moleskine notebook, two fountain pens, her computer, running shoes and shorts, a sports bra, socks, three Giordano T-shirts, a Chanel purse to take to meetings, and two rolls of duct tape. Ava went to the kitchen, took thirty Starbucks coffee sachets from a container, and tossed them into the bag.

At eight she called Uncle.

'*Wei*,' he answered.

'I found the money,' she said.

'The shrimp?'

'No, the shrimp have been sold already. I've located the money.'

'How much?'

'About five million.'

'Where is it?'

'British Virgin Islands.'

'That's not a surprise,' he said. 'Half of Hong Kong has bank accounts there.'

'I'm heading for Seattle tomorrow morning to see if I can find Jackson Seto and persuade him to give the money to Andrew Tam.'

'What do you think?'

'I have no expectations. I get into Seattle tomorrow morning around eleven. Both his office address and supposed home address are downtown, within a couple of blocks of each other. Who knows, I might get lucky.'

'If you don't?'

'I'm booked on Cathay Pacific tomorrow night into Hong Kong.'

'Are you staying?'

'Maybe a day or two. I want to check out Seto's Hong Kong address in Wanchai, and I might meet with Tam. I also want to talk to the guy who introduced Seto to Dynamic Financial Services.'

'Let me know how it goes in Seattle. I don't care what time you call. If you come to Hong Kong, where do you want to stay?'

'The Mandarin.'

'I'll book it for you just in case.'

'Thanks, Uncle.'

'And I'll meet you at the airport.'

'You don't have to.'

'I know, but I want to.'

She usually slept well. Her sleep mechanism was bak mei, the basic moves played and replayed in slow motion. That night was a little different. The core form was the panther, but this time she had a target: a tall, skinny Chinese man with a scrawny moustache and five million dollars in a bank account in the British Virgin Islands.

5

Seattle was a bust. The office was closed, empty. Seto had moved out of the apartment the month before.

Ava was back at Sea-Tac Airport well before her flight was scheduled to leave, so she killed some time getting a full body massage in the Cathay Pacific business lounge. She called Uncle just before boarding. He again insisted he'd meet her at the airport and she again told him he didn't have to. She knew how much he hated the new Hong Kong International Airport at Chek Lap Kok. He lived in Kowloon, no more than ten minutes by car from the old airport, Kai Tak.

Kai Tak had been theatre and drama, the planes approaching Hong Kong precariously through mountains and skyscrapers, crossing Kowloon Bay, their wing tips almost touching the lines of laundry on the balconies of the apartment buildings that pressed in on the airport. Then there was the bus ride from the tarmac to the tired old terminal, which had been built for 1950s levels of air traffic, and the long lines at Customs before one emerged into a small, cramped Arrivals hall where hundreds, if not thousands, of people lined the corridor, waving and yelling at the incoming passengers.

Ava wasn't as nostalgic about Kai Tak as Uncle. To her mind, the Arrivals hall at Chek Lap Kok might be huge and sterile, reducing people to ants scurrying under its soaring roof, but its almost brutal efficiency made up for any deficiencies in its character.

'I'll sit in the Kit Kat Koffee House,' Uncle said.

The business-class section of the airplane was more than half empty, and the window seat next to her was vacant. That was good; Ava wasn't one for casual conversation with strangers, and now she didn't have to find an excuse to avoid it.

It would be a twelve- to thirteen-hour flight, and factoring in the International Date Line, would get her into Hong Kong the morning of the following day. Ava hated that, because jet lag was almost inevitable. The only way she could avoid it was not to sleep at all on the plane, and for her that just wasn't possible. For reasons she couldn't understand, the moment a flight took off her eyes began to close. On a one-hour flight to New York in the middle of the day, she could sleep for forty-five minutes. During one seventeen-hour flight from Toronto to Hong Kong, she figured she had slept for fifteen hours.

The Seattle–Hong Kong flight turned out to be not that extreme. Ava managed to stay awake long enough to eat dinner and to watch a Hong Kong action film starring Tony Leung and Andy Lau. Then she fell asleep until the flight attendant woke her two hours before landing, to serve her breakfast.

When the plane landed, Ava found HKIA its usual ruthlessly efficient self. She was off the plane and through Immigration, Baggage Claim, and Customs within twenty minutes of landing. She spotted Uncle at the back of the Kit Kat, a plain, square box with round glass tables, metal chairs, and posters of coffee beans on the walls. He had a Chinese newspaper open in front of him and an unlit cigarette dangling from his mouth. Even in Hong Kong there were places where you couldn't smoke now.

He was tiny, not much taller than Ava, and thin. He was always dressed the same way: black lace-up shoes, black slacks, a white long-sleeved shirt buttoned to the neck. The monochromatic image was part convenience, part camouflage. It made him easy to overlook – just another boring old man not worth a second glance, except to those who knew.

Ava thought Uncle was somewhere between seventy and eighty, but that was as close as she could come to determining his age. Many people meeting him for the first time guessed that he was younger, and not from politeness. His face was fine-boned, with a small, straight nose and a sharply defined chin with a hint of a point; his skin had not begun to sag, and he had only the faintest of wrinkles around his eyes and on his forehead. His hair was cropped close to the scalp; Ava could see streaks of gray, but it was still predominantly black.

'Uncle,' she said.

He looked up from his paper, a smile cracking his face as his eyes fell upon her. She loved his eyes: pitch black pupils and dark chocolate brown irises set in a sea of white that seemed immune to lack of sleep or too much alcohol. They were eyes whose age was indeterminable: lively, curious, probing. Ava had learned rapidly that Uncle's world was defined through those eyes, not through his words. They could embrace you, mistrust you, detest you, adore you, question you, or not give a damn whether you lived or died. And she knew how to read them in all their subtlety. Ava had seen their many moods, although their darkest intent had never been directed at her. She was part of his unofficial family, after all, the only kind of family he had ever had.

She leaned down to kiss him on the forehead. 'You didn't have to come,' she said.

'I was eager to see you,' he said. 'You're as beautiful as ever.'

'And you look as young as always.'

He looked around. 'I don't like this place. We'll go to Central for noodles. Let me call Sonny. I'll have him bring the car down from the garage.'

They walked through the cavernous Arrivals hall, Uncle's hand resting lightly on her elbow. Two Hong Kong policemen watched them as they neared the exit. The older of the two nudged the younger and they nodded their heads in Uncle's direction. Ava saw the movement, looked sideways, and caught Uncle nodding in return.

Sonny was leaning against the front fender of the car. It was new, a Mercedes S-Class.

'What happened to the Bentley?' Ava asked.

'I sold it. Sonny said it was time to move into this decade.'

Ava had never known Uncle to be without Sonny, and she'd never met anyone who had. He was technically Uncle's driver, a monochromatic match to his boss in his black suit, white shirt, and plain black tie. He was tall for Chinese, a couple of inches over six feet, and heavyset. For someone that large he was quick – deadly quick – and he could be vicious when the circumstances required. He was one of the few people in the world whom Ava feared physically. And he wasn't talkative. If you asked him a question, you got a simple answer with no embellishments. Beyond that he didn't seem to have any opinions he needed to share.

When they approached the car, Sonny gave Ava a small smile and reached for her bags. She and Uncle climbed into the back seat as he put them in the trunk.

It was a quick ride to the city centre. Their route took them over the Tsing Ma Bridge, six lanes of traffic on the upper deck, rail lines beneath. The bridge always took Ava's breath away. It was close to a kilometre and a half long and soared two hundred metres above the water. The Ma Wan Channel, part of the South China Sea, glittered below in the early morning sun as sampans and fishing boats skirted the armada of huge ocean freighters waiting to be escorted into Hong Kong's massive container port.

They slowed when they reached the city proper, caught in the last of the morning rush hour. Hong Kong is not a city filled with private cars. Finding a place to park is not easy or cheap in a place where office and retail space is rented by the square inch, but there are red taxis everywhere, scurrying like beetles. Sonny drove carefully – too carefully for Ava, but he was a cautious man, maybe even deliberately cautious. It was as if he were restraining his true nature. She had seen this trait in him when he attended meetings with Uncle. He didn't do that often, but when he did, he remained standing off to one side, his eyes flickering back and forth as he followed the flow of conversation. Ava realized that his body language changed along with the tone of the meeting. If Uncle was having his way, Sonny was placid. Any opposition to Uncle's position caused him to tense, his eyes growing dark.

The financial and commercial heart of the Hong Kong Territory is divided into two main areas: Hong Kong Island and Kowloon, two dense urban settings connected by the Cross-Harbour Tunnel and the Star Ferry. Ava's hotel was on the Hong Kong side, in the Central district, set just back from Victoria Harbour and a short walk to the financial sector.

They reached the Mandarin within forty minutes of leaving the airport. Uncle walked into the hotel with her and sat patiently in the lobby while she checked in. She sent her bags to the room.

'There is a noodle shop a block from here,' Uncle said when Ava joined him. 'We'll walk.'

It always took her a day or two to adjust to Central foot traffic – the jostling, the pushing, everyone eager to get to the next corner, where they could wait in a throng before shuffling along to the next intersection, their pace dictated entirely by the mob around them. Ava and Uncle were hemmed in on all sides by a crush of people. Central streets weren't a place for the claustrophobic.

The noodle shop was a hole in the wall, ten tables with pink plastic stools. The place was full, but a man in an apron came out from behind the counter to tell two young men sitting by themselves to move to another table that was occupied but had vacant seats. He then waved Uncle and Ava to the empty table and bowed as Uncle walked past.

Ava ordered *har gow* – shrimp dumplings – and soup with

soft noodles. Uncle ordered beef lo mein and a plate of *gai lin*, steamed Chinese broccoli slathered in oyster sauce, to share.

'How is your mother?' he asked while they waited for their food.

'As lively as ever.'

'A crazy woman.'

Ava's mother was highly sociable and made friends as easily as other people changed clothes. Marian and Ava's friends weren't immune from her attention. It bothered Marian but never Ava; she saw it as just a natural extension of her mother's all-consuming interest in their lives. So it had come as no surprise when her mother, in Hong Kong to visit her own friends, called Uncle and said she'd like to meet him, to find out what kind of man her daughter was working for. If Ava had been working in Toronto for a North American firm, she would have been mortified, not because of what her mother had done but more because they wouldn't understand why she was doing it. But Uncle understood Chinese mothers; they met and got along well enough that from time to time Jennie Lee felt free to pick up the phone and call Kowloon. Just keeping in touch, she called it.

'She sends her love,' Ava said.

Uncle shrugged off the lie. 'Will you call your father while you are here?'

'I don't think so.'

The two men had never met but they knew of each other, as the wealthy and powerful of Hong Kong tend to do. 'Maybe just as well. I hear that the wife in Australia is causing him problems.'

Ava hadn't heard that news and the surprise registered on her face.

'It is smart of him, keeping them all separated. I don't know, though, where he finds the energy or the time to keep them satisfied.'

Their food came. She poured tea for both of them. The restaurant was full, a steady flow of people coming and going.

Uncle ate quickly, hardly bothering to chew his food. For a man who was otherwise outwardly serene and calm almost to an extreme, it was an unusual characteristic. She wondered sometimes if this might be truer to his nature than the bland, confident face he liked the world to see.

'There isn't any point in going to the Wanchai address you were given for Jackson Seto,' he said, pushing his empty plate aside. 'I sent someone there today. He hasn't lived there for at least six months.'

'Do you have another address for him?'

'No.'

'Hong Kong phone number?'

'No, but you might get better information from Henry Cheng. He is the one who connected Seto to Andrew Tam. You have an appointment with him tomorrow in his office at 11 a.m. He doesn't know why you want to talk to him, but he should be cooperative enough. One of my friends called him and made the arrangement.'

'Where is the office?'

He passed her a slip of paper. 'Kowloon side, Nathan Road.'

'I was thinking of going to see Andrew.'

'Why don't you wait until you see Henry Cheng?' Uncle

said. 'And even then it may not be a great idea. What can you tell him? That you've found out where his money is? What good does that do him? You might create false expectations.'

'I'll think about it.'

'You know, Andrew's uncle, my friend, used to call me every three weeks. Now he calls me twice a day. He is nervous for the nephew. The family does not have the kind of money where they can afford to lose thirty million Hong Kong. The repercussions would be massive. When he calls, I tell him I know absolutely nothing. And I'll keep telling him that until you tell me it is over, one way or another.'

'I need to find Seto.'

'Maybe Cheng can help.'

'And I need to find George Antonelli, the Bangkok partner.'

'Our friends in Bangkok have already been working on that. By the time you get there they should have all the information you need.'

'I don't think Antonelli has access to the money. From what I can gather, Seto has those controls.'

'But Antonelli can give you access to Seto.'

'Exactly.'

They walked slowly back to the hotel together, his arm looped through hers. The Mercedes was parked near the hotel entrance. Sonny stood near the car's front door, watching them as they approached. He opened the back door for Uncle and helped him into the car. Ava said goodbye and turned to walk into the Mandarin.

'Call me after you meet with Cheng,' Uncle said to her back.

6

Ava loved the Mandarin Oriental Hotel. The very first in the chain had been built on the Chao Phraya River in Bangkok in 1887. She had first discovered the hotel when she was dating a banker and had travelled to Bangkok with her for a four-day conference. They had splurged on their accommodation, booking the Somerset Maugham Suite in the Author's Wing. After the banker left for her meetings in the mornings, Ava took the hotel's private ferry across the river to its spa and indulged.

Her afternoons had been split between the wing's lounge, where she introduced herself to the works of Joseph Conrad and Graham Greene, and the restaurant terrace on the Chao Phraya. She was hardly a literary historian, but the fact that Conrad, Greene, Maugham, Noel Coward, and James Michener had all stayed and supposedly written there fascinated her. And the river was alluring in its own way. It was broad, brown, and sluggish, and as busy as a North American highway with ships, tugs, and barges working their way north from the Gulf of Thailand into the interior, while water taxis and ferries worked their way from east to west, dodging the bigger vessels as they went.

Most evenings her friend had an official function to attend, so Ava ate at the hotel by herself. There was a Chinese restaurant – the China House – on the hotel property next to the main building. It served perhaps the best Chinese food she had ever eaten up till then: abalone that had been gently braised for twelve hours, stir-fried black chicken, soy-braised pomfret.

The thing that had struck her most about the hotel was its level of service. It wasn't just that it offered good service – that was routine for every five-star hotel in Asia – it was more that the staff seemed to anticipate everything she did or wanted to do. During those four days she had never pressed an elevator button. On her first day there she ordered ice at four o'clock. The ice was there again the next day, the day after, and the day after that, always at four o'clock. And every staff member in the hotel seemed to know her name.

The only negative was the hotel's location, which was outside the city core. If you wanted to go anywhere else in Bangkok, you had to contend with traffic that was perpetually paralyzed. The hotel wasn't a place for someone who needed to get about quickly.

The Mandarin in Hong Kong did not have a location problem. After a quick shower and a change into her business attire, Ava walked out the front door and got to the Star Ferry in ten minutes. After a five-minute wait she was crossing Victoria Harbour to her meeting with Henry Cheng in Kowloon.

It was a pleasant day for Hong Kong, about room temperature, slightly overcast, with a light breeze. She sat at the back of the ferry, taking in the sun and looking at the skyline. There was nothing like it in the world – a solid wall of skyscrapers lining the harbour like some medieval fortress. The Hong Kong and Shanghai Bank. Central Plaza. Two international finance centres. The Hopewell Centre. The Bank of China building, designed by I. M. Pei. More than forty buildings over sixty-five storeys high. New York couldn't even come close.

The ferry docked in Timshashui on the Kowloon side. She thought about taking a taxi but had time to spare, so she walked instead. When she got to Henry Cheng's office on Nathan Road it was five minutes to eleven.

Kowloon isn't as aggressively modern as Hong Kong Island. The building on Nathan Road was only five storeys high, its brick exterior faded and chipped. She rode its single elevator to the top floor and found that Cheng's company occupied half of it – about three thousand square metres – a large office by Hong Kong standards. A hundred or so employees were working in an open-plan area. A handful of closed offices was at the far end, and a boardroom with its door open that Ava could see was empty. The receptionist noted her name and said in Cantonese that Mr Cheng was expecting her; would she please follow her to the boardroom.

Ava sat there and waited. The office tea lady stuck her head in the door and asked if she wanted anything.

'I'll have some green tea,' Ava said.

Henry Cheng was carrying a bottle of water when he arrived. He looked at Ava in her linen slacks and pink Brooks Brothers shirt with green jade cufflinks and said, 'You're not what I was expecting.'

'I'm not sure how to take that,' she said.

'It doesn't matter. Never mind,' he said, offering his hand. 'I'm Henry Cheng.'

'Ava Lee.'

He sat a couple of chairs away from her, tapping his fingers impatiently on the table. 'What can I do for you?'

He was short and chunky, and Ava guessed he was in his mid-forties. His hair was parted in the middle and swept over his ears in a style that might have suited someone twenty years younger, six inches taller, and forty pounds lighter. *He's still Hong Kong slick*, she thought, eyeing his Gucci loafers, tailor-made dress shirt with monogrammed cuffs, and D&G belt around a thirty-eight-inch waist. 'I need to know about Jackson Seto.'

'I know next to nothing.'

'You introduced him to Andrew Tam.'

'I mentioned Andrew Tam to Seto, and I called Andrew to tell him I was referring Seto to him. But I was never part of any meeting between them, and I had nothing to do with the business they did.'

'How did you meet Seto?'

'I met him through his brother, whom I do know very well.'

'What's his name?'

'Frank.'

'How did it come about that you met?'

'I was having lunch with Frank when Jackson came into the restaurant. He joined us and we started to have, you know, the normal kind of conversation businessmen have. Sometime during lunch Jackson mentioned that he was looking for some purchase-order financing and I brought up Dynamic

Financial. Andrew – if he hasn't told you – and I went to school together.'

'That's it? Nothing more than that?'

'That's all.'

'You never saw Seto again?'

'Never saw him, didn't talk to him.'

'Andrew suggested that you might have received a finder's fee.'

'No,' Cheng said forcibly. 'At the time the only reason I even mentioned Dynamic was that I thought if I helped Jackson, it might help me in my relationship with Frank. Little did I know.'

'What do you mean?'

'Frank is embarrassed by his brother. He wants nothing to do with him and is quite determined to keep him away from his social circle.'

'When did you find that out?'

'When I had lunch with Frank a few months after that first meeting.'

'Who is this Frank Seto?'

'He is married to Patty Chan, Carter Chan's only child.'

'Ah, the all-powerful Mr Chan. Is he still the wealthiest man in Hong Kong?'

'Maybe in all of Asia.'

'Nice catch.'

Cheng shrugged. 'Patty is ugly and fat, but she's going to be the richest woman in Hong Kong when Carter dies.'

'What does Frank do?'

'He tries to keep her happy.'

'No, I mean his job.'

'He tries to keep her happy,' Cheng said and laughed. 'Officially, though, he's the president of a real estate operation they own, Admiralty Properties. The office is on the Hong Kong side, Gloucester Road, overlooking the harbour. He wanders in there a few times a week.'

'Where does he live?'

'The family – the entire Chan family, including Carter, lives – where else? – at the top of the Peak. Security is very tight at the house. Actually, I should say houses, because it's more of a compound.'

'I get the picture,' Ava said. 'Still, I'd like to talk to him.'

'Good luck.'

'Would you—'

'No, I wouldn't,' Cheng interrupted. 'If you want to speak to Frank, contact him yourself. I've told you all I know. I understand that Andrew may have problems as a result of dealing with Jackson. I'm sorry about that, but none of it was my doing. Andrew had an obligation to do his own due diligence.' Cheng stood up. 'Now I have another appointment.'

Ava rode the elevator to the ground floor but waited until she was back on Nathan Road to call Uncle. She gave him a summary of her meeting with Cheng, then said, 'Can you arrange for me to sit with Frank Seto?'

'I don't know Frank Seto. I do know Carter Chan, but if I was face down on the street bleeding, Carter would probably kick me for good measure,' he said. 'I'll tell you who does know Carter, though, and probably Frank Seto too.'

'Who?'

'Your father.'

7

Marcus Lee didn't seem surprised to be hearing from his daughter, but then he never did. Whether it was six days, six weeks, or six months since their last contact, he always acted as if they had just had breakfast together.

'Hi, sweetheart,' he said, 'are you in Hong Kong?'

When she had phoned his office the receptionist had said he was in a meeting and wasn't to be disturbed. 'Could you tell him that his daughter Ava called?' she said.

'Ah, wait,' the woman said. 'For you, I can disturb him.'

For some reason it made her feel good to hear that, and then to hear him 'sweetheart' her when he came on the line.

'I am.'

'That's funny. I talked to Mummy this morning and she didn't mention that you'd be here.'

'A last-minute change of plan. I'm really heading to Bangkok, but I need to do something here first.'

'Where are you now?'

'I just got off the Star Ferry on the Hong Kong side.'

'You know, it's almost lunchtime. Do you want to join me?'

'Why not?'

'They have very good dim sum at the Shangri-La Hotel. Why don't you grab a taxi and meet me there in about ten minutes.'

When Ava arrived at the hotel, her father was already standing by the restaurant host, waiting for her. He was just under six feet and slender, with no hint of middle-age spread. His hair was still jet black and fashionably long at the back. *God, he's handsome*, she thought. He wore a charcoal grey suit with a white dress shirt and a red silk tie – the very picture of conservatism.

Her mother swore that Ava bore the closest physical resemblance to him of any of the children, even though she'd only seen pictures of the four sons from the first wife and knew nothing of those from the third. It wasn't just that Ava was lean and easy on the eyes. Her entire appearance was striking: a combination of good looks, the ability to carry herself well, and an aura of self-confidence.

Marcus Lee saw her and waved, then walked across the lobby to meet her halfway. He threw his arms around her and they hugged. She could feel a hundred eyes on them.

'You look gorgeous, sweetheart,' he said.

'Thanks, Daddy. You look great too.'

'I'm still running, still watching what I eat.'

'It shows.'

The restaurant was jammed but a table had been held for them. He ordered from the dim sum menu without asking her what she wanted. Her mother loved that about him, that he always took charge.

'I told Mummy this morning that I'm planning to come over to Toronto in May, when the weather improves. I'll stay maybe for the whole month. I hope you'll be there,' he said.

'It's a long way out, and with my work—'

'Anyway, I'm giving you notice. I told Mummy that maybe we could have a family holiday. You know, take your sister and her kids and you and go on a cruise, or down to the Bahamas.'

'How is everyone here?' Ava asked as if she hadn't heard him.

'Good, really good. Jamie and Michael are in business here. Neither of them is married yet, although Michael is now living with a girl for the first time. David is in Australia finishing up a Ph.D. and trying to find himself. Peter has just joined Barclays Bank.'

It always amazed her that he could talk about the children from his first marriage with such ease in front of her. What was as surprising was that her mother spoke about them and took pride in them as well, as if they were part of her extended family. Ava wondered if it cut both ways. Did they even know she existed?

'Yes, Mummy keeps me posted,' she said.

The waiter put a small tureen of hot and sour soup on the table. Her father filled her bowl.

'So, what brings you east again?'

'Business,' she said.

'Are you still working with Chow?'

'Yes, of course I am.'

'I can't help but wish you weren't.'

'But I am.'

'Be careful,' he said. It was the same thing he said every time Uncle's name was mentioned.

'Daddy, I'm an accountant,' she said.

His eyes flickered in her direction. She felt a nervous flutter in her stomach, her face flushed, and she found herself confronting the fact that this man was nobody's fool. He knew what she did for a living, and though she never discussed her work in detail, he'd been in business long enough and knew Hong Kong and China well enough to know what it could entail.

'So what is this business?'

'The usual. Someone took off with someone else's money, and I'm trying to track it down and have it returned to its rightful owner.'

'You make it sound so simple.'

'It is.'

'Do I know any of the principals?'

'I don't think so, and even if you did I couldn't acknowledge it.'

'So why did you call me, then?'

The question was asked gently but the point was direct; she couldn't lie to him. 'I need to speak to a man named Frank Seto. He is Carter Chan's son-in-law. I'm quite sure that if I approach him on my own I'll be put off. I was hoping you could help me.'

'I don't know Frank very well,' he said. 'Still, I can't imagine him getting himself immersed in anything untoward.'

'It isn't him. He has a brother who I'm trying to locate, and so far there's nothing but dead ends. I'm hoping that Frank can help me.'

Their food arrived: shu mai, fried turnip cake, scallops fried with salt, and steamed duck feet with mushrooms.

'I'm not sure my calling Frank will do any good. He might not remember me,' he said. 'On the other hand, Carter and I have had a long and uneventful relationship. In his own strange way, he may even consider me a friend. I'll call him and see what he can set up. You want to meet with Frank, correct?'

'Yes, thank you, Daddy.'

'Would you find it upsetting if I came along?'

She glanced up at him.

'It might make things easier all around,' he said.

'What would you tell him? I mean, what would you tell him about me?'

'That you are my daughter, of course. What did you think I would say?'

'I don't know. I mean, Mummy and me and Marian are in another world. This is your world here. I don't know who knows what about what.'

'You aren't a secret, if that's what you think.'

'I don't think I need a complete explanation,' she said.

'Well, anytime you do, just ask,' he said. 'I know it seems to Westerners that some of us Chinese have very complicated lives. Actually, the opposite is true. There are rules to this tradition of ours, and as long as everyone – and that includes the wives – plays by the rules, the family remains harmonious. What are the other options? Divorce? Secret mistresses? Messy and hurtful.'

She sat mute, a shu mai between her chopsticks.

'I know it's old-fashioned, but I was raised that way, and it can't be helped,' he said.

'No, I guess not,' she said.

They finished lunch and went into the hotel lobby. He turned on his cellphone. 'This could take a while,' he said to her. 'I have to get past a receptionist and then at least two personal assistants.' He was sitting directly under a harsh overhead light and still looked ten to fifteen years younger than he was. Ava saw several women close to her own age glancing at him as they walked past.

'Marcus Lee calling for Carter Chan,' he said. It took less than a minute. 'Hello, Carter, this is Marcus ... I'm well, thank you. And you and the family? ... Actually it's a family matter I'm calling about. I need a personal favour. My daughter Ava needs to speak with your son-in-law. It's about a matter that does not involve him directly, or you or any of your interests. She's a forensic accountant, and the issue concerns Frank's brother. I don't know much more than that ... He is? Can you give me a number where she can reach him?' He took a small notepad and pen from his inside jacket pocket and wrote down two phone numbers. 'And Carter, could you contact Frank yourself and ask him to speak with her? If she calls directly, well, you know ... Thanks, Carter.'

'Frank is in the UK,' he said to Ava. 'This is his Hong Kong cell number, and Carter says he normally has it on. The other is his hotel number. Carter will have someone call him and tell him to be cooperative. You should wait until that happens.' He checked his watch. 'It's about six in the morning there. Give it a few hours.'

He walked her out to the taxi stand. They hugged, his

intensity catching her off guard. 'I am really happy you called me,' he said. 'I love you, you know, and I'm very proud of you. Just be careful, huh?'

'Thanks for making that call. I love you too.'

'Try to join us in May, will you?'

'I'll try.'

8

Ava phoned Uncle when she got back to the Mandarin. She told him about her meeting with her father and about her possible access to Frank Seto. 'I'm leaving tonight for Bangkok,' she said. 'My flight leaves here at six on Thai Air. I've decided to take your advice and not see Andrew Tam.'

'I think that's best. I'll pick you up at the hotel at three thirty.'

'That's perfect. See you then,' Ava said.

She checked her watch. Not enough time to change and go for a run. She went online and searched Frank Seto. Ninety percent of the references were about his relationship to the Chan family, and the balance were reports about Admiralty Property deals. Seto didn't seem to exist outside of the Chans. There were photos of his wedding from multiple sources. He was as skinny as Jackson; the bride was twice his size. Some men like fat women, but all men love money. She wondered if Frank Seto had found the perfect combination.

The Mercedes was in front of the hotel entrance right on schedule. Sonny opened the back door for her and she slipped into the seat next to Uncle. He had a file folder resting on his lap. He waited until they were on the highway before he passed it to her.

'This came through this afternoon. Our friends worked quickly. Antonelli will be easy enough to contact. He is a creature of habit; he stays at the Water Hotel. I know you like the Mandarin, but it is miles from the Water and against traffic. They suggested the Grand Hyatt Erawan. You can walk to the other hotel from there.'

She knew the Hyatt, or rather she knew Spasso, the hotel's nightclub – one of the classiest pick-up joints in Bangkok.

Ava opened the file. There was a photo of Antonelli clipped to a page of data. He was short, fat, and bald and had a black mole on his right cheek. 'Not pretty, is he?' she said.

In the photo he was standing next to a gorgeous Thai girl. 'It is Thailand. He does not have to be,' Uncle said.

She scanned the documentation. 'He's American, Atlanta-born and -raised, and evidently still married. He has three sons in their teens. The family lives in Georgia. He wires money to them every month and seems to visit three or four times a year.'

'He and Seto have been in business together for close to ten years,' Uncle said.

'And in trouble before.'

'It seems to come around every two years.'

'And they get away with it.'

'So far, but then the people they scammed before were mainly Indian and Indonesian. Some of them tried to get their money back, but it is almost impossible to do it legally when so many jurisdictions are involved.'

'How much money?'

He shook his head. 'They started small and worked their way up. Andrew Tam is the biggest by far.'

She closed the file. She would read the rest on the plane.

'You'll be met at the airport.'

'I'd rather take a taxi,' she said.

He knew she preferred working alone unless she needed a specific kind of help. 'I made the arrangements,' he said.

'Cancel them, please. I still have to figure out how I'm going to handle things, and I don't want the pressure of worrying about someone waiting around for me. Just give me a name and contact information. I'll call when I'm ready.'

'They have the logistical material you requested.'

'I'll call if I need it. Hopefully I won't.'

9

It was a two-and-a-half-hour flight from Hong Kong to Bangkok. Ava slept for most of it. She had been to Thailand at least six times and it was by far her favourite place to crash. Whether she stayed in Bangkok, Phuket, Ko Sumoi, or Chang Mai, Thailand was always an oasis.

This was, however, her first time at the new airport, Suvarnabhumi. The old airport had always been the worst part of the trip, coming or going. Huge lineups at Immigration, slow baggage claim, waits of maybe half an hour for a taxi, and if it was raining you could be there for hours. Then a ride into the city that sapped whatever energy you had left.

So it was a bit of a shock for Ava when she breezed through the new complex. Like HKIA, Suvarnabhumi had been built and staffed to get you into the country as fast as possible. When she walked into the Arrivals hall, she almost ran straight into a sign that read UNCLE CHOW. She nodded at the young man holding it.

'*Sa wat dee ka*,' he said. He wore blue jeans and a black T-shirt that showed off his muscular frame. He was about five foot nine, and his hair was so close-cropped that the stubble on his chin was almost as long. He looked tired, his eyes tinged with red and swollen underneath, making them appear smaller than those of most Thais. Still, he gave her a quick and easy smile. Despite his casual dress, Ava knew he was a cop.

'I'm Ava,' she said. 'But I told Uncle that I was going to take a cab.'

'Arthon, and I never got that message.' He reached for her bags.

'No, I'll handle it,' she said.

'Do you want the ride?'

'Why not?'

He led her outside the terminal. His car was parked in a zone clearly marked NO STOPPING / NO PARKING. On the dash was an official-looking sign with a logo and the word dtamruat – she knew that meant 'Police'. Just behind the car, a man in uniform was putting a Denver boot on a silver Lexus. He and Arthon exchanged waves.

He seemed hesitant about which door to open. She went to the front passenger side and tossed her bag in the back. 'What a difference from the old airport,' she said.

'It wasn't so much fun when it opened. There were many birthing problems,' he said. Ava noticed a slight British inflection in his speech.

'You went to school in the UK?' she asked.

'Four years at Liverpool U.'

This is not your average cop, she thought. To go to university overseas meant at the very least that he came from money. He's probably Chinese Thai, she thought. None of Uncle's friends with whom she had worked didn't have Chinese roots.

'Are you by any chance Chinese?' Ava asked.

'I'm Chaozhou.'

'Do you still speak Chinese?'

'No, we're assimilated. Fourth generation now.'

Arthon pulled the car out of the airport almost directly onto an expressway. They sped into Bangkok, but then traffic slowed when they got into the city. It was always bad in the city. Seven-days-a-week bad. Twenty-four-hours-a-day bad. This despite an extensive infrastructure of expressways, sky trains, and subways.

Arthon was quiet, his eyes on the road. The only sound was a Neil Diamond CD playing on the car stereo. She was the first to speak. 'What have they told you about me?' she asked.

'All I was told was to give you whatever help you needed,' Arthon said. 'I read the file on your man Antonelli. He's a bit of a pig.'

'He sure looks like one.'

'The file says he lives at the Water Hotel. You can walk there from the Hyatt Erawan. The Hyatt is on Rajdamri Road. When you come out the front door, turn right and walk about a kilometre past CentralWorld to Petchburi and go left there. The Water Hotel is only a couple of hundred metres from the intersection.'

'I think I've been there,' she said. 'Is there a large market on the corner?'

'About four thousand booths selling every knockoff known to man. We raid it every month. Of course, we give them twenty-four hours' notice before we do.'

'And another market where you can buy bootleg DVDs and all kinds of computer software?'

'That's the Pantip Plaza, further down Petchburi.'

'Okay, I know the area. Now, does Antonelli have a routine?'

'According to our sources, on weekdays he comes down to the lobby lounge around 7:30 a.m.; has coffee and a biscuit, sometimes toast; works on his laptop; sometimes has a meeting. His driver and car show up around 8:30 a.m. He goes to Mahachai – that's northwest of Bangkok, about sixty kilometres. He has an office in a seafood plant there. He works there till three or four and then heads back to Bangkok to beat the traffic. He'll get back to the hotel by five, just in time for happy hour in Barry Bean's Bar, which is one level below the lobby. He'll drink margaritas until seven and then eat in the Italian restaurant upstairs.'

'So I can count on meeting him in the lobby?'

'That's what we're told. He's there every morning.'

'You said that he's a pig. What exactly did you mean?'

'So you haven't read the file?'

'Not yet.'

He looked sideways at her as if trying to gauge her appetite for steaminess. 'A short, fat, ugly American comes to Thailand and finds out that with enough money in his pocket he can be George fucking Clooney. That's Antonelli. He thinks he's George Clooney – George Clooney with some ugly twists. He started out with bar girls; some of those evenings ended badly because after fucking them he took to beating them. Charges were filed twice and then withdrawn when the Mama-Sans were paid enough. The fat man then switched over to boys for a while, and that was even worse. He hit one so hard he almost killed him. It must have cost a ton of money to get those charges dropped.'

The Grand Hyatt came into view. Arthon put on his turn signal. 'Read the report – it's all in there,' he said.

A ramp from the street led up to the Hyatt entrance. Arthon had to get in line. Security was tight. All the cars were being searched and their underbellies examined using mirrors on long poles.

'We had some terrorist scares last week,' Arthon said. 'They mainly stick to the south, but the word was that they were targeting Bangkok. Five-star hotels are always popular.'

As they approached the security checkpoint he rolled down his window and yelled something in Thai at a man in a black suit. They were waved through. He parked in front of the hotel and made a move to exit the car.

'No, that isn't necessary,' Ava said. 'I'm just going to check in and head for bed.'

He shrugged. 'Tomorrow?'

'Let's just play it by ear. I have to figure out how to handle Antonelli. I'll probably walk over to the Water Hotel in the morning as a starter. How about I phone you if I need you?'

'I live more than an hour away from this area,' he said.

'I'll keep that in mind.'

He passed her a business card. 'My office number is on the front, my mobile is on the back. Mobile is best.'

She took a quick glance at the card. He was a lieutenant. Ava was impressed.

10

Her room had all the Asian five-star bells and whistles: teak floors, Chinese black lacquer console and dresser, stylish modern beige leather chairs with expansive footrests, a desk with a leather captain's chair, and a king-size bed with a brilliant white duvet so plush it looked as if it could swallow her whole. The bathroom was all mirror and glass and marble, the walk-in shower large enough for six people. All the room lacked was the quiet dignity of the Mandarin.

Ava showered and climbed into bed in a T-shirt and panties. She extracted from her wallet the paper with Frank Seto's UK phone numbers and called his cellphone. It was late afternoon in London.

'Frank Seto,' he said on the second ring.

'Ava Lee.'

'I was told to expect a call from you.'

'Thanks for taking it.'

'My father-in-law and your father have been friends for many years.'

'So I'm told. I'm calling about your brother.'

'I have three brothers.'

'Jackson.'

'He is one of them.'

Ava knew then that whatever cooperation she got would be grudging. 'I'm trying to locate him,' she said.

'Why?'

'I have a client who has a business relationship with Jackson. There are some outstanding issues that need to be resolved and he hasn't been able to reach him. He hired me to help.'

'And what makes you think I would have any interest in Jackson's business dealings?'

'I haven't made that assumption.'

'And what makes you think I would have any idea how to reach him?'

'He is your brother.'

'In name only,' he said sharply. 'We have nothing in common. He's been a problem for our family for many years.'

'Yet you introduced him to Andrew Tam?'

'Shit, that was completely incidental. Andrew and I were having lunch when Jackson came into the same restaurant. Believe me, I'm not in the habit of hooking up Jackson with my friends or business associates.'

'He's burned some of them?'

'He burns everyone, sooner or later. He can't help himself.'

'I'm really sorry to hear that,' she said. 'It must be difficult for someone in your position.' He didn't respond, and she knew she had gone off mark. 'Anyway, Frank, I would be grateful if you could help me find him.'

'Weren't you listening? I have no idea where he is or how to get in touch with him.'

'Would your brothers?'

'No, and neither would my mother, so your enquiries should end with me.'

'I had a Seattle address for him, but the place is vacant,' she said.

'The last address I had for him was in Boston, not Seattle.'

'How many years ago was that?'

'At least five.'

'I also had a Hong Kong address for him, in the Wanchai district. Again it came up empty.'

'We were all born and raised in Wanchai, but the rest of us escaped. He keeps going back. He likes grunge, I guess. But I've only known him to stay in hotels there.'

'Any particular one?'

'No. He's strictly a two- or three-star-hotel kind of guy, and you know how many of them there are in Wanchai.'

'Do you have a phone number for him?'

'This is the number I have,' he said, and gave her the same cellphone number she had been trying to reach for days.

'Well, I guess I've run into another dead end,' she said.

'There isn't much I can do about that.'

'Evidently not. Well, anyway, thanks for taking my call.'

'Make sure you tell your father that I did,' he said.

'Are you always this rude?' she shot back.

'My brother brings out the worst out in me,' he said, and cut off the connection.

Ava turned her attention to the Antonelli file and began to read it in detail. He was now her primary interest. She had hoped she would be able to work her way around him, to avoid alerting Seto that they were coming after him and the money. Now she would have to go after him directly.

The file was quite detailed. Given the short notice, Uncle's Thai friends had done a remarkable job of using his passport to track his movements. The first official sighting of Antonelli in Thailand had been six years before. He had landed at the old Bangkok airport, got a six-month tourist visa, and then gone to southern Thailand, to the city of Hat Yai, in Songkhla Province near the Malaysian border, and checked into the Novotel Hotel. The visa was renewed six months later in Malaysia. A note in the file said that Antonelli probably drove there from Hat Yai – about an hour away – crossed the border, and then re-entered Thailand. It was all legal. Over the next eighteen months he renewed the visa three more times, flying back to Atlanta each time. On each trip to the US he didn't stay more than a week.

The Novotel had his passport on file for two years. It appeared that he had been involved in business with a fish processing plant in Hat Yai, but when the Muslim terrorists in southern Thailand targeted the city – the largest in the area, with a population of about a million people – and began blowing up hotels and shopping malls, Antonelli moved north to Bangkok. He stayed at an apartment hotel on Petchburi Road for the first three months and then moved three blocks to the Water Hotel. He had been there ever since.

After five months in Bangkok, his name showed up on two official documents. The first was a work visa through Seafood Partners. The second was a document registering him as a minority shareholder in the company; its majority shareholder was, as required by law, a Thai. The Thai owned a separate shrimp and fish processing plant, Siam Union and Trading. Ava assumed that the Thai's shares in Seafood Partners were a sham, declared simply to enable Antonelli and Seto to do business in the country. Over the next two years, Seafood Partners shipped multiple containers of shrimp to the US and became embroiled in dispute after dispute about short weights, mixed grades, and excess glaze.

The company also became an importer, buying whole grouper and snapper from India, the Philippines, and Indonesia, processing the fish, and exporting it to the US. The only problem was that it bought according to terms and paid well for only about six months. Then the company stopped paying invoices and started making complaints about every quality issue imaginable. Eventually the lawsuits were flying. Seafood Partners fought every claim, confident that time, cost, and the complications involved in cross-border legal action would discourage the exporters. They were right. One by one, the lawsuits disappeared.

But the Thai Department of Fisheries did not go away. All the quality issues related to the shrimp exports caught its attention. After a cursory examination, the department cancelled the licence of the processor, Siam Union and Trading, leaving Seafood Partners, even though it was the exporter of record, untouched.

Next, Antonelli flew to Atlanta for what looked like six months. He seemed to have returned when they landed the Major Supermarkets business. Ava couldn't believe that Major

Supermarkets had actually given them that business. Where was their due diligence?

She read on. Antonelli maintained a Thai bank account with a balance that rarely exceeded a hundred thousand baht, about three thousand dollars. His hotel bills were paid with a Visa credit card issued by a US bank. His car and driver had been paid for by Siam Union, and when that company left the scene, by the same Visa card used to pay the hotel bill.

There was no mention of Seto in the file, not in reference to the formation of Seafood Partners or in the lawsuits. She now wished she had asked the Thai police to run a casual check on him. At the very least she would have found out how often he came and went, and where he stayed when he was in Bangkok.

One thing that caught her eye was Antonelli's cellphone number, which had a Thai area code. She made a mental note to ask Arthon the next day if he had any way to access calls made to and from that number.

At the back of the folder were copies of the assault complaints filed with the police against Antonelli. None of them had remained active for very long. Ava leafed through them and stopped before the end. It was like reading sado-masochistic pornography. She wondered what the wife in Atlanta would think about his habit of beating up defenceless women and boys. Then again, maybe she knew.

The bedside clock said it was almost midnight. Ava tried to convince herself that she was tired and slipped under the covers. Fifteen minutes later she got up, put on her linen slacks and a clean Brooks Brothers shirt, and went downstairs to Spasso, which was one level below the hotel lobby. During the day and into the early evening, Spasso was the Hyatt's Italian restaurant. After 9 p.m. it began its transition to nightclub. Tables were cleared, the bandstand was set up, the bar was fully staffed, and security manned the door. It was one of the most popular high-end clubs in Bangkok, and Ava knew it would be going full blast until at least 2 a.m.

When she walked in, the place was jammed with the usual mix of young *farang* professionals – residents and tourists – and Thai girls on the make. This wasn't a place for backpackers. It also wasn't a place for bar girls from Soi Cowboy, Nana Plaza, or Patpong, the three most popular downmarket night spots in a city that advertised in-your-face sex clubs, night markets, lurid shows, and cheap by-the-hour hotel rooms for *farangs* who were squeamish about taking the bar girls back to their own hotel. The Thai girls at Spasso were amateurs, part-timers, teachers and students and the like, trying to make a few extra dollars and hoping, just hoping, to hit the jackpot – a *farang* boyfriend who would send monthly financial support when he got back home to North America or Europe, and who might give her the blue-eyed baby that had become a status symbol among these girls.

The foreigners in the club weren't all from the West. Ava saw some Japanese, a few Koreans, and a cluster of what looked like wealthy, hip Arabs. None of them were a natural attraction for the girls; they homed in on the Westerners. The Japanese and Koreans wouldn't get any action until the girls had explored all their Western options and found them wanting. The Arabs would have to wait as well, and they weren't being patient about it. One of them had ordered a large tub filled with ice and about forty shooters in test tubes. He held a shooter in each hand and waved at the girls to come and take what they wanted. He was getting the odd nibble but was having trouble getting the girls to stay.

Ava found a small table at the back of the club as far as possible from the stage, which had a set of drums and two guitars on it. To one side, propped on an easel, was a sign that read MANILA MAGIC. She groaned. Filipino cover bands were an Asian cliché. There wasn't a five-star hotel anywhere in Asia that didn't have one playing. The noise level in the room was already deafening; she could hardly imagine what the band would add to it.

She ordered a glass of white wine and sat back, content to dissect the action, trying to figure out who was going to get lucky. She could feel eyes turn in her direction. She ignored them, discouraging attention.

The band came onstage – three guys on the instruments and two female singers – and broke into a pretty horrid rendition of 'Proud Mary'. As she watched, a blonde crossed her line of sight. From the distance she looked about thirty. She wore black silk pants and a green silk blouse.

The blonde worked her way through the crowd towards Ava, and the closer she got the faster Ava's interest waned. She was closer to forty than thirty, and she had heavy thighs and a big ass.

'Hi, I'm Deborah,' she said. 'Can I join you?'

Ava hesitated and then realized she wouldn't mind the companionship. 'Sure, but I've got to tell you right off the top that you're not my type.'

The woman looked flustered. 'I'm sorry, I thought you were—'

'I am, but you're still not my type. Sit down anyway.'

'This is a tough place for girls like us,' Deborah said, holding her own glass of white wine.

'Where are you from?'

'Washington, DC. You?'

'Toronto.'

'Here on business?'

'Yes, and you?'

'Same.'

'Where are you staying?'

'Here.'

'Me too. This is my first trip to Bangkok, and I can't fucking believe how great these hotels are, how great the service is.'

'How long are you staying?'

'Another five days.'

'Well, Spasso is not where you should be. These girls are focused on *farang* cock. They're all very entrepreneurial, and they know that's where the money is.'

'So where should I go?'

'Over on Royal City Avenue – RCA – there are a couple of bars you might enjoy. One is called Nine Bar; the newest one is Zeta. I liked Zeta last time I was here. Most of the girls are young – you know, early twenties – and some of them are just figuring things out, still experimenting, enthusiastic and eager as hell but lacking technique. They would take to a woman like you.'

'Are they bar girls?'

'No, not really. They don't expect to get paid. Mind you, if you slipped them twenty or thirty dollars they would appreciate it. But it isn't necessary.'

'Would I have any problems if I went by myself? I mean, at home I'm quite circumspect. Dyke bars aren't my thing.'

'No problems.'

'Is it close?'

'Ten minutes by taxi. But then in Bangkok everywhere is ten minutes by taxi, according to the drivers, unless of course there's traffic,' Ava said and smiled.

'Thanks. I have to work early tomorrow morning, so I'm going to head out,' Deborah said.

'The girls will still be there tomorrow night,' Ava said.

'Can I buy you a drink before I go?'

Ava shook her head. 'No, I think I'm finally getting tired enough to go to bed. And besides, if I have to listen to another Filipino cover band murder Shania Twain, I think I'll go crazy.'

11

Ava popped a couple of melatonin tablets before going to bed and slept through until 6 a.m. It was too early to call Arthon, so she phoned her mother. She would be at home, since it was still too early for dinner and mah-jong. Ava told Jennie about having dim sum with her father. As always, Jennie over-reacted. Nothing pleased Ava's mother more than her daughters' contact with their father. She pretended that she was happy for their sakes, but Ava knew it was just as much about reaffirmation of her status as wife number two.

Ava boiled some water and made a cup of VIA instant coffee. She turned on BBC World, but after five minutes she gave up and reached for her running gear and a rubber band to tie her hair back. She was always of two minds about running in Bangkok. There was the safety, security, and clean air of the hotel gym, while her other option was to run outside and fight the smog, the smothering humidity, and the carnival of people. But she knew that the Hyatt was only about a kilometre from Lumpini Park, and she loved running there. When she stayed at the Mandarin Hotel, sometimes she would even take a taxi there and back. Lumpini it would be.

At six thirty the sun was visible but not yet oppressive. The streets were already lined with traffic but the smog hadn't had time to build to its midday thickness. She turned left from the hotel and headed to the park, dodging dogs and sidewalk cracks and rises.

In a city with virtually no greenery and few public recreational facilities, the park was a magnet for all kinds of athletes. Thousands of people were there, nearly all of them Thais. She joined the throng circling the park on a three-kilometre track, which was thoughtfully marked every two hundred metres in white paint. It was a catholic group, with no apparently dominant gender or age. The only people who stood out in the running group were the businessmen, who held their shirts and jackets in their hands so as not to get them sweaty.

The track was on the outer perimeter of the park. In the interior it was just as busy, with pockets of activities that made the place so interesting. There were tai chi practitioners, several groups of them, silently performing their rituals. Old men and women waving swords and fans in precise slow-motion patterns. Bird-lovers with their cages. People playing badminton, tennis, and a Thai form of lawn bowling or bocce. All this took Ava's mind off the running. In the gym she was usually good for five kilometres; at Lumpini she did three full laps before heading back to the hotel.

She showered, dressed in her business suit, put her slacks and shirts in a laundry bag and requested same-day service, and then went down to the lobby with the Antonelli file and her notebook. She reread the file as she sipped some ice water. How to approach him? How to get him to open the door to Seto? She had Antonelli's cellphone number. If Arthon could patch into his phone and trace calls to and from it, that could save her some time. She called Arthon and told him what she wanted.

'It won't be easy,' he said. She could hear street noises in the background. 'You can buy a SIM card anywhere here, and there are tons of pay-as-you-go phone-card companies. It isn't like the UK or North America, where you have only a handful of carriers. It could take me a while to find his carrier, and then I have to see if we've penetrated them already.'

'Please try,' she said.

'What are your plans for today?' he asked.

'I'm heading over to the Water Hotel in a few minutes. I'll see if I can engage Antonelli in conversation.'

'Using what pretext?'

'Feminine charm,' she said.

He didn't respond, and for a moment she thought he was mocking her. Then he said slowly, 'When you read the data on Antonelli, did you take note of the section that mentioned what he likes to do now on weekends?'

'I don't remember it particularly, but I assume he hits the bars.'

'More precisely, he goes to Nana Plaza.'

'And how is that different from Soi Cowboy or Patpong?'

'On the first two floors it's the same old bar-girl shit, but when you get to the third floor – that's another thing altogether. When we were in the car, I didn't get a chance to finish my story about him. Antonelli has graduated from women and boys and gotten into *katoeys* – ladyboys. The third floor at Nana Plaza is all katoey. The violence seems to have toned down since he switched. Maybe he's found what he was looking for.'

'Oh.'

'Like I said, he's a pig.'

It took longer than she had planned to walk to the hotel. Ava had to cross a couple of intersections, and the traffic lights were programmed to change about every five minutes. So you waited; if you tried to jaywalk you would meet inevitable death, because Bangkok traffic stopped for no one.

It was just after eight when she finally walked into the Water Hotel. It was supposed to be a five-star establishment, but she could tell from the lobby that it fell short. The furniture looked worn, and the staff uniforms showed frayed edges.

She spotted Antonelli right away. There was a lounge to the right of the lobby where they were serving coffee and tea. He sat on a sofa, his computer open on his lap, a cup and saucer and a plate of toast sitting on a small table beside him. He wore a *barong*, the loose Filipino shirt that is the fat man's friend.

His head was virtually bald, apart from a few straggly strands of hair stretched from ear to ear. He was even bigger than he had looked in the picture. His jowls swallowed up his neck, and the *barong* was stretched so tightly across his gut that she could see his white T-shirt between the buttons, which were threatening to pull apart. When he sat back on the sofa, his feet barely touched the ground. But as he typed, Ava noticed that his pudgy fingers moved quite deftly.

The lounge was busy, which gave her an excuse to sit almost directly across from him. She ordered coffee and waited for a chance to attract his attention. But Antonelli was focused on his computer, lifting his head only to look at his watch. When her coffee came, she took a sip and said, 'My God, is the coffee here always this bad?'

He took a quick glance at her but said nothing. Then he closed his computer, slipped it into a wheeled briefcase, stood up, and rolled out of the lounge. She watched him exit through the giant glass doors at the entrance. An elderly Thai man stood at the curb. He took the briefcase and put it in the back of a black Toyota SUV. Antonelli, with some difficulty, climbed into the back seat. Then the car drove off.

Well, wasn't that successful, Ava thought.

She phoned Arthon and told him what had happened. She could almost hear him smile. 'I'll give it another go in the bar tonight,' she said. 'In the meantime I'm going to go shopping, try to catch a nap, and wait for you to call me back with the cellphone information I need.'

'I told you that won't be easy.'

'One other thing,' she said. 'We asked you about Antonelli, but we are also trying to locate a guy named Jackson Seto. Antonelli is our primary source, but it would be useful to know what you can dig up on Seto and his movements both to and from and in and around Thailand. I've been assuming he's still in the US, which is why we didn't ask about him initially. That may have been a mistake on my part.'

'Jackson is an English name. Does he have a Chinese name – a proper name? Because if he does, his passport will likely be in that one.'

'I don't know.'

'We'll look under Jackson and see if anything comes up. Where will you be?'

'On this phone or at the Hyatt.'

It was too early to shop at Pantip Plaza, the techie mall almost directly across the street from the Water Hotel, so Ava walked back to the Hyatt. She got *wai*'d at the door, *wai*'d in the lobby, and *wai*'d at the elevator. *Wai* is the most basic form of respectful greeting among Thais, palms held together in prayer fashion and accompanied by a bow. The closer the hands are to the face and the lower the bow, the greater the respect being shown. As a woman in business attire, Ava seemed to generate a considerable amount of deference – *from everyone except George Antonelli*, she thought.

When she got to her room, she stripped down to bra and panties and hung up her clothes. Then she napped for a couple of hours. When she woke, she saw no reason to dress up, so she slipped on her track pants and a T-shirt. There weren't any *wai*s this time when she left the hotel.

At Pantip she ordered all five seasons of *The Wire* – fifteen DVDs – for forty dollars, and then she bought three film-editing software programs for one of her friends. The software cost three dollars for each program; her friend would save a couple of thousand dollars. While she waited for the DVDs to be burned, she went across the street and had a bowl of tom yam kung.

After Chinese hot and sour soup, which ranked as her uncontested favourite, tom yam kung was at the head of the second-tier list. Like a good hot and sour seafood soup, it is made with a chicken stock base and a generous amount of shrimp. Cilantro, straw mushrooms, scallions, fish sauce, lime juice, lemongrass stalks, and kaffir lime leaves are added to produce a flavoursome broth, its surface dotted with a crimson oil slick from the final ingredient, red chili peppers. The soup had a clean, clear aroma, like pure oxygen with just a hint of citrus.

After lunch she went back to Pantip to collect her DVDs. As she was paying for them, Arthon called. He had had no luck with Antonelli's phone, but they had compiled some information on Seto.

'Can I drop it off at the Hyatt?' he asked.

'Fifteen minutes,' she said.

'More like an hour,' he countered.

'I'll meet you in the lobby.'

12

Ava waited for Arthon for close to two hours. She drank several glasses of fruit juice and read all the newspapers in the lobby: the two English-language papers – *The Nation* and the *Bangkok Post* – a Chinese paper, the *International Herald Tribune*, and the Asian edition of the *Wall Street Journal*. The news was all the same: the economy was in tatters. This usually made for good business for Ava. Desperate times called for desperate measures.

Arthon came through the front door, leaving his car running right outside. He had clout, no doubt about that. He was better dressed than he had been the night before, in tight blue slacks and a form-fitting red Lacoste golf shirt, with sunglasses perched on his head. If she hadn't known him, she might have figured him for a dealer.

Arthon didn't apologize for being late – given the traffic, it is understood in Bangkok that meeting times are an estimate at best. 'I can't stay,' he said quickly as he handed her two sheets of paper.

'That's it?'

'Seto's comings and goings. That and his hotel stays are all we have on record. He's been here three or four times a year for the past six years, at first going to Hat Yai and then to Bangkok. He stayed at the Novotel with Antonelli when he was in the south, and at the Water Hotel when Antonelli moved north.'

'Seafood Partners?'

'If he was a partner, he was a discreet one.'

'When was he last here?'

'About five months ago.'

When he was organizing the Major Supermarkets scam, she thought.

'I have one more thing for you,' he said, passing her what looked like a passport photo. 'I didn't know if you had one.'

She looked at her target. Thick black hair streaked with grey and combed straight back with no part. Long, thin face with a small mouth, looking even smaller under a moustache that drooped on the right. His eyes were almost hidden by hooded lids. He stared right into the camera with a look of defiance.

'Now I have to go,' Arthon said. 'It's payday and I still have some collections to make. What are your plans for tonight?'

'Barry Bean's for happy hour. Maybe I can get Antonelli to talk to me if he has a few drinks in him.'

'Call me if you need me. I should be free by about seven.'

Ava got to the bar by six, figuring that happy hour would be in full swing. Barry Bean's was packed but there was no sign of Antonelli. She mentioned his name to her waitress and was told that 'Kuhn George' would be along eventually – he hardly ever missed happy hour. She chatted with a German bathtub manufacturer who was thinking about relocating his business to Thailand but was trying to do it without bringing his wife and kids. The problem was that his wife wasn't an idiot.

At seven the bar staff gathered in one spot, a bell was rung, and they yelled, 'Happy hour is over, happy hour is over.' Still no sign of Antonelli.

Ava called Arthon.

'Oh shit, I forgot this was Friday,' he said.

'What do you mean?' she groaned.

'On Fridays he goes to an Italian restaurant near Soi Cowboy. It's owned by actual Italians and is one of the trendiest spots in town. After dinner he shows up at Nana Plaza for his weekly romp with a katoey.'

'Does he bring her back to the hotel?' Ava asked.

'No. Security checks all the guests brought back to the rooms and holds their ID until they leave. Antonelli wouldn't want the staff to know he's into ladyboys. He uses a hotel attached to Nana that rents rooms by the hour.'

That might even be better, she thought. 'Arthon, it might be useful if we had proof of his little habit.'

'What do you mean?'

'Pictures,' she said.

He didn't hesitate. 'It's worth a try, but I'd have to pay someone, and maybe more than one person.'

'How much are we talking about?'

'Five thousand baht at least, maybe even ten.'

Two to three hundred dollars, Ava calculated. 'That sounds reasonable, but only if we actually get the pictures.'

'Let me see what I can arrange.'

'Call me later?'

'Whether I'm successful or not?'

'I need to know either way.'

Ava closed her phone and went upstairs to the Water Hotel's Italian restaurant that Antonelli frequented. It was deserted. The hostess was happy to have someone to talk to and was very forthcoming about Antonelli, or 'Khun George' – a verbal sign of respect, the equivalent of 'Mister' in English. It turned out that Khun George ate a lot, was very demanding, and tipped badly. Ava was finding it easy to work up a big dislike for him.

After dinner she walked back to the Hyatt. The streets were even more difficult to negotiate than earlier in the day because the night markets and restaurants – appearing as if by magic on the sidewalks – were in full swing. She shuddered when she saw the level of sanitation. There was no running water, and plates and cutlery were being washed and rewashed in the same tub. Ava had eaten street food once, and it had taken her two days to get over the food poisoning.

She thought about going down to Spasso, and then about going to Zeta. She ended up in her room watching HBO. At around eleven she fell asleep.

Although she felt like she had been asleep for a while, it was only eleven-thirty when the phone rang.

'Bingo,' Arthon said. 'And with one who hasn't completed the surgery – she has tits and a cock. Our guy burst into the room when they were in the middle of their fun, both of them completely naked and Antonelli staring right into the camera. He is one very ugly *farang* with no clothes on. His tits are almost bigger than hers.'

'When can I get the photos?'

'Tomorrow morning. I'll drop them off first thing.'

13

Arthon called Ava at eight the next morning to say he was on his way. She had already been up for two hours and had gone for another run in Lumpini Park. Saturday morning was even busier than Friday, and after two laps she walked the third so she could take in more of the sights and sounds. She hadn't known there were so many variations of tai chi.

When she got back to the hotel, she showered and changed and then camped out in the lobby to wait for Arthon. She was reading the *Bangkok Post*, which had an article in the lifestyle section about a katoey rock band. From the photo she couldn't have guessed that it wasn't just another gorgeous all-girl band.

Aside from his nasty violent streak, Ava had no issue with Antonelli's sexual tastes. She also knew Thailand well enough to be sure that the Thais wouldn't care either. Katoeys were a part of everyday life, an accepted third sex. Ava had been in public buildings that actually had three washrooms: for men, women, and katoeys.

A small cottage industry had developed around the katoey, and partly because of them the plastic surgeons in Thailand were some of the world's best. They had been lucky to catch Antonelli with one who hadn't yet completed the surgery. If she had, no one would have believed she was transgender.

Then again, Ava thought, *maybe we weren't lucky. Maybe Antonelli likes them half and half.*

Arthon arrived on time, wearing the same clothes as the night before. He looked tired, and Ava guessed he hadn't slept. He slumped onto the couch next to her and groaned.

'Rough night of police work?'

'I wish,' he said. 'It's month-end and I had to make my collections. I'm responsible for the gambling joints, and some of them don't open till midnight.'

'How much time do you spend on actual police work as opposed to running all these side businesses?'

'It's about fifty-fifty, although at month-end it gets crazy.'

'And I didn't think gambling was legal in Thailand,' she said.

'It isn't,' he said as he passed her a large brown envelope.

There were five photos. She winced as she looked at them. Antonelli was even more repulsive with his clothes off than she had imagined, and even though she already knew about his partner, it was still a bit of a shock for Ava to actually see her.

'Wonderful,' she said.

'Do you want me to be with you when you drop this on him? He might not be too pleased.'

'It should be okay. What you can do for me is find out his room number at the Water Hotel. I'll slip a picture under his door and then arrange to meet him somewhere public where he can't go off on me.'

'He's in room 3235.'

'Thank you.'

'I'm going home to get some sleep. If you need me, just call.'

'Here, I owe you this,' she said, giving him a roll of baht.

'Forget it. I talked to my boss and he said he'd kill me if I took anything from Uncle.'

She shrugged. 'Give it to a temple or something.'

'I can't do that,' he said. He stood up and stretched wearily. Ava noticed some of the female staff eyeing him. He noted them too and smiled and *wai*'d. *Wai*s all round ensued, and one of the women, who looked about sixteen, drifted towards him. A few words were spoken in Thai and then she laughed, took his card, and walked with him to the front door. Ava could only admire how aggressive these women were.

She went back to her room and changed her clothes; the linen slacks and pink Brooks Brothers shirt would create the right impression. She went outside, intending to walk to the hotel, but the sky was clear and the sun was brutal. She didn't want to get there covered in sweat so she took a taxi, even though the ride would take longer than the walk.

She caught the elevator to the thirty-second floor. The corridor was empty save for the room maid's cart. Ava stood outside Antonelli's room for a moment, her ear pressed against the door. She heard faint noises coming from what sounded like a television. She had left one picture in the envelope, on which she had written: *Meet me in the lobby downstairs. I'm Chinese, a woman, and I'm wearing a pink shirt.*

Ava slid the envelope under the door, rang the doorbell, and then used the nearby exit to run down the stairs. She got out on the thirty-first floor and pushed the elevator button, hoping she'd get to the lobby before him, and hoping even more that he wouldn't get into the same elevator car as her. It took less than a minute to arrive.

She walked into a lobby that was nearly deserted and chose a chair in the middle of the lounge. Across from it was a couch, with a broad coffee table in between. She ordered an espresso and waited. A few minutes later the elevator doors opened and Antonelli charged into the lobby. He was wearing a Georgia Tech tank top, baggy shorts, and a pair of blue Crocs. His legs were pale and surprisingly smooth. He hadn't brushed his hair, and the few strands he had left were sticking up in the air. He looked around the lobby; she could see a mixture of anger, urgency, and desperation on his face.

Ava waved at Antonelli and smiled. He headed towards her, the envelope clasped tightly in his hand.

'You, you bitch! You Chinese bitch! You fucking Chinese bitch!' he yelled when he was still ten metres away.

'Have a seat,' she said, pointing to the sofa.

He ploughed towards her, his face contorted, and for a second she thought he was going to try something physical with her. She shifted her feet, bracing herself for a countermove. He stopped when he was still a short distance away from her. 'You fucking bitch,' he spat.

Even from that distance Ava could smell breath that was foul from beer and God knows what else. His bared teeth were stained and coated with a yellow film. She guessed he hadn't taken the time to brush.

He brandished the envelope in front of him. 'You fucking Chinese bitch.'

'You're getting repetitive, and not accomplishing anything. I suggest you sit,' she said.

'You were the one who was here yesterday. I remember

you, you bitch. I thought there was something funny about you.'

'Obviously there was.'

He waved the envelope again. 'What is this about? What the fuck is this about? I don't know you. There is no fucking reason for this.'

The server hovered nearby with Ava's coffee, afraid to come any closer. 'You can bring it over now,' Ava said to her, and then turned to Antonelli. 'Do you want something?' she asked. 'I'm buying.'

'Fuck off.'

'Later. Right now we need to talk.'

'What do you think you're going to do with this?'

'You are George Antonelli, correct? And you have a partner named Jackson Seto, and the two of you have been stealing money from a client of mine. That's why I'm here.'

'I have no fucking idea what you're talking about.'

'Yes, you do, but really it doesn't matter one way or another. I have very little interest in you or your hobbies. What I need to do is find Jackson Seto. I want you to help me.'

'I still have no idea what the fuck you're talking about.'

Ava pulled the file Arthon had given her from her purse and placed it on the table. 'I know all about you. I know how long you've been here, who you've worked with, how many scams you and Seto have pulled. I also know about the wife and kids back in Atlanta. Their address and phone numbers are in the file.'

Antonelli sat down and reached for the folder. He opened it and started to read. She waited, watching his face for a reaction. His jaw tightened, and he licked spittle from the side of his mouth.

'What the fuck are you trying to do?' he said finally.

'It's very simple – I need to locate Seto. You know where he is, or at the very least you know how I can contact him. You have two options. You tell me what I want to know, or I'm going to make a hundred copies of that photo – and the five others that I have – and send them to your wife, your kids, your Atlanta neighbours, your parents, any siblings you have, your in-laws, and anyone you're doing or have ever done business with. My experience is that Americans, particularly Americans in the South, and Baptists at that, are slightly less liberal about matters like this than Thais are.'

He closed his eyes. *A good sign*, Ava thought. He was imagining the worst. He was calculating the odds. 'How do I know—'

'You don't,' she interrupted. 'But I am in the habit of keeping my word. Just help me find Seto and the photos will be burned.'

'Fuck.'

'I'm sorry it had to be like this, I really am. If I could have found him any other way this wouldn't have been necessary,' she said.

'What will you do if you locate him?'

'Get the money back.'

'What if I direct you to him and you can't get the money back? What will happen to the photos?'

'Just get me to him. Do that and you're completely off the hook, I promise.'

114

Antonelli chewed a fingernail while he thought. 'You got a pen?'

She took out her notebook and Mont Blanc. 'Go ahead.'

'I'll give you his email address. He rarely checks it and normally doesn't answer directly. I email him and tell him I need to talk, and he phones me. But you can try. You never know.'

'All right.'

'Right now he doesn't have a North American or Asian phone number that works. You'll have to call 592-223-7878.'

'What area code is that?'

'Guyana.'

'He's in Guyana?'

'Obviously.'

'Why Guyana?'

'We used to buy bangamary and sea trout there. We'd ship it to Atlanta, tray-pack, and sell it to the black and Hispanic markets. It was a good business for a while. Jackson has a house there, and a kind of wife, and he knows enough of the right people that he feels safe there. Whenever things get tight, he always fucks off to Guyana.'

'You're sure I'll find him there?'

'He was there yesterday.'

'Why does he feel safe there?'

Antonelli smiled. 'Guyana is a shithole, filled with people who either helped make it a shithole or people who thrive in shitholes. Even for me – and I've seen a lot of shitholes – it's more shithole than I can stand. And Jackson has surrounded himself with the nastiest bunch of shitholes he could find. As long as he pays them, they'll do what he wants.'

'What about the police?'

'Most of the people he's paying *are* the fucking police.'

'Do you have an address for him?'

'Malvern Gardens. I don't know the number but there are only about ten houses in the subdivision. It's fucking grand by Georgetown standards, and he's the only Chinese there.'

'Georgetown is the main city?'

'Yep. A shithole.'

'I get the picture,' she said.

'You think you do,' he said. 'Wait till you get there. However bad you think it is, it will be that much worse.'

'If I get there and it turns out that Seto knows I'm coming—'

'I won't tell him.'

'I mean it. If he has any clue—'

'Look, I don't want those photos in the wrong hands. You know that. You are a hundred percent fucking sure about that, aren't you? So I'm trusting that you will honour your word. That's all. Do I think you're going to be able to ambush Seto and get him to fork over the money? No, I don't. I don't think you've got a fucking chance in hell. So with that thought in my mind, why would I risk screwing you over? I'll not say a word to him. Nothing. You go and do whatever the hell you want. You just can't blame me if it doesn't work out.'

'Give me your phone.'

'Why?'

'Just do it, please.'

He tossed his cellphone to her. She caught it and flipped it open. 'I'm going to call the Guyana number you gave me,' she said. 'I'm also going to put the phone in speaker mode.' She checked her watch. 'It isn't too late there. Hopefully he'll answer. If he doesn't, then what? Voicemail?'

'Yeah.'

'Either way, just tell him you're going away for a long weekend and that you'll be out of touch until the middle of next week. Is that plausible? Would you do that under normal circumstances?'

'I have.'

She hit the numbers, put the phone in speaker mode, and placed it on the table between them. It rang four times before a muffled voice answered, 'What the hell do you want, George?'

'Jack, just wanted you to know I'm heading down to Phuket for some R and R. I'm not taking my laptop, so you won't hear from me till next week.'

'Whatever. Have fun.' The phone went dead.

Ava was surprised to hear that Seto still had a trace of Chinese accent. His brother spoke flawless English and she had expected the same of him.

'Okay, you happy?' Antonelli said.

'One last thing,' she said slowly. 'Money. Do you have access to the money?'

'No,' he said. 'That's all Jackson.'

'Has he sent you money?'

'He sends me money every month, but just enough to cover my overheads, my expenses.'

'You don't profit-share?'

'We have a seventy-thirty split, and you don't have to guess who gets the seventy. Normally we wait till year-end, around Christmas, before we dip into it. By then we know how much we actually have. You know, there are a lot of fucking ups and downs in our business.'

'So it seems.'

'And you could be one big fucking down.'

'Let's hope,' she said, standing. She put the notebook and the envelope back in her purse. 'Thanks for your help.'

'What I hope is that I never hear your fucking voice again,' he said.

'The feeling is mutual.'

14

Antonelli's description of Guyana began to fade the moment Ava went online to find a flight to Georgetown. The most obvious carrier, she thought, would be a national airline. Every country has one. Except Guyana – theirs had gone bankrupt in 2001. And then there had been another, quasi-national one that went broke as well.

The predominant carrier that flew to Guyana was Caribbean Airlines, and all its inbound flights originated in Port of Spain, Trinidad. The best way to get to Port of Spain was through New York or Miami. She knew that Thai Air had a direct flight from Bangkok to New York. It left at midnight and got into New York in the late afternoon. There was a flight to Port of Spain that arrived at 7 p.m. She would have to overnight in Port of Spain and catch a morning flight to Guyana.

She checked the seating availability in business class; all the flights were wide open. She emailed her travel agent to arrange the flights and book her into the best hotels she could find.

Checkout time at the Hyatt was noon. She called downstairs and negotiated a late checkout for half the normal daily rack rate.

Ava had missed two phone calls while working online, one

from Arthon and the other from Uncle. She phoned Arthon. He was pleased, if a bit surprised, that things had gone so well. She told him to keep a set of the photos in case they were needed. He said he had been going to anyway, and she wondered what that implied for Antonelli.

When she called Uncle, he asked her how it had gone with Antonelli. That was his way of letting her know he was always in the loop, and that indeed it was his loop.

She described her meeting in detail.

'Where is this Guyana?' he asked.

'What, you don't have friends there?'

'I won't know that until I know where the place is.'

'It's in South America. On the northeast coast, surrounded by Suriname, Brazil, and Venezuela, and a stone's throw from Trinidad. And I know that only because I looked it up.'

'This is encouraging,' he said, meaning that she had located Seto. Geography was lost on him.

'Do you want to say anything to Tam's uncle?'

'No, not until you have the money,' Uncle said. 'Ava, where you are at the Hyatt, the Erawan Shrine is right next to you.'

'It is.'

'Go there, will you? Light some incense, leave some flowers, make a donation, and pray for us all.'

'I didn't know you were a Buddhist.'

'I'm not, but neither is the shrine. It is actually Hindu, and it is devoted to the Thai version of Brahma – I can never remember his Thai name – and his elephant, whose name I do remember, but only because of the hotel. It's Erawan.'

'I'll go.'

'Good. It's a lucky shrine. I've been there twice, and both times the results were more than I could have hoped for.'

The shrine was on the corner of Ratchadamri Road, one of the busiest corners in one of the busiest cities in the world. The area was large, about twenty metres square, and was fenced, so Ava had to squeeze in through a gate. Even at one in the afternoon, with the sun at its peak, the shrine was filled almost to overflowing with concentric circles of worshippers standing around the statues of the six-armed Brahma and his elephant.

Ava bought a garland of flowers, an orange, and three incense sticks. She placed the flowers and the orange at Brahma's feet, where hundreds of gifts already lay. She lit the incense, held it in between her palms in the *wai* position, and began to pray, rocking gently back and forth, her lips moving, her words gentle.

It was mainly Thais who were praying. The tourists stood on the outskirts, taking photos of the worshippers and the troupe of Thai dancers who performed there every day, dancing to please Brahma so that he in turn would be kind to the supplicants.

Ava prayed for more than five minutes, naming all the members of her family and her closest friends. She asked for health and happiness, repeating the words like a mantra. When she had finished, she felt at peace. She put a hundred-baht note in the dancers' collection urn and returned to the hotel.

Since it was a Saturday the hotel had a couple of weddings booked. She couldn't move through the lobby without bumping into someone wearing a uniform or a gown. She figured that only people affiliated with the police or the military could afford to get married at the Hyatt. Their base pay was meagre, but the perks and kickbacks made up for it. Uncle said he had never met a retired police officer who wasn't a millionaire. She assumed that the same applied to the military.

If she had been feeling more sociable she could have quizzed Arthon about how it all worked. He had been pretty blasé about picking up contributions from casinos that weren't supposed to exist. She had heard that the street beggars worked like franchises, being assigned a specific spot to work their pathos and kicking back half their proceeds to the police. There wasn't a bar in the city that didn't contribute to the police pension fund. Every stolen car ended up being either sold or cannibalized by a special cop squad. The money moved upstream in an established and fully controlled pattern.

Still, she loved Thailand. Organized corruption was always superior to corruption with no rules. Uncle avoided doing business in places such as the Philippines and India and parts of China for that very reason.

Back in her room Ava switched on her computer and began a search on Guyana. This was new territory: a place in the world where Uncle's extensive network did not reach. Very quickly she deduced that George Antonelli hadn't been exaggerating all that much, if at all. The country – officially the Cooperative Republic of Guyana – had a population of about 800,000 people, most of them huddled along a sixty-kilometre strip of coastline, and a per capita income of less than $1,200. That ranked it 155th in the world, and she hadn't even heard of many of the countries that came in lower.

The country had one airport, with only a handful of airlines flying into it. It had no passenger railway. It did have more than eight thousand kilometres of road, but only about six hundred kilometres were actually paved, and on those it seemed that potholes were as prevalent as tarmac. A diesel-generated power grid provided about sixty percent of the country's actual needs; blackouts were a scheduled daily occurrence. Ava made a note to buy a flashlight. The water quality was also iffy. She made a note to buy water purification pills.

The population was predominantly East Indian, the descendants of indentured servants. But there was also a very large black population, the descendants of slaves. The two groups had a long history of antagonism. The rest were remnants of the original Carib Indians, a tiny group identified as European, and a small group of Chinese. The country had a remarkably high crime rate but also boasted one of the world's tallest wooden structures, an Anglican cathedral.

All in all, it didn't sound like a holiday destination.

Ava called downstairs to the concierge and told him she needed to buy a flashlight and some water purification pills. He told her she would find everything she needed at CentralWorld.

The shopping complex is on Ratchadamri Road almost kitty-corner from the Erawan Shrine, a five-minute walk from the hotel. CentralWorld is eight storeys high, and with more than half a million square metres of shopping space, it is the world's third-largest shopping complex. Ava found what she wanted, but only after a half-hour hunt.

Her shopping done, she settled in at the mall for her first full Thai meal since her arrival. She had just ordered when her cellphone rang. The caller was using a number blocker. She answered, since not many people had her number – only those she actually wanted to have it.

'Ava, this is Andrew Tam.' He sounded nervous. 'My uncle hasn't been able to get hold of your uncle. He is concerned about how things are proceeding.'

'Andrew, please tell your uncle that when I'm on a case, I don't give my uncle daily updates. It's like I told you: when I have something to report, I'll call.'

'It's getting quite tense around here. I'm under tremendous pressure from my family. I also have a meeting with my bank next week, and they're going to be asking some awkward questions. I'm not a very good liar.'

'So this is about you, not your uncle.'

'I am worried.'

'Andrew, I have located the money. I know where it is. Now I have to go and get it. That sounds easier than it might turn out to be, which is why I haven't called you. Until I actually have the money, I have nothing and you have nothing.'

'You've found it!' he said, grasping at the good news and ignoring the caveats.

'I have.'

'Fantastic.'

'Not until I get it.'

'This is a great start, though, isn't it? I mean—'

'Andrew, stop,' she said. 'Look, you can tell the bank and your uncle whatever you want. If you need to buy some time, do it. I have found the money and I'm going after it. That doesn't mean anything until I get it. You do understand that? I'm not going to make any promises, I'm not going to give you timelines.'

'Well, all I can say is that we believe in you.'

She sighed. 'What you mean is that you have no choice but to believe in me. That's a different thing. You don't know me, you don't know me at all. I don't like dealing in blind faith, which is why you haven't heard from me, and which is why, Andrew, you will not hear from me again until I can tell you either that I have the money or that I can't get the money. And when I say you won't hear from me again, it also means that under no circumstances are you to call me again. Are we agreed?'

'Yes,' he said.

'Now, there is one thing I do need from you. I was going to relay it through Uncle but – since we're talking already – I need your bank information. On the chance that I can get to the money, the best way to move it will be a wire transfer. So email me all the particulars from your bank. I'll need the bank name and address, the account name and address, and the bank's IBN number and its SWIFT.'

'I'll send it today.'

'Tomorrow will be fine.'

'Do you mind if I ask where the money actually is?'

'I'll call you when I have some hard information. Until then, try to relax.' She closed the phone.

There were times when Ava disliked the way she had to act. Tam was a nice enough guy; he was just looking for any comforting news he could get. She had learned the hard way that clients who were desperate – and hers were nearly always desperate – heard what they wanted to hear. A glimmer of hope would become a done deal. And if by chance she didn't deliver, all of a sudden she was the villain, the heartbreaker, the liar.

When Ava got back to the hotel, she packed her bag and got ready to go to the airport. The travel agent had already booked and confirmed the flights by email. She had also put her into the Hilton Hotel in Port of Spain and the Phoenix in Georgetown, and had arranged for hotel limos to meet her when she landed.

Ava smiled when she read the agent's comment about the Phoenix: It has three stars, but every other hotel is one or two. What kind of place is this? But she didn't smile when she read what followed: Every travel guide says to exercise extreme caution in Georgetown. Going out alone, even during the day, is not recommended.

15

Ava landed in Port of Spain right on schedule at 7 p.m. It was already dark. Trinidad is in the southernmost reaches of the Caribbean, and fifty-two weeks a year, the sun falls like a stone behind the western mountain range at 6 p.m. From the air and all lit up, the city looked bigger than she had imagined. She guessed it was also a hell of a lot prettier from where she sat than it was on the ground.

She coasted through Immigration, Customs, and baggage claim, stepping out into air that was Thailand-humid but filled with unfamiliar odours. Rotting leaves. Dead birds. Dog shit. Gas fumes. She couldn't put a fix on it, but she nearly gagged. When Ava walked through the Arrivals gate, she saw a large black man standing at the curb in front of a Lincoln Continental. He was holding a sign with her name on it. She signalled to him, he opened the back door, and she climbed in.

'That's some smell,' she said.

'Mainly dead vegetation,' he said.

She didn't need more detail. 'How far to the hotel?'

'About half an hour.'

For once she hadn't overslept on the plane. She had caught about eight hours en route to New York and that had been it.

She was sleepy, which was good, because she wanted to be fresh the next day.

'Are you here on vacation or business?' he asked.

'Business.'

'Staying long?'

'Just overnight. Tomorrow I head for Guyana. My business is there.'

'Guyana. That is ... one ... crazy ... place,' he said.

'Have you been?'

'Don't have to go to know. We hear the stories – there are always stories. Nothing works. Can't trust no one. Can't go out at night with even a ten-dollar watch on your wrist. We get some of them here, Guyanese. They come with suitcases filled with shrimp and go from hotel to hotel and restaurant to restaurant trying to sell it. As if the chef at the Hilton is going to buy shrimp from some guy selling it out of a suitcase.'

'Someone must be buying it or they wouldn't keep coming,' she said.

He looked at her in his rear-view mirror to see if she was making fun of him. Ava wasn't laughing.

'The only good thing about Guyana is that it makes the rest of us in the Caribbean look good. No matter what kind of stunts our politicians pull or how many drug dealers we have or how bad our crime is, it's always worse in Guyana.'

She knew that Port of Spain sat on the Caribbean Sea, but as they began to work their way along the highway into the city she could see no sign of it. She rolled down her window and listened. Nothing. 'Where's the sea?' she asked.

The driver pointed left to a row of what looked like

warehouses and abandoned factories. 'It's there, behind those buildings.'

On her right house lights glimmered weakly above a large brick wall that flanked the highway for at least two kilometres. 'That's the wall of shame,' the driver said, noting her interest.

'It isn't a sound barrier?'

'More like a sight barrier. That's Beetham Estate behind the wall, our biggest slum. You'll find squatters, shacks, people who live on scraps. Not a place to wander into. The government built the wall just before the Summit of the Americas was held here so the foreign dignitaries wouldn't have to look at Beetham on the way into the city. Building the wall was cheaper and quicker than doing anything about the slum. Hide it, pretend it isn't there. Mind you, not many taxi drivers are complaining. It used to be that if your car broke down on this part of the road the animals from Beetham would be on you in two minutes. Now with the wall it takes them a bit longer.'

As they drove into the city, office towers, hotels, and small shopping complexes emerged from the night. Most of them were to the right of the highway, away from the sea. *What kind of place is this?* Ava thought. In Hong Kong, any kind of waterfront view, no matter how slight, drove up the real estate prices. Here it was as if they had decided they needed to distance themselves from the Caribbean.

The driver left the highway, turned right, and cut uphill through a series of narrow streets lined with houses and shops only a sidewalk away. It was a bumpy ride. Many of the streets were cobblestoned, and the driver had to come almost to a complete halt to navigate deep V-shaped trenches cut across the roadway.

At the top of the hill the road opened onto a broad expanse and the driver began to circle what was obviously a park. There was only a half-moon and not all the street lights were working, but as they drove along Ava was taken aback by the scale and variety of architecture they passed. 'This is the Savannah, the Queen's Park Savannah,' he said, meaning the park. 'Used to play cricket here every Sunday, but now I just come for Carnival.'

'What about these buildings?' Ava asked.

'That's All Saints' Church, and over there is the American embassy.'

'No, I mean those,' Ava said, pointing to a row of mansions that looked as if they belonged in Victorian-era London.

'The Magnificent Seven, we call them. They were built over a hundred years ago by European businessmen who were all trying to outdo each other. That one there is now the president's house, and the rest I really don't know,' the driver said.

They continued around the circle to get to the Hilton, which was adjacent to the Savannah and close to the Royal Botanic Gardens. The hotel's curious hillside structure was reflected in the interior. The lobby at the front of the hotel was on the ground floor, and Ava's room at the rear, which still had a view of the lights encircling the Savannah, was two floors below. Aside from the architectural eccentricity, when she opened the door to her room she found herself in a classic Hilton hotel room: clean, middle-class, dependable.

She ordered a Carib beer and a club sandwich from room service and then called Hong Kong. It was just past ten in the morning there, and Uncle, as usual, was at breakfast. 'I'm in Trinidad. I leave for Guyana tomorrow.'

'We don't have anyone there,' he said.

'I didn't think we would.'

'The closest we have someone is in Venezuela.'

'I'll handle it myself.'

'Ava, if you think you need help I'll call Venezuela.'

'I don't need help,' she said. 'I'm staying at the Phoenix Hotel in Georgetown. I don't know if my cellphone is going to work there, so if you can't reach me that way, call the hotel. I don't know how long this is going to take, so don't get worried if you don't hear from me for a few days.'

'You are sure he is there?'

'As sure as I can be.'

'My friend saw me last night. We were at massage and I couldn't avoid him. He said you talked to Tam.'

'He caught me by surprise.'

'Well, nothing we can do but finish this project.'

'How many haven't I finished?'

'A few . . . but then they were usually dead by the time we got to them.'

On a previous case the client had assigned more than one group the job of recovering their money. Twice she had been in meetings with targets, easing them towards repayment, when the competitors intruded, blood in their eyes. She convinced one set to leave by promising to share part of the commission with them. The other had to be neutralized more forcefully.

'Do they have anyone else working this job?'

'No, no, no, it is just us. I am very careful about that now.'

'All right, then I'm off to bed. I have an early start tomorrow.'

Ava showered and then shampooed the smell of airplane out of her hair. She pulled on clean panties and a T-shirt and then sat on the bed to watch the local news. The lead story was about how Trinidad had become a major part of the South American drug pipeline to the US, which was reported with a mixture of shock and pride. The opposition leader, who was black, came on the screen to charge four cabinet ministers, who were all East Indian, with corruption. Lifelong politicians who had never made more than thirty thousand dollars a year, they had each somehow amassed a personal net worth in excess of ten million dollars. One of the cabinet ministers was interviewed in front of what appeared to be a local school. He looked directly into the camera and claimed to have gotten lucky in the stock market. *It's amazing*, Ava thought, *just how many politicians get lucky in the stock market.*

She turned off the television and crawled into bed, her mind randomly flitting ahead to Guyana. She had no idea what to expect when she got there, in terms of either the country or Seto. She knew well enough from trips to hinterlands in India, China, and the Philippines that her life's usual amenities might be in short supply, but it would be another thing entirely to experience deprivation of clean water and food she could actually identify. Guyana, from what she'd read, certainly held that potential. She could only hope she was wrong.

Then there was Seto. All he was right now was a passport

picture, a fragment of a voice, and an address in a neighbourhood she didn't know in a city and country in which she had
no connections. She could land tomorrow and find him gone.
Maybe Antonelli had figured that keeping $2.5 million was
worth a little – no, a lot of – humiliation. Or maybe when she
got there she wouldn't be able to find a way to get to Seto. *But
when has that ever happened?* she thought. *Not often. Actually,
never.*

There was always a way; it just depended on what level of
risk was warranted by the money at the other end. The risk
and the reward weren't always in balance, and Ava liked to
think she was pragmatic enough to recognize when that was
the case and to make the appropriate decision. Five million
dollars, though . . . her commission share of $750,000 was an
awful lot of money, an awful lot of reward.

16

Ava's wakeup call came at six. She brushed her hair and teeth and put on her Adidas training pants, a clean bra, and a T-shirt. She pulled a copy of the *Trinidad Tribune* from underneath her door and left it on a table near the window. There was a kettle in the room; she turned it on and then sat down to read the paper while the water boiled.

There was a rehash of the television story from the night before, with pictures of all of the accused cabinet ministers. They looked like half a cricket team gone to fat. Ava skipped that story and read about the government's concern over the rising crime rate and their search for a new police chief. A Canadian from Calgary was one of the candidates. Ava thought that had to be a bad idea. How could a Canadian understand the social dynamics and financial imperatives of a place such as Trinidad?

She poured hot water into a mug and made herself some instant. She had drunk one coffee and was halfway through the second when the room phone rang to tell her the car had arrived. She took the elevator to the lobby and was greeted by a different driver, who looked East Indian. As he drove away from the hotel and onto the road that circled the Savannah, she asked him what he thought about the corruption charges against the cabinet ministers.

'The blacks,' he said, as if that explained everything.

She asked about the drug trade.

'As long as the drugs don't stay here, who cares? It could be good for the economy.'

Ava turned her attention to the passing city. The Magnificent Seven looked almost decrepit in the daylight, the bright morning sun exposing faded paint, chipped bricks, and raised roof shingles. The Savannah had lost some of its allure as well. She noticed that there was less actual grass than patches of bare ground pocked with clumps of crabgrass and weeds. Ava thought about something Uncle had said about older women in the morning light without makeup, then pushed it aside.

They rode quietly along the main highway. The factories and warehouses looked less oppressive now, and Beetham Estate seemed even more shabby. When they got to the intersection that took them to the airport, the car stopped for a red light. As it sat idling, a scrawny woman, her naked body streaked with mud and dirt, her hair matted, her breasts lying flat against her torso, jumped out and began pounding her fists on the hood. Her face pressed against the glass of Ava's window as she screamed obscenities. Ava recoiled.

'No worries,' the driver said. 'She's here every day. Just a mad woman.'

'She needs help,' Ava said, still alarmed.

'No money, no help,' he said. 'This is Trinidad. Go downtown at night, there are a lot more people like her. Maybe not so crazy, but crazy enough.'

'Shit,' she said.

'So where are you going?' he asked as the car pulled away from the intersection, leaving the screaming woman behind.

'Guyana.'

'Why?'

'Business.'

'The only business in Guyana is monkey business.'

'That's not my business.'

'Just don't drink the Kool-Aid,' he said, and laughed.

'What?'

'Kool-Aid – don't drink it. You don't remember Jim Jones?'

'Vaguely.'

'An American preacher. He brought his entire church to Guyana and set up a commune. It didn't work out well.'

'How so?'

'They had troubles. The entire group drank Kool-Aid laced with poison. They all died. There were nine hundred of them, as I remember, maybe more. The joke around here is that if you had to choose between Kool-Aid and living in Guyana, Kool-Aid would win out most times.'

17

Ava walked out of Cheddi Jagan Airport into an atmosphere that even in the morning was fetid. She looked for a sign with her name on it. She noticed the person holding it before she actually saw the sign: a lone white man with blond hair, towering above a sea of black and brown faces.

She waved at him and he burst through the waiting group. He was wearing a red polo shirt with PHOENIX sewn over the heart, brown cargo shorts, and white socks pulled up to his knees. He walked awkwardly, with his knees almost locked, and his upper body was also stiff, biceps pushing out his sleeves, broad chest, thick neck. *Weightlifter*, she thought. *Steroids*.

'Welcome to Guyana,' he said, reaching for her bags. He had a big, loopy smile on his face, and bright blue eyes that were nothing but friendly.

He led her through the crowd with his elbows stuck out to help clear her path. He threw the bags into the rear seat of a black Jeep with a gold phoenix stencilled on all four doors. Ava guessed she was expected to ride up front.

The car was running and the air conditioning was going full throttle. She shivered and sneezed. Some of the worst colds she'd had in her life had been the result of going from heat and humidity into freezers posing as retail stores. When she asked him to turn the air conditioning down, he looked at her as if she were demented but did what she asked anyway.

'I'm Jeff,' he said.

'Hi, Jeff. How far is it to the hotel?'

'About forty-five kilometres,' he said.

'Half an hour?'

'You haven't been here before, have you?' he said. She detected a New England accent.

'No.'

'Didn't think so. We'll be an hour, maybe longer.'

'That much traffic?'

He laughed. 'Yeah, sort of.'

They hadn't travelled more than a kilometre when they ran into a line of cars slowly bobbing and weaving from one side of the two-lane road to the other. Jeff joined the conga line. 'They're trying to avoid the potholes,' he said. 'There are a few stretches of road between here and Georgetown that aren't riddled with them, but not many. So we're going to go as fast as the slowest car ahead of us. That's the way it is. Sorry.'

'I'm glad you have a Jeep.'

'There are some potholes even the Jeep couldn't get out of, especially in town.'

Some of the holes cut across both lanes, and that caused extra delays as the incoming and outgoing traffic sorted out who had the right of way. Ava tried not to feel nauseated, focusing her attention on the scenery. It was mainly country, low-lying land dotted here and there with what looked like rice paddies. In the distance was the familiar sight of a sugar-cane field. Sugar and rice – the agricultural staples of the poorest countries in the world.

The monotony of the landscape was punctuated every couple of kilometres by a village or, more often, a group of ten to twelve shacks. They were built almost right up against the edge of the road. There wasn't a brick in any of them. Most of them had some kind of wooden frame, the walls an interlaced mixture of planks of different woods, tarpaper, and corrugated tin. The windows were covered with strips of cloth.

Some residents stood leaning against the houses, watching the cars slalom past. Others sat outside on stools, goats tied to pegs bumping against them, children and chickens running around freely. Ava jumped a few times when she saw a child come too close to the road, but Jeff didn't flinch or slow down his twenty- to thirty-kilometre-an-hour crawl.

The area reminded Ava of parts of the rural Philippines where no one worked and each day was spent watching life drive by. She wondered how many of the people living in these shacks had travelled more than ten kilometres from where they lived.

The road began to improve a little after an hour, and Ava guessed they were getting close to Georgetown. Jeff had been quiet and intense during the drive, and Ava hadn't wanted to disturb his concentration. Now she said, 'I don't mean to be nosy, but I thought I detected a bit of a New England accent.'

He didn't take his eyes from the road. 'That's smart of you.'

'I went to school in Massachusetts for two years.'

'I'm from Gloucester.'

'How did someone from Gloucester find their way down here?'

Now he looked towards her, hesitated, then said, 'I'm – I was – a fisherman. I came down here on a shrimper out of Florida. We were buying our catch at sea, paying cash to Guyanese boats. What the skipper didn't tell us was that those boats were financed by local gangsters, and they weren't too thrilled about our little black market, about us stealing from them. We were in the middle of a deal when two speedboats came out of nowhere and put us out of business.'

'How did they do that?'

He glanced at her again. 'They shot the captain and the other two men on the Guyanese boat and threw their bodies into the sea. They took our boat, scuttled it, and set us adrift in a lifeboat.'

'Shit.'

'Big-time shit. We somehow found our way to Georgetown. The skipper went to the cops and they acted as if what had happened was the most natural thing in the world. They told us we were fucking lucky to have made it to shore and maybe we ought to let it go at that. The skipper and the rest of the crew flew back to Miami, but I decided to stay here a while. That was five years ago. It ain't Miami but the work is steady, the beer is cheap, and the women are slutty.'

'Those sound like great reasons to stay.'

Jeff shrugged. 'I didn't mean to sound like an asshole. It's just the way it is here.'

'I didn't take any offence,' Ava said. She noticed they were driving through larger concentrations of housing.

'Georgetown,' he said.

The driving began to occupy him again as the potholes expanded in number and size. As they manoeuvred their way into the city, Ava was immediately taken by the fact that nearly every building was made of wood. A lot of the houses were ramshackle affairs two or three storeys high, with three or four apparently boxed together and some on stilts. Most of the wood was grey, bleached, weather-beaten, not unlike houses she'd seen on Cape Cod, except the houses on Cape Cod had glass windows, not wooden shutters or strips of cloth. In New England there had been flashes of colour as well, something Georgetown was almost devoid of, aside from a wall that had been painted in red with GOD IS IN CHARGE. ALL IS WELL.

The storefronts were a bit more colourful, their wooden exteriors decorated with hand-painted signs advertising a variety of wares and services. Their windows and doors were protected by thick metal screens, and inside it looked as if the service counters and cash registers were separated from customers by a metal fence that extended from countertop to ceiling. People were passing money through one slot in the screen and getting goods back through another.

'If they didn't do that,' Jeff said, motioning to a string of storefronts, 'they would be getting robbed every other day.'

They were driving through the middle of the city now. Large white edifices began to appear, and they passed a building that housed various courts of law. From afar it looked elegant, but as they came closer Ava saw that paint was peeling off its exterior and some of the window shutters were broken and hanging at odd angles. There was a patch of dry, cracked earth between the sidewalk and the building, with a statue of Queen Victoria sitting on it. Both of the hands had been cut off and the torso was covered in graffiti. Ava looked away. There was something particularly depressing about public institutions – symbols of a nation – that were allowed to fall into such disrepair. It said as much about the people they represented as the structures themselves.

Ava next saw a wooden church spire soaring above the city's skyline.

'St George's Anglican,' said Jeff. 'It's forty metres high at the peak of the spire, the tallest wooden cathedral in the world.'

'And what is that?' she asked, her attention now caught by a clock tower in the other direction.

'Stabroek Market, the bizarre bazaar. You name it, you can buy it there – everything from pineapple to shoes to furniture, jewellery, and even a whole pig.'

'The clock tower, what is it made of?'

'Corrugated iron. The whole building is made of iron, some corrugated, some cast. What would you expect when it was designed by an engineer and built by an iron company?'

'Interesting,' Ava said.

'Interest wears off soon enough.'

They reached the end of High Street. Jeff turned right and then did a quick left. 'The hotel is straight ahead,' he said.

The Phoenix Hotel was framed on either side by nothing but sky. It was a big white wooden box, six storeys high and four times as wide. A line of palm trees dotted the front of the property and marched around the outer edge of the circular driveway. A water fountain stood in the middle of the drive-way: six dolphins spewing a cloudy-looking liquid.

Jeff pulled into the driveway and stopped in front of the hotel. The front doors had been thrown open and Ava could see directly into the cavernous lobby, which had a second set of open doors at the far end that offered an impressive view of the Atlantic Ocean.

She climbed out of the car and faced the hotel. To the left she could see a muddy brown river moving sluggishly towards the ocean.

'That's the mouth of the Demerara,' Jeff said.

'Like the rum?'

'One and the same. The distillery is upriver.'

She looked again at the colour of the river and made a note to avoid the rum. Near the river and slightly back towards town, she saw some familiar flags flying. 'And over there?' she asked, pointing.

'Foreign embassies.'

The American embassy was closest to the hotel and the Canadian was next in line.

Jeff carried her bags into the lobby. There was a breeze flowing from the ocean side, and huge fans churned overhead. Ava still felt hot, and she could only imagine how sticky it would get if the breeze subsided.

To her left was a café and a registration desk that was nine metres long and had one clerk standing behind it. To her right was a large sitting area filled with wicker furniture, the cushions rumpled and faded. Farther down was a bar with bamboo chairs and tables that were in better, if not pristine, condition.

As they crossed the lobby towards Registration, a large cockroach scurried across the hardwood floor almost directly in front of her. It startled her and she jumped. 'Did you see that?' she said.

'No, I didn't see anything,' Jeff said.

'It was a cockroach.'

'We don't have cockroaches,' he said.

'It had to be three inches long, with a gold body, black spots, and a black head.'

'Son of a gun, that does sound like a cockroach,' he said as he dropped her bags at the front desk.

She tipped him twenty dollars. He looked uncertainly at the bill in his hand. 'This is way more than the normal rate around here.'

'I insist. I appreciated the way you drove.'

'Thanks.'

'Jeff, tell me, do you ever make yourself and the Jeep available to guests for non-airport runs?'

'What do you have in mind?'

'Nothing too far out of the way, I would imagine. I may need a ride to a place called Malvern Gardens. Heard of it?'

'Yeah, I know it.'

'And I may need you to wait with me a while when I'm there.'

He shrugged. 'I don't think that's much of a problem. The usual rate is ten dollars an hour.'

'For you and the Jeep?'

'Yeah, but you have to pay for any gas I use, and I have to tell you, gas is expensive.'

'What are we talking about?'

'Five dollars a gallon.'

'No problem.'

'Do you have any idea when you might need me? I've got another airport run to make today and I've actually got to get going.'

'There's no rush. How about I let the doorman know after I figure things out? Check in with him when you get back.'

'That'll work.'

Ava turned to the registration clerk and gave her name. For almost two hundred dollars a night – almost the same as the Grand Hyatt in Bangkok – she got an ocean view, a single bed, and a television, but no cable. There was internet access in the business centre on the ground floor, but none in the room. If she wanted to make a long-distance call she would have to let the switchboard know so they could activate the service for her. There was no mini-bar or fridge in her room, and if she wanted ice she had to call down to the bar. She did get coffee and toast in the morning. When she asked about mobile phone service, she was told that if she had Bluetooth she could use her phone in Georgetown.

Ava rode the elevator to the fourth floor, unhappy with the hotel's concept of 'three star'. Anywhere in Asia, every service she'd asked about at the registration desk would have been provided. When she opened the door to her room, the Phoenix's rating tumbled to one star.

There were two single beds covered in pink chenille spreads, and the floor was covered with white tile. It reminded Ava of a hospital. The dresser and bedside table were tattooed with cigarette burns, and the bedside lampshade was slightly frayed, as was the shade on the single overhead light.

Ava went into the bathroom. No bathrobe, no slippers. Two thin towels and one facecloth. There was one bar of soap, wrapped in paper, and no shampoo. She checked the shower. No mould. She flushed the toilet. It worked.

Back in the room she gazed resignedly at the room's only feature that she liked: a rattan chair by the window. She sat in it and looked out at the Atlantic Ocean. The water was choppy, crashing against a seawall that extended over to the Demerara on the left and as far as she could see on the right.

It could be worse, she thought. At least it was clean, and she wasn't there for the hotel anyway. Somewhere out there Jackson Seto was waiting to be found.

18

Since her meeting with Antonelli, Ava had been debating how to approach Seto. She had thought of phoning him first, maybe pretending to be a seafood buyer and setting up a meeting on that basis. There were a couple of problems with that idea. First, she didn't really know enough about the business to survive any rigorous questioning. And second, why would anyone come to Guyana to buy seafood without making preliminary arrangements?

No, her first contact had to be incidental. It hadn't worked with Antonelli, but he was into ladyboys. Not many heterosexual men could resist showing interest in Ava, so she had to find a way to get next to Seto and take it from there.

She walked down to the lobby and looked for the concierge or the doorman, neither of whom was on duty. She asked the front desk clerk where they were. 'They're on break. Be back around one,' the woman said.

'I need to buy a few things. Is there a mall around here?'

'The best place would be the Stabroek Market. It's just down the street to the right. You can't miss it – look for the tall clock tower.'

'Yes, I've seen it.'

'I wouldn't go dressed like that,' the woman said.

Ava was wearing her running shoes and a T-shirt and track pants. 'Why not?'

'I mean the jewellery. You should leave it here.'

Ava had on her gold crucifix, her Cartier watch, and a green jade bracelet. 'It's the middle of the day,' she said.

'Don't matter. That watch – it's real?'

'Yes.'

'I thought so. It's a magnet. You'll get all kinds of unwanted attention, and if they go for the watch they'll take the necklace and bracelet too.'

Ava took them off and put them in a pocket that zipped closed. 'Better?'

'Just be careful.'

Outside the front entrance the heat was brutal and oppressive, and Ava thought about using the hotel Jeep, but she could see the clock tower and figured that Stabroek Market wasn't much more than a ten-minute walk. She was fine until she had gone about a hundred metres and the ocean breeze had dissipated. The sky was cloudless and the sun beat directly down, radiating off the tarmac; the heat seemed to penetrate through the soles of her shoes. She began to sweat, her eyes burning, beads dripping from the end of her nose, her panties absorbing what they could and then sending the excess down her legs. It was hotter than Bangkok, more humid than a Hong Kong summer. And then there was the smell. She held her breath as she walked past the decaying garbage and dog shit on the sidewalk.

When Ava was about twenty paces from her destination, she heard a buzz in the air, a mixed symphony of voices haggling and car horns blaring. It wasn't until she stepped onto Water Street that she had a full view of Stabroek Market. The building encompassed a large area of about sixty to eighty thousand square metres; it was, as advertised, completely encased, including the roof, in red iron. To Ava it looked less like a shopping centre than a steel foundry.

The noises she'd heard came from outside the building, where people were hawking goods from tables and stands shaded with tarps to fend off the sun. It was crowded, the stands were jammed close together, and people were milling about as they tried to avoid the bicycles and buses that circled the perimeter. Ava pushed her way past mounds of pineapples, plantain, bananas, coconut, okra, sweet potatoes, long beans and spinach, sides of pigs and goats, and chickens clucking in cages. They were selling clothing outside as well, but not the knockoffs found in most Asian markets. These looked like second-hand garments that had been collected by a charity in the developed world and sold by the pound to some trader. Apparently there was a market for old Toronto Maple Leafs jerseys.

Ava went inside the market building to search for food and air conditioning. There were pockets of cold air here and there, and she lingered while she decided what to eat. She toured the stalls, trying to choose between chicken curry, duck curry, lamb and goat curry, rice and beans, and roti. She was about to give a curry a try when saw a vegetarian stand. She ordered three fried lentil patties with hot sauce and washed them down with mauby, a local soft drink made from tree bark.

After she finished eating, Ava wandered through the market. It was eclectic, to say the least. Most of the fruit, vegetables, and meat available outside were also for sale inside, along with more second-hand clothing, shoes, furniture, dishes, household utensils, fish, shrimp and a surprising amount of gold. She had read that Guyana had deposits of the metal. And here it was, mined, refined, and then fashioned into some of the crudest jewellery she had ever seen. It was super-bling – large, chunky necklaces and bracelets moulded into zodiac signs and commercial logos for brands such as Nike, Calvin Klein, and Chanel. But crude or not, the jewellery looked to be made from twenty- or even twenty-two-karat gold.

Ava didn't find what she wanted until she got to the very end of the market. It was dark there; the stalls were pressed closer together and there was no overhead light. She had to work her way around a throng of local shoppers, and as she did, she could feel eyes following her progress. The desk clerk hadn't been wrong.

She wandered into one of the stalls and was greeted by an East Indian woman wearing a sari, rolls of flesh cascading over her waistband. She seemed surprised to see Ava, and turned away as if she expected her to leave again. When Ava didn't go, the woman finally acknowledged her with a raised eyebrow.

'I want one of those,' Ava said, pointing to a selection of knives locked in a glass case.

'Which one?'

'I can't tell. Could you open the case for me?'

The woman struggled to her feet and took a key from a

150

drawer. She looked around suspiciously as she unlocked the case. When it was open, she motioned for Ava to come closer.

They were nearly all automatic switchblades, and it was a surprisingly good collection. She recognized Heckler and Koch, Blackwater, Schrade, Buck, and Smith and Wesson. Ava took her time appraising them and then asked the woman to pass her a Schrade. The blade was bit too short. 'I prefer stilettos,' she said.

The woman lifted the felt-lined tray; underneath was a row of Italian stilettos. 'Everything from six inches to fifteen inches,' the woman said.

'I think eleven inches will do just fine.'

The woman passed her the knife. It was lightweight and fitted easily into her palm. She touched the button and the beautifully crafted blade hissed into view in a microsecond. 'How much?'

'One hundred and fifty American.'

'One hundred.'

'One twenty-five.'

'One hundred.'

'One twenty, final.'

'Done,' Ava said.

It was hotter than ever when she exited Stabroek. A taxi with its windows open sat at the curb. She got in and told the driver to turn on the air conditioning and take her to the Phoenix.

'I don't have air conditioning,' he said.

'Drive anyway.'

'It is too close. You should walk.'

She passed him ten dollars. 'Drive.'

At the hotel the doorman was back on duty. He was leaning against a wall, looking out at the empty lobby. She hadn't seen any other guests coming or going and was beginning to wonder if she was the only one staying there. He acknowledged her arrival with a nod. She nodded back and walked over.

'Is Jeff back from the airport yet?'

'No, but he should be here soon enough.'

'When he does get back, could you please ask him to call my room? Tell him I'd like to use the Jeep this afternoon.'

She stripped off her clothes when she got to the room. There was a full-length mirror on the back of the closet door, and she caught her image in it. She was proud of her body and worked hard at maintaining it, but not to excess. No power-lifting for her; she liked her leanness. She liked even more her proportions, which were just about perfect. She had a thing about girls with thick ankles or long torsos – they weren't for her.

Ava's sense of well-being disappeared when she stepped into the shower. The water spewing from the showerhead was a light chocolate brown. She waited for it clear. It didn't. She sniffed the water and detected a chemical odour. She waited for another minute, and when the colour still didn't change, she left the bathroom and phoned the front desk. 'The water in my shower is brown,' she said.

'Yes?'

'Did you hear what I said?'

'The water is always brown. We get it from the Demerara.

We have our own purification system – the water is perfectly safe, but we can't do anything about the colour.'

Ava hung up and climbed back into the shower. She closed her eyes, shut her mouth, and tried not to breathe through her nose, soaping and rinsing herself as quickly as she could. Getting to Jackson Seto was becoming more urgent.

When she got out of the shower, she put on a fresh T-shirt and track pants and waited for Jeff in the rattan chair. She passed the time reading a copy of the *Guyana Times*, which had been at her door when she came back from the market. The lead article was about some club owners who were complaining about police raids. The clubs were indeed illegal, but the owners maintained that the police were being too heavy-handed during raids and were driving away tourists. What made it even stranger was that the minister of culture and tourism was quoted as saying that the club owners had a point. The next page was one giant police blotter: a list of crimes committed over the past twenty-four hours. Arrests for drug dealing, robbery, mugging, and physical assault were pretty common.

Ava heard a knock at the door. She opened it to see Jeff standing there. He had changed his clothes and was now wearing jeans and a tank top. On his right shoulder was a tattoo of a lightning bolt.

'I called but no one answered,' he said.

'I guess I was in the shower.'

'You want to go somewhere?'

'Yes. I mentioned Malvern Gardens earlier and you said you know where it is.'

'I do.'

'That's where I want to go.'

'It's a housing estate.'

'I know.'

'Do you have an address?'

'No, we need to find that out. The guy who lives there is named Jackson Seto.'

'Wait a minute,' he said, and squeezed past her into the room. He opened the bottom drawer of her dresser and pulled out a phone book. 'He lives at number eight.'

As they rode the elevator to the ground floor Ava said, 'Before we go, there are a few things we need to make clear. For starters, I'm probably going to be sitting in the car with you for a while, and I have no idea how long. I'm looking for this guy Seto, and all I know is that he lives at 8 Malvern Gardens. When he does appear, we're going to follow him and see what happens. Are you okay with that?'

'What if you don't see him?'

'Then we'll go back tomorrow and do it all over again.'

'Is this legal? I mean, are you a cop or something?'

'It's perfectly legal and I'm not a cop.'

'Can I ask why?'

'No.'

He gazed down at her. 'Well, I can't say you look like much of a threat to anyone.'

The Jeep had been left idling at the hotel entrance. Jeff started up High Street and then cut left. The road was littered with potholes, and one was so big it could have swallowed the front end of the vehicle. 'Don't they ever fix those things?' Ava asked.

'No.'

'Do they try?'

'Not so you'd notice.'

When they reached the end of the street, they were confronted by a structure about six or seven storeys high made entirely of corrugated iron. Ava could see rows of razor wire along the top. The building had no windows, just a door barricaded by a semicircle of concrete pillars. Standing to the left of the door with their backs pressed against the wall was a line of women.

'What's that?' she asked.

'Camp Street Prison,' he said.

'It must be an oven in there.'

'No one much cares.'

'And the women?'

'Waiting for visiting hours.'

As they moved away from the city centre, the mix of retail stores gave way to rows of stucco, stone, and even brick houses, most protected by tall concrete walls with rolls of razor wire glinting fiendishly across the top. 'I've never seen so much razor wire,' she said.

'It's the choice of the budget-conscious middle class, who can't afford a personal guard or a security service. Ever come in contact with it?'

'No, of course not.'

'It'll rip you to shreds.'

They had left the city proper and were driving through countryside when a housing development, as isolated as an oasis in the desert, appeared on the right. From a distance all

Ava could see was a brick wall and red tile roofs; she thought, *Gated community*. But as they drew closer she saw that the road leading into Malvern Gardens wasn't barred. Jeff stopped the Jeep between two stone pillars at the entrance to a cul-de-sac. There were five houses down each side and two at the end. The two-storey brick-and-stone homes were enormous, reminding Ava of high-end suburban developments in Toronto. Each sat on a one-acre lot surrounded by a stone wall about 2.5 metres high that was crowned with large shards of glass and razor wire. The only way into each compound was through heavy metal gates with sharp points at the top and more razor wire strung through them.

'This is Millionaires' Row,' said Jeff.

The house numbers went up by fours. Seto's house was the second on the left. It had a latticed gate, and as they drove past Ava saw an old Mercedes and a Land Rover parked in the driveway. Someone was home.

She pointed back towards where they had turned off the main road. 'If we park behind one of those pillars we can see everyone coming and going from the house,' she said. 'And if they turn left to go to the city, we'll have a clear view.'

Jeff turned the Jeep around and parked behind the pillar. From that angle they could see Seto's gate and the end of his driveway.

'Now what?' he asked.

'We wait.'

'Do you mind if I sleep?'

'Go ahead.'

Jeff got out and climbed into the back seat to lie down. 'I

sleep lightly, so don't worry about having to wake me if we need to move.'

She had kept her watch in the zippered pocket of her pants. She pulled it out and put it on. It was 3:30 p.m.

Jeff slept until just past five, when he woke with a start.

'Nothing yet,' she said.

'I need to piss.'

'Be my guest.'

He went behind the car, his back turned to the Jeep.

'What time does it get dark?' she asked when he climbed back in.

'Six.'

At five thirty Seto's gate swung open. Ava drew a deep breath. The Mercedes backed out onto the road and then crept towards them. Ava saw that the driver was a young East Indian woman, heavily made up, with lots of jewellery on both wrists and at least three gold chains around her neck.

'That's a disappointment,' she said.

The gate remained open. *Somebody else is going to leave*, she thought. After a couple of minutes a wiry Asian man in jeans and a black T-shirt ambled out onto the road. He took a quick look around and then motioned towards the house. *He looks Vietnamese*, she thought.

'Get out of the car,' she said to Jeff. 'Go around back and pretend you're still peeing.'

He went without question.

The Land Rover emerged from the driveway. It stopped and the Vietnamese man climbed in. As it turned the corner both passengers took a hard look at Jeff. Ava was slumped down in her seat but was able to get a clear view of them. Jackson Seto was driving.

Jeff waited until the Rover was well down the road before getting back in the Jeep.

'Now what? Do you want to follow them?' he asked.

'I'm not sure. Where do you think they're going?'

'A hundred to one they're headed for the city.'

'It's just about dinner time. Is there a restaurant district?'

'Nearly all the decent places are in a four-square-block area.'

'Any of them Chinese?'

'A couple.'

'Let's give it fifteen minutes and then we'll head into town. We'll cover that area and see if we can find their cars.'

'And if we can't?'

'That's my problem for tomorrow.'

The sun was setting as they were driving back to Georgetown. Jeff hit a couple of potholes, and Ava was sure they were going to lose a tire.

Georgetown had taken on a different look. It took Ava a minute to realize that it was because only part of the city was lit while the rest was blanketed in almost total darkness. 'Is there a power outage?' she asked.

'I guess you could call it that, except it happens every night. They only have enough power for half the city. So they alternate between east and west on a nightly basis. Tonight the east end gets electricity and the west end has to make do with candles. Most of the businesses have their own backup generators.'

'What a place.'

'Yep.'

'The area we're going to, will it have power tonight?'

'Yeah, we're lucky,' he said, and then turned towards her. 'I hope you don't mind me asking, but I've been curious all afternoon. Just what is it we're doing, following this guy?'

'It's just business.'

'What kind of business?'

Ava stared at the road. 'I think it's better if I don't share that with you.'

'Better for who?'

'Me.'

Jeff shrugged. 'We're getting close to the restaurant district. I'll circle.'

It took less than five minutes to find both cars, which were parked outside a restaurant called China World. 'The Chinese are so predictable,' Ava said. 'You could drop them in Paris on a street lined with three-star French restaurants and they'd still go looking for something Chinese, even if it was a hole in the wall.'

'Are you going in?'

'No, we'll wait for them to come out.'

They waited for an hour. The girl exited first. She was big, about five ten, and was wearing jeans that showed off muscular thighs and a high, firm ass. A tank top accentuated her large, round breasts, and Ava could see that she didn't need a bra. She blew a kiss towards the restaurant door, got into her car, and drove off. 'That's a body,' Jeff said.

The Vietnamese man came out next, with Seto a few steps behind. *He's Seto's bodyguard*, she thought, *or some kind of hanger-on who doubles as a bodyguard*. He was small, but she knew that didn't mean anything. His type could be tough, vicious, and fearless to the point of stupidity. He was a complication she didn't need.

Seto too was a thin, reedy shadow. He was maybe six feet tall, but he slouched when he walked, making him look shorter than he was. He was wearing a pair of high-waisted black slacks secured by a belt that was on its last notch. Ava thought he looked almost emaciated; she could see that his chest was concave beneath his white dress shirt. His face was alive, though, his dark brown eyes darting here and there like a rat's, his mouth drawing hard on a cigarette.

They climbed into the Land Rover and drove away. 'Let's follow them for a bit,' she said.

They had barely gotten the Jeep in motion when she saw the Land Rover pull into a parking spot no more than two blocks away. The neon sign over the door read ECKIE'S ONE AND ONLY CLUB. Seto got out by himself, walked past the bouncer, and disappeared through the door.

'You know this place?' she asked Jeff.

'Everyone knows Eckie's. It's the best club in Georgetown, one of the few places that doesn't need cheap beer and sluts. They import some good DJs, and it's where the high-priced girls – amateurs and pros – go. Tourists and locals with money are the target.'

'Who owns it?'

'I have no idea.'

'Who is Eckie?'

'Don't know. I've been there a few times and I never met anyone called Eckie.'

She sat quietly, weighing her options while watching the

Vietnamese bodyguard smoke. The few approaches she could think of were flawed. Confronting him in the bar wasn't much of an option. No one knew her, and if there was a fuss they would likely support the local – and that was without his bodyguard jumping in. If she tried to talk to Seto outside, Vietnamese involvement was a certainty, and it was too soon for her to trigger that kind of response without knowing more about to whom and how Seto was connected. Antonelli had said that Seto had strong ties with the police in Georgetown; she needed to find out how far up the chain those ties went. Still, doing nothing wasn't an option.

'Could you get me a local SIM card?'

'Yeah. Tomorrow morning okay?'

'That's fine.'

'You're not going into Eckie's?'

'No, there's nothing for me to do tonight.'

'So now what?'

'I'm going back to the hotel.'

When they got to the Phoenix, Ava climbed out of the Jeep and turned to Jeff. 'Call me when you have the SIM card. I assume you're free tomorrow if I need you.'

'The day is clear so far.'

She passed seventy dollars through the window.

'Thanks.'

'Jeff, I don't want you to discuss any of this with anyone. Not a word. The name Jackson Seto doesn't exist for you.'

'You didn't have to say that.'

'It's always better to make things clear,' she said, and threw another twenty-dollar bill onto the passenger seat.

19

Ava woke up early and was downstairs by six. The coffee shop wasn't open, so she drifted over to the business centre. It wasn't open either. She went to the front desk. 'Can you open the business centre for me?' she said.

'It don't open till seven.' A young man in a sports jacket two sizes too large was manning the desk.

'Do you have a key?'

'Yeah.'

She put ten dollars on the counter. 'Open it for me now, please.'

There were forty emails in her main account. She worked her way through them in ascending order. Tam had sent her his bank information and overly enthusiastic good wishes. Her mother wanted her to know that she had had a big night at mah-jong. Uncle hoped she was safe. Her best friend, Mimi, was going to break up with the guy she'd been seeing for the past few weeks.

She logged onto Yahoo and, using her mother's home address, opened an email account under the name Eatfish12. She then sent an email to Jackson Seto. It said that she worked for a trading company in Toronto that was interested in importing cheap fish, and that she had been told Guyana was a good source. She was currently in Trinidad doing some sourcing but could get over to Georgetown on short notice if he thought there was an opportunity. She added that she had been referred to him by a friend of a friend who knew George Antonelli. She didn't think there was much chance he would answer. Still, it was worth a shot.

She wandered back into the deserted lobby. The coffee shop was still shuttered. The desk clerk held up ten fingers, so Ava flopped into one of the chairs and turned on her cellphone. Uncle had called. She hit the redial button.

'I'm just making sure you are okay,' he said. She knew he was with other people; he never used her name when he was.

'I've found him. I mean, I've seen him. Now I just have to figure out how to get to him.'

'Difficult?'

'I don't know yet. I don't know enough about him or his habits. He has a Vietnamese bodyguard, which is not good. His house is like a mini fortress. And if he is as connected here as Antonelli claims, I can't count on the authorities – whoever they are – staying out of our business if it gets aggressive.'

'Do you want me to send help?'

'No, let me find out more.'

'Call me every day, then. I'll worry otherwise.'

When Ava hung up, she noticed that an overweight middle-aged man had joined her. His large gut was accentuated by the tight T-shirt tucked into his jeans. The shirt read, GUYANA SUCKS. He had tattoos on both arms: RED DEVILS down one and MANCHESTER U down the other. He walked over to the coffee shop and rattled the closed grate. A young East Indian woman stuck her head out, saw him, and swung it open. Ava followed him in.

The coffee shop was small, but she tried to find a table as far away from him as possible. It didn't do much good.

'So what the hell are you doing here?' he called over to her.

She wasn't adept at identifying English accents, but even without the tattoos she could have figured out that he was from northern England and definitely working class. 'I'm here on business,' she said, wishing she had a book or a newspaper to hide behind.

To her surprise he got up, walked over to her table, and sat down. 'I'm Tom Benson,' he said.

'Ava Lee.'

'So what are you doing in this hellhole?'

'Some business – financial. In and out.'

'I should be so fucking lucky,' he said, pronouncing it more like *fooking*.

'Really.'

'Been here six fucking months and probably good for another six.'

'And how is that?'

'The power. I'm here to fix it, if it can be fixed.'

'You don't seem to be having much success, if last night is any indication.'

The waitress came to the table. 'Coffee and toast,' he said, 'and make sure you use bottled water for the coffee.' He looked at Ava. 'Don't order the eggs or any of the meat. It's given me at least two lots of food poisoning. And you have to ask for bottled water or they use that shite from the river. They tried

164

to sneak it by me once, but I went to the fucking kitchen and caught them. Now I pop in and out of the kitchen every so often to keep them honest.'

'I'll have what he's having,' Ava said to the waitress.

'I work for Rolls-Royce. They used to be in the diesel generator business, like about a hundred fucking years ago. This city has the last of those generators that are still working. They should have been replaced years ago but no one gives a shite, and even if they did they probably don't have the money. So the Guyana government went to the British government and said, "We have this problem. Could you arrange to send someone over to fix it?" The British guys went to Rolls-Royce and said, "Send someone over. We'll pay for him." So here I am.'

'Six months?'

'Yeah. The second week I was here, I figured out one of the major problems and told the Power Authority – what a joke they are – they needed to order some parts. They have to be custom made, see. They told me they ordered them from an outfit in the US, some high-end tool-and-die operation. I'm still waiting for those fucking parts.'

'So what do you do? I mean, how do you fill your days?'

'At eight thirty they'll send a car and driver for me. I'll go to the office, make my long-distance calls back home, fuck around on the internet, and then around eleven drag my arse into the boss's office and ask him if the parts have arrived. He'll say no and I'll have the driver bring me back to the hotel. I usually sit by the pool drinking beer all afternoon, and then I head into town for dinner. I didn't have this belly when I got here. I also had a girlfriend back home, and she's packed me in.'

'So why do you stay?'

'The money mainly. I'm living here for virtually fucking free. All I have to pay for is my beer. Then, of course, there are the girls,' he said, looking to gauge her reaction. When she registered none, he went on. 'I mean, for a bloke like me this is heaven when it comes to the girls. At home you practically have to beg before you can get a shag. Here I flash a few dollars and, voila, I have my pick of the lot – every night if I want.'

'Sounds like fun.'

'Not always. Sometimes it can get dicey.'

'Meaning?'

'This is a rough place, even for someone like me. Have to be careful. I was robbed twice before I figured out it was a good idea to leave my watch, wallet, room key, and everything but the money I needed for the night here in the hotel. If you're going out anywhere, you should do the same thing. They'll fucking come at you for a plastic Timex, never mind a Cartier,' he said, pointing at hers.

'Thanks.'

'No bother.'

Breakfast arrived. He didn't let the waitress leave until he had sniffed and tasted the coffee.

Ava took a sip of hers. It was instant coffee, Nescafé, she thought. She wondered whether, if she brought her VIA instant in, they'd make that for her.

'Tom, do you know a club called Eckie's?'

'Sure, it's my favourite. Better class of girls. Imported beer.'

'Who owns it?'

'I wouldn't know.'

166

'Have you ever seen a Chinese man hanging around the club?'

'A few.'

'This one is tall and skinny, really skinny. His hair is streaked with grey and he's got a moustache that's a bit off balance and a pointy, thin face like a rat.'

'Oh fuck, he's a madman, that one. Drinks like a fucking fish and treats the girls like shite. He tosses money around like crazy too, which gets the girls all excited, but I've never seen him actually leave with one or nip into one of Eckie's back rooms.'

'I thought you said it's dangerous to have too much money on you.'

'For me, for you, for any other fucking tourist. He's a local, that lad. I've seen the cops come into the club and give us all the fucking evil eye except for him. He has connections, he does.'

'The police are, what, corrupt?'

Benson started laughing, slivers of wet toast spilling from his mouth. 'Jesus, what do you think?'

'That's why I asked.'

'Look, the army, the police, the security people – it's all one big happy gang here. You can't tell one from the other.'

'So the Chinese guy is paying them off?'

'One way or another, but that's true for anyone in this country who has money. You don't get money and you sure as fuck don't keep money unless you're looking after the powers that be.'

'And who are they, the powers that be?'

'I don't fucking know and I don't fucking care. As long as I'm left alone, the cops and the army and the rest of them can fiddle away.'

'That seems sensible,' she said.

They walked to the elevator together. She sensed that he was going to come on to her and wasn't surprised when he said, 'Would you like to go out tonight? You know, hit some clubs?'

'Tom, I'm not really your type,' Ava said gently. 'Believe me, I'm not.'

At ten o'clock Ava slipped her notebook and her Canadian passport into the Chanel bag and went downstairs. Dressed in a black knee-length skirt, black pumps, and a white Brooks Brothers shirt, she looked every inch a conservative, serious businesswoman.

She went straight out of the hotel up to Young Street, turned right, and walked two and a half blocks to a white wooden house the size of a small apartment building that flew the Canadian flag. She assumed that the embassy offices were on the ground floor and the residences above. She had expected to meet security at the double doors, but there was none. In the small air-conditioned vestibule, a young black woman sat at a reception desk behind a plastic shield that was perforated at mouth level.

Ava walked towards her, the woman eyeing her as if she were a thief. 'Hello, my name is Ava Lee. I'm Canadian and I'm here on business. I've run into a bit of trouble and I need to speak to the ambassador,' she said, flashing her passport.

'There is no ambassador. We have a high commissioner, and he sees no one without an appointment.'

'This is an emergency. If he isn't available, is there anyone else who can help me?'

'I'm not sure—' she began, and then was interrupted by the appearance of a man who didn't look to Ava much like a diplomat.

He stared at her from behind the shield, his hand resting on the woman's shoulder. Ava smiled and held up her passport. 'I'm having some problems and I hope you can help.'

There was a slit at the bottom of the shield. He pointed to it. 'Slide your passport through there, please.' She did. He took it and examined her picture and all her visas and entry stamps; then he spread it apart to check the binding.

'What's the problem?' he said.

'Do I have to stand out here?'

He thought about it. 'No, I guess not.' He reached down and hit a button. The door to the offices buzzed and swung open.

She walked through and held out her hand. 'I'm Ava Lee.'

'Marc Lafontaine.'

He was a hulk of a man, layered with muscle. 'You're not the high commissioner, are you?' she said.

'I'm with the RCMP.'

'Ah.'

'I'm the security around here.'

'You may be exactly the person I need to talk to.'

'No one ever wants to talk to me.'

'Don't be so sure.'

'What is it you want to discuss?'

'Out here? You don't have an office?'

'Pushy, aren't you?'

'Desperate is more like it.'

That caught his attention. 'Follow me,' he said. 'We normally don't let people back here, but you don't look like a threat.'

His office was modest, containing a metal desk, a wooden swivel chair, and two four-drawer metal filing cabinets. On a coat rack in one corner, his uniform hung inside a plastic dry-cleaning bag. She noticed there were three stripes on the sleeve. Two photographs of three young girls sat on top of one of the filing cabinets. 'Are those your daughters, Sergeant?'

'Yes, and call me Marc.'

'Are they here with you?'

'They're in Ottawa with their mother.'

'I see.' She looked at the pictures and then at him. He had short auburn hair cropped close to his scalp, thin eyebrows, a long nose, and a chin that was distinctively pointed. All the girls shared that chin. 'They look like you,' she said.

'We don't get many Canadians walking in off the street the way you just did. Tell me why you're so desperate. That is the word you used, right?'

'That may have been a bit of an exaggeration. It's a bit too soon to tell.'

'Are you going to make me guess what this is about?'

She had dealt with Mounties several times before. They had not been very imaginative but they had been rigorously honest, and she knew they valued the same in return. She had no intention of lying to him; she just needed to gauge how much she could tell him. 'As security, I imagine you have to deal with the local police and the like.'

He nodded.

'Well, I need to know how the system works here.'

'You are going to tell me why, aren't you?'

'I represent a Canadian company that was bilked out of a substantial amount of money by someone currently residing in Guyana,' she said carefully. 'I'm here to try to collect some or all of that money.'

His face didn't register any emotion; he had probably heard this story before. 'That's why there are lawyers. I can recommend a couple if you want,' he said.

'This has gone beyond lawyers,' she said. 'Besides, the scam took place in the US, the money is probably in an offshore account, and the culprit is here. You can imagine how complicated any legal action would be, involving four separate jurisdictions.'

'I can. Now you haven't told me just what you do. Are you a lawyer?'

'I'm an accountant, a forensic accountant.'

'So you tracked the money.'

'I did.'

'And you know who took it and where he or she is?'

'His name is Jackson Seto. He has a house in Malvern Gardens, on the outskirts of Georgetown, and he's there right now.'

'I know Malvern Gardens. Him I've never heard of.'

'Why would you?'

He shrugged. 'You'd be surprised.'

'Anyway, I need to tackle Seto head-on.'

'What's stopping you?'

'I've been told by several sources that he's connected to the people who run things in Guyana, that he probably has some measure of protection.'

'If he lives in Malvern Gardens it wouldn't surprise me to know he's connected.'

'To whom?'

'What do you mean?'

'How do things work here? You just can't land at the airport, pay off a few cops, and all is well. There has to be some kind of established system, yes?'

'Very established.'

She waited. 'Is it my turn to guess?' she finally said.

He looked troubled.

'You know, if we need to be off the record, that works for me. Both ways, of course,' she said.

'Do you want to start?'

'Are you serious?'

'Yes, I am.'

With anyone else she might have asked for more assurance of discretion, but she knew from experience that he would take offence. Mountie honour is a prickly thing.

'As I said,' she began, 'I'm here to try to collect money that was stolen from a client. To do that, I need to meet with Seto to try to persuade him that it would be in everyone's best interest if the money were returned.'

'And how exactly would you do that?'

'Well, I would try to reason with him initially, and if that failed ...' Time to take a little leap of faith. 'Then I would pressure him in any way I could, and that might include some physical interaction.'

'Physical interaction?'

'I'm not as gentle as I look,' she said.

'How extreme might this physical interaction get?'

'He's no use to me dead, crippled, maimed, or otherwise unable to function.'

'You're serious?'

'Absolutely.'

He shook his head, a tiny smile tugging at the corners of his mouth. 'I am so glad I came to work today.'

'I don't actually find this amusing.'

'I'm sorry,' he said, still shaking his head. 'It's just that I'm sitting across from a young, beautiful woman who can't weigh much more than a hundred and ten pounds, who tells me she's an accountant and then tells me she's here to rip this Seto guy a new asshole.'

'That's the way it is,' she said. 'My problem – my potential problem – is that if I have to go beyond reasoning with him I'm going to run into his friends, and my experience in the developing world is that I won't stand a chance. They'll run me right out of the country, or worse.'

'Here it would probably be *or worse*.'

'So I need to know who they are.'

'Why?'

'So I can make them my friends, or at least disentangle them from Seto.'

'Just how much money does this guy owe?'

'About five million.'

'Wow.'

'So who do I need to talk to?'

He pushed himself to his feet, walked to the door, and closed it. 'This is off the record – we are agreed on that?'

'I wouldn't have told you what I just did if that wasn't the case.'

He sat down, leaned back, and looked at the ceiling. 'It's called the Guyana Defence League. During the 1960s the communists were active here and Cheddi Jagan was prime minister for a while. At the time that made Guyana only the second communist government in the Americas, after Cuba, and the US sort of went ballistic. They pushed – and financed – Jagan's former political partner, Forbes Burnham, into going up against his old colleague; they had been allies in forcing the UK to surrender their colonial power. There were strikes, riots, boycotts, and a lot of random violence against Jagan and his people. The fact that he was East Indian and Burnham was black only made it worse.

'Anyway, Jagan ended up in jail and Burnham became prime minister, supported by the Americans. At the time there was only a small police force in Guyana. The Americans needed assurance that the communists wouldn't be coming back, so they invested heavily in building an army and creating a clandestine special forces unit. Because the country is so small, they came up with the idea of grouping all these security forces together, creating the Guyana Defence League.

'The communists came and went. Burnham was in and out of office. Even Jagan – who was now a social democrat – got a chance to be the leader again. Through it all, the Guyana Defence League remained intact and developed methods of operation that are still in play today. Basically, the person who heads up the special forces is the top man. The military report to him, the police report to him. He moves officers back and

175

forth at will among the various services. So when you're dealing with the police, you aren't really. Everything flows upstream.'

'Including money?'

'Especially money.'

'I've just left Thailand, but it feels like I haven't.'

'I'm sure the scale is different,' Lafontaine said. 'This is a small, poor country. There's only so much graft to go around, and the politicians feed at the same trough.'

'Who heads up the Defence League?'

'Commissioner Thomas for the police, and General Choudray heads up the military. One's black, the other East Indian, and that's the way it always is: one of each. The strange thing is, they report to a white guy, the infamous Captain Robbins.'

'A white guy – that's curious.'

'Isn't it. When I arrived here, I met him at a High Commission function. He has two daughters at school in Toronto – Havergal College – and Canada is his country of choice in terms of making investments. I thought he was just a fat, jolly businessman until the High Commissioner pulled me aside and told me to be careful, very careful.

'He's had the same job for twenty years. There isn't a man in any of the forces who is not beholden to him for his job, and in this country, with unemployment at around thirty percent, that's no small thing. He also knows where all the bodies are buried, and he's probably responsible for a number of them himself. There isn't a politician whom he doesn't know inside out, and I can't imagine there's one who would defy him. It has been tried, though. Last year there was an East Indian minister of mines who decided the royalties that were going to the Defence League should end. His house was broken into and he, his wife, and his mother-in-law were shot dead. They never found the perpetrators.

'So, Ms Lee, if Seto has protection, it emanates from Captain Robbins, directly or indirectly.'

'How do I meet Captain Robbins?' she asked.

Lafontaine smiled again. 'You're serious, aren't you? I mean, really serious. I keep looking at you and thinking you're pulling a practical joke on me.'

'Do you have a phone number for him?'

He opened a Day-Timer that sat on his desk. 'Write this down, though I don't think it will do you any good. He doesn't take calls and he never returns calls unless he wants to talk to you, not vice versa.'

'Thanks for all this,' she said after writing down the number in her notebook.

'We're here to serve.'

'That's always been my experience with the Mounties. You're a very professional group.'

He nodded in acknowledgement. 'Where are you staying?'

'The Phoenix Hotel.'

'Neighbours.'

'Sort of.'

'Tell me, would you like to have dinner with me while you're here? You could keep me up to date on your progress.'

She looked over at the pictures of his children.

'I'm divorced,' he said.

Two propositions in one day, Ava thought, and unless she was wrong, Jeff was a potential third. For reasons she didn't understand, *gweilos* found her attractive. In Hong Kong she could stand on a street corner holding a sign reading PLEASE TAKE ME OUT TO DINNER and not get this much action.

'I wouldn't mind having dinner with you, but in keeping with our honesty policy I have to tell you I'm gay.'

'I did say dinner; I wasn't assuming anything else,' he said, but the flush that crept up his cheeks told her differently.

'How about I keep in touch with you? Can I get your cell number?'

He handed her a business card. His title read ASSISTANT TRADE COMMISSIONER.

'I'll let you know how it goes with Captain Robbins.'

21

Jeff was standing at the entrance of the Phoenix wearing slacks and a Polo golf shirt. He looked happy to see her, and she knew she was going to end up saying no to him as well.

'I have your SIM card,' he said.

'How much do I owe you?' she said as she took it.

'Twenty.'

She gave him thirty.

'Will you need me today? I have to make a run to the airport around one. After that I'm free.'

'I'm not sure. Call me when you get back.'

The room was way hotter than when she had left. The maid had turned off the air conditioning. She turned it back on and for good measure jacked it way down.

She undressed; her clothes were damp even though it was no more than a three-minute walk from the High Commission. She put on her running gear. It was really too hot to run, but she needed to think, and running freed her mind. Before leaving the hotel she checked her emails at the business centre. Nothing from Seto. That was no surprise.

From the literature in the room she knew there was a walkway along the seawall. The path was grass, and running on grass was easy on her legs. Add the sea breeze to that and she thought maybe it wouldn't be too tough, despite the heat.

The Georgetown seawall had been built during the nineteenth century by the Dutch, the original colonists, before the British ousted them. Georgetown, and in fact most of the northern coastline, was below sea level. The Dutch were experts at keeping the sea at bay, and they had constructed an impressive bulwark of stone about two metres wide and a metre high.

Ava began jogging towards the Atlantic. It was close to low tide, and between the wall and the ocean was a large expanse of sandy beach. On her right was Seawall Road, which was lined with embassies and consulates. There was hardly any traffic on the road and virtually no one on the path. Ava could see maybe two or three kilometres ahead. A woman was on the beach tossing sticks to a dog, and farther down she could see two figures sitting on the seawall.

She had run about a kilometre before the seated figures became distinct. They were two East Indian men, sitting maybe twenty metres apart. As she drew near she noticed she had attracted their attention. She thought about stopping and turning back, then told herself she was being silly. It was the middle of the day, and they were in a wide open area.

When she was five metres from the first man she saw him stiffen, and her senses prickled. She sped up to get past him. Just as she did, the second man jumped off the wall onto the path. She was trapped between them.

One of the men was about five foot ten and had to weigh at least two hundred pounds. He wore ragged blue shorts and a

T-shirt that read DRINK COORS. The other, who was a bit taller and not much thinner, was wearing soiled jeans and a singlet that exposed his chest and armpits. Ava noticed he had only one eye. It was fixed on her, and it wasn't conveying kind intent.

She stopped and turned so that she was facing the wall and had a clear view of the two of them.

'This can be easy or hard – your choice,' the one to her left said, a knife now visible in his right hand.

Ava saw no reason to respond; the outcome would be the same. The other man didn't seem to be armed, so she decided to take on the one with the knife first.

They inched towards her, trying to maintain equal distance. Ava moved left to bring her closer to the one with the knife. He waved it in the air until he was about half a metre from her. Then he reached down to grab her hair with his left hand, the knife held back, poised to strike.

She retreated backwards about half a step. When he tried to close the distance, she stepped forward. Her right arm rocketed towards him with the force of a piston. The extended knuckle of her index finger crashed into the bridge of his nose. She wasn't sure which she noticed first, the crack of cartilage or the gush of blood. He sagged to the ground, dropping the knife as both hands moved to cradle his nose. She picked up the weapon and threw it over the wall.

The other man hadn't moved as she put his friend out of action. Now he edged towards her, his fists balled. He didn't move very well; his hips seemed to propel his legs. She knew she could avoid his swings but she wasn't about to give him the chance. When he was within striking range, her right arm shot out again. This time she used the base of her palm to strike at the centre of his forehead. He reeled back and she leapt after him, her left fist driving into his Adam's apple. He collapsed, his eyes rolled back, and his hands clutched his throat as he gasped for air. She had known people to die from that blow.

The whole incident had taken no more than thirty seconds. She looked around. There was no one in view, no cars on the road. She turned and began to jog back to the hotel, past the woman throwing sticks to her dog.

22

'How was your run?' the doorman asked when Ava arrived back at the Phoenix.

'Okay,' she said.

She had bought two bottles of water to take to her room. She didn't recognize the brand and then saw it had been bottled in Georgetown. She added a water purification pill to each of them. When the pills had done their work, she sat in the rattan chair and looked out at the ocean. She was ready to phone Captain Robbins. She didn't expect him to take her call, but she did expect him to return it. That was when she would be challenged to capture his interest and get him to meet with her, or at the very least to send someone who had his trust.

She punched in the number and waited. Just when she thought it was going to flip into voicemail, a woman's rich, cultured voice said, 'The office.'

'I would like to speak to Captain Robbins, please,' she said.

There was a long pause, and Ava wondered if Lafontaine had given her the correct number.

'I'm afraid that Captain Robbins is not available.'

'Well, could you have him return my call, please? My name is Ava Lee and I'm affiliated with Havergal College. Do you need me to spell Havergal?'

'No, I know Havergal,' she said. 'Is there anything I can help you with, or is there a specific message you would like me to pass to the Captain?'

'No, I need to speak to him directly.'

'He has the number for the college. He can call you there.'

'No, I'm at a conference and I'm using my mobile. Let me give you my contact information,' Ava said, and gave her Toronto cellphone number.

'Is this about either of his daughters?'

'I'm not at liberty to say. Please have him call me when he can.'

'I will pass on the message.'

Then Ava phoned downstairs to ask about laundry service. The front desk told her it could be back in her room by that evening. She left the bag outside the door for pickup and climbed into the shower. The water seemed less thick, less brown, and she stayed in longer than usual.

Her cellphone beeped when she emerged from the bathroom – a message. *Already*, she thought.

It was Captain Robbins' receptionist, asking her to call back.

She dried her hair and dressed while reviewing her pitch in her head, deciding just how much she should or shouldn't say. That was always difficult to determine when you were dealing with someone you didn't know, and in this case, knew nothing about except that he just might be the most powerful man in Guyana.

'The office.'

'This is Ava Lee.'

'Just one second, Ms Lee.'

Robbins was on the line almost instantly. 'This is Robbins. What can I do for you?' He had an accent that sounded familiar but wasn't like anything she had heard in Guyana.

'My name is Ava Lee and I'm afraid I've called you under some mildly misleading pretences. But I really need to speak to you and I was told that you're a difficult man to get hold of.'

There was silence from his end.

'I am a Havergal graduate, by the way, and I'm in Georgetown on business, not Toronto, though that is my home. I apologize for taking this approach.' She waited for the sound of the phone being disconnected.

'Ms Lee, who gave you this number?'

'The Canadian High Commission. I went to them for help and they said you were the man I should speak to.'

'That's highly unusual. What kind of problem can you have that the Commission can't help with?'

His voice was plummy, even richer than his secretary's. His speech was slow, even, and full of confidence, in control.

'It's a business problem with a considerable amount of money involved,' she said, invoking the magic word.

'And you think I can help?'

'I've been told that if anyone can, it's you.'

'Someone thinks too highly of me. Still, it would be churlish not to try to assist a Canadian visitor recommended to me by the High Commission, and a visitor who happens to be a Havergal graduate at that. Where are you staying in Georgetown?'

'At the Phoenix.'

'This is obviously a discussion that we shouldn't continue

over the telephone. Are you going to be at the hotel this evening?'

'Certainly.'

'I'll send someone there to meet with you. His name is Patrick West. I'm not sure when exactly he will be free, so try to leave the entire evening open if you can. I'll give him your mobile number, and I know he has the Phoenix's number, so if there's any change in plans he can contact you.'

'Thank you so much.'

'No promises, mind you, but Patrick is a good man and quite resourceful. He has my confidence, so make sure you're completely open with him.'

You clever girl, she thought as the line went dead.

The afternoon was going to drag, so Ava set out to fill it with as much activity as she could. She took a taxi back to Stabroek and wandered aimlessly for an hour. In an area close to the market she found a bookstore. Most of the offerings were second-hand but she found a copy of *Tai-Pan*, James Clavell's historical novel about the early days of Hong Kong.

She was hungry but reluctant to experiment again with the local cuisine. The bookseller recommended the Kentucky Fried Chicken outlet just around the corner. She couldn't remember the last time she had eaten fried chicken of any kind. Still, there weren't many funny things they could do to it, so she decided to eat there.

Jeff was sitting in the lobby when she got back to the hotel. He waved to her. He was on the verge of becoming a nuisance.

'Are we in business today?' he asked.

'I have some things I need to do here,' she said. 'You can help out, though.'

'How is that?'

'Go back to Malvern Gardens and keep tabs on Jackson Seto. You'll have to park somewhere else this time or they'll get suspicious. I think you should drive past the entrance and then turn the car around and park it in the direction of Georgetown. Stay about a hundred metres away. They shouldn't notice you if they leave.'

'If they leave, I follow?'

'Only if you're sure it's okay. Keep well back. There aren't that many places he can go anyway.'

'You want me to call you if anything happens?'

'Sure. Use the Guyana number you have for me.'

She checked her emails again before going upstairs. Still nothing from Seto.

Her backup cellphone was fully charged. She slipped the Guyanese SIM card into it and turned on the phone. She placed it and her regular mobile on the small table next to the rattan chair. She still had some hours to kill. Hopefully James Clavell would help.

23

It was dark when Ava was woken by a ringing phone. The Clavell book was open on her lap to page thirty. She looked at both her mobiles before she realized it was the hotel phone.

'Yes?' she said.

'Ava, this is Marc Lafontaine. I'm just finishing work and I'm still wondering if you would like to have dinner with me.'

She was still groggy from her nap and his name didn't register at first. Then it clicked and she almost groaned. Half of her wanted to hang up and the other half realized she might need him again before this project was finished. 'I can't leave the hotel,' she said. 'I have a meeting here tonight and I'm not sure of the time.'

'We can eat at the hotel. It's not that bad.'

'All right, but if my appointment arrives while we're eating I'll have to leave.'

'I understand. I'll see you in the lobby in, say, fifteen minutes?'

'Okay.'

She brushed her teeth using bottled water and then splashed some on her face. Her linen slacks were still presentable and she had a white cotton shirt she hadn't worn yet. She thought about putting on makeup for her meeting with Patrick West, and then decided against it. The more innocent she looked, the better.

There was a bar and lounge beside the lobby. Marc Lafontaine was sitting at a table with a Carib beer and a bowl of peanuts in front of him. 'Glad you could join me,' he said. 'We don't get many Canadians coming through here, and truthfully it gets pretty lonely. I'm grateful for the company.'

She knew he meant it, and she felt a twinge of guilt for having thought about blowing him off.

He looked at the two cellphones as she placed them on the table. 'Busy girl, eh?'

'I'm trying to be. I managed to get in touch with Captain Robbins and I'm scheduled to meet one of his people here tonight at some time or another.'

'You've got to be kidding! You actually got through to Robbins?'

'I did.'

'That's amazing.'

She smiled. 'Well, that's the easy part.'

'Do you want a drink?'

'White wine would be fine.'

'I'll have to go to the bar to get it. There's no table service here.'

He returned with her wine and another beer for himself. 'They have a restaurant on the second floor. It's Georgetown's version of fine dining. I've eaten there three or four times and not gotten ill. The only thing is, they normally have only a quarter of the menu available, so I ask them what they do have rather than wait to be told they don't have something.'

'Sounds good. I just want to tell the front desk where I am before we go upstairs, in case the Captain's man comes asking for me.'

The restaurant was empty except for them. A sign by the entrance said PLEASE WAIT TO BE SEATED. Ava wondered who had thought that was necessary.

They were taken to a seat by a window. The lights from the part of Georgetown that had electricity sparkled in the night. 'It looks almost attractive,' he said.

She told him about meeting the Englishman Tom Benson that morning, and about his daily trek to the power company. Lafontaine laughed and told her that Benson's attitude was the only way to deal with Guyana and still stay sane. If you expected things to change, you were a fool.

She talked about Asia and about how North Americans in particular often went with preconceived notions of how hard life must be there, only to find themselves in Hong Kong or Singapore or Bangkok or Shanghai. The lifestyle in those places was more refined and luxurious than what they would find in just about any city in North America.

The waiter appeared with menus. 'Just tell us what you have,' Lafontaine said.

They had a choice of grilled snapper, broiled chicken, baked pork chops, and roast beef. There was only the one fish, and Ava chose it. Lafontaine ordered the chicken.

She asked him about his children in Ottawa. As Lafontaine began to talk about them, he suddenly caught himself. 'There's something I really need to talk to you about,' he said. 'I hope you won't think I'm being rude.'

'What is it about?'

'This morning when you told me that you were gay, you were being serious, yes? Not just keeping me at arm's length?'

'Marc, I could not have been more serious.'

'I believe you,' he said. 'The thing is, homosexuality is illegal in Guyana. In fact, it's punishable by life imprisonment. Now, I haven't heard about anyone being prosecuted, but the law is on the books. And they really frown on any display of affection between two people of the same sex.' He stopped, clearly uncomfortable. 'I'm not trying to pry into your life or anything, but you need to be careful here, circumspect.'

'I wasn't planning on going to gay bars,' she said.

'That's good, because there aren't any.'

'Thanks. Enough said.'

Ava directed the conversation back towards his children. They were all teenagers and drifting away from him. She listened to him lament the fact and realized he knew absolutely nothing about girls. She was about to give him some suggestions when her Guyanese phone rang.

'Hi, Jeff,' she said.

'He left the house about an hour and a half ago and went out to eat – guess where – and then went to drink and party – guess where.'

'Same as last night.'

'He's a creature of habit.'

'Good. Pack it in. There's no reason to hang around there any more tonight.'

'What are you up to?' he asked, his voice cracking ever so slightly.

'I'm having dinner with a friend from the Canadian High Commission, and then I have a meeting with a Guyanese government official. I'll see you tomorrow and settle our accounts.'

Out of the corner of her eye she saw the restaurant host hovering. The moment she ended her phone call he walked to the table. 'There are some people downstairs waiting to see you,' he said.

'Call downstairs and tell them I'll be right there,' she said. 'And bring me the bill.'

'I'm paying,' Lafontaine said.

'No, you're not,' she said. 'You've done quite enough for me today as it is.'

While they waited for the bill to arrive, Lafontaine said, 'People? I thought you were meeting one person.'

'Me too.'

'Would you mind if I walk down with you?'

'Not at all.'

There were three people sitting in the lounge: two large black men who looked as if they had come directly from the gym to an *Esquire* photo shoot, and a very pale, rotund man with a sly smile and a glint in his deep blue eyes.

'Christ, that's Robbins,' Lafontaine said.

The three stood as Ava and Lafontaine approached, and she was shocked by how physically imposing Robbins was. His men were both over six feet tall, but Robbins was a shaved head taller. His belly mounded under a black satin shirt draped over black jeans; his face was round and jowly. His heaviness made him look, if anything, more dangerous.

And then there was his skin – it was the colour of paper. In a country where everyone was some variation of brown, he was a ghost.

His eyes found her and didn't let go.

'Ah, Sergeant Lafontaine,' Robbins said, his eyes still on Ava. 'So it was you who gave Ms Lee my phone number.'

'Captain.'

'What shall I say to you for unleashing this young woman on us?'

'I don't know what you mean.'

'And why would you? Look at her – a Havergal graduate, tiny, well-mannered, a Chinese doll. And then . . . Ah, I'm not being polite. This is Patrick and this is Robert,' he said, motioning to his men. 'I thought you should meet them,' he said to Ava, 'and truthfully, they wanted to meet you.

'My plan, Mr Lafontaine, was to send Patrick to meet with Ms Lee, but after what happened today I couldn't resist the opportunity to meet her myself. Robert, why don't you explain?'

'I was called by the police today after they picked up two men at the seawall,' Robert said.

Robbins interrupted. 'It seems that a young Chinese woman was jogging there when she encountered these men. They are known to us, and not as particularly good citizens. Some minor theft charges, some more serious rape allegations, though never proven . . . Still, they told an interesting story. They claim they were sitting on the seawall, minding their own business, when this young woman ran by. They do admit they ogled her, and maybe made some inappropriate comments, but certainly did nothing to warrant the attack that ensued. One of them had his nose destroyed. The other had his windpipe crushed and is lucky to be alive. These are not small men, Mr Lafontaine. I daresay even you or I would have found it a challenge to take on the two of them at the same time. You do jog, don't you, Ms Lee?'

'Once in a while.'

'The victims, or villains – call them what you will – said the woman in question came from this hotel. And as far as we can ascertain, Ms Lee is the only Chinese woman in residence.' Robbins stared at her, his expression not the least unkind. 'So tell me, how do you explain the damage you inflicted on these men?'

'I restrained myself,' Ava said.

Robbins exploded with laughter. Patrick and Robert followed suit. Marc Lafontaine looked as if he had wandered into the wrong wedding reception.

'Marc, I have business to discuss with Captain Robbins, and I don't think you should be here,' she said softly.

'Ms Lee is quite right. We do have business to discuss, Mr Lafontaine,' Robbins said, wiping tears from eyes. 'This is no place for you.'

Lafontaine started to say something but Ava cut him off. 'I'll call you if I need you.'

They watched him leave, the three men still chuckling. Robbins said, 'When I heard this story, how could I send Patrick to meet you alone? What if he offended you?'

'Don't make fun of me or the situation I was in. They were going to rape me. I dealt with them, that's all.'

'Apologies,' Robbins said. 'Sit, please.' Robbins sat down as well; his two men stood on either side of his chair. 'I have daughters, as you know, and I am sensitive to the situation you found yourself in this afternoon. I'd like to think that anyone who tried that with my girls would be equally indisposed. Except I can't imagine my girls inflicting that kind of damage. You are an amazing young woman, Ms Lee. That's why I wanted to meet you in person. I thought you would be built like a shot putter, yet here you are, not much more than a hundred pounds soaking wet.'

'I appreciate that you came,' she said.

'I'm drinking beer. What can I get you?'

'Nothing, thank you. I'm quite sated.'

'You speak like a Havergal graduate.'

'I am one.'

'I believe you. So what is this business you're involved in? It doesn't sound like something a Havergal grad would pursue.'

'I'm a forensic accountant. I find money that has been misappropriated and try to return it to its rightful owner.'

'And there's misappropriated money in Guyana?'

'No, the money is in the British Virgin Islands, but the thief is here.'

'Name?'

'Jackson Seto.'

Robbins' eyes showed no sign of recognition, and she felt a surge of optimism. If he didn't know the name, Seto couldn't be all that high in the food chain.

'Boys, do you have any information for me?' Robbins asked.

Patrick leaned forward and whispered in Robbins' ear.

The Captain looked at her and said, 'Could you excuse us for a moment, Ms Lee? We need to chat amongst ourselves.'

She left the lounge and sat in the lobby, her back deliberately turned to them. In what seemed like less than a minute there was a gentle tap on her shoulder. Patrick was looking down at her. 'The Captain will talk to you now.'

Now it was just the two of them; the men had moved to the lobby.

'Seto is a friend of a friend,' Robbins said.

'I want to be a better friend.'

The Captain put his fingertips together, placing them against his nose. 'To whom?'

'That's your decision.'

'Tell me what your plans are for this Seto.'

'I have to convince him to give the money back.'

'Using logic?'

'Yes.'

'And if that fails?'

She shrugged.

'And what would we be expected to do?'

'Stay out of it. Keep everyone out of it.'

'That sounds simple enough.'

'That isn't to say that I might not need active assistance at some point.'

His eyes glittered, and she wondered why he seemed so amused.

'There is a substantial difference between turning a blind eye and becoming actively involved in whatever it is you have in mind,' Robbins said.

'Everything has a price.'

'You are a mercenary, Ms Lee.'

'I am an accountant,' she said.

'Exactly.'

'Obviously I can't be sure what kind of help I might need until I can actually get to Seto and spend some time alone with him.'

'Give me an idea, though, will you?'

'I'd like all the information you have on him. You must have a dossier somewhere.'

'That's not difficult.'

'He has a Vietnamese bodyguard. I would like to have him put out of circulation for forty-eight to seventy-two hours.'

'Go on.'

'Seto seems to go to Eckie's Club every night. I'll try to talk to him there. If he isn't cooperative I'll need a place to take him. I can't very well bring him back to the hotel. His house would be ideal but I'm not sure that will be doable, so I want to have a backup plan.'

'This is getting more expensive. You know that, yes?'

'If I do need to start moving him around I'll need some physical assistance, so you might have to assign someone to me.'

'Is there more?'

'Not for now.'

'Those are a lot of ifs.'

'I always think it's better to plan for the worst.'

'You do know that he pays a fee to some friends to look out for his interests?'

'I'll pay more.'

'But you'll only pay once. He pays annually. Then there are all those ifs. How do we factor those into the equation?'

'I want you to assume that I'll need all the help I've outlined here and to give me a figure that accommodates them and makes everyone happy about upgrading friends.'

He put the beer bottle to his lips and drank delicately. 'I'm not good at numbers,' he said.

Ava was not going to be the one to put the first offer on the table. It was Uncle's primary rule of negotiation: let the other party start. Not that she needed that advice. Her mother had practised that her entire life, in every transaction, big or small, that she had ever made. Even at the Chanel store in Toronto, her mother regarded the sticker price as merely an opening bid in the negotiation process. Ava had absorbed that life lesson. She turned her palms upward, as if helpless to know where to start, caught his eye, and let him know she was waiting for him.

He breathed deeply, a sigh of exasperation. She could almost see him calculating. How much money was she here to get? How much could Seto have gotten away with? He was in Guyana, after all, not the Cayman Islands, so it couldn't be a fortune. What percentage of it could he claim?

'Two hundred thousand will get you all the assistance you need,' he said.

She had expected a larger sum. 'That's too much, Captain. My clients would never agree to pay that amount.'

'Then ... ?'

She couldn't insult him. They had paid for help before,

sometimes up to ten percent of the amount owed. But that had been based on a successful recovery. This was a payment with no guarantees attached. All she knew was that without the Captain she probably had zero chance of success.

'One hundred thousand – US dollars of course,' she said.

'Cash?'

'We prefer wire transfers.'

'Upfront.'

Uncle hated paying upfront. The most he had ever agreed to was half upfront and half at the conclusion. But the Captain hadn't been making a request – those were his terms. She sensed that trying to negotiate those terms would put a crimp in what had so far been a relatively painless exercise. Uncle was going to have to put up with it.

'Yes, upfront.'

The Captain's face broke into a smile. 'Okay, let me speak with my friends. If they're happy with the arrangement I'll let you know and give you the details of how the money should be transferred.' He nodded in the direction of Robert and Patrick. 'You've met the boys. If we go ahead I'll lend one of them to you as a . . . liaison. Do you have a preference?'

'Who is senior?'

'Patrick.'

'He's the one I'll take.'

'Assuming we do business,' the Captain said.

'Assuming.'

24

Ava called the number Lafontaine had given her and got his voicemail. She left a message apologizing for the way their dinner had ended. Nothing else. If things went as planned, she wouldn't have to speak to him again.

Uncle answered her call on the first ring. 'Ava, when will you be finished with this project?'

Ava was caught off guard. Uncle never rushed a job. 'I'm not sure. Two days, maybe three. I made progress today ... Has something happened?'

'We have landed a huge client. Have you heard of Tommy Ordonez?'

'The Filipino billionaire?'

'That's him. He is ethnic Chinese; the family name is actually Chew but he changed it to fit in with the Filipinos. He has a brother here in Hong Kong, David Chew, and another in Vancouver, Philip Chew. Tommy is the eldest, so all of the family money flows through and around him. He called me today through a friend.'

'Tommy Ordonez got screwed in a deal and needs us to chase money for him?' she asked.

'Don't be foolish – he never gets screwed,' Uncle said. 'The brother in Vancouver is the one who was unwise. Someone, who obviously doesn't know he is Tommy's brother, took the family for more than fifty million in a land swindle. If it were the Philippines or China or anywhere else in Asia, Tommy would look after it himself. Canada is another world. So a friend referred him to me. We have the contract. I had to cut our rate, but not that much.'

'I need at least three days, and that's not a promise,' she said.

'If Tam weren't the nephew of my friend ... You think three days?'

'Minimum.'

'Where are we?'

'I've found him. I think I've bought off the local muscle. Now I need to get my hands on Seto and get the money back to Tam.'

'How much to buy off the locals?'

'One hundred thousand, upfront, all of it by wire.'

'You know—'

'I know,' Ava said, louder than she intended. 'It can't be done any other way, and without them I'm nowhere. This is like a Chinese provincial backwater where one guy controls every- thing and nothing happens unless he says so. In this case, the main guy won't give the green light unless the money is sent to him upfront.'

'He is that powerful? He is that insistent?'

'Yes and yes.'

'Okay, Ava, I understand. Where do I send it?'

'I won't know until tomorrow.'

'As soon as you know—'

'Uncle, I want to get out of here more than you want to make Tommy Ordonez the happiest man in the Philippines.'

'Sorry,' he said.

She wasn't used to getting apologies from Uncle. Normally if he made an error – and that was seldom enough – he'd correct it and tell her about the change in the situation without acknowledging a mistake had been made in the first place. And she, of course, would accept the change as a given and never mention the events that had preceded it. It was enough that they both knew; there was no reason for her to be disrespectful by remarking on it and no reason for him to explain himself. She guessed that he was feeling guilty about pushing Tommy Ordonez at her when the Tam job was still on the boil.

'Let me finish here,' she said, 'and then we'll make the Chews one big happy family.'

Ava crawled into bed with the James Clavell novel. She slept amazingly well and didn't wake till just past eight. Skipping breakfast and Tom Benson, she went for a completely uneventful run. When she got back to the hotel, Patrick was asleep in the lobby, his head on the back of the chair, his mouth half open.

She tapped his arm. He snorted and his eyes flicked open, immediately alert.

'I was on a run,' she said.

'Yeah, they told me,' he said. 'Here, the Captain wanted me to give this to you. It's what we could come up with on Seto last night.' He handed her an envelope. 'He's been coming here on and off for years, mainly to do fish business, but recently just to hang. He's never been a problem.'

'Is that because someone decided to leave him alone or because he was saintly?'

'Who knows, but if he was left alone it was because he never went over the line.'

'Who's the woman?'

'Anna Choudray. They've been together for about six years. She was a bar girl when they met. They aren't married but he must like her a lot 'cause she's the legal owner of the house in Malvern Gardens, lucky her. The Vietnamese is Joey Ng. He travels under an American passport, the same as Seto. He isn't new; he's been here with Seto quite a few times.'

'I was told this is where Seto comes when things get too hot elsewhere.'

'Could be. Like I said, he's trouble-free here.'

She wiped sweat from her brow. 'I need to shower and change. It will take me about half an hour. Will you stay and have breakfast with me?'

'Of course.'

'This means that the Captain has accepted our arrangement?'

'I wouldn't be here otherwise.'

'And you are my ... liaison?'

'That isn't the word he used but the meaning is the same, I guess.'

'Banking information?'

'In the envelope.'

The shower could wait. Ava went directly to the business centre, opened the envelope, and sent an email with Robbins' bank particulars to Uncle and the Hong Kong accountant who handled their wire transfers. It was mid-evening there and nothing would move until the next morning, which meant that, given a twenty-four-hour transit time, the wire wouldn't get to Robbins until two full days from now. She didn't fancy spending two days doing nothing, so she asked the accountant to scan and email her a copy of the wire transmittal. It was being sent from the Kowloon Light and Power Bank, which was owned by some friends of Uncle, to the Cayman Islands branch of a Canadian chartered bank. Kowloon Light and Power was substantial enough that she was sure the Canadian bank wouldn't have any issues with the amount. In that case, maybe Robbins would accept the copy of the transmittal as confirmation and let her get started before he actually had the money.

It took her close to an hour to get things sorted out. That didn't seem to bother Patrick, who had fallen asleep again. A slight nudge wakened him. 'Do you want some coffee?' she said.

'Sure, but not here. The coffee here is horrible.'

They climbed into a Toyota truck sitting in the no-parking zone in front of the hotel. He weaved through the now all-too-familiar downtown terrain.

'I've already sent the bank directions. The wire should be done within the next twelve hours. I'll get you a copy of the confirmation once it's gone,' she said.

'I don't need to know any of this, so it's best not to talk to me about it any more. Just put the information in a sealed envelope. The Captain likes to keep details like that between himself and people like you. My directions are more basic.'

'Such as?'

'Take Ng out and do what I can to help you with Seto.' He looked hard at her. 'The Captain says you're a debt collector. He says you must be a very special kind to come here by yourself and be able to wire a hundred thousand dollars as if it were nothing.'

'That's what I do for a living,' she said. 'Now, taking Ng out – how hard will that be?'

'Not a problem for us. How about Seto for you?'

She liked Patrick already. He was direct without being rude or aggressive, and he was confident and assertive.

'I'll meet him at Eckie's and try to convince him that it's in his best interests to cooperate with me,' she said.

'What will you say? "Pretty please, give me back whatever gazillions of dollars you scammed"?'

'Something like that,' she laughed.

'Does it ever work?'

'You'd be surprised. Once they know I've found them and once they know I've located the money, most of them understand that I'm the best chance they have to give it back and maintain – how shall I say it? – their physical well-being. Mind you, this is me dealing with the Chinese – and all our clients are Chinese – in Hong Kong or New York or Toronto or Vancouver. They always assume that I've been sent by the triads, and that if they don't cut a deal with me they'll have four guys with machetes sitting beside their beds.'

'The Captain thinks you are triad.'

'I have no guys with machetes sitting back at the hotel,' she said, smiling. 'And I have no tattoos. Everyone knows that triads have tattoos.'

'Do you think Seto will be as cooperative as your Chinese in Hong Kong?'

'Actually no, I don't. He thinks he's protected here. So I think I'm at Plan B already.'

'So not much chit-chat?'

'No.'

'What will you do?'

'Tell me first, how will you handle Ng?'

'Under our national security law we can detain anyone we suspect of anti-government activity for up to a week without laying charges and without providing a lawyer. They don't even get to make a phone call. We'll use that law to put Ng on ice for as long as you need. Now tell me about Seto.'

'He seems to go to Eckie's every night. We'll confront him there. He's a scrawny little piece of shit – you shouldn't have any problem putting handcuffs on him and getting him out the door. We'll take him to his house. If the woman is in the club, she'll go with us. If she isn't, we'll deal with her at the house.'

He didn't speak again until he stopped the truck at Donald's Doughnut Shop. She looked around; the neighbourhood was even more rundown than central Georgetown.

'I live over there,' he said, pointing to a small red bungalow at the end of the street. 'It's my mother's house.'

They got out of the truck and entered the shop, sitting in the booth farthest from the door. The coffee wasn't instant but she didn't complain. Her doughnut was virtually oozing fat. She ate it silently.

'Seto owns a piece of Eckie's,' Patrick said between bites.

'That's how our people got to know him at first. Eckie's is not completely legal. By that I mean clubs in general aren't exactly legal, so if you want to operate one you have to make arrangements with the right people.'

'Are there bouncers at the club, or might any of his partners choose to interfere with us?'

'If they know we're involved, everyone will stay out of the way. No see, no hear, no nothing.'

'Then let's hope he goes to Eckie's.'

'If we weren't involved, how would you – I mean, what do you do in other cases when people aren't co-operating?'

'There are always options,' she said. 'The most important thing is figuring out ahead of time what will work. If I think a direct approach will succeed, then I become direct. If I think there's going to be resistance, then I'm more discreet, less visible. In a case like Seto's, if I were acting alone I would use something like chloral hydrate to strengthen my position.'

He raised an eyebrow. 'Jesus, I haven't heard that mentioned in a while.'

'I know, it's a little old-fashioned. But it's effective. There's something about waking up with your hands and feet bound, your eyes masked and mouth covered, that makes people want to be cooperative. It brings an unknown quality; it lets me create a bit of fantasy. Since I have you, that won't be necessary, but I'll still tape his eyes and mouth until we get to the house.'

'No problem,' he said.

'Where are you from?' she asked suddenly. 'You and the Captain have a similar accent. I can't place it but I know it isn't from here.'

'Barbados – we're both Bajans. My grandmother was his nanny, if you can believe that. He moved here more than thirty years ago and made his name, made his fortune. I was a boy in trouble back home when Gran called the Captain and asked him to take me on. So I came with my mother and my sister. It isn't Barbados, but we're doing okay.'

'The Captain is an impressive man,' she said.

'The Captain runs this poor excuse for a country,' he said. 'He keeps the animals in check.'

She fought back an urge to comment on the potholes, brown water, and irregular power. 'Thank goodness,' she said.

'What are you going to do today?' he asked.

'I have a little shopping to do. Other than that I can't do very much until the Captain gives me the green light.'

'I know.' Patrick yawned. 'I had a late night. I think I'll go to the gym and get myself revved. You want to come?'

'No, I ran this morning. I'm good.'

'We were talking last night, Bobby and me, about the way you handled those two creeps. They're handy, both of them, so we couldn't figure out how you did it. I thought maybe you could show me at the gym.'

'I practise bak mei,' she said. 'It isn't something you teach someone at a gym.'

'Never heard of it.'

'It's a Chinese martial art.'

'Like karate, kung fu?'

'Like kung fu but not kung fu. No one makes movies about bak mei.'

'What is it, then?'

'It's very old, very Chinese – Taoist in fact. It has never caught on in the Western world because it isn't pretty and it can't be made into a sport. It's purely functional, designed to inflict damage. And it can be lethal when applied to the extreme. I went relatively easy on those two.'

'Do you use kicks?'

'Only below the waist.'

'Nice,' he said. 'How did you learn this stuff?'

'I was already into martial arts and I was good, good enough that one of the teachers pulled me aside and asked if I had heard of bak mei. I hadn't. He explained that it was a secret art – in the old days, a forbidden art – and that it was only taught one-on-one: father to son, teacher to student. He asked me if I wanted to learn. When I said I did, he sent me to see Grandmaster Tang. I haven't stopped learning since.'

'Show me some moves.'

'It isn't something to be demonstrated.'

'No juking and jiving?'

'Afraid not.'

Patrick, thinking Ava was joking, waited, expecting her to get up and move into a fighting position. When she didn't, he said, 'You aren't any fun.'

'That's true enough.'

'What do you want me to do?' he asked.

'I think I'd just like to go back to the hotel.'

'You aren't any fun at all.'

'That's still true.'

An hour later, Ava was in her rattan chair with the James Clavell on her lap. Time would not move fast enough. She read for two hours and then was so restless she couldn't stay put any more. She went down to the business centre, signed on, and then thought about Tommy Ordonez. It was one of her rules never to start thinking about the next case before the one she was working on was completed. She had done it twice and both times it had brought bad luck. She hesitated and then thought, *What the hell*. She was at least as curious as she was superstitious.

She googled Tommy Ordonez. He seemed to own half the Philippines. This job was enticing both in size and in terms of the participants. But why had Ordonez gone to Uncle? On any number of levels it didn't make any sense. Ava wondered what kind of deal Uncle had cut with him, or rather them. The older she got, the more inflexible she found herself becoming. If their rate was thirty percent, what did it matter if they were collecting ten million or a hundred million? The client was out the larger amount, and if she was their last hope, thirty percent was nothing. She loved Uncle and had enormous respect for him, but there were times when he was too accommodating with people who were above him in the power scheme. At some point she would have to talk to him about that. Not now, though.

For maybe the tenth time since she had been given Seto's account number at Barrett's Bank, she logged onto the Barrett's website. She hit the ACCESS YOUR ACCOUNT button and punched in the S&A account number. The program asked for the pass-word. As before, she didn't even attempt to guess at one. She was leery of bank websites. They were sensitive in the extreme; if she entered the wrong password she was afraid it would trigger a reaction, and any reaction would not be to her benefit. She just wanted to confirm that the account was still active, and it was.

She figured the wire would be sent that evening and she would be able to get confirmation to the Captain the next morning. The money might even land in his account that day if she was lucky. If not, she would try to sweet-talk him into letting Patrick and her and whomever else they wanted to involve go after Seto tomorrow night.

Things had gone very well with this project. The money had been almost ridiculously easy to find, and Seto had become a sitting duck once she had located him. The only wrinkle had been the Captain and his crew. But if everything went according to plan, Tam would have most of his money back within twenty-four hours, and she would be on a plane back to Toronto the morning after.

25

The wire had been sent the night before, and Ava had printed two copies of the confirmation. She called the Captain's office and was put directly through to Robbins.

'Ava, do you have some good news for me?'

'The wire went through last night. I have a copy of the confirmation. Can I bring it to you?'

'Is Patrick there?'

'I don't know. I haven't been downstairs yet.'

'He should be there. Give it to him and ask him to bring it over to the office.'

'I can bring it there myself.'

'No, my dear, please just give it to Patrick.'

'The money might be deposited into the account today,' she said.

'That would be nice.'

'If it isn't, I'm hoping you might take the copy of the confirmation at face value and let us deal with Seto tonight.'

'That's possible,' he said. 'I don't like dragging things out unnecessarily. Let me see the wire and I'll tell Patrick how we are to proceed.'

'Thank you.'

Patrick was in the lobby reading a newspaper. He smiled

when he saw her and held the paper out for her to see. There was a picture of the man whose nose she had crushed. 'He claims he was walking along the seawall when he was viciously attacked by a woman with a cricket bat. The paper is urging people to be cautious until the police find the suspect.'

'How stupid is that, to draw attention to himself that way?'

'He has a little life. For this morning at least he is in the spotlight. It happens all the time here. Something atrocious happens and instead of keeping quiet, the victims feel compelled to tell the world, or at least to tell Georgetown.'

'Here,' she said, handing him a hotel envelope. 'Could you take this over to the Captain? He's waiting for it.'

Ava was in the coffee shop working on her second cup of Starbucks instant, which the waitress had agreed to make, when Patrick returned. The office, she figured, had to be in the neighbourhood.

He sat down, a contented look on his face. 'The Captain sends his regards. We have the go-ahead for tonight.'

She beamed. Good dim sum wasn't much more than a day away.

'How about Seto's friends? What have they been told?'

'The Captain has already had a chat with the one who counts. He'll make another courtesy call today to let him know it's going down tonight. The word will get out.'

'Not prematurely?'

'You don't know the Captain,' said Patrick. 'Things get done the way he wants, when he wants – always. You have his word, and I'm here as proof of that. No one is going to warn Seto. No one would dare. The wrath of Captain Robbins is a terrible thing to experience.'

'So how do we proceed?' she asked.

'My people are keeping an eye on Seto. The moment he leaves Malvern Gardens we'll know.'

'If he doesn't follow the usual routine?'

'We'll work something out.'

His casual manner took her aback. She was accustomed to working alone, to sweating every detail, to being thorough to the point of obsessive. Now she had to work with a team over which she had no control, and she had to accept that her plan was subject to the whims of not just Seto.

Patrick sensed her discomfort. 'Ava, this is Guyana. At the end of the day, one way or another, you'll get Seto, because the Captain has said that's what will happen. If it's at Eckie's, great. If it's somewhere else, what does it matter?'

'What do you want me to do this afternoon?'

'Whatever you want. Go for a swim, go for a run, beat up some locals. I'll pick you up here at six and we'll go downtown, park near the restaurant, and wait for Seto.'

Ava decided to go for another run. When she got back to the hotel, she showered and then went downstairs. She had toast and jam in the restaurant and killed some time on the computer, but it was still only four o'clock when she got back to her room. She turned on the television for the first time and watched old reruns of *M*A*S*H* and the *Bob Newhart Show*.

Six o'clock came and went without a word from Patrick. She

checked and double-checked the kitbag she had packed with the odds and ends she would need for Seto. She also started getting her luggage organized for the trip home.

At six thirty she thought about calling Patrick and then held off, fearful of looking too anxious, like an amateur.

It was almost seven when her cellphone buzzed.

'Yes?'

'He's on the move, headed for downtown. I'll pick you up in five minutes. Be outside.'

Patrick was at the entrance by the time she had worked her way downstairs. He looked at the kitbag in her hand and said nothing.

'Ng is with him, and the woman,' he said as they left the hotel.

'The woman is good,' Ava said.

They parked half a block from the restaurant and slumped down in the red Toyota truck. They didn't have to wait long. The Land Rover rumbled into the street and Ng parked it directly in front of the restaurant and jumped out. Seto took a bit longer and then stood by the back door, holding his hand out for the woman as she descended.

'How can they eat here every night?' Patrick asked.

'It's a Hong Kong thing,' she said. 'People there have incredibly small apartments, and getting outside is part of daily life. The fact that they also love to eat gives them the perfect excuse. There must be more restaurants per capita in Hong Kong than any other place on earth. And when they find a restaurant they like, they keep going to it.'

'I should try this place sometime,' he said.

'There will be two menus: one for Chinese, the other for ... well, for non-Chinese.'

'In that case I'll pass.' Patrick looked around. 'We can get out of the truck now if you want; they can't see us from inside. There's a roti shop over there that isn't bad. From the window we have a good view of the restaurant.'

As they were about to get out of the truck a black Nissan sedan pulled alongside. The tinted window on the passenger's side slid down slowly and a black man with grey hair eased his head out towards them.

'Park near Eckie's,' Patrick said to him. 'They should be about an hour in the restaurant. Wait until Seto goes into the club before making a move on Ng. There's a woman with them. If she goes into the club we'll look after her. If she doesn't, you'll have to get her. Separate her from Ng. We'll need her with us.'

The man nodded and rolled the window back up.

'They're a good team – experienced,' he said to her as the Nissan left to position itself near Eckie's. 'The Captain has given you some quality.'

For what I'm paying, I should hope so, she thought.

The roti shack had three tables, all of them empty. They sat by the window, keeping the China World entrance in their line of sight. He ordered chicken curry and roti. She asked for plain fried rice and a ginger beer.

'Tell me,' Ava said, 'how does a man like Captain Robbins get into a position of such power in a country like this?'

'Do you mean how does a white man get into a position of such power in a country where ninety-five percent of the population is either black or Indian?'

'Yes, that's precisely what I mean.'

Patrick bit his lower lip. It was a question he could answer if he chose; he just had to decide whether he wanted to or not.

'The Captain was a policeman in Barbados. He came here as part of a Caribbean exchange programme. That's one thing people don't understand about Guyana. Geographically it's in South America and we've got Venezuela and Brazil as neighbours, but culturally, socially, linguistically, we're part of the Caribbean. I mean, there are always Guyanese on the West Indies cricket team.

'At that time the Brits had already left, the blacks and East Indians were jockeying for power, transferring their hatred for the Brits to one another, and the Americans were sticking their noses – and putting their money – into the politics here. It was quite a mess. The Americans were looking for someone neutral, someone they could trust to be a pipeline for straight information, someone who could act as an honest broker between the blacks and Indians. There weren't many candidates. According to the Captain, he was about it. That's how it started.'

'But to make it last as long as he has ...'

'He did that himself. He didn't need the Americans to support him. You have to understand, he's about the only person in Guyana whom all the groups can support – because he's neutral, because colour doesn't matter to him. They trust him.'

'And fear him?'

He ignored her question. 'Those politicians – black and brown – they like to hear themselves talk. The Captain is always the quietest person in the room. He tells me, "Patrick, listen, just listen. You'll be surprised how much you can learn." Then there are the generals in our so-called army and the inspector general of the police, all of them with titles and uniforms and medals. You saw how the Captain dresses: blue jeans and plain shirts. That's his way. He doesn't need to play dress-up, he doesn't need to impress anyone. He's been in charge for more than twenty years; he doesn't need a fancy title. But you know, when he walks into a room with all those generals wearing all their medals, they're the ones who stand at attention. And they stay that way until he sits. I'm biased, I know that. He's like family to me. But I'm man enough to recognize a bigger man.'

'I was told that he knows everyone's secrets, that he knows where all the bodies are buried, that the politicians are completely beholden to him,' said Ava.

'Would you expect anything less?' Patrick said. 'The politicians are window dressing, no more than that. The Captain keeps them on a leash. I don't ask how he does it; no one in Guyana does. We're just happy that he's here, keeping them under control. If it means he has to put a bit of fear into them, we're the better off for it.'

'I wasn't being critical, just curious,' she said.

Their food arrived. She picked at the rice. Patrick ate his chicken, dabbing the roti into the curry. When it was gone, he ordered another. 'One more thing about the Captain,' he said between bites, 'is that he is really smart. I don't mean book-smart – though he is that too – I mean people-smart. He can figure out anyone in ten minutes.'

'What did he say about me?' she prodded.

'That you aren't what you appear to be, but by the time most people figure that out it's too late for them.'

She shifted her attention from the plate to look at Patrick. His eyes were locked on the front entrance of China World. She didn't ask any more questions.

26

It had been dark when they'd arrived, their side of the town being designated powerless for the evening. However, most of the stores and restaurants on the block were lit up. Ava could only imagine what it would be like walking the side streets on a moonless night. No wonder the crime rate was through the roof.

The name CHINA WORLD flickered in the window of the restaurant. The Chinese characters below the English lettering translated as 'heavenly food'. She couldn't remember ever seeing a Chinese restaurant whose English and Chinese names meant the same thing. Before she could file that thought away, she saw Seto framed in the window. He was talking to a short Chinese man in an apron.

'I think he's about to leave,' she said.

Patrick called a number from his cellphone. 'Wake up, boys,' he said.

'See the small guy in the apron?' he said to Ava. 'He's one of our leading drug dealers; does most of the imports. He's also a friend of a friend. Until now it didn't occur to me that he might be involved with Seto and Ng. After all this is over I'll have to ask.'

The trio exited the restaurant and climbed back into the Land Rover. Ava held her breath.

They followed the car as it lumbered two blocks and parked at Eckie's. Seto and the woman climbed down. Ava saw him say something to Ng, who was still in the Land Rover. The black Nissan was four spots farther along.

Patrick used his cellphone again. 'Give them about ten minutes inside and then get Ng,' he said. He reached over and opened the glove compartment. Ava saw a semi-automatic in an shoulder holster and several pairs of handcuffs. 'We'll need two sets, I imagine,' he said as he put on the holster.

'I want to tape their eyes and his mouth before we get them in the truck,' she said.

'Just his?'

'Someone has to tell us the entry codes for the gate, and I'm sure the house is protected as well.'

He nodded. 'There's an alleyway behind the club with an exit leading to it. I'll park the truck there. There's no point in drawing more attention to ourselves than necessary.'

They sat with their eyes fixed on the Nissan. At exactly the ten-minute mark the doors opened and two very large men, one the man with grey hair, emerged. They wore black jeans and black T-shirts. Ava glanced sideways at Patrick – he was dressed the same way. Two nights before, both he and Robert had been in black. *They're cops*, she thought.

She watched as the one with grey hair tapped on the driver's-side window of the Land Rover. It rolled down. The cop flashed some ID and motioned for Ng to step out.

Ng didn't move. She saw the cop's neck muscles stiffen as he stepped back. He screamed, 'Fuck you, you Asian piece of shit,' as he raised a boot and kicked the car door.

Ng stuck his head out the window and said something. The cop pulled his gun and aimed at him. The door swung open and Ng jumped to the ground. Again she could see him talking, and she could imagine what he was saying. She was sure the word *friend* was being dropped.

The Captain's men outweighed Ng by at least a hundred pounds each, and when one of them grabbed him by the collar and ran him towards the club's wall, he hit it with a thud. In the light cast by the flashing Eckie's sign, she could see blood on Ng's forehead and under his nose. She tried to muster some sympathy for him but came up short.

The cop yanked Ng's arms behind his back, handcuffed him, then jerked him backwards, making him fall onto the sidewalk. Then he grabbed him by the hair and hauled him to his feet. Ng's head was turned towards the Toyota. All Ava could see in his face was confusion and fear.

'Are you ready to go?' Patrick said.

'Drive.'

He cut down a side street and into the alley. On what looked like a fire door someone had crudely painted ECKIE'S. 'Our exit,' Patrick said.

They got out of the truck and walked back to the front door. Ava felt a rush of adrenalin.

The club was badly lit, but she could make out a circular dance floor surrounded by booths. There was also a bar, two sets of curtains, and an exit. What little light there was, was trained on the dance floor. At best the booths were in semi-darkness.

'I can't see a thing,' Ava said.

'There they are,' Patrick said, heading towards the booth closest to the bar. She trailed behind him, almost unconsciously trying to stay invisible.

Seto didn't notice them. He was kissing Anna Choudray, his hand stuck down her blouse, fondling her right breast; the nipple was half exposed. Patrick paused and Ava wondered if he was enjoying the sex.

'Seto,' Patrick shouted, holding a badge in midair. 'I need you and the woman to come with me.'

Ava noted that this was voiced as a demand, not a question, and she knew that her hundred-thousand-dollar investment had been well spent.

'What the fuck?'

'Just get up,' Patrick said.

'Or what?'

She could see Seto clearly now. He wore a black suit with a crisp white shirt. She figured he couldn't weigh more than a hundred and thirty pounds. His eyes skittered left and right as if he was trying to figure out if this was a joke. 'Don't you know who I am?' he yelled.

'I know exactly who you are,' Patrick said. 'Now you and the woman get up or I'll come in there and help you.'

'Fuck you,' Seto said.

Patrick reared back and punched Anna on the side of the head, catching her on the ear and driving her into the back of the booth with an audible thump.

'*Fuccccckkkk!*' Seto screamed. 'Don't you know who I am? Talk to General Swandas, for fuck's sake. I'm with him. Call him. *Call him.*'

'This has gone several levels above the general,' Patrick said. 'Now for the last time, get your skinny ass out of there and bring the woman with you.'

Seto looked at the gun Patrick was now holding in his girlfriend's face. 'You wouldn't—'

'You have five seconds.'

Seto slid sideways, bringing her with him.

'Turn around,' Patrick said.

Seto pulled the woman to her feet. She held her hand over her ear, tears flowing down her cheeks. Patrick handcuffed him first. When he put the cuffs on Anna, he had to wrench her hand away from her head. 'Sorry to do this, but if your asshole boyfriend was more cooperative this would not have been necessary.'

'This is a mistake,' Seto insisted. 'Call the general.'

'Here, you call him,' Patrick said, holding out his phone to Seto. 'If he answers and agrees to help you, I'll shoot both you and the woman right here.'

Seto's face collapsed, his confidence gone, the fear visible in eyes that darted around the club looking for help – which wasn't coming. 'What do you want?' he said.

'In time, in good time,' Patrick said. 'First we have to get you out of here.'

He led them to the fire door. Ava couldn't help noticing that every eye in the club was focused somewhere else. It was as if they didn't exist.

She had her kitbag in her hand. 'Put them against the wall,' she said to Patrick when they were outside. She took out a roll of duct tape and wrapped it around their eyes. 'Turn him around now,' she said. She tore off a small strip and sealed his mouth. 'Okay, let's go.'

Ava and Patrick helped them get into the back seat. Anna pressed herself against the window as if she were trying to get as far away from Seto as possible. She was sobbing so hard she was having difficulty catching her breath.

Ava reached back, grabbed the woman's knee, and squeezed until she had her attention. 'Listen to me. When we get to the house, you're going to tell us the entry code and whatever information we need to get in the front door. I'm telling you this now so you have time to think about it and be prepared when I ask. I don't want to ask twice.'

Anna didn't reply.

Ava squeezed harder. 'I need you to say yes.'

'Y-yes.'

To Ava the drive to the house seemed to take forever; she could only imagine how long it felt for Seto and the woman. Neither she nor Patrick spoke. They both knew how intimidating silence could be.

When they pulled up to the gate, Ava asked, 'Anna, is there anyone in the house?'

'No.'

'Good. Now tell me the code.'

'Eighty-eight, eighty-eight, eight.'

'How Chinese,' Ava said.

'What do you mean?' Patrick asked.

'Superstition. The number eight in Chinese is pronounced *ba*, and that sounds like the word for wealth. Two figure eights resemble the way 'double joy' is written. Having an eight in your address, on your licence plate, or in your phone number is thought to bring good luck, and the more eights the better. Except, of course, for Seto in this instance,' Ava said as she punched in the numbers.

The gate swung open. Patrick parked the Toyota next to the Mercedes. 'The house code?' Ava asked.

'The same as the gate,' Anna said.

They walked to the front door. Ava held the woman by the elbow and Patrick had a firm grip on the back of Seto's suit jacket. The walkway was uneven, making the blindfolded pair stumble; Ava held her charge steady and Patrick yanked Seto straight.

The house was remarkable in at least one way: when they entered, Ava saw a staircase directly in front of her, running straight from the door to the second floor. For anyone Chinese it was an unthinkable design. It would take only a minimal understanding of feng shui to know that it would bring the worst possible luck to the owners of the house. She figured that Seto, or most probably the woman, had bought the house as is.

To the left of the unlucky staircase was a dining room furnished with six chairs and a naked table. No sideboard, no plants, no pictures. It looked as if the room had never been used. The rectangular room on the right was about forty square metres in area, and all it contained was a cheap-looking leather couch, two beanbag chairs, and a large LCD television.

Ava walked towards the kitchen at the back of the house, pushing Anna in front of her. The room held a glass table with three napkins on it and a bowl of fruit, plus a counter large enough for a double sink and a prep area on either side. There was a cutting board and a set of knives in one prep area and the other had a substantial spice rack and jars of flour, sugar, and cereal.

'Bring Seto back here,' she shouted to Patrick.

Seto scuffled into the kitchen. The house was air-conditioned but there were beads of sweat on his forehead. 'Take off his jacket,' she said.

Patrick undid the handcuffs, removed the jacket, and then put the cuffs back on, adding a hard tug on Seto's arms for good measure.

Ava set Seto on a chair, lifted his hands over the chair back, and pulled them down behind. She then knelt down and grabbed his ankles. She spread them until they were aligned with the chair legs and taped his ankles to them.

'Pass me the jacket,' she said to Patrick. She quickly went through the pockets, extracting a wallet.

'Now, where is his computer?'

'Upstairs,' the woman said.

'Let's go,' Ava said. 'Patrick, stay with Seto.'

There were four rooms on the second floor. Two were being used as bedrooms, one was empty, and the fourth was a makeshift office. Ava took Anna into the master bedroom, which was furnished with a king-size four-poster bed made of heavy mahogany and matching massive wooden dressers; one wall was entirely mirrored.

The bed was littered with decorative pillows. Ava pushed them onto the floor and then told Anna to climb onto the bed.

Then Ava taped her ankles together and taped her mouth. 'Now stay here. Don't move,' she said.

Ava walked into the office and sat at Seto's desk. It had two drawers on each side and a laptop computer on top. Ava turned on the computer, and while it was booting up she went through the drawers. They were mostly empty, except for one, in which there was a copy of a plane ticket and two cancelled boarding passes. Seto had come to Georgetown from Port of Spain via Miami. There were also two passports. One was American, in the name of Jackson Seto, and the other Chinese, in the name of Seto Sun Kai.

She opened his wallet. There were four credit cards, all in the name of Jackson Seto, and a Washington state driver's licence in the same name with the address she had visited in Seattle. He also had a Hong Kong ID card under the name Seto Sun Kai.

The computer flickered to life and asked her for a password. That could wait; she turned her attention to the rest of the room. The only things that interested her were six cardboard filing boxes pushed up against a wall.

When she opened the first box, she could see that Seto was neat and organized. Everything was filed alphabetically, and when she looked in the Barrett's Bank folder, the paperwork was ordered by date. She took the folder over to the desk and quickly scanned the documents from the oldest – a copy of the signature card from when he had opened his account – to the newest, which included a recent online bank statement. She had her notebook in her kitbag, and the account number on the statement matched the one she had written down.

The account was in the name of S&A Investments. There was only one authorized signature: Seto's. She checked the dates. The account had been open for more than ten years but had been almost inactive until three years ago, when deposit activity picked up. The wire transfers of Tam's money were the largest deposits by far, but Seto had been squirreling other funds away all along, mainly in the range of ten to twenty thousand dollars. Some much larger deposits had been made over the past year; she assumed that was the money Seafood Partners had been scamming from the Indian and Indonesian fish guys.

The two Tam wire transfers brought the account total to more than seven million American dollars. It was the kind of surprise Ava enjoyed.

She went downstairs to join the boys. Patrick sat quietly on the kitchen counter, jiggling his legs to some music in his head. 'Did you find what you were looking for?' he asked.

She put Seto's passports, his Hong Kong ID card, and the Barrett's file on the kitchen table. 'I didn't do badly.' She moved closer to Patrick. 'I'm going to speak to him in Cantonese,' she said.

Seto was slumped in the chair, his chin almost on his chest. She reached for the tape on his mouth and ripped it off. He yelled in pain.

'Seto Sun Kai, what made you think we would not come after you? And what made you think we would not find you?'

He shook his head as if he was confused, then licked his lower lip. She wondered if it had sunk in that she had used his Chinese name.

'Why would you or anyone else come after me? I haven't done anything.' His voice was hoarse, his mouth dry from stress.

Ava took a glass from the cupboard and filled it from the tap. The water was a lighter colour than the hotel's. *Must be the neighbourhood*, she thought.

'Here, drink,' she said, holding the glass to his lips.

He hesitated.

'It's your own fucking tap water,' she snapped.

He took a careful sip. 'Where is Ng?' he asked.

'Gone and not coming back.'

'I don't believe you.'

'Believe this: you don't have friends here any more. No one is going to come to your aid. This is strictly between us now, and how it goes and how it ends is your choice.'

'Who sent you?'

'I work for people who are friends of Andrew Tam. You remember Andrew Tam?'

'Where are you from?'

'Hong Kong.'

He became still. She knew he was now fully aware of his situation. She knew he would be thinking about how to extract himself from it. She knew that when he finished examining his options, he would be left with the one she wanted him to choose. But she also knew it wouldn't stop him from trying other ways out.

'We did business, just business, Andrew and me. There were some problems with customers and I had to step in and salvage what I could, for all our sakes.'

'So you're telling me you were looking after Andrew's best interests.'

'We had inventory that was shit. I had it reworked and repacked, that's all. It couldn't have been sold any other way.'

'And you discussed this with Andrew?'

'There wasn't time. And besides, he was just the money man. What did he know about the actual business?'

'Not enough, I guess,' she said. 'This product, did you sell it all?'

'I did.'

'Did you get paid?'

He paused. She could almost see his mind whirring away, calculating just how big a lie he could safely tell. 'For most of it,' he said.

'How much did you get paid?'

His head rolled back as if she were holding a knife to his throat. 'About three million,' he said, squeezing the words out.

'When did you plan to send it back to Andrew Tam?'

'When things settled. I haven't had time; we just got paid.'

'But you do plan to send it back to Andrew?'

'Of course, of course.'

'Seto Sun Kai,' Ava said gently, 'you are a thief and a liar.'

She reached into her kitbag and removed the stiletto, flicked it open, and pressed its point into his thigh. It pierced his trousers and then his skin. It was a prick, not much more. Still, he jumped, startled. His leg twitched. 'Don't,' he said.

She moved the knife up his leg and stuck the point into his genitals. He flinched and strained to move back.

The knife tracked up his chest and onto his face. Ava

rested the tip in the soft flesh just above his eye. Sweat from his brow trickled down his nose and both sides of his face. She was about to say something about the knife but realized it wasn't necessary. Seto understood well enough without the theatrics.

'Seto Sun Kai,' she said calmly, 'let me tell you what I know and then let me tell you what I need to know. I know why you had a problem with the shrimp. I know the games you and George Antonelli played with it. I know how the shrimp were moved, who repackaged them, and where they were sold. I know how much you got for them. I know about the little bank in Texas where the money was sent. I know that the little bank wired the money to an account in the British Virgin Islands. I have copies of the transfers, so I know to which bank they were sent and I know the account in which they were deposited. I know you are the sole signing authority on that account. Now, there are two things I don't know. Do you want to guess?'

He shook his head, sweat dripping onto her hand and the knife.

'I don't know the password to your computer upstairs, and I don't know the password for your BVI bank account.'

Seto grimaced and said nothing.

She waited. A minute passed, maybe more.

'Seto Sun Kai, I'm waiting.'

'It isn't that easy,' he said.

She felt her first flush of irritation. 'I really don't want to hurt you, or the woman upstairs,' she said, increasing the pressure on the knife tip.

'The password for the computer is "waterrat",' he said in a rush.

'Your zodiac sign?' she asked.

'Yes.'

'And for the bank account?'

'Eighty-eight, sixty-six, eighty-eight, sixty-six.'

'Thank you.'

'It won't do you any good,' he said.

She noticed that he was beginning to sweat again and his voice had tightened. This wasn't where she had thought they were going. 'And why not?'

'There's a limit to the amount of money I can take out of the account electronically.'

'You can access the account through the Internet, yes?'

'Yes.'

'You can transfer money out of the account, yes?'

'Yes, but like I said, it's restricted.'

'What do you mean?'

'I can only withdraw up to $25,000 per day.'

She saw his left foot begin to shake. He was scared, and she began to think he might be telling her the truth. 'I don't believe you.'

'That's how we set it up. We never had that much in the account until last year, so it was never a problem.'

Ava picked up the Barrett's file from the kitchen table. She leafed through it, taking out the monthly statements and the attachments, and read them more closely than she had upstairs. Patrick watched her, confused about what had just transpired.

After ten minutes she said, 'There was a withdrawal eighteen months ago of $335,000, and then another ten months ago of $200,000, and then a third just three months ago of another $400,000.'

'How many are there for $25,000 or less?' he said.

'Admittedly, a hell of a lot more.'

'Anything under $25,000 I did electronically. I was sending money to George's accounts in Atlanta and Bangkok and to my account in Seattle. Those other three withdrawals I did in person.'

'What do you mean?'

'I went to the BVI. I went to the bank. I presented a written request for a certified cheque along with my American passport and one other form of photo ID, usually my driver's licence. They drew up a release form and I signed it. They photocopied my passport and driver's licence and dated the copies, and I signed those too. Then they gave me the cheque.'

'Who does that any more?' she said.

'The account was opened before internet banking took off,' he said. 'And Barrett's is a conservative bank. They're paranoid about money laundering and gave me a hard enough time just opening an account.'

'What if you dropped dead?'

'George has the power of attorney, and that is recorded at the bank. He would need to show up and go through the same shit I did.'

'Can't you request a change in the amounts?'

'Only by doing it in person.'

Seto was telling her the truth. She knew he was – there was

234

no reason for him to lie. But that didn't help quell her anger: anger about making too many assumptions, about thinking the deal was closed, about having dared google Tommy Ordonez. She had jinxed herself. She had broken one of her own rules and now she was paying for it. The only mistake she hadn't made was to tell Andrew Tam his money was on the way.

'Patrick, look after him for me,' she said abruptly. 'I have to go upstairs for a minute.'

He looked at her questioningly but she was already halfway out of the kitchen.

She went upstairs and checked in on Anna on her way to Seto's office. She was curled on the bed, crying softly to herself. Ava closed the bedroom door so she wouldn't have to listen.

The computer was still on. Ava typed WATERRAT and the screen opened up. Then she tried to access the internet and was told it wasn't currently available. She waited. On the fourth attempt she finally got online.

She went to the Barrett's Bank's home page and clicked on ACCOUNTS. She input the account number and then the password. The S&A bank account came to life. She checked the balance: $7,237,188.22. There was a list of options for her to pursue, and one of them was WIRE TRANSFER. She clicked on recipient details. She was going to type in Andrew Tam's bank information until she realized she had left her notebook downstairs, so she typed in her own bank data. Under AMOUNT TO BE SENT she requested $50,000. Then she hit the send button. The request was immediately flagged.

Ava appeared calm and focused when she walked back into the kitchen.

'What the hell happened?' Patrick asked.

'I have a problem,' she said.

'I guessed.'

'I need to think about it for a while.'

'I have good ears if you want to talk it through.'

She was about to dismiss the idea when she realized that she was going to need help no matter what she decided to do, so she might as well bring him on side sooner rather than later. 'Let's go into the living room,' she said.

They sat side by side on the leather couch, which smelled of cigarette smoke, and she told Patrick about her problem. The only thing she didn't – and wouldn't – tell him was the total amount of money involved.

'It sounds to me like you're going to have to take him to the BVI if you want to get that money back,' he said. 'Or spend the next few months transferring $25,000 a day, though I can't even begin to imagine the things that could go wrong with that idea.'

'It has to be done quickly or chances are it won't get done. Is there any other choice?'

'What do you think?'

'I think I'm screwed,' she said.

'How's that?'

'As I said, the quicker you move, the better your chances are to succeed. In my business you strike when guys like Seto are vulnerable, scared, and within your control. The longer the process takes, the more they begin to think they can find a way out. But how do I get him to the BVI without getting their Customs or police involved? All he has to do is open his mouth and scream bloody murder. And believe me, it will occur to him – if I can get him there. He'll talk himself into thinking he can get away with this. He'll figure if he can lose me, he has enough money to hide somewhere we can't find him. We always do find them in the end, but the problem is that the money is often gone by then.'

'And if you can get him there, how do you deal with the bank?'

'There's no point worrying about the bank unless I can get him to the BVI.'

'You need to talk to the Captain,' Patrick said.

'What can the Captain do?'

'I'm going to call him,' he said. 'Don't go anywhere.'

She sat in the kitchen while she waited for Patrick to return. Seto kept rotating his head as if he had a stiff neck. She felt like snapping the fucking thing.

The front door opened and Patrick stepped back inside. 'I have to go meet with the Captain. I'll be back in a while.'

27

Patrick didn't come back until after ten o'clock. Ava hated the thought of the two men discussing her business without her. The longer he was gone the more irritated she became, and by the time the door opened again she was really angry. Patrick walked in with the two men from outside Eckie's, the cops who had taken Ng.

'You and I are going to see the Captain,' he said. 'The boys will look after things here until we get back.' He saw the look on her face and said, 'I tried to call. Your cellphone was off.'

She realized he was right about the phone, and bit back an irritable remark. Then she picked up the Barrett's file and forced it into her kitbag. She wasn't leaving anything behind for them to look through.

'What did he say?' she asked as she climbed into the Toyota truck.

'Who?'

'For God's sake, Patrick, you know who.'

'He said he wanted to see you, that's all. I explained the difficulty and he said he wanted to see you. Nothing more than that.'

'So this could be for nothing?'

'I can't say for sure, but normally the Captain doesn't waste his time on nothing.'

She felt a twinge of hope. 'Where are we going?'

'The doughnut shop. It's close by.'

The entire area was in utter darkness except for the odd flicker of a candle or flare from a flashlight. The shop, though, was lit up like Times Square. The massive figure of the Captain filled its window, a plate of doughnuts in front of him.

'I'll wait here,' Patrick said as he parked the truck.

The Captain gave her a little wave when she walked in. 'I ordered you coffee,' he said, pointing to a cup. 'Patrick said you liked it.'

In the bright light he looked even whiter than she remembered. And in the small confines of the shop he looked even larger, a mountain of a man, and she was again taken aback by how startlingly blue his eyes were. If she had been meeting him for the first time, the impression would have been overwhelming.

She steadied herself and sat down. 'We have to stop meeting like this,' she said.

His eyes twinkled, amused maybe, curious certainly, involved most definitely. 'We have a problem, I hear.'

She noticed his use of *we*. This was, at the very least, going to cost her money. 'We do,' she said.

'Unfortunate.'

'For no one more than me.'

'Seto was either rather clever or rather stupid. Patrick wasn't sure which because he said you spoke to him in Chinese.'

'It was necessary for him to understand that I had been sent from Hong Kong.'

'And all that entails, implied or otherwise.'

'Implied.'

'But still effective.'

'Normally.'

'So you got what you wanted except for a minor twist?'

'If you want to call it minor.'

The Captain bit into a chocolate-coated doughnut. 'I eat these every day and then rush home to take my cholesterol medication,' he said.

'Do you have a way to resolve this minor twist?'

'Yes, I probably do. But as I said to Patrick, what's the point of exerting all that effort – and spending all that money – getting you and Seto there if the bank won't cooperate?'

'I'll handle the bank.'

'You sound so confident.'

'Just get me and Seto there and I'll find a way to handle the bank.'

'You will find a way or you have a way? The difference is not inconsequential. I mean, you're asking to us spend a considerable amount of capital – both financial and personal – assisting you to get to the British Virgin Islands. What if you fail? How do we get compensated?'

'How much do you want?' she asked.

'No, no, no,' he said, looking offended by the question. 'You're going about this in entirely the wrong way. This is not just about money. This is about making use of friends and contacts whom I don't want to embarrass if things go awry. Friends and contacts whom I don't want subjected to questions from their lords and masters. Friends and contacts I still want to have five years from now.'

'So this isn't about money?'

'I said this is not *just* about money.'

'What do you want from me?' she asked.

'A plan. I want you to give me a plan for extracting the money from the bank. If I think the plan can work, then we can move on to the other details.'

It was, she thought, not an unreasonable request. It was even, she thought, a perfectly sensible request. He could have demanded more money, found a way to shuffle her and Seto to the BVI or somewhere close by, and then washed his hands of them both as he pocketed the funds. The only problem was that he was now becoming a partner, and the cost of business had just skyrocketed. It was a good thing Seto had that extra two million in his account.

'I'll have something by tomorrow,' she said, having no idea how.

'Good. Tell Patrick when you're ready to chat and I'll make myself available.' He waved his arm at the shop. 'We meet here more often than not – we own it. There's a camera overhead and microphones dotted about here and there. I like to bring my political friends here. They think I'm slumming,' he said smoothly.

Ava wasn't sure she believed him. If it was true and he thought sharing that confidence with her would earn trust, he was going to be disappointed. In her eyes the Captain was now more dangerous.

'I'd like to go back to the hotel; I don't need the distractions at the house. Can you leave your men there overnight?'

'Consider it done.'

28

Ava bought a bottle of white wine at the hotel bar and carried it in an ice bucket to her room. The air conditioning had been turned off again. She swore as she restarted it. Then she poured herself a glass and settled into the rattan chair. 'Time to think,' she said to herself.

It took her an hour to create a scenario that just might work. She called Patrick. 'Where are you?'

'At Seto's house.'

'Could you come and get me?'

Ava was quiet in the truck. She could tell that Patrick was anxious to ask her questions. But there was nothing to be said until she had a firmer grasp on the plan, and when she did it would be the Captain she would speak to first.

Seto was sitting in the kitchen, still handcuffed and taped to the chair. She thought he was sleeping until he raised his head at the sound of feet crossing the tiled floor. She touched him on the arm and said in Cantonese, 'I need your email password.'

'Waterrat.'

The man has no imagination, she thought. She had the Barrett's Bank file in her hand. She opened it and looked at some of the most recent correspondence. Several names and email addresses were involved.

'Who is your primary contact at Barrett's?'

'Jeremy Bates.'

'Is he the manager?'

'Yeah. It's a small staff. Jeremy handles most of the clients.'

She climbed the stairs to his office. One of the cops sat on the floor outside the master bedroom. 'Everything okay?' she asked.

'The woman started wailing a while ago. I had to shut her up.'

Ava didn't ask how.

The computer was still online. She accessed Seto's email account and brought up his address book. There was a Jeremy Bates listed. She checked it against the email address she had in the Barrett's file. They matched. She then hit MESSAGES SENT, typed in BATES, and requested a search. There were close to twenty emails that had gone back and forth. She took notice of Seto's style. His tone was more formal than she had thought it would be. Also more candid – Seto hadn't been reluctant to discuss his financial affairs.

She began composing an email to Jeremy Bates.

Hi, Mr Bates,

I'm coming to Road Town on February 26 or 27. I will be making a wire transfer to Hong Kong in the amount of $7,000,000. I would appreciate it if you could have the paperwork organized for me.

I will be bringing a Ms Ava Lee with me to the office. She is the accountant for the firm in Hong Kong that we are doing business with. Ms Lee is there to confirm the wire transfer in the amount specified. You have my permission to share any and all information regarding the S&A account with her.

Once our travel arrangements have been confirmed I will contact you to set a date and time for us to meet at your office.

Yours sincerely,
Jackson Seto.

She clicked the SAVE DRAFT icon.

It was lunchtime in Hong Kong. She phoned Uncle. 'I'm still in Guyana and I'm still working on getting this project finished,' she said quickly. 'It's going to be two days more, maybe three, maybe four. I'm getting there, but progress is slower than expected.'

'Any specific reason for the delay?'

'I have to go to the BVI.'

She could almost feel his grip tightening on the phone. 'That wasn't the plan,' he said.

'The plan had to be changed. The outcome will be the same.'

'Are you going alone?'

'No,' she said. 'Seto is coming with me, and I'm going to bring Derek down to help.'

'Is it that complicated?'

'I just need an extra pair of capable hands,' she said. Uncle would be even more nervous now, knowing she had to bring Derek Liang into the picture. He had worked with her on five

244

other occasions, and every one of them had been problematic or worse.

'If you think it is necessary,' he said quietly, after a pause.

At the very outset of their relationship, Ava had been present at a meeting between Uncle and a Macau businessman who wanted to hire them. Despite his need for their assistance, he played his cards close to his chest, giving them the absolute minimum amount of information. Uncle had grown impatient with the man's vagueness and began asking questions that became more and more pointed. Finally the man threw up his hands and said, 'Believe me, you have enough information. Trust me, trust me – you have everything you need.'

Uncle had refused the assignment. As they rode the hydrofoil back to Hong Kong he said to Ava, 'Whenever someone says, "Believe me," or "Trust me," and can't give you a reason to do so that you can wrap your arms around, run the other way. For me they are the most dangerous words anyone can utter; they are the refuge of the weak.'

In all the years since, those words had never crossed her lips. The day she had to ask for his trust would be the day she was no longer working with him. And she liked to believe that the same was true in reverse. Even if Uncle was full of reservations, he would never express them. His confidence in her was complete, and even if things went horribly bad – which they sometimes did – he never second-guessed her.

'Yes, I do think it is necessary.'

'Is there anything else?'

'Do you remember the time I used Fong Accounting as a cover?'

'Yes.'

'I need to do it again.'

'Do you still have the business card?'

'I do.'

'What are the circumstances?'

'When I get to the BVI, I'll be calling on Seto's bank, Barrett's, and I'm going as an accountant. The bank may call Fong to confirm my identity. It's a long shot that they will, but it's better to play it safe.'

'What name is on the card?'

'Ava Lee.'

'Okay, I'll talk to Mr Fong and we'll set it up. Is there anything you'd like the office to tell any callers?'

'I'm travelling in the Caribbean – on business, mind you. And you could tell them to offer to provide my cellphone number if the caller wants to reach me.'

'Is that all?'

'No. We'll need to send more money to our friends in Guyana.'

He didn't react right away. She could only imagine the questions that were raging through his head. They were already out of pocket more than $100,000 and now she was asking him to send more. Bringing Derek in would cost at least $10,000. If she didn't collect from Seto, how big a loss would they be looking at?

She cut him off before he could speak. 'Uncle, I've found more money than Tam is owed – a lot more. We'll get our full commission plus a bonus on top of that.'

'What is the amount we need to send?'

'I don't know; I'm still negotiating,' she said. 'All I know is that Tam's money isn't going to be recovered anytime soon unless we make the investment.'

'When will you know?'

'Tomorrow. No later than tomorrow.'

'I'll expect your call,' he said.

'Uncle, I'm sorry about this. I know you're anxious to get started with Tommy Ordonez.'

'He'll have to wait. You look after yourself. You be careful.'

Ava next dialled Derek Liang's cellphone number. She didn't reach him until the third attempt. When she did, she could hardly hear him speak over the music that was booming in the background. He was a karaoke junkie and fancied himself as Jackie Cheung, Hong Kong's biggest Cantonese pop star. She yelled at him to go outside.

She had known Derek for six years. They had been introduced by their bak mei instructor, who thought that his only two students should get acquainted. Derek joked that their teacher had visions of them mating and producing the ultimate fighting machine. Even if her sexuality wouldn't get in the way of that happening, Derek would be close to her last choice as a partner. He was the only son of a wealthy Shanghai trader and had been sent to Toronto to get a university education. He had dropped out during his second year and devoted himself to martial arts, customized sports cars, karaoke, and women. She didn't think she had seen him twice with either the same woman or the same car.

But Derek was smart and he was tough – very tough. Over six feet tall, lean and chiselled, well-spoken in English and three Chinese dialects, and a tasteful, conservative dresser when he chose, he made a hell of an impression. He and Ava had posed as a couple several times. Hand in hand, they drew stares everywhere they went. Now they were about to do it again.

'I need you to go to the British Virgin Islands,' she told him.

'When?'

'Tomorrow, if possible.'

'I'll be meeting you there?'

'Yes, but I'm not sure when I'll arrive. Could be a day or two later.'

'I'm sure I can find something to amuse me.'

'We'll need a suite – a big one, as big as you can get. Someone else will be travelling with us. Can you look after getting the suite?'

'Of course.'

'Email me when you've made the arrangements.'

Ava paid Derek two thousand dollars a day plus expenses. The first time they worked together he had tried to refuse the money. He said he didn't need it, which was true enough. Ava had ranted at him in Cantonese, which is close to the perfect language for hurling abuse, with its harsh consonants and piercing tone. He took the money and never questioned the arrangement again. For her it was strictly business. If he worked for no money, she would be indebted to him. If she paid, he was indebted to her.

She opened the email she had drafted to Jeremy Bates and read it over. Ava decided it didn't sound authentic and tried again.

Dear Mr Bates,

I am arriving in the BVI in the next day or two. I am bringing
with me a Ms Ava Lee, who I am introducing to you via this
email. She is the accountant for a firm in Hong Kong that
we are going to partner with. I am going to be doing a wire
transfer in the amount of $7,000,000 to the firm. Ms Lee
will be with me to confirm the transaction, and I would
appreciate it if the bank would treat her as my associate.
She has complete access to all of our banking records,
and by way of this correspondence I am authorizing the
bank to provide her with any and all additional information
she needs. As soon as our travel arrangements are
finalized, I will contact you to set up a time for us to come
to your offices.

Sincerely,
Jackson Seto

That's better, she thought, and hit SEND.

It was almost midnight. Ava wasn't tired, so she headed downstairs to find Patrick. He was on the couch, watching television.

'Could you call the Captain for me, please?' she asked.

'Now?' he said, looking at his watch, a Panerai that would
have cost about five thousand dollars if it were real.

'Yes, tell him I'm ready to chat. I don't want to wait until
morning.'

'I'm not sure this is a good idea.'

'Give me his number and I'll call him myself.'

Patrick lifted himself off the couch with a grunt. 'Wait here,' he said.

He went outside to phone the Captain. She wondered what they could be discussing that they didn't want her to hear. He was back inside in less than a minute, holding out the phone to her. 'He wants to talk to you.'

She took the phone. 'Hello.'

'Go somewhere we can speak in private,' the Captain said.

Ava climbed the stairs to Seto's office, closing the door behind her. 'I'm alone,' she said.

'I didn't expect to hear from you quite so quickly.'

'It's mid-morning in Hong Kong. If we're going to wire more money it could be done in the next few hours. Why waste an entire day?'

'So you have concocted a plan?'

'I know how to get back what is owed.'

'You are a clever girl.'

She assumed he was being sarcastic. 'It can be done, and with no fuss.'

'Would you like to share it?'

'I have to manage Seto; I have to keep him on ice,' she began, and then outlined her plan. 'If this works – and I don't know why it wouldn't – it will come down to my ability to convince the bank manager to release the funds. And I think I've already created the framework for that to succeed.' When she finished detailing what she had done, she added, 'I need you to understand that I'm not about to do anything that will put you at risk with any BVI officials or with Barrett's Bank. It will be my name and my reputation on the line.'

'It sounds reasonable,' he said, 'but it still requires a leap of faith.'

'Yes, I know, but I have thought this through. It is entirely doable.'

'Ms Lee, I am inclined to believe you,' he said quietly. 'Maybe because it's so late and my mind is not fully functional.'

Maybe because you stand to make at least another $100,000, she thought. *Maybe because all this stuff about making sure I had a workable plan was just so you could strengthen your bargaining position*. 'Thank you, Captain, I really appreciate your support,' she said.

He ignored her posturing. 'So now we need to talk about the details.'

'How do you propose getting us there?' she asked.

She had expected him to sidestep her question but he didn't. 'By private plane. Actually a government plane. Nothing fancy – a turboprop – but the airstrip on Beef Island can't handle much more than that. It's about two and a half hours from here. The best time to land would be evening. It'll be quieter, and the fewer people who see you the better. Customs and Immigration will have to be notified of your arrival. We'll look after that, of course. You'll be waved through,' he said.

'Sounds good.'

'This doesn't mean that anything goes, though. You do understand that?'

'Explain.'

'Well, we can't have Seto taped up like a mummy. No handcuffs either. Our friends there expect us to be discreet . . .

Can you keep Seto under control without those inhibitors? We can't have him causing a ruckus.'

'Seto will be sleeping by the time we land,' she said. 'A friend of mine will meet us at the airport. His name is Derek Liang. I need you to tell the BVI officials who he is and arrange permission for him to meet me at the plane when we land.'

The Captain laughed, a laugh that turned into a cough. 'I really must give up these cigars,' he said.

'Bless you.'

'No, bless you, Ava Lee. You are indeed a clever girl. Does the presence of this Mr Liang mean you won't need our physical assistance on that end?'

'Not after I get Seto on the plane.'

'Can I ask just how you intend to get him to sleep?'

'I had coffee with Patrick at the doughnut shop a few days ago. Check the tape,' she said.

'I have,' he said.

'So you know.'

'I know.'

'Then why ask?'

'I wasn't sure I believed it.'

'You can.'

'Evidently. Well, now that we have landed you safely and you have taken a very passive Seto past Immigration without any fuss or bother, that leaves us with the small matter of money. You can understand that the plane is expensive. And our friends in the Virgin Islands have a grossly superior standard of living. They won't be satisfied with just a few dollars for turning a blind eye to what is essentially a kidnapping.'

She had thought of taking a different approach, of giving him a choice between a set fee and a percentage of what she would recover. If she was unsuccessful collecting the money, then giving a percentage would lower the hit she and Uncle would have to take. But that would make it necessary for her to tell him how much money was involved. And if she did, she would tell him the truth; she didn't discount the idea that his BVI contacts were good enough to enable him to find out. And of course, if she was successful he would make even more than he could with a set fee. It would be found money, of course, but it was still coming out of their pockets. It all boiled down to how confident she felt about her chances at Barrett's.

When she was leafing through Seto's records, she had noted that Jeremy Bates seemed to be a recent arrival at the bank. His name didn't crop up until the past year. Before that Seto had dealt with a Mark Jones. This meant that Bates hadn't been involved in establishing the withdrawal procedures. He would know about them, for certain, but maybe he would find them as cumbersome and old-fashioned as she did. Maybe he'd take a more flexible attitude if she could establish the right framework. It felt right, she decided. It would work.

'Name your fee,' she said.

'We'll need $200,000,' he said.

'Captain, you're killing me,' she said.

'Ms Lee, this time we are not negotiating with you. That's the sum. Pay it or enjoy your vacation in Guyana with Mr Seto, because I assure you he is not leaving this country under any other circumstances.'

She knew he meant it and she knew she was going to wire

the money, but it wasn't in her nature to capitulate so readily. She sighed. 'I'll have to talk to my people. I can't agree to this without their permission. Can you give me ten minutes?'

'Take twenty if you need it.'

She switched to her own phone, but not before checking the previous calls made on Patrick's. She wrote down in her notebook the number she presumed was the Captain's direct line.

Uncle took her call on the first ring.

'We'll need to send $200,000.'

'Same banking information?'

'Exactly.'

'It will get done in the next half-hour,' he said without hesitation.

'Have the wire confirmation scanned and emailed to me, please.'

'It will be done at the same time.'

She knew how hard this was for him. 'Uncle, this will work,' she said.

'How much extra money do you think there will be?' he asked, simultaneously confirming his trust in her and letting her know that his decision to wire the $200,000 wasn't based on a potential windfall profit.

'About two million.'

'Do you have any sense of the timing?'

'It will take Derek at least twenty-four hours to get to the Virgin Islands. I can't do this without him, so there's no point in my leaving here until the day after tomorrow. They want us to arrive in the evening, so the soonest I can get to the bank is probably three days from now.'

'Keep in touch.'

'Every day,' she said.

Ava checked her emails for the next half-hour, catching up with her family and friends. The weather was brutal in Toronto, and her mother was making her usual winter threat to move back to Hong Kong. As she was reading her sister's plea for Mummy to stay put – why Marian took these threats seriously amazed Ava, as her mother had no friends there any more, and besides, if she did show up their father would cut her off financially – an email arrived from Derek. He had booked a flight through San Juan that would get him into Tortola at six o'clock the next day, sooner than she had thought possible. He had struck out with hotel suites but had found a three-bedroom serviced apartment with a one-week minimum stay and had booked it.

An apartment is perfect, she thought. Maybe Derek was going to be her good luck charm. She figured he must have gone straight home from karaoke after her call. She seemed to be the only thing in his life he took seriously. Ava phoned him at home. He didn't seem surprised to hear from her so quickly.

'The place sounds great,' she said.

'It wasn't easy to find.'

'Derek, I may try to fly into the BVI tomorrow night as well. I would try to structure it so I'd land around ten. That would give you time to get organized.'

'What do you want done?'

'I'm coming in on a private plane. I'd like you to meet me on the tarmac with a wheelchair.'

'I'm sure I can find a wheelchair somewhere,' he said.

'They'll have them at the airport.'

'But how do I get to the plane? You know what security is like these days.'

'That's being arranged. BVI Customs and Immigration will have your name. They'll let you come and meet me. I don't have all the details yet, but I'll get them and a contact name for you in case you have any problems.'

'Sounds simple.'

'Doesn't it always – just before things get screwed up.'

'Ava, can we trust these people?'

'I'm paying them enough.'

'Still ...'

'They also think I'm triad.'

'You mean you're not?' he said jokingly. Even if she wasn't, the idea that she might be connected to the triads was enough to give most people second thoughts about screwing around with her. More than once she and Derek had been faced with the threat of violence, only to have Ava short-circuit it with, 'We're the nice ones. You really don't want to meet our friends.'

'Not that I know of,' she said. Then she asked him about his departure the next day and said she'd call him before he left to confirm her schedule and to give him the other information he needed.

Now it was time to call the Captain. She punched his number into her phone. No harm in letting him know she could contact him directly.

He didn't answer until the fifth ring, and Ava wondered if he was playing with her. 'Ms Lee, I see you have my number.

I'm assuming you also have some heart-warming information for me.'

'The money is in the process of being wired. I'll have a copy of the transfer in a few hours. With any luck the money will be in your account tomorrow,' she said.

'Do you mean today? It's already well past midnight.'

'Today. And I'd like to get out of here today as well. Do you think that's possible?'

'I hadn't counted on your being quite so efficient,' he said. 'The plane is scheduled to be used by our minister of agriculture today for a quick trip to Port of Spain.'

'He can fly commercial. I can't.'

'You know, I don't have a reputation for being accommodating,' he said, 'but for some reason I can't seem to say no to you.'

Three hundred thousand dollars so far is a pretty good reason, she thought. 'My people in Hong Kong appreciate your help. If you ever need their assistance, all you have to do is ask,' she said.

'I can't think why I would ever need them,' he said.

'You never know.'

The line went quiet. In the background she heard the clink of ice hitting glass. He had been a bit friendlier than usual, jovial almost, and she figured it was the booze. 'Captain, can I get out of here tonight?' she said.

'Why not?'

'Thank you.'

'Let's talk in the morning, shall we? Call my office around ten and we'll work out the details.'

She thought of Derek. 'I would like to know the name of our

contact in the British Virgin Islands, right now, if possible. My associate will be in transit by ten and we'll be out of touch until I land. I don't want to arrive at the airport and find myself alone with Seto.'

'There are two, actually. A chap called Morris Thomas will be at the airport. He is the senior Customs and Immigration officer. We will notify Morris of your schedule the moment it's absolutely firm, and he will make himself available for you and your Mr Liang. There shouldn't be any difficulties, but if there are, phone Jack Robbins.'

She wrote down the number.

'And in case you're wondering, Jack's my younger brother. So you're going to be in very good hands,' he said.

After hanging up, Ava sat quietly in Seto's office staring at his screensaver: a photo of a busy seaport. Derek's question about trusting these people resonated in her mind. The problem was that she was in too deep to extract herself without making things worse. There came a time in every case when she had to have faith in her own judgement. This was the time. It was all too easy to imagine everything that could go wrong – she simply wouldn't let herself go there. Instead she said aloud, 'The $300,000 is secure. The plane will be there. Seto and I will get to the British Virgin Islands. There will be no issues at the airport. Jeremy Bates will be cooperative. Andrew Tam will be a happy man.'

Then she called Derek and told him about Morris Thomas and Jack Robbins.

'See you tomorrow night,' he said brightly.

'Tomorrow,' she said.

29

'You pig, you fucking pig!'

Ava walked into the kitchen to find one of the Captain's men throwing paper towels at Seto's feet, where an impressive pool of urine had gathered.

'Couldn't you just take him to the bathroom?' she said.

'He didn't ask.'

Patrick wandered in from the den, wiping sleep from his eyes. 'We can't leave him like this. He'll stink up the place.'

'I'll get the woman,' Ava said. 'Give me the keys for her handcuffs.'

When she entered the bedroom, Anna was asleep. There was dried blood on the side of her head from the blow Patrick had administered. Beneath it Ava could see the beginning of a hell of a bruise. She touched Anna's arm, not wanting to alarm her. The woman woke with a start anyway, fear leaping into her eyes.

'Anna, I'm not going to hurt you. I need your help downstairs with Jackson. Just wait here a minute.'

Ava went into the bathroom and wet a facecloth. The woman was struggling to sit upright but was having some difficulty because of the tape that bound her legs together. Ava peeled it off Anna's ankles and told her to turn around. 'Now please, don't do anything stupid,' she said as she unlocked the cuffs. She handed her the cloth. 'Here, wash your face. There's some dried blood on your right cheek and ear.'

Anna winced as she dabbed her face.

'Do you need to pee?' Ava asked.

'Badly.'

'Go and use the bathroom. Just leave the door open.'

Anna staggered slightly when she stood up. Ava could see that she was completely deflated and wasn't going to cause trouble. 'Wash your face a bit more as well, if you want,' she said to her.

It took about five minutes for Anna to sort herself out in the bathroom, and by then Ava had made a mental list of everything she wanted her to do. 'Let's go downstairs,' she said. 'Your boyfriend peed himself. I want you to bring him up here and wash and change him. One of the boys downstairs can supervise.'

Patrick and the cops were sitting at the kitchen table with disgusted looks on their faces. 'Take the tape off his ankles,' Ava told the woman. She could have taken the handcuffs off too, but she didn't want to lessen his feeling of helplessness. She didn't want him to think for even a second that there was any chance of a reprieve.

'Patrick, the woman is going to take him upstairs to wash and change. Go with them, will you?'

He looked as if he wanted to argue with her. She turned her back on him and spoke to Anna again. 'Do you have a passport?'

'Yes.'

'Where is it?'

'Upstairs in my dresser.'

'Where is Ng's passport?'

'He keeps it in his room. I don't know where.'

'Now listen to me. When you finish with your boyfriend, I want you to pack a small suitcase for him. His toilet kit, change of underwear, shirt, and whatever he sleeps in.'

'You don't have to go into the bathroom,' she said to Patrick as they started up the stairs.

'Thank you, boss,' he said.

She found Anna's passport in the top drawer of the dresser. It took her a bit longer to find Ng's, which was hidden under his mattress. She tore all the pages from both of them, ripped them to shreds, and threw the scraps into a garbage can in Seto's office. Those two wouldn't be leaving Guyana for a while.

She checked her emails. Derek had sent his itinerary. She then signed on as Seto on the off chance that Bates had responded. Nothing. Seto did have about thirty unread emails. She saw the one she had sent from the Phoenix. There were also two from George Antonelli. She opened them; they contained details about a tilapia deal they had been offered.

Seto was standing in the middle of the bedroom. Patrick had removed one of the cuffs and Seto was holding his hands up so Anna could slip a clean shirt on him. He was incredibly skinny, bones protruding through skin. When he was dressed again, Patrick re-cuffed him.

'Do I have to tie you up again?' she asked Anna.

'No . . . please don't.'

'We'll leave him here with you. You can take the tape off his eyes when we're gone. There will be someone outside the door and someone else downstairs, so don't get creative. I don't want to see you hurt any more, and there is nothing, absolutely nothing, you can do to help him. Is that understood?'

'Yes.'

'They should be okay till morning,' she said to Patrick. 'Can you drive me back to the hotel?'

While Patrick told his men what was going on, she gathered up her notebook and kitbag. A quick check showed that Seto's passports, driver's licence, and Hong Kong ID card were still in the bag.

'I assume from the conversation in the house that you'll be leaving us tomorrow?' he said as they began the drive back to the Phoenix.

'That's the plan.'

'And you're taking him with you?'

'I am.'

'Do you need any help when you're there?'

'The Captain asked me already, and the answer is no.'

'Too bad. Not much travelling in my job.'

'Travelling is overrated. After a while the planes, hotels, and restaurants all become interchangeable.'

'This must have been different,' he said.

She smiled. 'Different is a good way to describe it.'

Patrick's phone rang. He looked at the incoming number. 'It's a call from the house,' he said.

'I hope nothing's happened,' she said, slamming herself for having let the woman stay with Seto.

She could hear the cop's voice but not what he was saying. Thoughts of disaster began to creep into her head.

'No, leave them alone. What's done is done,' Patrick said finally, and ended the call.

'Is everything all right?' she asked.

'My guy heard noises from the bedroom, so he opened the door. The woman was giving Seto a blowjob. I guess the handcuffs were a turn-on.'

30

Ava finished the bottle of wine when she got back to her room. Then she waded into *Tai-Pan*, hoping the turgid writing would quickly put her to sleep. No such luck. She didn't nod off until past 4 a.m., and she was awakened at seven thirty by the clatter of machinery outside. From her window she could see a crew of men fixing potholes in front of the hotel. *If they want to take on the rest of Georgetown too, it could be a lifelong occupation*, she thought.

Tom Benson was in the coffee shop, and this time she didn't avoid him. An entire day stretched in front of her, and it was going to drag. She could use every diversion she could find.

'I'm leaving tonight,' she said as she sat down.

'Lucky you. Successful trip, was it?'

'So far.'

'I may be leaving soon myself. They told me yesterday that my parts may actually be in transit. Assuming the boat don't sink and the silly buggers at Customs let them into the country, I may have my hands on them in about two weeks. Then it's a matter of a week for installation, and presto, this fucking hellhole has seventy percent of the energy it needs instead of fifty.'

'Amazing.'

'Isn't it, in this day and age.'

'Now if you could only do something about the water.'

'I know. Even after all this bloody time I still can't get used to it.'

'The only place I can think of that is almost as bad is a town in the Philippines, on Negros Island. I was staying in a hotel where the water had so much sulphur that the entire place smelled perpetually like rotten eggs.'

'It wasn't as dangerous as this place, was it?'

'They closed the front desk at ten o'clock at night and turned off most of the lights. They had a soft-drink dispenser in the lobby, and I remember going down one night to get a Coke and being confronted by a guy with a shotgun. His backup was another guy patrolling the entrance with an Uzi. They were the hotel's security system. Now, remembering that this hotel was a dump, what does that tell you about how safe the town was?'

'Did you knock around any of the locals there?'

'I beg your pardon?'

'There's a story all over the hotel about how you beat up two hoodlums who came at you. You're quite the heroine. I'm kind of glad I didn't come on too strong to you.' He stood up and held out his hand. 'Safe journeys.'

'Same to you, Tom.'

'You're one I'm going to remember. Can't say that about many I didn't shag.'

'I'll remember you too.'

Ava sat by herself for the next half-hour reading the local newspapers. The East Indian politicians were calling the black

265

politicians crooks and the blacks were calling the East Indians thieves. *And somewhere*, she thought, *Captain Robbins is pulling everyone's strings.* There had been four muggings, seven break-and-enters, and two attempted homicides the night before. When she left, they could add one kidnapping to the crime statistics.

Jeff was in the lobby chatting up the front desk clerk when Ava left the coffee shop. She waved at him. 'Going to be here for a while?' she asked.

'I have a pickup at noon.'

'I'll catch up with you before you leave,' she said.

Ava changed into her running gear for one more jog along the seawall. That was something about Georgetown she might actually remember fondly. The air was heavy for sure, but it was clear, and the smell of sea salt was almost cleansing. *There is something to be said*, she thought, *for a non-industrial society*.

Her normal run was about five kilometres. She decided to go farther and bought some bottled water in the lobby to take with her.

The doorman nodded to her as she left. 'I'll put the word out that you're going for a run – give the baddies a chance to get out of your way,' he said.

Ava ran sixteen kilometres, which turned her into a sweaty mess. The air conditioning in her room, for once, was on when she got back. So was the message light on her phone. She threw a towel around her neck and checked the calls. Uncle, Captain, and Marc Lafontaine: a trifecta.

The Captain was at his office and she was put directly

through. *The money's arrived already*, she thought. 'The payment is in our account,' he confirmed. 'I admire your efficiency. Patrick will come by the hotel at six. You'll pick up your baggage on the way to Cheddi Jagan. I've scheduled your departure for eight. Good luck to you.'

'I'll say hello to your brother,' she said, but the line was already dead.

It was late in Hong Kong. Uncle would have already had his massage and dinner and would be settling in to watch replays of the horse races from Happy Valley Racetrack. The phone rang four times and she was ready to give up when he answered with his familiar, comforting '*Wei.*'

'It's Ava. The money has reached them already, thank you. I leave tonight and I'll be at the bank tomorrow morning.'

'I'm glad. Let's end this project one way or another as soon as we can. My friend has called me twice tonight, but I've avoided his calls. Tommy Ordonez has called as well. I told him it will be a few days before we can do anything. It is easier when we are dealing with strangers.'

'You know Ordonez from before?' she asked.

He realized he had misspoken. 'He is a friend of a good friend. They come from the same village. I met him in Jakarta at a conference about ten years ago. Nothing more than that.'

I bet, she thought. 'I want to end it tomorrow,' she said.

'If you can't, talk to me before getting into this any deeper.'

'Uncle, how much deeper can I get?'

'No more money.'

'I understand.'

'And don't put yourself at risk.'

She could think of two or three replies, all of them disrespectful. 'I won't,' she said.

The shower wasn't only brown, it was cold, and after waiting five minutes for it to warm up she gave up and towelled herself off. It was too early to get dressed for the trip so she put on her Adidas track pants and a Giordano T-shirt. She'd save her business suit for the journey.

She sat on the bed and dialled Marc Lafontaine's number.

'Are you okay?' he asked.

'I'm getting ready to leave. I'm flying out tonight.'

'Did you get what you wanted?'

'Some of it. I'll know better tomorrow.'

'The odds?'

'Fifty-fifty. But the Chinese always say fifty-fifty.'

'What do you mean?'

'When my mother buys a lottery ticket, I ask her what she thinks her chances are. She always says the same thing: fifty-fifty – I either win or I lose.'

'True enough.'

'Only if you have no faith in mathematics.'

'So what are your true odds?'

'Ninety to ten, in my favour.'

'Good. I'm glad I was able to help.'

'Without you I wouldn't have gotten close. Thank you.'

'How did you find the Captain?'

She became cautious. 'This is off the record?'

'It isn't going anywhere.'

'He's a very complicated man, but at the root he is probably completely corrupt and amoral. His only concern is for himself, and that, I think, is the beginning and end of his story.'

'Could you be less subtle?'

'If he ever invites you for coffee and doughnuts at Donald's, don't go. And if you do go, keep your mouth shut. They record every meeting there.'

'I've been to Donald's. So has the High Commissioner. He thought it was quaint.'

'They record every meeting,' she repeated.

'Jesus,' he said.

'And there you are,' she said. 'The last thing he is, is quaint. He's a dangerous man.'

'So how did you manage—'

'I paid him a lot of money for something he didn't care about in the first place.'

'Jesus.'

'He does have some weaknesses. You could exploit them if you decide you ever need to.'

'Meaning?'

'He banks with Royal York and has an offshore account in the Cayman Islands. Lean on the bank and they'll lean on him. If you need an account number, I have it.'

'Why are you telling me this?'

'I appreciate the assistance I received from the head of security at the Canadian High Commission in Georgetown. In fact, when I get home, I'm going to write to Foreign Affairs in Ottawa to tell them just how good he was.'

'You don't have to do that.'

'You didn't have to help me the way you did.'

'It's my job.'

'I haven't met many Canadian diplomats who think that way. Most of them treat you as a nuisance, someone who's trying to disrupt their day.'

It was nearly lunchtime and she thought about inviting him to join her. Then she thought better of it; using him just to kill time wasn't polite, and Ava had been raised to be polite. 'I have to go now, Marc. I have some work to do in the business centre. Great meeting you.'

Ava hung up, grabbed her notebook, and went downstairs. As usual, the business centre was empty. And also as usual, it took her four attempts to get online.

She accessed Seto's email account. Jeremy Bates had replied to the message she had sent the night before. He said he would be quite happy to meet with Mr Seto and Ms Lee in the bank's offices. *Bless you*, she thought, and replied that they would be there tomorrow morning around ten.

Next Ava checked her own email account. She had twenty-five new messages, most of which were unimportant. Mimi was wondering when she would be back in the city. There was one from Marian complaining about their mother; she read half before deleting it. She started writing an email to Mimi, Marian, and her mother saying she would see them in a few days, and then she stopped and hit the DELETE button. She wasn't going to jinx herself again by anticipating. One thing at a time.

She checked Seto's inbox again. Bates had responded to her message, confirming the 10 a.m. meeting. *He doesn't get many people dropping in*, she thought.

Ava knew little about the British Virgin Islands, only that the territory was a haven for offshore accounts. She did a quick web search. A group of small islands close to Puerto Rico, the largest of which was Tortola, and it was only twenty kilometres long and five kilometres wide. The capital, Road Town, had a total population of twenty thousand, and it seemed that at any given time there were as many tourists as residents there. It didn't sound to her like a place where someone could stay inconspicuous for very long. She could meld into most backgrounds, almost disappearing into herself, but Derek was another matter. He walked, talked, and looked like someone who just had to be someone.

It was almost noon and she realized she hadn't heard from Patrick. She called his cellphone.

'Hey, I'm at the house,' he said.

'Is everything okay?'

'Fine. We changed shifts this morning and I wanted to make sure the new guys knew the rules.'

'Seto?'

'Quiet.'

'The woman?'

'She's standing next to me, making us lunch.'

'Let me talk to her.'

'Hello.'

'Are you all right, Anna?'

'Better, anyway.'

'Things will be back to normal soon. Now, did you pack Seto's suitcase?'

'I did.'

'Good. Let me talk to Patrick again.'

'Hi,' said Patrick.

'When are you leaving there?' she asked.

'After lunch. I have things to do at the office.'

'You're getting me at six?'

'Those are the orders.'

'I'll be at the front entrance.'

'See you then.'

She had one last thing to do online. She went to the American Airlines website. Derek's flight had left Toronto on schedule. So far, so good.

31

At a quarter to six Ava was in the lobby with her bags. Patrick had arrived early; he was sitting in the lounge with a bottle of Carib and a bowl of peanuts.

She wanted to leave Jeff an extra tip but there was no sign of him. The doorman was still on duty, and she debated leaving it with him. She decided not to and instead asked the desk clerk for an envelope and discreetly put a hundred-dollar bill into it. She sealed it, wrote Jeff's name on the front, and passed it back.

It was just getting dark when she and Patrick left the Phoenix. 'Pothole time,' she said.

'It gives the city some character, don't you think?' Patrick said. 'Rome has the Vatican, London has Buckingham Palace, New York has the Statue of Liberty, and we have the world's largest and most vicious potholes.'

'They are memorable.'

'You see what I mean.'

The Captain's men, Anna, and Seto were sitting at the kitchen table when they got to the house.

'Where's the suitcase?' Ava asked.

The woman pointed to a corner of the kitchen.

Ava collected the bag and put it on the table. She opened it and went through the contents. It contained everything she had requested, and nothing more.

'I assume you know where we're going,' she said to Seto. 'You can say goodbye to your girlfriend now.'

Anna gave Seto a passionate hug. He received it without much enthusiasm. *She is the last thing on his mind*, Ava thought. *But what comes first, money or survival?*

'I need the men to stay with her for another twenty-four hours,' Ava said to Patrick. 'No phone calls, no internet. Nothing.'

'You heard her,' he said.

They bundled Seto into the back of the truck. 'I haven't taped your mouth or eyes this time, but one wrong word out of you and I will,' she said to him.

For the first time since they had picked him out of Eckie's, she saw something other than fear and compliance in his eyes. He was getting over the shock. He was beginning to think maybe there was a way out for him. She would have to fix that.

It took them more than an hour to get to Cheddi Jagan Airport. The only light was from a crescent moon and the roadway was almost pitch black, forcing Patrick to creep along at thirty kilometres an hour.

She kept looking at her watch. Derek should have landed at six. She called every fifteen minutes until, at seven thirty, he finally answered.

'You good?' she asked.

'Not a problem. The plane was a bit late, but I'm already in a taxi and headed for the apartment. I'll be back at the airport by ten.'

'I'm on schedule.'

'See you there.'

Just before they reached the terminal, Patrick turned away from it. Ava shot a quick glance at him; he looked calm. She waited. He took the road marked FREIGHT, and she relaxed a touch. On the tarmac, under floodlights, she saw a turboprop with GOVERNMENT OF GUYANA stencilled on the side. Parked next to it was a white Cadillac Eldorado that was at least ten years old. She could think of only one person who would drive a car like that.

Patrick stopped his truck directly in front of the plane. As he did so, the driver's door of the Cadillac opened and Captain Robbins got out. Ava could see inside the car – the Captain was alone. She quickly scanned the area around the plane. No one else was visible.

'Let's get out,' Patrick said.

She jumped down from the cab and took a few steps in the Captain's direction while Patrick emptied the truck of Seto and their bags.

Robbins lumbered towards them, his size even more imposing in motion than it was sitting or standing. He didn't look flexible or fast, but the power he emanated was overwhelming. Patrick, tall and muscular as he was, looked like a boy by comparison.

'I came to say goodbye,' Robbins said.

'Thanks.'

The Captain gazed upwards towards the plane's windscreen. The pilot looked down at them and Robbins motioned to him. The pilot joined them on the tarmac.

'This is Ms Lee,' Robbins said to him. 'You are taking her and this piece of shit to the British Virgin Islands. She is the boss when it comes to anything to do with him. Stay out of her business. Just land them there safely, drop them off, and get back here tonight.'

'Yes, sir.'

'Who is your co-pilot?'

'Hughes.'

'Make sure he understands as well.'

Robbins looked at Seto. 'As for you, I think you'd be wise to cooperate.'

He turned back to Ava. 'Do whatever you want with him when you're finished. I can't imagine we'd miss him,' he said with a smile.

She glanced at Seto. His eyes were locked on the Captain. She saw a touch of anger in them and wished Robbins hadn't taunted him.

'Thanks again for all your help,' she said.

He shrugged. 'Patrick, take him on board. I want to speak to Ms Lee privately.'

Now what? she thought. This could not be good.

Robbins waited until the tarmac was clear before he handed her a slip of paper. 'These are the names and cellphone numbers of my daughters in Toronto. Their names are Ellie and Lizzie. I would appreciate it if you could contact them when you get back. I've already told them you're a friend and that if they ever get into any trouble they can call on you for help. I think they would like to hear that from you in person. We do worry about them.'

She was surprised by his assumption, and by the level of trust he was displaying. 'I would be happy to. We Havergal girls have to stick together.'

'Glad to hear it. Now off with you. Good hunting, and say hello to my brother for me.'

The plane had been built as part of a commuter fleet; it was designed to seat thirty-six people in twelve rows of three. It had been converted into an eight-seater, with two rows of four seats facing each other across a table. Patrick had put Seto in a window seat. Ava sat on the aisle, kitty-corner from him.

'Good luck,' Patrick said as he left.

'See you around,' she said.

The pilot stuck his head into the passenger cabin. 'The flight is about two and a half hours long. I'll turn off the seatbelt sign ten minutes after takeoff. There's a galley up front with drinks and snacks. Help yourself.'

She had put two bottles of water and two Cokes in her bag just in case. 'Any liquor?' she asked.

'A variety.'

'That will be just fine,' she said.

Seto leaned against the window, his eyes closed. The plane revved its engines and moved onto the runway. Ava braced herself as they taxied, then drew an extra breath when they left the ground, the soft lights of Georgetown twinkling in the distance. After all the crap she had gone through, the departure seemed anticlimactic.

She waited until they had been in the air about an hour before disturbing Seto. He was still slumped against the window with his eyes closed. She didn't know if he was sleeping and didn't care. She stretched a leg towards him and gave him a kick.

His eyes crawled open. It looked forced – he had been awake.

'I need you to listen to me,' she said. 'Sit up and pay attention.'

'Jesus,' he said, twisting his neck and shaking the leg she had kicked.

'When we land, I'm going to take off the handcuffs before we leave the plane. We'll be met on the tarmac by a friend of mine. He's tough, mean, and completely loyal to me. One word out of line from you, any bad body language, and he'll lay you out. Our intention is to walk calmly through Customs and Immigration. I'd like you to walk with us, but if we have to carry you, we will. Do you understand?'

'I get it.'

'Now, tomorrow will be more of the same. You and I have an appointment with Jeremy Bates at the bank. We're going to wire Andrew Tam the money you stole from him. I'll go over the details with you in the morning. All you have to do is cooperate, and by tomorrow night you'll be on a plane back to Guyana or wherever else you choose to go.'

'I get that too. I already told you I was going to give it back anyway,' he said.

'Yes, I heard you, and maybe I believe you.'

'These cuffs, can you take them off now? What the hell can I do up here?'

'Don't rush,' she said. 'Tell you what, though, how about I buy you a drink? You want a drink?'

'Sure.'

'What do you want?'

'See if they have any Scotch.'

Ava walked into the galley. The bar was better stocked than the lounge at the Phoenix. There were three Scotches: Johnnie Walker Red, Black, and Blue – the premium one. 'They have Johnnie Walker Blue,' she told him.

'I'll take it neat,' he said.

She came back into the cabin. 'I'll get it in a minute. I have to go to the bathroom first.' She took her kitbag from under her seat and went to the washroom. On the way back she stopped in the galley, leaving on the counter two hundred-millilitre shampoo bottles filled with chloral hydrate.

Ava poured herself a modest shot of cognac, a Remy Martin VSOP, and then filled a quarter of a glass with Blue Label for Seto.

She walked back with the drinks and held the whisky to his lips. He slurped rather than sipped. 'Give me a break with these cuffs,' he said.

'Too soon.'

'C'mon.'

'Look, I'm sorry it has to be this way. I can't take any chances.'

She put the glass to his mouth again. The Scotch disappeared. 'You want another?' she asked.

'Why not?'

In the galley she tipped half the contents of one shampoo bottle into the glass and then added the Scotch. The colour was all Scotch. She sniffed. The smell was all Scotch.

Seto was sitting up straight now. The liquor seemed to have revitalized him.

'Slow down,' she said. 'I don't want you falling-down drunk.'

'I can handle my booze,' he said.

He followed her advice anyway, and it took him about ten minutes to finish his drink.

She went into the galley and refilled his glass with more chloral hydrate and Scotch. When she brought the refill back into the cabin, he looked up at her with a stupid grin. His eyes were beginning to glaze over, and she realized that the second dose might not be necessary. *What the hell*, she thought. *Why waste it?* To her shock he managed to finish the entire glass before collapsing forward. Ava pushed him back against the seat. She figured he'd be out for at least five or six hours.

So far, so good, Ava thought, looking down at the comatose Seto. Another hour and a half and they'd be on the ground, and she'd have Derek to help. Any worries about getting Seto through Customs and keeping him under control were starting to ebb, only to be replaced by anxiety about the next day and the bank. Regardless of how docile Seto was, she knew it was going to come down to Barrett's and her ability to handle Jeremy Bates. She opened her notebook and took the bank files from her bag. The email she had sent in Seto's name had established the framework for the meeting; now she just had to be calm, controlled, and credible. The problem was, she knew that wasn't going to be enough. Somehow, some way, she had to convince Bates to take a leap of faith. Not a blind one entirely, but for a serious banker a leap with a risk, however you cut it.

Ava reviewed the story she intended to spin, making notes as she did. Where were the holes? What questions would Bates ask? *The basic premise seems plausible enough*, she thought, and she had no trouble answering the questions she imagined Bates would ask. Then Seto snorted, and for an instant Ava thought he was having trouble breathing. She watched him until his body eased and he was quiet. She looked at her notebook again, but her concentration had been broken. She was tired, she knew, and the next hour might best be spent giving her mind a break rather than playing out endless scenarios with Jeremy Bates.

She closed her eyes and leaned back against the seat. *One more day*, she thought, *that's all I have to get through.*

32

The plane's descent towards Beef Island Airport was rough, and Ava woke with a start, unaware that she had nodded off. She took a hurried glance at Seto. He was dead to the world.

The landing was smooth, the taxi longer than she would have thought necessary for a plane that size. When the engines were turned off, she looked out the window and saw that the terminal was still a hundred metres away. She reached over and unlocked Seto's handcuffs.

The pilot opened the door to the cockpit and came into the cabin. 'I called in and they were expecting us. But you can't leave the plane until they get here and give you clearance.' He looked at Seto. 'Is he okay?'

'He slept most of the way. I think he's worn out.'

The pilot went to the exit door and pulled the security handle, then swung the door open and lowered the steps onto the tarmac. Ava felt the warm air rush in, the smell a curious mixture of oils and gases rising from the runway. She put her notebook in her bag, straightened her shirt, pulled back her hair, and reset the ivory chignon pin.

The pilot peered out into the darkness. Ava didn't know what to expect from Customs; she just hoped Derek had acquired a wheelchair and that they'd let him bring it to the plane. She didn't fancy carrying Seto to the terminal. She checked her watch. They had been on the ground for five minutes. What was causing the delay? The pilot must have been thinking the same thing, because he turned to look at her and gave a shrug.

Another couple of minutes passed, and Ava was about to join the pilot at the door when he said, 'I see them. They're coming.'

She stood and stretched. 'Is there a wheelchair?' she asked. 'Yeah.'

They were still going to have to carry Seto to the stairs and down onto the tarmac. Ava said to the pilot, 'My friend may need help to get him into it.' She reached into her bag, looked for her money stash, and counted out four hundred-dollar bills. 'Here, this is for you and your co-pilot. Split it any way you think is fair,' she said, handing him the cash.

The pilot moved back into the doorway. Ava stood behind, looking around him into the darkness.

Three men were walking towards them. None of them was Derek.

Two of the men were in uniform, one of them pushing the wheelchair. The third man trailed behind, lumbering, the walk an effort. He was massive, a head taller than the others and twice as broad. Ava turned away from the door and leaned against the wall. Where the hell was Derek? *Probably inside the terminal*, she thought, fighting to suppress far more negative thoughts.

'Hello,' she heard a voice call. It had a distinct Bajan accent.

'We need some help with one of the passengers,' the pilot said. 'You'll have to carry him from the plane.'

'Not a problem,' the same voice boomed.

The pilot moved back and Ava found herself looking into a huge face that was all too familiar. The man had Captain Robbins' bright blue eyes and large, fleshy lips. He lacked the Captain's near-translucent skin, but his dark tan was accentuated by deep furrows that looked like white trenches etched into his brown scalp. The blue eyes flickered around the cabin before they rested on Ava. 'You must be Ava Lee,' he said. 'I'm Jack Robbins.'

'Hello,' she said.

'You're right on time,' said Robbins, pulling himself up the stairs. His head just cleared the doorway, and when he stood inside, it skimmed the ceiling. His frame seemed to fill the front end of the plane. Maybe it was his proximity to her or the close quarters, but to Ava he seemed even more physically imposing than his brother. Maybe not quite as fit, not quite as agile, but certainly just as impressive. His plain white short-sleeved cotton shirt draped like a tent over his gargantuan belly and baggy blue jeans, and his feet were spilling out of unbuckled leather sandals. He glanced at Seto. 'Is that the cargo?'

'Yes,' Ava said, her eyes now drawn to Robbins' hands, which were covered by clear latex gloves drawn tight around his wrists.

Robbins had to turn sideways to get down the aisle. Ava stepped back, keeping out of his way. He reached down, grabbed Seto under the armpits, and lifted him in the air as if he were a small child. Ava half expected him to carry the man on his hip or over his shoulder. Instead he held him out at arm's length, Seto's head level with Robbins' chest and his feet dangling just above the ground. 'Let's get him out of here,' he said, turning and walking towards the door.

Ava reached for her bags and for Seto's. She didn't know what else to do. She had no idea what to think. Her confusion was so obvious that the pilot said, 'Is everything okay, Ms Lee? Because if it isn't . . .'

If it isn't, then what? she thought. *You'll take me back to Guyana?* 'Just fine,' she said.

As she started down the stairs, Robbins was putting Seto none too gently into the wheelchair. The other two men, who were wearing uniforms with the insignia of Customs and Immigration, looked up at her without much interest. 'I'm Ava Lee,' she said to them. 'Is one of you Morris Thomas?'

'Thomas sent them to help. He's in his office. That's where we're heading,' Robbins said.

They walked across the tarmac. One of the men pushed the wheelchair while the other chatted to him quietly. Ava was next to Robbins. His face was passive and he was completely silent.

When they neared the terminal, the wheelchair was swung to the left, away from the main entrance. About twenty metres along they came to double glass doors that read CUSTOMS AND IMMIGRATION. EMPLOYEES ONLY. Ava felt her spirits lift slightly.

They walked into a large open office that was deserted and then past a row of desks to the back. MORRIS THOMAS was stencilled on a grey steel door. 'Leave the wheelchair outside. One of you stay with it,' Robbins said to the men. He reached for the handle, twisted, and swung the door open. 'After you,' he said to Ava.

A thin black man in a blue shirt sat behind a desk that further diminished his size. *He has to be sixty*, Ava thought, taking in his wiry grey hair, a face lined with worry, and red-tinged eyes with pouches the size of tea bags. 'This is Ava Lee,' Robbins said to him.

Thomas glanced up at her, his eyes filled with pity, or at best some form of weary resignation. Ava knew immediately that things would not go as planned. 'A pleasure,' she said.

'Can I have your passport, please?' Thomas said.

There were two chairs in front of the desk. Robbins lowered himself slowly into one as Ava rooted through her bag. 'Here you go,' she said.

She put her bags on the floor, took the chair next to Robbins, and watched Thomas make a show of turning the pages of her passport. It held forty pages, the largest the Canadian government issued; she'd already filled thirty-two pages and was going to need a new one before the expiry date. 'A world traveller,' he said, closing it.

'It's the nature of my business,' Ava said.

Thomas looked at Robbins, pursed his lips, and reached down to open a desk drawer. Ava watched him slip the passport into the drawer and close it. 'You have a friend who arrived here earlier this evening, a Derek Liang,' he said.

'Yes,' Ava said, struggling to maintain her composure. 'Captain Robbins told me he had made arrangements with you for Derek to land. I had expected to see him here.'

'There were some problems with his paperwork,' said Thomas slowly. His eyes avoided hers and Robbins'.

'What kind of problems?' she asked.

Thomas rolled his head from side to side. 'His papers weren't in order. We couldn't let him stay. We picked him up at the apartment he had rented and put him on a plane headed back to Puerto Rico.' He looked at his watch. 'He left about fifteen minutes ago. And just so we're clear, we notified the Puerto Rican authorities that he shouldn't be allowed to stay there either. I believe they intend to put him on the first flight back to Canada, which should leave around midnight tonight. To Montreal, I think.'

Ava glanced at Robbins. His eyes were half closed, a slight grin tugging at the corners of his mouth. 'This wasn't what was agreed upon,' she said.

Thomas raised his right hand and motioned to Robbins, his part in the proceedings done.

The big man checked his watch, a Patek Philippe that was lost in the folds of flesh around his wrist. Ava wondered if it was real. Then she saw the back of his hands for the first time: red splotches of skin interspersed with black and green scabs. She turned her head away quickly.

'There's been a change in plans, Ms Lee. My brother is scheduled to call here any minute now, so if you will be patient I'd appreciate it.'

'Do I have another option?' she asked.

'No.'

'Jack, you don't need me any more, do you? Because if you don't mind I'll take myself home,' Thomas said.

'Say hello to Betty for me.'

'I will,' Thomas said, rising from his chair.

'Leave one of the men, will you?'

'I'll leave both.'

'Only need the one.'

'Okay. Just close the door when you go. It locks itself.'

When Thomas left, the room seemed suddenly empty. Ava shifted in her chair, and then to her shock Robbins' gloved right hand shot out and grabbed her upper arm. He squeezed, his fingers digging through her flesh until they reached bone. She flinched, more from surprise than pain. 'My brother warned me about you,' he said. 'I'm just telling you it would be stupid to try anything with me.'

'I had no intention—' she began, only to be cut off by the sound of a cellphone ringing to the tune of the *William Tell* overture.

'It's me,' Robbins said. He listened for a few seconds. 'No, it went well. She's sitting next to me.' He paused and then passed the phone to Ava.

Ava wiped the mouthpiece against her shirt. 'This is Ava Lee.'

'Before anything else is said, let me immediately apologize for this untimely departure from our plans.'

She heard the clink of ice against glass. He was at home. Drinking. 'Captain, what exactly is going on?'

He laughed, or coughed; she wasn't sure which. 'I felt it necessary to make some changes to our arrangement.'

'So your brother told me, though he was somewhat lacking in detail.'

'The thing is, Ms Lee, you didn't play fair with me.'

She sensed at once where this was headed, but she wasn't going to go there first. 'As I remember, Captain, I paid you

$100,000 for services rendered, and then another $200,000 for services that so far have been unfulfilled. So in terms of being fair, I think I'm the one who should be complaining.'

'You aren't the least bit curious as to why I feel aggrieved?'

'We have an agreement, one that I've completely honoured. I don't need to know any more than that.'

'The thing is,' he said again, slurring the *s*, 'I've found out that you've been less than forthcoming with me.'

Ava closed her eyes. Had this been his plan all along? Had he arranged to get her and Seto to the British Virgin Islands just so he could squeeze her? Had the note with his daughters' names and phone numbers just been theatre? 'Captain, I have no idea what you're talking about.'

Ice clinked. 'I stopped by Seto's house on the way back from the airport tonight and had a chat with his woman,' he said slowly. 'Don't know why I did it, actually; it just came to me that it was the thing to do. Anyway, she was quite open with me after a little persuasion. It seems that our friend Seto had made quite a score for himself. According to her, he's managed to turn a recent profit in the amount of about five million United States dollars.'

She didn't know if she believed a word of it, but her position wasn't going to change. 'There was no profit. There was just theft,' she said.

'So you concede the amount?'

'Captain, I never misled you about how much money I was chasing. I don't remember ever mentioning an amount.'

'And you know, I don't think you did either, so that's true enough. The fault is mine, of course. I couldn't imagine Seto being that successful. But now, belatedly I admit, I find out that he is evidently more clever than I thought. And so here we are, Ms Lee ... Let me ask you, given this new information, do you really think it's fair that I should have to settle for just $300,000?'

'Yes, I do,' Ava said.

'You disappoint me, Ms Lee. I mean, really, without our very active and unique support, where would you be? I'll tell you: you'd be sitting at the Phoenix Hotel with no hope of getting at Seto or his money. Yes, I think that's exactly where you would be.'

'Possibly,' she said.

'And even if you had contrived to get your hands on him, where were you going to go with him? Nowhere, I tell you, although you might have ended up in Camp Street Prison for kidnapping, or worse.'

Robbins' voice had risen an octave, his words coming faster. Ava waited for a few seconds, not jumping to respond. When she did, she said as softly and deliberately as she could, 'I assume you want to make a proposition.'

'Of course I do. I think that we have to revisit our agreement, that we need to make it less one-sided.'

'You're looking for more money?'

'It's only fair.'

'It isn't my money to give. It belongs to my client,' she said.

'That's a quibble. All I know for certain is that the money is in a bank account belonging to Seto. How it got there is your word against his. In fact, the case could be made that you tried to bribe a Guyanese government official to help you fraudulently deprive a Guyanese resident of his hard-earned assets.'

Ava bit back the anger that was swelling up from her stomach. Seto had been an idiot to tell the woman. She had probably confessed everything the moment the Captain asked his first question. As for him, well, he was turning out to be exactly what she had feared he was. She just wished he could have been contained for another day or two. But there was nothing positive to be gained in getting angry about any of it. She tried to shift the conversation. 'You know, Captain, all this talk about money is still completely hypothetical. There is no guarantee that the bank will release any funds at all to me.'

He laughed, phlegm catching in his throat and causing him to cough. 'I have absolute confidence in the approach you described to me,' he said, catching his breath. 'I found it entirely sensible, and when I factor in your persuasiveness and your appeal, well, I think the approach goes well past sensible all the way to irresistible. So humour me, please, and let's talk about money, hypothetical or otherwise.'

'What do you have in mind?'

'Half,' he said bluntly.

The figure took her aback. He was even greedier, even more aggressive than she'd imagined. 'Captain—'

'I want $2,500,000.'

Ava held the phone against her neck as she did two quick calculations. The first was how much negotiating leverage she had. The answer was short and brutal: absolutely none that she could think of at the moment, and the moment was all that mattered now. They had her passport and, more important, she was in a place where she had no connections, no support, no backup. All it would take was one quick phone call to the bank from some BVI crony of Robbins and the entire deal would be blown apart.

The second calculation was how much money she would have left if she drained Seto's bank account and paid Robbins what he wanted. Not enough to make Tam whole, but he would get bandaged up. 'Captain, that amount is way too high,' she said.

'Don't be stupid. I think half is fair for all the trouble I've gone to. In fact, when I really think about it, half is generous on my part.'

He'd been under control until then, not pleasant but not harsh either, just confident and insistent. Now she detected the first real threat in his tone. He was drinking, and dollar signs were dancing in his head. *This isn't the time to aggravate him*, Ava thought. *It's time to pull back.* 'I've already given you $300,000.'

'What?'

'I've paid you $300,000, and I think that needs to be factored into any agreement.'

He laughed again, and when he spoke he was back in control. 'Always negotiating, aren't you? But you are correct, of course. So where does that leave us?'

Both of them went quiet. Ava had no idea what he was thinking. All she knew was that she had to negotiate some kind of deal or she wasn't going to leave the airport. And there was only one deal on the table. She needed to get into Road Town; she needed to get to the bank; she needed to buy time. 'Discounting the $300,000 would mean we pay you $2,200,000,' said Ava.

'Are you saying you will pay or you might pay that amount?'

'Will.'

'Ah, I knew you were too clever to do anything else.'

'I still need to call Hong Kong—'

'No,' he said. 'No Hong Kong. No calls. You and I have made the deal and we'll leave it that.'

'I'm not sure—'

'I'm sure,' he snapped. 'No Hong Kong. No calls. You go to the bank tomorrow and work your charm. Have them send the $2,200,000 to my account and then you can send whatever you want overseas and explain everything later to your people there. I'm sure they'll understand why it was necessary to do things this way. I mean, a bird in the hand—'

'You know, it isn't going to be as simple as you think,' she said as calmly and softly as she could, and then waited for another eruption.

She heard him breathing, and then another clink of ice. 'I think you need to explain exactly what you mean by that,' he said, the edge creeping back into his voice.

'Transferring the money directly from Seto's account to your account could cause a problem,' Ava said.

'Why?'

'Well, I've already established the parameters for my meeting. The banker has been told – by Seto, he believes – that the money is being placed in an investment in China. He thinks Seto and I are going to show up at his office tomorrow morning to execute the paperwork. Instead, I'm the only one who's going to be there. I think I can talk my way around Seto's absence, but even if he thinks I'm credible, he still needs to see Seto's identification and he still needs Seto's signature on a whole bunch of documents. Will he accept the signatures without actually seeing Seto? That's my hope, Captain, but it is by no means certain. He's going to be suspicious enough when I show up without Seto, and even more suspicious when I deliver him signed documents but still without Seto. Now, by sending money to the Cayman Islands, what you want me to do is compound all that uncertainty by changing the terms of the arrangement Seto emailed to him.' Ava stopped to let the Captain absorb the information.

She felt Jack Robbins looking at her. He was obviously listening. 'Given those circumstances, I can guarantee, Captain, that the moment I tell him we now want only half of the money to go to Asia, and the other half to be sent to a bank account in the Cayman Islands, alarm bells are going to ring in his head. And, Captain, we don't want any alarm bells, because no capable banker can ignore them, and a bank as good as Barrett's will have someone very capable running a branch as sensitive as this one. It's all in the optics, Captain. Change the optics and you change the reaction. Change the reaction and you put the outcome at risk. The optics now are okay – not great, just okay. If we alter the plan now, it would only hurt us both.'

She knew none of that would have occurred to him. Now she hoped he wasn't too drunk to think things through.

'If what you say is true . . . ' he finally said.

'It is true.'

'Okay, assuming it is, and assuming you follow your plan, how do I get my money?'

'We'll wire it to you from Hong Kong,' Ava said. 'If tomorrow I can get the bank to send us the money, we'll have it the day after. We'll send you your share right away. So we're talking, what with the time change, three days?'

'Three days,' he repeated.

'And I'll be here, of course. I'm not going anywhere. My passport is in Morris Thomas's drawer.'

'I know where your passport is.'

Now is the time, she thought. 'So, Captain, as much as I hate to ask, do we have a deal?'

The Captain fell silent. He was making her wait. She knew he was going to say yes, but he had to remind her who was dominant. 'I'd like you to give your cellphone to my brother,' he said.

'Why?'

'Just do it.'

She opened her bag, took out her phone, and handed it to Jack Robbins. 'Done,' she said.

'What do you think of my brother?'

'You can certainly tell you had the same mother.'

'Actually, his personality is closer to hers than mine,' the Captain said. 'In any event, you'll get to know him better, because he's going to be staying with you for the next three days, or for however long it takes us to conclude our business.'

'That's completely unnecessary,' she said.

'It's what I want.'

295

'Captain, you have my passport and you have my cellphone. Where exactly do you think I'll go? What do you think I'll do?'

'I don't know what you could get up to. All I know is that you're resourceful, and I don't want to have to worry about you.'

'If it has to be—' she began.

He cut her off. 'Good. Now put the phone on speaker mode.'

She pressed the speaker button and then held the phone out to his brother. It seemed to get swallowed up by the gloved hand. 'Go ahead,' he said.

'Jack, Ms Lee and I have reached an agreement that I think is fair. In fact, you could consider us business partners. Now, she has to run to the bank at least once tomorrow. You're the chauffeur and the bodyguard. Make sure no harm comes to her. Make sure that she is well looked after otherwise.'

'She'll be fine.'

'As we talked about earlier, you'll stay at the apartment they rented. No phone calls. No computer. Nothing. She doesn't communicate with anyone but you, me, and the bank ... Now, Ms Lee, please put the phone back on regular mode.'

'Okay, it's just me,' she said, holding the phone away from her face and wondering what skin ailment forced Jack Robbins to wear latex gloves.

'It's very simple: we have your passport and you're not leaving the islands without it. And to be completely honest, you're not leaving the islands even if you do have it, because Thomas has put your name on a watch list. If you try to leave you will be stopped and detained. I didn't need to say that, but I thought you should know that we're being careful.'

'I understand,' she said, not pleased to hear how thorough he had been. 'What you said to your brother about the computer, though – that could be a problem. How do you expect me to send instructions about a wire transfer to your account?'

'Did you send instructions by computer for my $300,000?'

'I did.'

'Are they still in your system?'

'They are.'

'Well, when you're ready to send new instructions, show the old ones to Jack and then follow the exact same routine. He'll be watching, of course.'

'Of course. One other thing, Captain – something I do have to ask. What happens if, even with my best efforts, I can't convince the bank manager to release Seto's money?'

'That's not the outcome I expect.'

'You have too much faith in me.'

'You'll get it done.'

'But if I can't?' she persisted.

'That's a conversation for another day,' he said. Then he went quiet.

Has he gone? Ava wondered. 'Captain?'

'I want you to behave for my brother,' he said, as if he were talking to a child.

'Of course.'

'And Ms Lee – Ava, I want you to know that I have the greatest respect for you. This isn't personal; this is just business. We – me and you – are professionals, so I know you'll see the fairness in it.'

'I understand,' she said.

'As for my daughters,' he went on, 'I meant what I said when you were leaving Guyana. When this is over and we each have our money and you're back safely in Toronto, I'd like you to call them, I really would.'

'Captain, don't worry about your daughters,' Ava said.

33

The customs officer pushed Seto through the terminal, with Robbins tailing and Ava alongside him, carrying her own bags. A black Crown Victoria idled outside. The window was open and Ava saw a middle-aged man with a tattooed arm dangling out the driver's-side window.

'Davey, help me with this guy and then put the wheelchair in the trunk,' Robbins said.

Davey leapt from the car, all five foot six of him. He was scrawny and had a patchy beard. He wore stovepipe jeans, high-top running shoes, and two earrings. The only thing he lacked was a mullet. He opened the back door and watched Robbins shove Seto across the seat. 'Put your bags in the trunk and then get in the front with Davey,' Robbins said to Ava.

They crossed the Queen Elizabeth II Bridge, which separated Beef Island from Tortola, and wound their way to Road Town. It was a slow trek. The roads were narrow, the car was big, and the route was mountainous. The car was American-made and the steering wheel was on the left-hand side but the road rules were British. It made for awkward turning, especially on the tight corners that came at them every hundred metres. The first time Davey honked his horn as they approached a curve, Ava jumped, anticipating a collision, but he did that before every curve as a precaution.

The car was otherwise quiet. Davey concentrated on his driving. Robbins sat like a lump behind her. Ava glanced into the rear-view mirror and saw him staring at the back of her head; then she imagined his breath on her neck. She tried to clear her mind, tried to start thinking through the mess emanating from Guyana, but Davey's driving was so herky-jerky and the road so potentially lethal she couldn't sustain any level of concentration.

It took twenty minutes to meander their way to the city. Road Town is built at the base of a mountain, and as they drove down towards it Ava saw that the lights were arranged in what looked like a circle. 'That's pretty,' she said, breaking the silence.

'That's Road Harbour. The town is built around it, like a horseshoe,' Davey said.

Ava was surprised by the thoughtfulness of his description. 'How many people live there?'

'About ten thousand.'

'Looks bigger, but then most cities do at night.'

'This place looks okay in the day too. They've done a good job developing it. Your boyfriend picked a nice place for you. It's right over there, next to Wickham's Cay,' he said, pointing.

He must have picked up Derek at the apartment, Ava thought, rerunning the timeline since her departure from Guyana. Customs officials must have gone along too, because she couldn't imagine Derek letting just Davey and Robbins kick him off the island. She looked in the direction Davey had indicated but all she saw was a wall of lights. 'Any good restaurants near the apartment?' she asked, thinking it wouldn't hurt to make a friend.

'Enough with the chatter, Davey. You aren't being paid to be a tour guide,' Robbins said.

They approached Road Town from the east, taking a route that traced the harbour to the west. She saw signs for Wickham's Cay II and the inner harbour as they passed through a combination of residential, commercial, and government buildings. The architecture was Caribbean generic, mainly low-rise white stucco housing with the odd dash of coral pink or powder blue. The homes were to the north, set back from the harbour, while the restaurants, markets, government buildings, and commercial offices, with long lists of tenants posted on their exterior walls, crowded near and around the water. Davey turned left off Main Street, following the arrow to Wickham's Cay I.

Guildford Apartments, a white stucco three-storey building, was right on the cay. To Ava's eye it looked as if it had been built in a week.

Davey stopped right in front of the building. It had a double glass door that looked into the lobby and a reception desk that was unmanned. 'How is security?' Ava asked.

'What do you mean?' said Robbins.

'I mean, is there any? Do we really want to be answering questions about Seto's current state? I don't know about you, but I don't want to be drawing unnecessary attention to myself.'

Robbins shrugged. 'There aren't any guards. They have a

small front desk that's open from nine in the morning to nine at night. They lock the doors the rest of the time and you let yourself in with your room key.'

'Cameras?'

'What does it matter?'

'How often do they service the apartments?'

'Again, what the fuck does it matter?' Robbins snapped.

'Seto is going to be handcuffed and taped around the ankles and mouth for at least part of the time. We don't want staff wandering in and out.'

'We'll ask them in the morning,' he said.

Davey opened his door and went to the trunk. Ava followed. She took out her and Seto's bags while Davey hauled out the wheelchair and unfolded it. 'That's a creepy-looking guy you've got in the back seat there. Looks like he should be peddling drugs to kids or selling porn,' he said.

'He's in the fish business, so you aren't far off,' Ava said, thinking that Davey might be trying to make a friend as well.

Robbins got out of the back seat feet first, his arms on either side of the door straining to pull out the rest of his body. He joined them by the trunk and reached inside for a briefcase. 'I'm staying the night with the girl,' he said to Davey. 'Be here in the morning to pick us up.' Then he turned to Ava. 'What time is your meeting?'

'Ten,' Ava said.

'Barrett's, right?'

'Yes, Barrett's.'

'Quarter to ten should be fine,' he instructed Davey. 'Now help us get this guy upstairs before you bugger off.'

Davey pushed the wheelchair to the door. Robbins inserted the plastic room key and then stepped back as he pulled the door open. As they walked into the lobby, a side door opened and a young black woman with a name tag that said DOREEN, RECEPTION almost ran right into them. She looked at Robbins, staring at his gloves, then at Ava, at Davey, and then Seto, whose head was hanging down, his chin on his chest, drool coming from his mouth. 'My friend has a terrible case of food poisoning. We need to get him to the room and into bed,' Ava said.

'What room?'

'Three-twelve,' Robbins said, holding up the key for her to see. 'Liang.'

The girl hesitated, then said, 'Have a nice evening,' as she walked out the front door.

As they rode the elevator to the third floor, Robbins asked, 'What did you knock him out with?'

'Something that should last another eight hours or so. We'll tape and handcuff him anyway to be safe. I wouldn't want him roaming around or running off in the middle of the night. I'll give him another dose in the morning.'

'Do you really need him?'

And if I didn't, Ava thought, *what would you do with him?* 'Did your brother tell you what I have to do at the bank tomorrow?'

'I have a rough idea.'

'Well, until then I don't know if I need him. If things go perfectly, I don't. In the meantime, we have to keep him on ice just in case he has to make some kind of appearance.'

The apartment door opened into a white-tiled living room with a couch, two pine chairs, and the room's main feature, a forty-eight-inch Panasonic Viera television. On the right was the kitchen, with a wooden table, four flimsy-looking folding chairs, and a sliding door that led out to a balcony. There was one bathroom to the left, the sink visible through the open door. There were three bedrooms between the bathroom and kitchen. 'Let's put him in the middle room. If there's a fuss we'll be sure to hear it,' Ava said to Robbins.

He looked at her as if she were trying to trick him. 'Stick him the middle,' he said to Davey.

Davey wheeled Seto into the bedroom and Ava followed with her Shanghai Tang bag. 'Throw him on the bed and take off his pants and shirt,' she said. As Davey undressed Seto, she went into her bag and took out a roll of duct tape. She wrapped his ankles together and then put a strip across his mouth. The handcuffs went back on. 'Could you tuck him in now, please?' she asked.

Robbins watched them from the doorway. When they were done, he motioned to Davey. 'A quarter to ten. We'll meet you outside.'

Ava stood in the living room and watched the small man leave. Robbins walked into the kitchen and opened the fridge. 'Your boyfriend bought some stuff on his way here. Too bad he didn't have time to try it.' He took out a Stella Artois and brushed past her on his way to the couch. He spread himself across it and turned on the television.

From where she stood Ava could see bags of chips and nuts on the counter. She hadn't had any dinner and wasn't about to ask Robbins if she could go out. She went into the kitchen and picked out a bag of smoked almonds. She didn't drink beer, so she hoped Derek had bought some soft drinks. To her surprise there was a bottle of Pinot Grigio. She gave silent thanks.

'I want the bedroom with the king-size bed,' Robbins shouted from the couch.

Ava turned. He was staring at her from across the room, looking at every part of her except her eyes. Almost absently, his hand reached for his head and he stuck his fingers into the furrows in his scalp and slid them back and forth, the latex gloves easing the path. Ava turned away, repulsed. She put the wine back in the fridge and left the kitchen with her bag of nuts. She picked up her other suitcase and went into the bedroom closest to the bathroom. Two twin beds. She was about to close the door when he yelled, 'Leave it open. I need to be able to see you.'

She dropped the bag on the floor and went back into the living room. *Enough of this crap*, she thought. 'Listen, you fucking jerk. If you heard your brother properly, we're supposed to be partners. I have a big day ahead of me tomorrow and I need to get organized, I need to get my head in the right space. So I'm going to close my bedroom door until I decide I want to open it again. If you have a problem with that, call the Captain and explain to him just exactly why you need to have it open, and then the Captain can explain to me how that is going to contribute to our getting our hands on some money tomorrow.'

He barely looked at her. 'Whatever,' he said.

Ava turned away. She knew she would have to put up with him until the money had found its way to Hong Kong. After that . . . well, she'd play it by ear.

With the door closed, Ava opened her Louis Vuitton suitcase. She took off her watch, undid her cufflinks, detached the ivory chignon pin, and put them neatly inside their pouch. She stripped down to her bra and panties, carefully folding her slacks and shirt and putting them back in her bag with the jewellery. Then she put on her Adidas training pants and a black T-shirt. She looked in her Shanghai Tang bag and found her notebook and a pen, then saw her computer back staring at her. She did a quick visual search of the room for a computer link and saw none. Even if one was available it wasn't worth the risk, at least not yet. On the side and near the bottom of the Tang bag was a zipper. She opened it and reached inside. It was still there: a Hong Kong passport in her name. If the Captain was right about Thomas it wasn't going to do her much good if she wanted to leave the island by air. Not that she was ready to leave anyway. *Do the banking; just get the banking done*, she told herself.

She picked up the notebook and pen and opened the door. Robbins hadn't moved from the couch. Ava went to Seto's bedroom and poked her head in. He was still tucked in bed, his head visible above the covers, looking almost happy.

She closed Seto's door and turned. 'There's a balcony just outside the kitchen,' she said to Robbins. 'I'm going to take a bottle of wine, my notebook, and my pen, and I'm going to sit out there and get ready for tomorrow.'

Robbins pulled himself semi-erect, his belly hanging over

306

his knees. His face was pinched; he started to say something and then stopped.

Ava took that as 'I don't care' and walked to the fridge. She took out the wine, found a glass in the cupboard above the sink, and slid open the balcony door.

It wasn't a large space: there was room enough for two canvas chairs and a small plastic table between them. She plopped into a chair and stretched her legs towards the railing. It was a beautiful evening. A light breeze was blowing in from the harbour, carrying a mixture of sea air and flowers. The balcony overlooked the water, and there was enough light from the boats and the surrounding buildings for her to see that the harbour was packed with sea craft of every size. Ava knew nothing nautical, couldn't tell a catamaran from a yacht or a skiff from a sailboat, and was equally lost in terms of the lengths and values of boats. But she was impressed with Road Harbour anyway, because it seemed to have something of everything bobbing on the water. It was soothing, watching the boats, and as she became calmer the reality of her situation began to settle in, moving past shock towards acceptance and from there to dealing with circumstances by priority. The number one priority was Jeremy Bates and Barrett's Bank. Without success there, Robbins' threats were irrelevant and Andrew Tam was toast. She needed to focus on the bank.

Ava poured herself a glass of wine and opened her notebook. For ten minutes she reviewed the strategy she intended to use, again looking for weaknesses and anticipating questions. It wasn't perfect and couldn't be, given Seto's state, but the basic approach she had outlined did make sense, regardless of Robbins' intrusion. She needed to get the bank to transfer the money, and that was all in her hands, under her control. What would happened afterwards, where and how the money would change hands ... well, that was open for evaluation, and that was what she began to think about.

Since landing at Beef Island she'd been in a state of suspended disbelief, going through the motions, trying to keep the surprise of it all at bay. Robbins had done a good job springing it on her, and she had to acknowledge that she was in a bit of a jam. No Derek. No passport. No phone. Jack Robbins parked on the sofa. But how much danger was she really in? Nothing had changed in terms of Seto and the bank except that Robbins wanted a cut of the money. If that was all he wanted, then it was manageable. And she had to assume that was all he wanted. The only question was how to handle it.

She could, of course, do exactly what she had told Robbins she would do. But there were certain problems attached to that, not least of which was whether she could trust Robbins to be satisfied with $2.2 million. What if, once he knew she had moved the money to Hong Kong, he got even greedier? What if he continued to hold her passport over her head and demanded even more money?

And then there was the ethical issue surrounding Andrew Tam. It was his money. He was entitled to all of it. From a practical viewpoint, she and Uncle had never guaranteed any return, let alone full return, but Ava couldn't lie to herself about the fact that the money was intact and within reach, and that with a little ingenuity she might be able to get it all. Why give Robbins anything if she could find a way around it?

How cooperative, how gullible would Robbins be once he knew she had successfully engineered the wire transfer to Hong Kong? Assuming he was going to be satisfied with the $2.2 million, was he prepared to instruct Thomas to give back her passport and let her leave the country once he had proof that the wire had been sent to his Cayman account, rather than wait until the money actually reached it? He had been willing enough to do that in Guyana. But that was there, and those were much smaller stakes. How much did he actually trust her?

So there would be a Plan A and a Plan B, she decided, and then caught herself before going too far down that road. *Let's focus on tomorrow*, she thought, reopening her notebook. In the back she had taped Seto's Washington state driver's licence. She took it out and placed it at the bottom of an empty page; then, starting at the top, she filled the rest of the page with Seto's signature. By the bottom of the page it was beginning to look authentic.

Ava finished her glass of wine and poured another. Below she saw a knot of ten people on the dock walking towards a boat that looked like a small floating hotel. They looked like couples, old friends, arms entwined or thrown loosely around necks. They weaved as they walked, their voices rising towards her, the happy voices of happy people who had probably just finished a gourmet meal and six bottles of wine. *Well, I have my wine*, she thought, *and a nice evening and a great view. Things could always be worse.* If only she hadn't googled Tommy Ordonez.

34

Ava crawled into bed fully dressed, her mind jumping back and forth between Jeremy Bates and Robbins. She began taking long, slow breaths and tried to focus on her bak mei exercises. It was difficult to maintain that kind of concentration; it took her half an hour, maybe longer, to finally fall asleep. When she did, her father came to her in a dream. They were in a hotel, ready to leave for an airport. He said he was going to check out and asked her to collect their bags from their room. Except she couldn't find the room. She wandered from floor to floor, her frustration and panic increasing. She was ready to run to the lobby to get his help when someone else entered her dream.

Ava didn't dream that often, and when she did, her father was always in it. The locations, the situations, the other people changed from dream to dream. None of that mattered. It always came down to her and her father and one of countless variations of him leaving and her trying to catch him or imploring him to stay. She never caught him. He never stayed.

Ava sensed a presence, a subtle change in the light triggering her response. She was on her back, arms by her sides, head resting on two pillows. She opened her eyes and saw him standing in the doorway, the light from the living room glowing around him like an aura. She thought she could hear him breathing. Her own breathing had stopped. She lay perfectly still, her eyes unblinking, locked on the doorway. Ava's arms were outside the covers but her legs weren't. She calculated the distance between the door and her bed, and knew that she had the time she needed to react if he decided to come into the room, even if he came charging into the room.

She thought about saying something, and then thought, *No, let him think I'm still asleep. Let him try to do whatever it is he has chosen to do, and then I'll do what I choose to do.* How badly would she hurt him? There was no limit in her mind. Money or no money, she wouldn't let him get close enough to even think he had a chance. Then the Captain could decide which he valued more, his brother or a payday.

Minutes passed, or maybe it was just a few seconds – Ava had no real sense of time. Robbins stood immobile in the doorway, his massive backlit head stretched towards the bed. She couldn't see his eyes and wondered if he could see hers, wondered if he knew she was awake.

Then he moved, turning, one hand reaching for the doorknob. Ava's legs twitched; her body coiled, her mind cleared. He took a step back. Then she heard a deep breath and was plunged back into darkness as the door closed.

Now she could not sleep. She had no idea what time it was and didn't care. She forced herself to think of something other than the man in the next room. Jeremy Bates and Barrett's Bank were her choices. She conjured question after question and threw back answer after answer until the sun slipped between the slats of the blinds that covered her window. The room gradually filled with sunlight and just as gradually dulled her nighttime fears. Ava looked towards the door. That hadn't been a dream.

She slid out of bed, the tiles cold on her feet, increasing her urge to pee. She took out her toiletry bag, walked to the bedroom door, and opened it with purpose. Six empty bottles of Stella sat on the coffee table. Robbins had left the sofa but he hadn't left the room. He was in one of the pine chairs, which he'd pushed against the apartment door. His head was back, mouth open, as he breathed and snored in spurts.

Ava went into the bathroom and locked the door. It took her half an hour to pee, brush her teeth, shower, wash and dry her hair, and put on the lightest touch of makeup. She couldn't remember ever enjoying bathroom time quite so much. As she was finishing up, she heard shuffling in the apartment and knew that Robbins had left his chair. She listened, trying to figure out where he was. She had no intention of opening the bathroom door and walking into him. Then the noises he was making became indistinct and she had two thoughts: he was in his bedroom or he was standing outside waiting for her.

She opened the door carefully and saw him almost at once. He was standing at the entrance to Seto's room. 'You need to look after this guy,' Robbins said.

Ava had almost forgotten about Seto. She went to his door. He was flailing on the bed, kicking the covers free, revealing a pair of jockey shorts that didn't flatter his stick-like legs. When she saw her, he motioned with his head for her to come close. She pulled the tape from his mouth. 'I need to pee,' he gasped. His eyes were still glazed from the drug, but she could see that the flash of anger, the hint of growing confidence that had begun to emerge in them the night before had completely disappeared. He was a whipped puppy again, just the way she liked them to be.

'Take him,' she said to Robbins, who had come into the room and was standing only a few feet behind her. 'Behave,' she said to Seto.

'I want nothing to do with him,' said Robbins.

'I can't do it, and we can't have him here all covered in piss if I have to bring the banker back.'

She watched as Robbins thought it out through his beery haze. 'Fuck,' he finally said, brushing past her and reaching down for Seto. He picked him up by the armpits again and, holding him at arm's length, carried him from the room. Seto looked back at Ava, his eyes rolling in panic.

While they were in the bathroom she prepared another dose of chloral hydrate in a glass of water. She had only a bottle and a half left. She hoped she wouldn't have to use it all.

Robbins carried Seto back the same way he had taken him and threw him onto the bed from a metre away. Seto bounced and then lay sideways across the bed. Ava helped him sit up and held the glass to his mouth. 'Drink,' she said.

He shook his head.

'Drink it or I'll get Mr Clean here to hold your mouth open and I'll pour it down your throat. Look at it this way: you'll be sleeping through a whole bunch of unpleasantness. This is a kindness, not a punishment.'

Seto looked up at Robbins, then at the glass Ava held. His lips parted and he drank. The roll of duct tape was on the bedside table. She tore off a strip and re-taped his mouth. 'This will be over soon enough,' she said to him.

Robbins followed her from the room, breathing heavily, the stench of beer and body odour wafting from him.

Ava said, 'I need to get organized for the meeting this morning. I'm going to get my paperwork and sit in the kitchen. I would appreciate it if you stayed away from there until I'm finished.'

'Do I bother you that much?'

'Your smell does.'

He raised an armpit, sniffed, and then smiled. 'I'm not leaving you alone.'

She went into her bedroom, closing the door behind her. She knelt by the bed and said a little prayer invoking St Jude, the patron saint of lost causes. Given the Roman Catholic Church's stance on homosexuality, Ava had quietly cut her ties with the institution. But she couldn't entirely revoke her childhood. She saw no relationship between prayer and the Church, or between St Jude and the Church. She prayed to him often when she was working, not because she was involved in that many lost causes, but more because he was also the patron saint of desperate situations, and those were something with which she was more familiar.

Her prayer finished, she laid out her clothes and accessories for the day. She decided on the pencil skirt, thinking that a show of lightly tanned, nicely shaped legs wouldn't hurt. The white Brooks Brothers shirt fit a little tighter than the other two, and her black bra would be vaguely visible through it. The green jade cufflinks and the ivory chignon pin were musts, as were the Cartier watch and the gold crucifix. They completed the image she wanted to project: professional, successful, and attractive in an understated, conservative way.

She opened the Chanel bag she took to meetings and put the business cards from Fong Accounting and all of Seto's ID into it. Grabbing two sachets of VIA instant, her notebook, and the Barrett's Bank file she had taken from Seto's office, she left the bedroom and went to the kitchen. Robbins was back in the chair at the door. She thought he was sleeping until his eyes flickered open.

Ava put on the kettle, and while she waited for the water to boil she slipped onto the balcony, leaving the door open behind her. The sun was well above the horizon, beaming down on Road Harbour, the Caribbean a shimmering sky blue with streaks of green and the boat hulls gleaming. It was already warm, at least in the mid-twenties, but a light trade wind ruffled the morning air. Ava decided the balcony was for her. She left the notebook and files on the table and returned to the kitchen to make her coffee.

She drank half a cup standing by the stove, added a bit more coffee, topped up the water, and went back outside. She went through the bank file first, reacquainting herself with the account history. Thank God Jeremy Bates wasn't entirely new. If she'd drawn a manager who hadn't dealt with Seto before, her job would have been that much more difficult, if not impossible. At least Bates knew what Seto looked like.

Then she opened her Moleskine notebook and reviewed the notes she'd made after Seto had described the procedures for withdrawing more than $25,000 at a time. She wasn't worried about being able to cover the transaction with a plausible paper trail. It seemed to her that Seto's signature on a wire application, along with presentation of the appropriate identification – with copies signed and dated if necessary – would give the bank everything it needed. The important, overriding question was, would the bank insist on seeing Seto actually sign the documents? *But why would they?* she thought. They had his signature on record for comparison. She would be able to present his genuine ID in a couple of forms, with copies signed and dated. Not right away though, not at the first meeting. The worst thing she could do would be to overwhelm Bates with documentation.

The most important thing was for her not to rush, not to appear the least bit anxious. Slow and steady, slow and steady. Spin Bates the story. Establish her credibility. Show him Seto's ID. Establish the relationship. Get Bates primed to organize a wire but don't try to close at that first meeting. It would take two meetings, maybe even three. As long as she could keep nudging him along … tiny steps, tiny steps. Let him tell her what they needed and how they needed it. Let him think he was in control of sending the seven million dollars to Hong Kong.

The only problem was that Robbins thought five million was in play. She knew – at least, if he was smart – that he'd want to confirm the wire that Barrett's sent to Hong Kong. If he knew it was seven million his price would go up. She needed to convince the bank to send two wires, and that was doable. The way she figured it, if Plan A worked she'd be able to look after Tam and pocket an extra commission for herself. If things moved on to Plan B, Tam would still recover most of his loss.

She closed her eyes and rested her head against the back of the chair. The sun was naked in the sky, the heat building. She loved the sun on her skin, but it dulled her senses, lulled her to sleep. *Time to go in, time to go to work*, she thought, pulling herself up from the chair.

The apartment's living room was empty. Robbins' bedroom door was open but she could see no sign of him inside. Then she saw him standing in the bathroom at the sink. He was naked to the waist, rolls of fat rippling like ruffles on a splotchy white dress. He had a cloth in his gloved hand and was rubbing his left armpit. Robbins' eyes flickered in the mirror, staring back at her. Ava avoided his glance and went on into her room. Maybe he wasn't a complete animal after all. Or maybe he just couldn't bear his own stench.

She took her time brushing her hair, fixing the chignon, applying a hint of lipstick, and slipping into the clothes she had laid out on the bed. It was almost a ritual. When she was done, she stood back and looked at herself in the mirror on the dresser. She had left the top three buttons of her shirt undone. She turned sideways and then bent over to see how much breast showed. Too much, way too much for an accountant and too much for the banker. She buttoned one of them. The Cartier watch went on last, and she saw that it was already nine thirty. She did one last check of her Chanel bag to make sure she had everything she needed and then she was ready to go.

Jack Robbins sat on the sofa, his bare feet up on the coffee table. He had shaved as well as washed and had exchanged the baggy white tent shirt for a baggy black tent shirt. He stared at Ava, making no pretence that her breasts weren't his main interest.

'It's time,' she said.

Robbins stopped at the door to shove his feet into his sandals, his hands pressed against his belly so he could see them.

'We need to talk to Reception before we leave,' Ava said.

'About what?'

'Maid service. We don't want it.'

'I called downstairs already. It's cancelled until further notice.'

Ava was surprised he'd remembered

Davey was waiting for them, the Crown Victoria the largest car in sight. He smiled at Ava as he opened the back door for Robbins.

They left Wickham's Cay and drove into town. In daylight it was at least as pretty as it had been at night, clean and compact, with well-paved narrow streets with actual sidewalks and sections of picket fencing. The town was a mix of British colonial and Caribbean architecture, all on a scale that suited a territory of about fifty small islands and cays with a population of around twenty thousand. Davey kept up a laconic running commentary as they went. He pointed out the two-storey Legislative Council building, with its ground floor fronted by five arches and the second by a balcony that ran its length. 'The court is on top,' he said.

Ava listened, none of it really registering. It was nice not to be in Georgetown, but that wasn't going to help her with the bank.

Fyfe Street was in the middle of town, the bank housed in Simon House, a four-storey powder blue stucco commercial building. The street was predictably narrow, the sidewalk meagre. Davey drove the car onto the sidewalk and parked it so close to a wall that Ava doubted he could open his door. But then, he didn't have to leave the car. She looked at her watch. It was five minutes to ten. 'I have no idea how long this is going to take,' she said to Robbins.

'We're not going anywhere,' he said.

The bank was only one of a large number of tenants in the building. On the outside wall, on both sides of a white double door with elaborate brass handles, were lists of the occupants. There were two signs in brass, Barrett's and an insurance company. The insurer had the third floor to itself and Barrett's had the fourth. The other businesses, about twenty of them, each had a white-painted wooden sign about the width of a sheet of paper. They all seemed to be involved in offshore registration, providing a legal address and a cubbyhole for mail for God knows how many firms.

Ava stepped through the door into a small lobby with corridors running off on either side. There was an open elevator that looked as if it had been built in the 1950s. She got in, hit the button for the fourth floor, and then waited for the door to close. As the elevator creaked its way upward she realized it wasn't air-conditioned; she felt sweat beading on her forehead. She swore as she wiped at it, not wanting to look nervous.

The door opened onto a reception area that had two red leather couches along the wall to the left and a coffee table stacked with magazines. The wall on the right had pictures of London: Big Ben, Westminster Abbey, the Tower of London. Between the walls there had to be ten metres of Persian carpet. Straight ahead, also about ten metres away, a young woman sat behind a massive mahogany desk that was bare except for a phone and a magazine she was leafing through. Behind her, a wood-panelled wall ran from floor to ceiling. The Barrett's logo – cast in bronze – occupied its centre; it was at least a metre across and two metres high. Behind and to either side of the desk, two steel-plated doors, painted beige to blend with the walls, barred any further entrance into the bank's premises.

There was no one else in the room. There wasn't a sound save for the woman turning the page of her magazine.

It gives the right impression for a private bank, Ava thought. Spacious, unpretentious, elegant in a subtle and solid kind of way, certainly quiet, and no hurly-burly, nothing screaming at you to take out a car loan or refinance your mortgage. It looked like the kind of place where you'd have to know someone before becoming a customer, the kind of place that knew how to keep secrets.

The woman looked up from her magazine and Ava saw that it was *People. The Economist* would have been more appropriate, she thought. 'Hello, my name is Ava Lee. I have an appointment with Mr Bates.'

The woman smiled. 'Mr Bates is expecting you. Actually, you and a Mr Seto.'

Not many drop-ins here, Ava guessed. 'Mr Seto is indisposed. I'm here by myself.'

'I'll let Mr Bates know. I'll be back in a minute.'

The woman left the desk and walked to the door on the left. She punched in a six-digit security code, turned, and disappeared.

Ava looked through the magazines on the coffee table and found an *Economist* as well as a week-old copy of the *Financial Times*. She was debating which one to read when the beige door opened and the woman reappeared. 'Could you follow me, please,' she said.

Ava trailed her down a hallway lined with closed doors. At the end, standing in an open doorway, was a tall, slim young man who bore a remarkable resemblance to the actor Jude Law. *That can't be Bates*, Ava thought. The man managing the bank's interests in the world's largest offshore tax haven had to be more senior, tried, tested. Ava had the feeling she was being sloughed off. A ripple of panic danced in her stomach.

'Hello, I'm Jeremy Bates. So pleased to meet you,' he said.

Ava took his extended hand, assessing his off-white monogrammed shirt, blue and yellow Ferragamo silk tie, slate grey light wool tailored slacks with their sharp, straight crease, and glistening black lace-up shoes. *Those shoes are handmade*, Ava thought, *and Bates is no working-class boy*.

He was just over six feet, and as he looked down Ava saw that he was eyeing her just as closely. She gave him her shyest smile and said, 'Thank you so much for seeing me.'

'I was expecting Mr Seto as well,' he said, stepping aside and motioning for her to come into his office.

'He is terribly ill,' she said.

'We'll sit at my conference table,' said Bates. 'Nothing serious with him, I trust?'

'Food poisoning. We ate a hurried meal before getting on the plane yesterday and something did not sit right with him. He's been either in his bed or in the bathroom since we arrived, and either running a fever or experiencing chills.'

'So he's here in Road Town?'

'Oh, yes, just not mobile.'

She sat, her eyes wandering around the office. It was massive, as large as the reception area, designed to impress. More mahogany in the desk and credenza, another Persian rug spread over wooden floors. A high-backed, heavily padded green leather chair sat behind the desk, with two smaller ones in front of it. There were three picture windows on the back wall and the side walls were lined with bookcases filled with what looked like company minute books. Then her eye caught something a bit more modern. In the upper right-hand corner, where ceiling met wall, she saw a tiny camera. She had no doubt that every meeting in this room was recorded.

'My business card,' he said, passing it to her.

'Thank you,' she said, noting his title: DIRECTOR, PRIVATE BANKING, BRITISH VIRGIN ISLANDS.

'Now, I have tea, coffee, and water. Do you have a preference?'

'Oh, nothing, thank you,' she said, finding herself still taken aback by his youth and good looks. His hair was dark blond, short, receding at the temples. He had brilliant blue eyes set a bit far apart, and his nose was long and slender.

'Fine,' he said, pouring himself a glass of water. 'Now tell me, Ms Lee, in what capacity are you affiliated with Mr Seto?'

She took her business card from the Chanel bag and held it at two corners as she presented it to Bates. 'Our firm is the accountant of record for Dynamic Financial Services. Dynamic finances purchase orders and letters of credit and generally facilitates trade among Southeast Asia, Europe, and North America. One of Mr Seto's companies, Seafood Partners, has used Dynamic's services extensively over the past six months and the principals have developed a close working relationship. About two months ago, Mr Seto decided to take an equity position in a scallop and shrimp plant in Yantai, on the northern coast of the Yellow Sea. He used Dynamic to broker the deal, and now we're getting ready to close.'

Bates looked at her business card and then back at Ava. She sat tall, Havergal style, her breasts thrust ever so slightly forward. 'That all seems very interesting,' he said, words she knew meant nothing.

'Well, it's never easy dealing with the Chinese,' she said. 'Dynamic, though, has extensive experience in that area. They always try, for example, to negotiate terms that leave the investors with exit options in case of problems. Quite obviously, they have contacts inside China that make this possible, contacts they have nurtured over a great many years. The fees they charge for brokering contracts like this, for being the stable bridge between the two parties, are exceedingly reasonable given the level of protection they offer.'

He had a pen, a notepad, and a closed file in front of him. He didn't write a single word as she spoke. 'Our bank has a presence in Asia, of course, and I have heard how difficult it is to do business there,' he said.

'It can be incredibly frustrating,' Ava said. 'We represented an American firm one time that was negotiating a contract in Shanghai. It dragged on and on for months, and every time they thought the deal was done, some new issue would emerge. Finally they thought everything had been put to bed and were told by the Chinese to bring their senior people to Shanghai for a signing ceremony. A week later their CEO flew into Hong Kong from New York to catch a flight to Shanghai. When he got to Hong Kong, he was met at the airport by his local staff. They had just received a fax from the Chinese company signed by someone none of them had met or even heard of. The fax advised them not to bother coming to Shanghai – the deal was dead. The Americans tried phoning, faxing, and emailing everyone they had met during the course of the previous months. No one would take their calls or respond to any of their communications.

'Dynamic made some phone calls for me and found out that the nephew of the Shanghai mayor had brought a German firm to the table the week before. All those months of work, all the complicated negotiations, all the money expended – it all went down the drain on the strength of a handshake between the nephew and the Germans.'

'What a story,' Bates said. 'You know, if you don't mind me saying, you seem very young to have this level of experience and responsibility.'

'I was thinking exactly the same thing about you,' she said. 'I was expecting to meet some old banker in a tweed suit.'

'A tweed suit wouldn't do in this climate, and actually I rarely wear a jacket of any kind,' he said, smiling. 'As for my age ... well, Barrett's is very aggressive when it comes to recruiting and very progressive in putting younger staff in positions that place demands on their learning curve. I've just turned thirty-eight and this is my second foreign posting. I was second-in-command of our Paris office before this.'

'I had put you as even younger.'

'Thank you, I guess, though that's not always good in this business. I get clients coming in here who keep insisting that they want to talk to my boss.'

'I get the same thing,' Ava said, shaking her head. 'I'm in my early thirties and still get treated as if I graduated from university last year.'

'I can't say I'm completely surprised. I mean, you do look younger than thirty.'

'Chinese genes.'

'For someone who is Chinese, your English is remarkably good,' he said, and then caught himself. 'I didn't mean that to sound condescending.'

'I was raised and educated in Canada.'

'I love Canada,' he said, leaning towards her. 'I have a brother living in Montreal and a sister in Vancouver.'

'I love it too, but for work purposes I didn't have much choice but to go back to Hong Kong.'

'Now, Mr Seto . . . He lives where exactly?'

'He has a residence in Seattle and another in Hong Kong, and of course he has a home in Guyana.'

'Yes, we've most often dealt with him from Guyana.'

Ava didn't want to go much further down that path. She opened her Chanel purse. It was time to raise the ante. 'Here is the banking information for Dynamic,' she said, sliding a sheet of paper to Bates. 'You already have their name and address. These are the bank's particulars, including the branch address and the IBN and SWIFT numbers. The account number is at the bottom.'

'Mr Seto wrote that he wanted to send a wire.'

'Yes.'

'For how much?'

'One for five million, and a second wire for two million.'

'Two wires?'

'Yes, the two million is to be sent to the holding company of the scallop plant as a deposit. Here is their data,' Ava said, passing over Uncle's banking information. 'The five goes to Dynamic. They'll hold it in escrow until the deal closes, and that hopefully will be within the next twenty-four hours.'

'Seven million total, then?'

Could that be his only question? He had no concerns about the separate wires? 'Yes, seven million.'

He opened his file. She saw copies of the emails she had sent from Seto's address on top. They looked bona fide, even to her. 'There is sufficient money in the account,' he said.

'I assume you'll prepare two wire transfer drafts for Jackson's signature?'

He picked up the two pieces of paper she had given him and put them in his file folder. 'Give me a few minutes. I'll get them started right away.'

Ava hesitated. He hadn't mentioned the passport requirement or the need to present other ID. She thought about letting it pass and then just as quickly decided not to. Bates might not be entirely up to date with the account safeguards, but someone would be sure to flag them. It was better for her to be proactive, to appear as transparent as possible. She needed all the trust she could generate.

'Excuse me, Mr Bates, I don't mean to slow things down, but Jackson did mention that the bank normally requires him to present his passport and other forms of ID, and to sign and date copies of them. I brought the originals with me just in case you needed them.' She reached into her purse and removed Seto's American passport, Hong Kong ID card, driver's licence, and credit cards. She spread them in front of Bates. 'Take whatever you need.'

He nodded. 'Yes, thanks for reminding me. Marilyn usually handles this kind of detail. I'll take everything to her and she can copy whatever she wants. She'll be preparing the wire transfer drafts as well.'

'How long do you think it will take?' she asked.

'You're in a rush?'

'No, no, it's just that I really need to make a couple of phone calls and I left my cellphone at the apartment.'

'You can use the phone here if you wish,' he said, pointing to the one on the conference table.

'They're long-distance calls.'

'Ms Lee, I think the bank can afford to pay for a few long-distance calls. Any line will do. Dial nine for an outside line, and then 011 and the country code.'

'Thank you, I really appreciate it.'

'And I'll close my office door. When you're finished, just open it to let me know you're free.'

Bates put Seto's passport and other ID into his file. Then he stood up and looked down at Ava. 'I must say, this is a nice break from my usual routine,' he said.

She watched him leave the room, grateful that he hadn't made her ask to use the phone. Conscious more than ever of the camera at work in the corner of the ceiling, she tried to look as natural and composed as she could. *Just pretend you're calling Mimi*, she thought, as she punched in Uncle's Hong Kong cellphone number, fervently hoping he'd pick up.

'*Wei*?' he answered.

'Uncle, it's Ava,' she said.

'I don't recognize this line. Where are you?'

'I made it. I'm in the British Virgin Islands,' she said, switching to Cantonese.

'Ava, I've been calling your cell. Why haven't you been answering?' he said, matching her language choice.

'I've made it but I'm having a bit of trouble.'

'I thought Derek was there,' he said.

'He isn't, and that's part of the problem. But I don't have time to get into all of it, so please listen very carefully to me.'

'I don't like this.'

'Just listen, please.'

'Are you in any danger?'

328

'Nothing I can't handle, so don't get anxious, please.'

'All right, I'm listening,' he said slowly.

'I'm at the bank and I'm close to getting Tam his money back, and a sweetener for us. If all goes well today, I'll be able to wire five million to him and two million to your account in Kowloon. Once the wires have left here, and that should be sometime in the next twenty-four hours, I'm going to send you an email asking you to send another $2.2 million by wire to the account in the Cayman Islands we've already sent $300,000 to – except I don't want you to send the wire. What I want you to do is get your friends at the bank to dummy one up. When our accountant gets it, I want him to scan it and send it to me and to another email address I'll provide.'

'Ava, this is all a bit more complicated than you expected, no?'

'Uncle, will you have any problem getting your bank to dummy the wire?'

'No, it is owned by friends of mine. But why are we sending more money to the Caymans, or pretending to, at any rate?'

'It's a shakedown. I don't want to get into the details right now. Just believe that it is something I need done.'

'I can get the bank to do it. That won't be a problem,' he said.

'Great. When I send you the email requesting the wire, I'll include the guy's email address and fax number so you can copy him when it's issued.'

'What makes you think he will accept the wire at face value?'

'Well, he has before. And he's not Chinese, so I'm assuming he has some faith in banks.'

'That sounds thin to me.'

'Uncle, I don't have time to explain everything. I'm using someone else's phone because I don't have mine, so let me finish what I have to say.'

'I'm listening, I'm listening,' he said.

'All I'm hoping the dummy wire will do is buy me the time I need to get out of here. As I said, I'm not going to ask you to send the dummy until I know for sure our money is secure. So if for some reason this guy doesn't bite, we just might have to send him his share. The extra two million I got covers most of it, and Tam can eat the rest.'

'How will I know what is what if I can't reach you?'

'When I send the first request – the one I want you to dummy up – I'll sign off simply as Ava. If I really need you to send the money, I'll send a follow-up email asking for confirmation that the money has been sent and sign off as Ava Lee. If you don't see my full name, don't send anything.'

'I don't like this,' he said.

'Uncle,' she said quietly, still conscious of the recording device, 'this guy is trying to take us for a ride. I don't like it, and I'm not about to roll over and play dead. I want Tam to get his money, all of his money. And I want us to get our share and then some. I know you're not taking a cut from Tam's end, but there's no reason you shouldn't have half of anything extra we collect. I mean, you did front $300,000.'

'What if the guy there catches on?'

'I'll tell him there was a glitch in the system and send you the second email. All it should mean is that I'll be stuck here for a few extra days.'

'You're confident about this?'

'Enough to try it.'

'And I still won't be able to reach you?'

'No, and don't bother. I can't use my cellphone or my computer on my own. Right now I'm in the banker's office. I should be able to email you the wire request soon. If you don't get it within the twenty-four hours and you don't hear from me, send in some troops. I'm staying at the Guildford Apartments in Road Town. The room is booked in Derek's name.'

'You know,' he said softly, 'I wish I hadn't talked to Tam's uncle about taking this job.'

It's a bit late for that, she thought. '*Momentai* – no problem, Uncle. Now I have to go. I'll email you when I can, and hopefully I'll be talking to you sometime tomorrow.'

As she hung up she felt suddenly quite isolated. When was the last time she and Uncle had been out of touch through any reason not of their own choosing? What other option did she have, she wondered as she phoned Derek.

His cellphone rang four times, and she was preparing to leave a voicemail when he answered, his voice defensive, as Uncle's had been. 'Who is this?'

'Derek, it's me, Ava. I'm in the British Virgin Islands. Where are you?' she said, again in Cantonese.

'I'm in Montreal. I'm catching a plane back to Toronto in a few minutes. Do you know what happened?'

'They told me your papers weren't in order.'

'Bullshit,' he shouted.

'I know.'

'I walked through Customs with absolutely no problem, caught a cab, and stopped at a market near the apartment to load up on some food and drinks. I was in the room for barely ten minutes before they came knocking – two customs officers and a guy who looked like a walking mountain. I tried to argue with them but they wouldn't listen. If they hadn't been customs officers I would have resisted. Sorry, Ava, but I just didn't see the sense in doing that.'

'No, Derek, you did the right thing, absolutely the right thing. No point in making things worse. They told me they shipped you back to Puerto Rico and then put you on a plane to Montreal. I'm glad you made it.'

'Hey, how about you? You okay?'

'Not so bad.'

'You need help?'

'That's why I'm calling.'

She heard voices in the background noise behind him. 'They're boarding my flight,' he said.

'This won't take long. Do you have a pen and paper?'

'No. Let me see if I can find something.'

'Wait, don't bother,' Ava said quickly. 'Turn off your cellphone when we hang up. I'll call back and leave a voicemail with some names and phone numbers. Derek, listen to me – I need you to be completely available over the next twenty-four hours. I may need you to pick up something for me, so keep your cellphone charged and on. If I have to call in the middle of the night, I want to know I can reach you. Right now you're my lifeline.'

'I don't like that word,' he said.

'I'm just being dramatic,' Ava said with a light laugh.

'But you're not joking about my being available.'

'No, I'm not,' she said.

'Shit, Ava—'

'Okay, Derek, enough. Go catch your plane and turn off your phone, and if you don't hear from me, don't worry and don't be disappointed.'

She hung up and waited, giving him two full minutes. When she connected with his phone again, she was put right into voicemail. Ava explained, slowly and carefully, what she wanted him to do.

35

Ava sat quietly for a moment, trying to compose herself, conscious of the camera tracking her every move. It was time to focus her attention back onto Jeremy Bates. The meeting had gone well, but she knew that was the easy part. There were still so many things that could go wrong. All it would take was one small doubt on his part and the words 'I really do need to talk to Mr Seto' and all the scheming in the world wouldn't do her much good. *Why did I think this was going to work?* she thought. She shook her head, caught herself, and rubbed her eyes. It was becoming a struggle to stay in the moment. There were all the things that could go wrong with Bates, and then of course there was Robbins. Had she overplayed her hand by calling Uncle? No, she told herself, she at least had a backup plan now, and Uncle never failed her. The thought of Uncle reminded her of Tommy Ordonez. Uncle hadn't had a chance to mention him during their talk, thank God, but now he intruded into her mind – the jinx that lingered. She pushed him away.

One thing at a time, she thought. *Get off the chair. Walk to the door. Open it.*

There was no one in the hallway, but she could see an open door halfway down the hall and hear Bates's voice saying,

'That looks just fine.' She turned and went back to her seat, her spirits improved already.

Bates wasn't far behind her, the file folder in one hand, a clutch of papers in the other. 'Here we go,' he said, putting the papers on the table in front of her. 'I had everything done in triplicate. One set for Mr Seto and you and two sets for me.'

Ava leafed through the documents. The two draft wire transfer requests looked perfect. All they needed was Seto's signature. They had copied his passport, Hong Kong ID card, and Washington state driver's licence. That meant fifteen signatures. She tried not to think about how difficult that would be.

'I'm hopeful I'll be able to get these back to you within the next few hours,' she said.

'Ms Lee—'

'Please call me Ava.'

'And I'm Jeremy,' he said with a slight smile. 'What I was about to say, Ava, is that it would be ideal if Mr Seto could accompany the documents in person.'

The fact that she was prepared for the request didn't make it any easier to hear. 'Jeremy, I'll obviously do everything I can to make that happen. I just can't predict what kind of shape he's going to be in.'

'Well, we can wait, you know,' he said. 'This doesn't have to be done today.'

'Yes, it does,' Ava said matter-of-factly. 'We can't miss the closing. If we miss the deadline, the Chinese will see it as a sign of weakness. We'll be forced into yet another round of negotiations and will probably face a higher cost.'

'This is quite difficult. From my end, I mean,' he said.

There was no threat in his tone, just a kind of sad resignation, but to Ava the message was clear enough. Jeremy Bates had drawn his banker's line in the sand. No Seto, no money. She knew from Bates's side that it was the right thing to do, and the only thing that gave her any comfort was the subtle way in which he had chosen to tell her. She respected him for his tact, and at heart she respected the fact that he wasn't willing to discard his sense of duty – even for her. 'I'll get Jackson out of bed and over here if I have to carry him myself,' she said.

'That would be best, Ava,' he said.

She gathered the papers together and put them in her Chanel bag. 'Well, I guess I should get going.'

'I'll walk you to the elevator,' he said, standing up.

'That's not necessary.'

'I insist,' Bates said.

They walked side by side, Bates more awkward than she. 'Where are you staying, by the way?' he asked.

'The Guildford Apartments.'

'Nice.'

'Yes, nice enough.'

'When do you leave?'

'If we wrap up today, then tomorrow.'

He pushed the elevator button for her. 'Now, would you let the bank buy you and Mr Seto dinner tonight?'

'I can't imagine he'll be up to it.'

'Then how about just you and me?' he said, not missing a beat.

'I would like that very much.'

He paused, his eyes wandering away from her. 'You'll call me, I trust, when Mr Seto has signed the documents. We can arrange another appointment then. My afternoon is quite open, so there won't be any delay on my end.'

'I'll call,' she said.

'Excellent, and when you do, we can confirm a place and time for dinner.'

'Of course,' Ava said, with more enthusiasm than she felt.

The elevator was still hot and still slow, but her mind was preoccupied with signatures and the very unconscious Jackson Seto.

The Crown Victoria was where she had left it, with Davey in the front seat, window open, bobbing his head to the sound of Neil Diamond's 'Cracklin' Rosie'. It made Ava think of Bangkok and Arthon. How long ago was that? And what was up with all the Neil Diamond? Robbins was sleeping, his head flung back, his mouth wide open. As she stood on the side-walk she could smell the aroma of fresh bread coming from a bakery across the street. She suddenly felt hungry and realized she had eaten only a bag of almonds since noon the day before. She looked up and down the street and spotted a fish-and-chip restaurant a few doors down from the bakery.

She walked to the front passenger side of the car and stuck her head in the window. 'I'm going to eat at that fish-and-chip place. If he wakes up, tell him where I am,' she said to Davey, and then turned and left before he had a chance to say a word.

The restaurant was plainness itself – linoleum floor, plastic chairs and tables – but it was clean, and the smell of cooking oil was muted. 'I'm surprised you're open,' Ava said to a tall, skinny man dressed entirely in white.

'Cruise ship docks in about half an hour. We'll get swamped.'

She scanned the menu, her fish-and-chip experience limited to the occasional after-club foray with Mimi and Good Fridays with her mother and Marian when the girls were small. She couldn't remember whether haddock or halibut was the premium choice, so she asked.

'Take the halibut,' he said.

'With chips and gravy,' Ava said.

'Mushy peas?'

'Why not?'

She felt a touch guilty when the plate was put in front of her. Loading up on grease was something – Guyana and KFC aside – she rarely did voluntarily. Now she put malt vinegar and salt and pepper on the fish and chips. A dollop of tartar sauce went on one side of the plate and ketchup on the other. She cut into the fish, the batter golden brown and surprisingly light, slathered a piece in tartar sauce, and ate it. The fish melted in her mouth.

Ava ate quickly, but she was still only halfway through the meal when the front door opened and Robbins lurched in. His eyes danced around the restaurant as if he were expecting to see something other than her sitting at a table. 'What are you doing?' he demanded, his voice husky with sleep.

'What does it look like?'

'You should have asked.'

'You were sleeping.'

His hand went to his head. Ava turned her attention back to her food, not wanting a glimpse of his fingers sliding in the furrows. But the vision was already in her head. She ate a few more chips, a sliver of fish, and a forkful of bright green mushy peas, then put her utensils down. 'That really was excellent,' she said to the man behind the counter.

He nodded as if he was used to hearing such compliments.

As she left the restaurant she said to Robbins, 'I need to find a place where I can make some copies of documents.'

Davey had moved the car to in front of the fish-and-chip shop. Ava climbed in. 'I need to make some photocopies,' she repeated.

Davey looked back at Robbins. 'Go to Quickie Copy,' Robbins said.

They drove back through town, past the turnoff for Wickham's Cay II, and continued around the southwest corner of the harbour. The copy shop was on Main Street, in the end unit of a small strip mall. Ava went inside with Robbins tagging along. She made an additional two copies of each of the papers Bates had given her. Her Jackson Seto signature was passable, she thought, but the extra copies gave her some insurance.

Back in the car she said, 'And I wouldn't mind stopping at a grocery store on the way back to the apartment.'

'Jesus Christ, this is getting stupid,' Robbins said.

'I can't exist on nuts and potato chips.'

'There's a market just around the corner from the apartment. I saw it as we were leaving this morning. It's right on the way,' Davey said.

'Okay, okay, but that's it,' said Robbins.

As Davey pulled up in front of the store, Robbins' cellphone rang. 'Wait,' he said to Ava. He listened for no more than a few seconds. 'Here, it's my brother for you,' he said, passing her the phone.

She held it away from her mouth. 'I left the bank about half an hour ago,' she said, knowing that was why he had called. 'Nothing is finalized, nothing is agreed. It was step one, that's all.'

'I was going to ask if you slept well,' the Captain said.

'And then you were going to ask me about the bank.'

'That is incorrect. I was also going to ask if my brother was good company.'

'And then you were going to ask about the bank.'

'True enough.' He laughed. 'So if it is just business you want to discuss, tell me how it went.'

'I didn't get thrown out of their offices, if that's what you mean.'

'That's the last thing I would have imagined.'

'You may be expecting too much of me, and it's way too soon to know how this will end. The banker, Bates, is very sharp and very conscientious. He's insisting on talking to Seto,' Ava said.

'And you're trying to tell me that could be a problem?'

'What do you think?'

'I see the potential risk.'

'That's an understatement.'

'Oh, I'm sure you'll be able to handle it, Ms Lee. I have nothing but confidence in you.'

Ava saw no reason to pursue such a pointless conversation. 'Look, I have to go. I have papers to sign and things to organize.'

'What is your schedule?'

'I'm going to talk to Bates again this afternoon. If he'll accept at face value the documents with my version of Seto's signature, I'll attempt to get the money wired to Hong Kong today. If that happens, and after I have confirmation, I need to email my end to initiate a wire back to you. Obviously I need to use my computer to do that, so you'll have to instruct your brother accordingly.'

'That won't be a problem.'

'Landing here wasn't supposed to be a problem.'

'Ms Lee, don't be churlish,' he said.

'Assuming we get to the point of sending a wire from Hong Kong – and I'm not guaranteeing we will – I'll ask my people to email you a scanned copy of the wire as I did before. And to be doubly safe, I would like to send you a fax copy. Do you have a fax number that's secure?'

'My brother has that number.'

'I don't want to ask him for even that much,' said Ava.

'Ah. He does lack charm, I admit. All right, I'll email it to you.'

Ava saw Jack Robbins stiffen and realized that he could hear what his brother was saying. That gave her pause. She had been about to nudge the Captain about returning her Canadian passport and calling off Morris Thomas after he received the wire transfer notification. Suddenly and completely, that felt like one of the worst ideas she'd had since leaving Toronto.

God, don't appear the least bit anxious, she thought. *And don't give him time to think about doing it. Try to catch him when he's just been told he's about to pocket two million dollars.* 'Thank you,' she said. 'You understand this means I have to get into my computer?'

'As long as it's related to our business and Jack is watching you, I have no objections.'

'Aren't you generous.'

'Ms Lee, you honour your commitments and I'll honour mine.'

She handed the phone back to Jack Robbins. 'I'm going to buy some food. Here, you talk to your brother.'

Robbins caught up with her as she was putting two bottles of sparkling water into her basket. 'Stop running out on me,' he said.

'Just trying to save time.'

'My brother wasn't finished with you.'

'Tough,' Ava said, and held out the basket. 'If you're going to follow me around you might as well carry this.'

Robbins stared, his eyes for the first time really looking into hers. They weren't entirely lifeless, she saw, more like disinterested, as if she was completely insignificant to him. She knew that goading him wasn't the best approach, but she couldn't bring herself to make nice. 'Let's go,' he said, ignoring the basket.

Ava walked down two more aisles, adding rice crackers, cheese, a jar of olives, and a small plastic container of hummus. Robbins stayed close behind her, his gloved hands jammed into his jeans pockets, saying nothing.

342

Outside the store she could see that the apartment building was no more than a couple of minutes away; she asked Robbins if they could walk. He opened the car door and said, 'Get in.'

Davey dropped them in front of the building. 'Do you need me later?' he asked.

'If I do, I'll call,' said Robbins.

Doreen, the young woman they had met in the lobby the night before, was behind the reception desk. She stared, rather rudely, Ava thought, as she and Robbins entered and walked to the elevator. What lurid thoughts were running through her mind?

The apartment was as they had left it. Ava went to look in on Seto. He had rolled over onto his side, kicking the bedcovers clear. His hair was dishevelled and starting to look greasy. Drool had dried on one side of his mouth. She covered him, hoping it wasn't going to be necessary to clean him up.

Ava heard a clatter from the living room and looked out to see Robbins clearing the Stella empties. She walked towards him as he deposited the bottles in the kitchen trash bin. 'I need this space,' she said. 'I have a lot of papers to sign and I need to concentrate, so I'd appreciate it if you could leave me alone. I don't want the television on. In fact, I don't want any distractions at all, so it would be ideal if you could hang out in your room until I'm done.'

She saw his body tense; this time he wanted to argue. Before he could react she brushed past him and sat at the kitchen table. He stood near the sink, staring down at her. She tried to ignore him, extracting from her purse the documents Bates had given her, setting out the extra copies she'd made, and laying out Seto's passport, Hong Kong ID card, and driver's licence in a row. 'I need to work,' she said, not looking up.

'Cunt,' he muttered.

Ava heard it clearly enough but pretended she hadn't. She searched in her purse for one more document, a copy of Seto's last withdrawal request from the bank, and then put it next to his other identification. She opened her notebook. 'I need to work,' she said.

He took two steps towards the living room, stopped to look back at her, and then shuffled across the floor to his room.

Ava sat quietly at the kitchen table for a few minutes, collecting herself. Robbins was becoming a distraction, and she blamed herself for letting him annoy her. She opened her notebook and looked at the signatures she'd penned the night before. *Not bad*, she thought, *not bad at all*.

There were a lot of things for her to like about Seto's signature. It was short, for one thing, simply *JSeto*. It also wasn't identical from document to document. Similar, of course, and recognizable obviously, but with minor variations. It gave her a little wiggle room. Despite those positives, she sat quietly at the table for a few minutes, gathering her nerve. She had done this often enough in the past and never failed, but her perfectionist streak could always find flaws. The truth was, any reasonable facsimile normally worked. She was just afraid of running into someone as anal as she was.

She started with a blank page in her notebook and began to practise. The signature was basically a big looping J, the bottom loop curling into the upper, and a relatively straight-forward S, followed by a straight line that tailed off to a dot. The J was dominant. If she got that right, imperfections in the rest would pass. The proportions were tricky, though, between the top and bottom loops, and when they were out of sync the signature looked contrived.

Ava began to write J's – just J's. She had filled almost the entire page before she managed to get three in a row that looked similar to the ones in front of her. She closed her eyes, envisioning it. *I have it*, she thought.

She started with the copies of his ID. With one eye fixed on the bank document he'd signed and the other on the paper in front of her, she wrote *JSeto* nine times in rapid succession. When she had finished, she discarded only the last two – the J was out of whack. *Take a break, step away*, she thought. She got up and turned on the kettle. While the water boiled she looked out onto the harbour, amazed by the level of activity.

Ava drank half her coffee on the balcony, clearing her head, and then went back to the table. She had written two more lines of J's in her notebook before she recaptured the balance she wanted. Then quickly she redid the two signatures that looked suspect and moved on to the wire transfer requests. Those went smoothly, the signatures indistinguishable, even to her paranoid eye, from what the bank had on record. *There, the easy part is done*, she thought, as she organized the paper-work into matching sets.

It was too soon to call Bates. There was no value in letting him think Seto had been well enough to affix the signatures so promptly. She'd wait. It was almost eleven thirty. One o'clock – no, one thirty worked better. *Give him time to have some lunch.*

She gathered the documents and slid them into their folder. Out of nowhere came a yawn, and Ava realized she was tired. She'd been awake since God knows when, and the morning had been draining. She had time to kill, and a rest couldn't hurt.

Ava didn't say anything or look into Robbins' room as she walked past to hers. If he couldn't figure out that she had finished working, that was his problem. She closed the door behind her and lay on the bed fully clothed. Her mind was more of a jumble than she would have liked. Bates was more than enough to occupy her, but Robbins – both Robbinses – kept intruding. She tried to shut everyone out, thinking bak mei, crane position: her foot poised to strike, her hands moving faster than light.

When she woke, it was with a start, her eyes darting to the doorway. It was closed. She was on her bed, still dressed, nothing out of place. She lifted her left hand and looked at her watch. Two forty-five. She sat on the edge of the bed, composing herself.

She opened her bedroom door and saw Robbins back on the couch, watching television. She went to the bathroom, locking the door behind her, and washed her face with cold water, slapping at her cheeks. Then she undid her hair, brushed and coiled it again, and put the ivory chignon pin back in place. She reapplied her makeup. Her eyes looked a bit puffy from sleep, but there wasn't anything she could do about that.

Robbins turned towards her as she re-entered the living room. 'I need to call the bank,' she said.

'Use that phone,' he said, pointing to the only one in the apartment, which was on the wall near the kitchen.

She called the number on Bates's business card, assuming it was his private line. Instead, the receptionist she had met earlier answered with a rolling 'Barrrrrett's.'

'Mr Bates, please. Ms Lee calling.'

He came on the line quickly, and she guessed he had been waiting for her call. As he'd said, she was a diversion from his usual routine. 'Ava, how are things progressing?'

'Hello, Jeremy. Well, not bad at all. Jackson has signed the draft requests and all the other documents that are needed.'

'Wonderful. So when will I see the two of you?'

She heard the emphasis, however slight and subtle, on the word *two*. Ava drew a small breath. She knew for certain, knew totally and completely, that no matter how she spun things, Jeremy Bates wouldn't be sending any wires until he actually saw Jackson Seto. Suggesting anything else, no matter how creative she could be, wasn't going to fly. She could try to charm him, of course, but she knew there were limits to charm, and when charm had to compete against money, it lost its lustre pretty quickly.

'Unfortunately, Jeremy, there is that continuing problem with Jackson. Frankly, I'm having a tough time getting him from the bedroom to the bathroom, let alone dressed and out the door to visit the bank. In fact, I may need to ask you for the name of a doctor.'

'Ah,' he said.

To Ava's ear, that simple interjection was filled with hesitation, questions, doubt. She felt a slight touch of panic, and spoke before he could shut any doors on her. 'There is another way, though,' she said, in as low-key a manner as she could manage. 'Why don't you come here to collect the documents? I know Jackson would like to see you to say hello.'

He didn't respond immediately, and for a second she thought she had misjudged the situation. 'You know, that's not a bad idea,' he finally said.

'The sooner, the better,' she said. 'He's exhausted and keeps nodding off.'

'About an hour?' he asked.

'Perfect. We're in apartment 312.'

'See you both then.'

36

Ava tried to put herself in Bates's position. Every transaction he conducted was a candidate for scrutiny, a potential target for the only person who might scare him: the bank's auditor. All the good bankers she had known made it a religion to cover their tracks, regardless of the size or nature of the transaction. Following banking regulations had become second nature to them. So to her mind, dinner invitation or not, Bates wasn't going to treat her differently from any other customer. It was her job to make sure he had everything he thought he would need if an auditor came calling. And she thought she had done that adequately.

He had the email from Seto saying that he wanted to send a wire and bringing Ava into the picture as a trusted associate. He had met Ava, and she seemed to be the person Seto had described. She knew, given the time difference, that he hadn't had a chance to call the accounting firm in Hong Kong to confirm her position, and from the way he had looked at her card and at her, she knew he wouldn't. He had seen all the originals of Seto's identification, and they matched everything they currently had on file. Now he was going to get the signed original copies of the wire transfer requests and signed and dated copies of the same ID. It was, all in all, Ava thought, a paper trail that would satisfy any auditor.

But there was still the important matter of Bates actually meeting Seto, actually witnessing him signing the necessary documentation. It was a chink in the due diligence process, she knew, that might cause Bates problems if he had to explain the situation later. But that would be later, when hindsight would make it easy to adapt what had actually occurred into what was supposed to have transpired. And even then, he could say with all honesty that he had seen Seto. The fact that he was comatose could be explained. Seto was ill, after all, and Bates had made the point of physically going to his apartment to meet with him. He couldn't be blamed for the fact that Seto was sleeping at the time. Due diligence had been done. The bank couldn't reasonably expect more of him.

It's going to hold, Ava thought as she stood up, feeling satisfied.

'We're going to have a visitor, and I need your help,' she said to Robbins.

'Huh?'

'The banker is coming to meet me and Seto. We need to get organized.'

'Like how?'

'Come with me,' she said, heading for Seto's bedroom.

He was still out cold, but it had been more than six hours since she'd given him the previous dose of chloral hydrate. She wasn't about to take the slightest chance that he'd wake up when Bates was there. 'Sit him up and see if you can revive him enough to drink,' she said.

While Robbins grabbed Seto under the arms and hoisted

him up, Ava rooted through the toilet kit Anna Choudray had packed for him. She found a toothbrush and a hairbrush. She threw the hairbrush on the bed and left the room with the toothbrush.

In the bathroom she mixed another dose of chloral hydrate and set it aside. She soaked a facecloth, put toothpaste on his brush, and with a towel under her arm went back to join the two men.

Robbins was shaking Seto as if he were a rag doll. Seto's eyes rolled open, but for only a few seconds at a time before closing. They were blank, uncomprehending. Ava wondered if the dose would be necessary, a thought that was banished when he slurred, 'What the fuck ...'

'Hold his mouth open,' she told Robbins.

Brushing Seto's teeth was nearly impossible because his head kept moving around, but at least when his mouth was open there was now a faint smell of toothpaste. When she was done, she took the facecloth, wiped away the remnants of paste, scrubbed the dried drool from around his mouth, and then for good measure opened the cloth and rubbed his entire face. 'I'll be back,' she said.

Seto seemed to have nodded off again when she returned. 'He needs to drink this,' she told Robbins.

Robbins pried open Seto's mouth again. She poured. He gagged, and she slowed down the process until he was taking little sips. He got halfway through the glass before he couldn't swallow any more. She stopped; a drowned Seto wouldn't do her any good. 'Hold him upright for just another second,' she said.

Ava went to work with the hairbrush. When Seto finally looked decent, she reached behind him to undo the cuffs. 'Lay him down.'

She unwrapped the tape from his ankles. Fortunately neither they nor his wrists were marked to any degree. She pulled the bedcovers halfway up his chest, leaving both arms out, resting comfortably along his sides. She stepped back. He was thin, wan, pallid – like someone who was very ill but was being well looked after.

His suitcase was still on the floor where she had dropped it the night before. She put it in the closet. 'That should just about do it,' she said to herself.

Ava went into the living room, closing Seto's door. 'I can't have you here when the banker comes,' she said to Robbins.

'I'm not leaving,' he said.

'Then we have a problem. Do we need to call your brother?'

'I'll go to my room. The door will be closed. But I'm not leaving the apartment.'

Ava tried to think of a convincing argument that he was being unreasonable and failed. 'Just be quiet, then.'

'I didn't bring my drums,' he muttered.

She carried her file folder to the kitchen, opened it, and placed Bates's two sets of documents on the table. She checked the signatures against the passport and the Hong Kong ID card. The only way they wouldn't pass, she thought, was if the person looking at them had predetermined they weren't genuine. They weren't perfect, she knew; they were just good enough. And if Bates, God forbid, questioned any of them, she could always use Seto's illness as an excuse.

'Hello, hello,' a voice said from the intercom by the door. 'There's someone here to see a Ms Lee.'

Ava looked at her watch. Bates was early. She walked to the intercom. 'Send him up, please.'

Robbins rose from the sofa and walked silently to his room.

Bates looked slightly uncomfortable when Ava opened the door. She hoped the idea of being in the apartment alone with her – well, almost alone – was behind it.

'I've never been in one of these apartments before,' he said. 'I've heard good things.'

'Well, they give you value,' she said, directing him towards the kitchen. 'Can I get you anything? Bottled water, coffee?'

'I'm fine.'

'Let's sit then.'

He looked at the documents on the table.

'They're all signed. Two sets for you, one for us.'

Bates sat at the table and began to peruse them. He went through both sets, which surprised her. Then he took a copy of one of the wire transfer requests and placed it alongside the copy of Seto's passport, checking the signatures. He did it far more intensely than Ava would prefer, and she felt a quiver of doubt.

'It all seems to be in order,' he finally said.

'Are you ready to meet with Jackson?' Ava asked.

'That would be excellent.'

She led him to the bedroom door, gave it a light tap, and listened. 'He may be sleeping,' she said, rapping harder. She counted to ten. 'I think he's sleeping. We'll go in anyway.'

Seto's covers had slipped a touch. She tiptoed towards the

bed. Bates followed behind her, looking uncomfortable again and doing his best to be quiet. Ava leaned down. 'Jackson,' she whispered. 'Jeremy Bates is here. Do you want to say hello?'

'He looks very pale,' Bates said.

Ava nodded as she gently shook Seto's shoulder. 'He's terribly dehydrated. I've been making him drink as much water as he can handle.'

'Food poisoning can be debilitating,' said Bates.

'Jackson, Jeremy Bates is here. He wants to say hello,' Ava said more loudly.

'Oh, leave him, please. Leave him,' Bates said. 'I have everything I need.'

Ava backed away from the bed, bumping into Bates and stumbling. He reached out to steady her, his right arm slipping under her breasts. That's when she heard a thud. To her it sounded as loud as a bag of bricks being dropped three metres onto a tile floor. She flushed.

'Sorry about that,' Bates said. 'I thought you were going to fall.'

'I might have,' she said, scarcely believing he hadn't heard the noise.

She led him out of the bedroom, closing the door behind her. 'You mentioned earlier you might need a doctor?' he said.

'I don't think that's necessary now. He's slowly coming around. I've had food poisoning myself, and it's usually twenty-four hours of misery and then another twenty-four to forty-eight hours of recovery. I just hope he'll be okay to fly. We're supposed to leave tomorrow night. I may have to postpone if he isn't feeling up to it.'

'There are worst places to be stuck,' Bates said.

'Admittedly,' she said with a little smile.

They walked back to the kitchen table and the documents. Bates gathered up his sets. 'Do you think it will be possible to send the wires today?' she asked.

'I don't see why not,' he said casually.

'Wonderful. We would really appreciate it.'

'You will want copies of the actual transfer, I presume, and confirmation that they've been sent?'

'Yes, I would. We need to let Hong Kong know as soon as possible that it's a go from this end.'

'Why don't I bring them with me tonight when we meet for dinner?' he asked.

That was smooth, she thought. 'Jackson won't be up to it.'

'Well, we'll have to manage without him, won't we?'

'Yes, we will. I'm looking forward to it,' Ava said, not missing a beat.

'There's a French bistro called Les Deux Garçons on the first street before the bank. Are you comfortable with French food?'

'I eat everything.'

'Fantastic. Do you need me to pick you up?'

'No, please don't. I'm going to spend the rest of the day sightseeing. I'll find my own way.'

'Seven o'clock, then?'

'Yes, perfect. I'll see you at seven.'

She waited by the door until she heard the elevator close. She was walking towards Robbins' room when he emerged.

'Dinner?' he said.

'What the hell was that noise?' she said, cutting him off.

'You handled it, right?'

'If he had had any suspicions at all—'

'But he didn't, or it sure didn't sound like he did. Dinner at seven, huh?'

'I had no choice.'

'We'll drive you and we'll wait outside. And don't give me any story about having to go back to his place for a drink.'

'There's no chance of that,' Ava said. 'It's dinner and out. I just want to get this thing finished and get myself on a plane back home.'

37

They left the apartment at quarter to seven. Ava had spent the rest of the afternoon and early evening going back and forth between the balcony, bedroom, and kitchen, her restlessness even getting on her own nerves.

Davey knew the restaurant and drove her to within a hundred metres of it. Ava looked up and down the street, not wanting Bates to see her getting out of the car. When there was no sign of him, she got out and moved away from the door. Robbins rolled down his backseat window. 'We'll be right here,' he said.

She got to the restaurant door at seven on the dot. There was no sign of Bates at the entrance. She stuck her head inside. It was a small place, only about fifteen tables, and unless he was in the washroom he hadn't shown up yet. A short, round, cheery-looking woman with a menu cradled in one arm glanced at Ava, waved, and then walked towards her. 'Ms Lee?'

'Yes.'

'Mr Bates called for you. He wants you to phone him at this number.'

Ava's paranoia kicked in. *This can't be good.*

'I'll have to use your phone. I left mine at the apartment.'

'Certainly,' the woman said, pointing to a phone on the hostess stand.

Bates's phone rang six times, and Ava was ready to give up when he answered.

'It's Ava,' she said.

'Sorry, I didn't recognize the number. I should have known you'd call from the restaurant.'

'Is there some kind of problem?'

'Ava, apologies. Actually there is.'

There was only one obvious question, and she wasn't going to ask it because she didn't want to hear the answer.

'A very important customer from New York dropped in unexpectedly with a long list of things he wants done, right away, of course,' he said. 'He's insisted I join him for dinner at his hotel at eight. And I'm not in a position to refuse.'

Ava could feel her tension melting. 'That really is too bad.'

'You know, you can join us if you wish. I'm sure he won't mind, since we've concluded most of our business already.'

'I can't leave Jackson alone that long.'

'I understand,' he said slowly.

She paused. 'Jeremy, did my wires get transmitted in the midst of this other activity?'

'Of course. They went out late this afternoon.'

'Wonderful. Thank you.'

'My pleasure.'

'And the copies for our records?'

'They're right here in front of me. You're only a couple of minutes from the bank. Would you care to walk over?'

'Sure.'

'There's a night bell in the lobby. Ring it when you get here. I'll have to come down and let you in.'

She left the restaurant and retraced her steps to the Crown Victoria. Robbins stood outside, leaning against the car. 'What's going on? You get stood up?'

'He can't make it – some other business – but the wire has been sent and I'm going over to the bank to get a copy of the confirmation.'

'We'll drive you.'

'I'll walk. You know where I'm going. Follow me if you want.'

She took her time, enjoying the fresh evening air, the breeze from the Caribbean drifting inland. *In a different time, under different circumstances, I might actually enjoy this place*, she thought.

The Crown Victoria passed her on Fyfe Street, drove past the bank, and parked about twenty metres past the double doors to Simon House. Robbins stared at her through the rear window.

Ava walked into the lobby; the corridors to the left and right were closed off, sealed by what looked like fire doors. She pressed the night bell next to the elevator, stood back, and waited. It took Bates a couple of minutes to reach her. She had half expected him to bring the documents with him, but he was empty-handed except for the plastic card that activated the elevator during off-hours. 'Let's go upstairs and we'll get things sorted,' he said.

Sorted? She wasn't crazy about his word choice. Neither was she comforted by his body language, which seemed stiffer, more awkward. *Something's happened*, she thought. She just couldn't think what.

Bates led her past the Barrett's reception desk and into his office. The bank was deserted.

They sat in the same chairs they had occupied that morning. It seemed to her like a very long time ago. There was a brown envelope on the table. Bates placed a hand on it.

'Ava, there is something I need to discuss with you,' he said, his eyes averted. 'I wouldn't do this normally, but I think we have struck up a good enough relationship that I feel I can share some information that has come to my attention.'

She saw that he was tense, his lips tightly drawn. She fought back a sense of foreboding, flashing an encouraging smile in his direction. 'Please, Jeremy, feel free.'

'I received a phone call from a bank in Dallas late this afternoon, just after we sent your wires. It's the bank that recently sent us electronically two very large transfers from Jackson Seto. The call was in confidence – a courtesy, one bank colleague to another – and I have to ask you to honour the spirit in which it was made.'

'Of course. You can be assured of my discretion,' Ava said.

'The bank ... the banker advised me that they were contacted by an investigator from the US Treasury Department about a week ago with regard to Mr Seto. The Treasury official said that Mr Seto was being investigated on suspicion of money laundering.'

'Good God, I can't imagine—' she began.

'Ava, how long have you known Jackson Seto?' Bates asked. His eyes were full of concern.

'A few months, no more than that, and only because Dynamic introduced us and wanted us to help with the financial side of this transaction.'

'I think it's only fair to tell you that I ran some checks on Dynamic and your accounting firm after that phone call.'

'That's understandable.'

'Both companies, of course, reported well – long-standing, excellent reputations – so I'm not suggesting even for a second that either would be involved in some illegal operation.'

'I should think not,' Ava said.

'Seto is another matter,' Bates said. She noted that the honorific had disappeared. 'His account has been a minor concern for some time, and I say minor because until recently there wasn't that much money going through it. I went through some of the bank's files. We've had calls from lawyers and the like before, asking questions about him and his account. There were claims that he misappropriated funds. There was no proof, of course, and the chap who was here before me let the matter slide. Even if he hadn't, of course, the bank would hardly be able to just give the money back.'

Ava sighed. 'I had no knowledge of any of this, and I'm sure Dynamic doesn't either. As far as I can tell, Seto was referred to them, and vouched for, by a cousin of the CEO.'

'Well, now you've been warned.'

'Has the Treasury Department taken any action?'

'No, not according to the Dallas banker, and he should be in a position to know.'

'So it's supposition at this point?'

'Precisely.'

361

'Still, I'm going to speak to my boss and make sure he talks to Dynamic. Knowing him and them as well as I do, I imagine they will distance themselves from Seto as quickly as they can. We are committed to concluding this transaction, but after that I can't see them conducting any more business with him.'

'I'm of the same mind,' Bates said, a trace of anger in his voice. 'My bank has an operating code of ethics that is the very first thing new recruits have drummed into them. We have survived and thrived for more than two hundred years by doing business completely within the letter of the law. If the US government ever charged Seto with money laundering and our bank was somehow implicated, I can tell you it would end the career of everyone who had put a finger to it.'

He's worried, genuinely worried, Ava realized. 'Jeremy, I'm absolutely sure nothing will come of this,' she said softly. 'Money laundering is easy to say and hard to prove. Has the Treasury Department contacted you yet?'

'No.'

'There you go. If they were really bearing down on Seto I'm sure they would have contacted you by now. The Dallas bank told them where they sent his money, yes?'

Bates nodded.

'So the fact that a week has passed and they haven't followed up with even a phone call does tell you something. You won't hear from them. I'm sure of it.'

'I thought that as well.'

'Anyway, Treasury Department or not, we will cut ourselves free of him after this.'

'As will the bank. I'm going to close his account as soon as your wires clear. When you see him, tell him I need to talk to him privately. He can come here or I will come to the apartment.'

Ava sat back. 'Jeremy, do you think you could delay doing anything until I leave? This is quite uncomfortable for me. I was going to stay with him until he was well enough to travel, but now I have to call Hong Kong and probably adjust my plans. I would appreciate it if you could hold off until I have some direction.'

'Of course,' Bates said, his hand reaching across the table as he passed over the envelope.

Ava touched his fingers and then pulled back. She looked at the brown envelope. 'Are those my copies?' she asked.

'Yes, of course. Forgive me for getting distracted,' he said.

She opened it and took out the confirmations. Both had been registered at 4:15 p.m. 'Thank you so much.'

'It was my pleasure. I'm just sorry about dinner. Maybe tomorrow night?'

'If I'm here – and I think I will be – I'd love it.'

He walked her to the elevator, his hand lightly touching her elbow, a display of interest that confirmed what she had already decided: it was time to leave Tortola.

As the elevator door closed, Jeremy Bates left her life as completely as if he'd never been in it. During the ride down and halfway across the lobby, the Robbins brothers consumed all her attention. But it wasn't until she was nearly out the door that it dawned on her she was taking some things about them for granted. She stopped, opened the envelope, and took out the wire confirmation for the two million that had gone to

Uncle. She folded it into a small square and tucked it inside her underwear.

The car was where she had last seen it. Davey saw her first and said something to Robbins. The big man whipped his head in her direction, his eyes drawn to the envelope. Ava gave thanks to whatever impulse had made her remember the second wire.

She climbed into the front seat and said, 'I'm starving. I need to eat.'

'Was the money sent?' said Robbins.

'Yes, I told you it was.'

'Is that the confirmation?'

'Yes.'

'I want to see it. Pass me the envelope.'

'Do you have your brother's permission?'

His voice rose. 'You need to stop fucking around with me.'

Ava turned around to face him. 'I'm not fucking with you. I'm doing business with your brother. I'm not showing this to anyone unless he tells me to.'

Robbins stared at her. Ava could see that he was trying to make up his mind whether she was being respectful towards the Captain or pissy towards him. 'I'll call him,' he said.

'That's the wise thing to do,' she said.

He climbed out of the car and crossed the sidewalk to a white stucco wall. He leaned against it, the phone appearing in his gloved hand. Davey looked sideways at her as if to say *Be careful*. Ava realized it was the first time she'd actually been alone with the driver. 'Why does Robbins wear those gloves?' she asked him.

'Ugly, huh?'

'Certainly not pleasant.'

'Nothing freaky, if that's what you're worried about. He got what he thought was eczema a few weeks ago. It comes and goes, except this time it didn't go. The doctor told him he's got some kind of ringworm. He got some medication but he has to wear the gloves for a few days.'

'It hasn't done anything for his disposition.'

'Hey, with or without the gloves, Robbins is a piece of work.'

'How long have you worked for him?'

Davey laughed. 'What makes you think I work for him?'

'I assumed.'

'He's got his own day job and I got mine. This is just a short-term gig for me. I crew for a living. This is the busiest charter port in the Caribbean. I'm off again in two or three days. We got some honeymooners going island-hopping for a week.'

'What does he do?' Ava asked.

'He's a cop.'

'I should have guessed.'

'Why? He sure as shit doesn't look like one.'

'And what does your typical cop look like?' Ava asked.

'Not like the Michelin man.'

Robbins lumbered towards the car. Davey said, 'Best for us not to talk so much. He's a suspicious son of a bitch.'

'My brother wants to speak to you,' Robbins said from the door, holding his phone over the back of the front seat.

'Captain,' Ava said.

'I understand congratulations are in order, Ms Lee.'

'The money has been sent.'

'Well done, very well done. Now do me a favour and pass the confirmation to my brother. He'll need the phone back as well.'

Ava handed them both over. The big man retreated to the wall again. She started to speak to Davey, but he turned his head away.

She watched as Robbins read the wire details to his brother. When he was done, he climbed into the car, a fat, sloppy grin spreading across his face. He handed her the phone.

'Yes, Captain,' she said.

'I imagine you're eager to inform Hong Kong of your success?'

'You know I am.'

'I've told my brother that you're free to use your computer. Please show him the transfer requests you did before and then follow the same model.'

'The only difference, obviously, is that I'm going to ask our accountant to fax and email you directly a copy of our bank's wire transfer to your Cayman account.'

'That's understood. I must say, Ms Lee, it's a pleasure doing business with someone who values efficiency as much as I do.'

'Well, speaking of efficiency,' Ava said, 'while I'm on the computer I wouldn't mind booking a flight out of here for sometime late tomorrow.'

'I guess that won't do any harm,' Robbins said slowly. 'But until things are concluded, you understand, our current working arrangement will remain intact.'

'I didn't expect anything different.'

'Good. Now let me speak to my brother again.'

Jack Robbins listened for a minute, closed his phone, and said to Davey, 'Take us back to the apartment.'

'Hey, I need to eat,' Ava protested.

'We'll have something delivered.'

38

Ava really did have to eat. The memory of the fish and chips was long gone, and the rice crackers and hummus she'd snacked on during the afternoon hadn't done much to fill the void in her stomach, a void that had expanded as the tension of doing business with Jeremy Bates and the bank subsided.

She wanted Chinese. Robbins told her there wasn't any in Road Town, and when she said that was impossible he turned to Davey. 'Tell her, will you?'

'There ain't none.'

'How about Italian?' she asked.

'You like pizza?' Davey asked. 'The Capriccio is good,' he said to Robbins.

'Drop us off at the apartment and then head over there. Better get three large, with sausage, mushrooms, and olives. That okay with you?' Robbins said to Ava.

'Thin crust?'

'Two regular, one thin crust. Call when you get to the building. We'll come down and get the food.'

As Ava and Robbins walked back to the Guildford she could feel that he was less tense now as well. She wondered if his brother had said anything in particular to him. When they got into the apartment, he said, 'Where do you want to set up the computer?'

The cable connection was in the kitchen, next to the phone. While Ava got her computer and notebook from her bedroom, Robbins went into the fridge for a Stella. He was sitting at the kitchen table, the bottle already half empty, when she came back and started to get set up.

The connection was good and Ava quickly got online. 'I'm going to sign into my email account now,' she said.

He came over to her side, his head almost touching her shoulder. 'Don't crowd me, please,' she said. He pulled back about six inches.

Her inbox had more than thirty messages. 'I have to open that one from your brother. It has his fax number in it,' she said, ignoring the others. She opened her notebook to the Guyana page where she'd recorded the Captain's bank account information, and wrote the fax number underneath. Then she hit the MESSAGES SENT tab, scanned down, and found her first email to Uncle with Robbins' bank information.

'There, that's what I sent before,' she said to Robbins, not remembering exactly what she had written in addition to the bank details. Not much, it turned out. At least no editorializing, nothing negative about the Captain.

'Okay,' Robbins said.

Ava clicked on the COMPOSE button, typed in Uncle's email address, and then copied the email she had shown Robbins, changing only the amount of money to be wired and adding a request that a copy of the confirmation be emailed and faxed to Captain Robbins at the address and number provided.

When she had finished, she said, 'Here, read this and make sure it's all right. In fact, why don't you call your brother and read it to him? That way neither of us has to worry about being accused of screwing up.'

'That's not a bad idea,' he said.

'Good. While you do that, I'm going to the bathroom,' she said, standing up. He pulled back to let her pass. She didn't know which she needed more, to pee or to get out from under the hovering Robbins. Even in mute mode he was still oppressive.

Ava was about to sit on the toilet, skirt pulled up and panties around her knees, when the copy of the second wire transfer fell to the floor. God help her if she hadn't remembered it back at the bank. She would have been hard-pressed to talk her way around that problem. It would have cost her more money at the very least, and more important, it would have destroyed any trust the Captain had in her. She picked it up and tucked it back into her underwear.

When she came out of the washroom, Robbins was at the table again, a second beer freshly opened. 'Did you reach your brother?' she asked.

He nodded. 'You can send the email.'

'I want to change first. I don't feel like eating pizza in these clothes.'

'Whatever.'

She took off her jewellery first, putting everything neatly away. Then she slid off her skirt and reached into her panties for the folded piece of paper, which she put in the pocket of the Shanghai Tang bag that held her Hong Kong passport. She unbuttoned her shirt, thinking that with any luck she was done with dress shirts for a while, and reached for her last clean T-shirt.

'Your brother did tell you that I can stay online and book a flight after I send this email?' Ava asked as she re-entered the living room and walked towards the kitchen.

Robbins nodded and then got to his feet to stand behind the chair where she'd been sitting. Ava resumed her place. The email was still exactly as she had drafted it. She hit the SEND button. 'There we go – the easiest two million dollars Captain Robbins ever made,' she said.

The apartment intercom sounded. Davey's familiar voice said, 'Pizza man.'

Robbins went to the door and pressed the button. 'Can you get in?'

'Not without a key.'

'Okay, I'm coming downstairs,' he said and then looked at Ava.

'I'm looking for flights. I'm not going anywhere,' she said.

He hesitated.

'What am I going to do, for God's sake, jump off the balcony?'

'Be back in two,' he said.

Ava found an American Airlines flight to San Juan. From there she could catch the midnight flight to Montreal or any one of a number of connections to Toronto through Miami, Chicago, or Newark. She did a rough calculation. If they moved fast in Hong Kong, Robbins would have his copy of the wire by morning – the middle of the night, actually. That might allow her to get a morning flight to San Juan, an early afternoon flight to the US, and a connection that would get her into Toronto in the evening. *Why not?* she thought, as she signed off on that itinerary.

Just as she finished, Robbins was back with three large pizza boxes in hand. He put them on the counter, the aroma filling the small kitchen. He opened the top one and put it aside. 'That's yours,' he said.

Ava salivated as she took a plate from the cupboard. As she did, Robbins took her place at the computer. He hit the MESSAGES SENT tab. The email to Uncle was top of the list. He switched to DELETED MESSAGES. Nothing. Ava forgot about any growing notion that Robbins trusted her, even in the slightest.

She watched until he was finished. When he stood up, she leaned down and turned off the computer. *It's almost over*, she thought, as she put three slices of pizza on her plate, poured a glass of sparkling water, tucked her notebook under her arm, and headed for the balcony.

39

Ava didn't sleep well. She had gone to bed early, way too early. She hadn't been tired, just bored. With Jeremy Bates out of the way, the money sent to Hong Kong, and the Captain at least half managed, her mind was now purring along in low gear. Robbins had parked himself in front of the television and she wasn't about to join him. She had no phone and didn't want to have to ask permission to turn on the computer again. That left the view of the harbour from the balcony, but bobbing boats have their limitations, especially in the dark. Around nine she went to check on Seto. He was still sleeping, but she figured the chloral hydrate would wear off soon, so she taped his ankles and mouth again and reapplied the handcuffs. Then she went into her bedroom and opened the James Clavell novel.

She had been reading for no more than ten or fifteen minutes when her eyes began to close. The first time she woke it was just past midnight, and she was on top of the bed with the lights on. She opened the bedroom door and saw that Robbins had fallen asleep on the couch, the television still running, four empty beer bottles on the coffee table. She made a quick bathroom run, turned off the lights, and crawled under the top cover.

Sleep was now more difficult; thoughts about the day ahead kept intruding. She pushed them aside, only to have Tommy Ordonez slip in through the gaps. She hoped she wouldn't have to spend any time in the Philippines. Guyana had offered enough hardship to last her for a while. And then Captain Robbins intruded on her consciousness. Had she overplayed her hand with him? No, she thought, his greed aside, they had connected at some level. He was a man who understood how things really worked, what motivated people to do things they wouldn't normally consider voluntarily – the right things for the wrong reason, although his definition of what was right might differ sharply from hers. Still, they had connected. They had some measure of mutual respect, respect that had nothing to do with approving what the other actually did. It was more for the manner in which each operated. Style points, Ava thought – they gave each other credit for style points.

The next time she woke it was two thirty. For ten minutes she fought to get back to sleep and then gave up. She turned her light on and picked up James Clavell again. She read for more than an hour before sleep encroached enough for her to turn off the light and give it another try.

It was dawn when she opened her eyes. She looked at her watch: ten minutes past six. She closed her eyes and began to pray to St Jude. She had barely started when the tones of the *William Tell* overture interrupted. It went on and on and then cut out. She went to her door and opened it a crack. Robbins was still asleep. The volume on his cellphone was louder than she remembered, but not loud enough to wake him.

She started her prayer from the beginning, only to have

William Tell start up again. 'Answer the phone,' she said under her breath. As if on cue, the tune ended and she heard him say, 'What is it?'

She was almost finished when he knocked on her door.

'Yes?' she said.

'My brother needs to speak to you,' said Robbins.

Ava thought about the time, and an immediate feeling of disquiet crept through her. Why would he call so early? Had something gone wrong on the Hong Kong side? No, she thought. Uncle never failed her. 'I'm coming,' she said.

A few last words to St Jude, the name Robbins in her prayers for the first time, and then she went to the door.

'Here,' Robbins said, handing her the phone, and then turned and walked to his bedroom.

Ava went to the kitchen and sat facing the balcony, the harbour glittering in the morning sun. 'Good morning, Captain.'

'Good morning, Ms Lee.'

'It's rather early for a phone call.'

'Well, I'm too perturbed to sleep.'

Ava felt a surge of worry. 'How so?'

'The Hong Kong wire.'

'You didn't get it?' she asked, her disquiet expanding.

He paused. 'I got a copy of a copy. I got it by email and fax.'

'Was the amount wrong? The date? Did they make a mistake with the bank information?'

He said, slowly and carefully, 'You know, Ms Lee, I don't know which annoys me more, the fact that you tried to play me for a fool or the fact that, even though you've been caught, you keep trying to play me for one. At this very moment I think it's the latter, and I warn you not to persist along those lines.'

Ava closed her eyes. *Why did I try it? How the hell did he catch on so soon?* She wished him away, wished away her attempt to keep the money, but she was not yet ready to concede a single thing. 'I can't even begin to respond to that until you tell me what the problem is.'

'There is no money.'

'I beg your pardon?'

'And there you go again with your bullshit,' he said, his voice harshening.

'I don't understand,' she persisted, glad he couldn't see her, the sweat beading her upper lip.

'You didn't send the money.'

'Captain—'

'My relationship with my bank is as strong as the one I imagine you have with your bank in Hong Kong. They give me twenty-four-hour service, something I never thought I needed – until I started doing business with you. Well, when I couldn't sleep this morning, I called them, gave them the wire transfer number, and asked them to check its progress. Ms Lee, they had no record of the wire, nothing anywhere in their system. Nothing, absolutely nothing.'

Ava drew a deep breath, struggling to keep her voice even. 'I can't understand how that's possible unless there was a glitch during the transmission process. Let me contact Hong Kong and check it from that end,' Ava said. 'I assure you—'

'—that it is shit. The only thing you can assure me of is that every word you've said to me is shit.'

'Captain—'

'My bank called your bank,' he said with finality.

God, she thought, *surely no one actually told them about the dummy wire?*

'A very friendly young woman on the international desk at your bank told the friendly young woman from my bank that there was no record of the wire on file. No record, no wire. Simple enough, I think.'

That wasn't the worst thing he could have been told, she thought, her mind spinning, searching for an explanation, any explanation, that would at least buy her a little time. 'Given the nature of the transfer, my people may not have used standard procedures,' she said. 'You need to let me call or email Hong Kong.'

Robbins went quiet. *He's thinking*, she thought, with a glimmer of hope. 'Yes, I think we both know that you need to contact Hong Kong, and this time to tell them to actually send the money,' he said slowly. 'The one thing I grant is that you know how to stick to a story. The thing is, the more I listen to it, the angrier I get.'

'Captain, please—'

'What? You thought this would actually work? You thought so little of me as to try something this stupid?'

Oh God, Ava thought. When was the last time she had misjudged a situation quite so badly? When was the last time she had misjudged a man so badly? 'I can fix this,' she said, still not wanting to admit culpability, not wanting to bring up Plan B.

He ignored her, and Ava felt him slipping away. 'You know, you shouldn't have tried this. We had an arrangement and I was fully prepared to honour my end. Now you've changed all that, and I have to decide what I'm going to do.'

'I can fix this,' she said.

'Yes, I have no doubt you can fix it, but the details may change. I'm not going to rush into anything with you, so have no fears about my being rash. I'm going to take some time to think this over. In the meantime, you need to do some thinking about what you've done. I think you need to make penance. You need to be punished, Ms Lee. You need to be taught a lesson.'

'Captain, I can't even begin to tell you how bad I feel about the way this process has been mangled. Just give me the chance to get it fixed.'

'That half-hearted apology doesn't quite make up for the transgression,' he said.

She knew what he wanted, but she just couldn't give it to him. It was one thing for him to be ninety-five percent sure of what had happened and another for him to be one hundred percent certain. She had to leave a shred of doubt. She couldn't prostrate herself. 'I'm sure that as we talk this through—'

'No, we're finished talking for now. I need to think and you need to reconsider your position and your attitude towards me. I have spoken to my brother and asked him to help you rethink everything. His ways may be a little rough but I expect you to take it like a big girl, and when he's finished we can look at this again through fresh eyes.'

'That is—' she began, but he was gone, the phone line dead. She put Robbins' mobile on table, her mind in a muddle. *What the hell is he talking about?* she thought. Then she screamed as the back of her neck and her right shoulder exploded. The pain brought her to her feet, but before she could turn her left leg collapsed and she fell forward against the kitchen wall.

He was behind her, a thick leather belt in one hand, a baton in the other. How had he managed to move so quietly? she thought. She twisted to press her back against the wall. She knew it was the belt that had hit her shoulder and the baton that had jabbed into the soft flesh behind her knee. For some reason the details became important. He held the belt by the buckle so that he could hurt her without scarring her flesh. The baton was close to a metre long, longer than any she'd ever seen, and it was made of fibreglass, a high-tech innovation hardly necessary for the purpose it was meant to serve.

'It's never a good idea to screw around with my brother. He isn't a turn-the-other-cheek kind of man,' Robbins said.

'No one screwed with your brother.'

'That isn't what he thinks, and that's all that matters to me. He told me to strap you, and that's what I'm going to do,' he said. 'If you're cooperative it'll be over before you know it.'

She shook her head.

He held up the baton. 'I know how to use this but I'd rather not. The belt won't break anything, but this might, so I advise you to lie still for the belt. It's your choice, though.'

She flexed her leg. It ached, but she could move it.

He was at least two metres away, the distance giving him time to react to anything she might try. The baton was poised and the belt hung by his side, waving back and forth. 'You need to think about the big picture,' he said, enjoying the sound of his voice. 'I give you a bit of a beating and my brother plays nice with you again. Not such a bad deal, the way I look at it.'

She shook her head again.

The belt lashed out, catching her across the top of her thigh. Ava shifted her feet.

Robbins took a step back, cautious. 'Don't let my size fool you. I can still move quickly,' he said.

She slid slowly to the ground. He stared down at her, his eyes now tightly focused on her for the first time since she'd met him. Ava lowered her head. Her arms fell to her sides. Slowly she pressed the small of her back firmly against the wall, tightened her glutes, and pushed her hands into the floor. 'This isn't necessary,' she whispered.

'My brother thinks it is, and I agree with him. You are a sneaky little cunt, a cunt who got caught,' he said, raising the belt.

'Don't,' she said.

'I'm losing my patience,' he said, the belt drawn completely back.

She sensed rather than saw the motion, and when he took the necessary step forward to hit her, she uncoiled. The belt went flying past Ava's face as she left the wall, her right heel driving into his groin. He groaned and staggered but didn't fall, the baton flailing in her direction.

The kitchen was cramped and Ava was still hemmed in against the wall, vulnerable to even the wildest of swings. She jumped to the right, the baton grazing her left arm. His head was turned and all she could see was his right eye. She thrust.

He moved at the last second, too late, and her fingernail pierced it, drawing blood almost instantly. He screamed, his belt hand going to his eye, finally giving her room and time to manoeuvre.

She moved farther right, away from the still-thrashing baton. Her right hand formed a fist, the middle knuckle of her index finger extended like the end of a pile driver, and then she leapt, the knuckle driving into his ear. He rocked on his heels, backing up some more.

Ava couldn't believe that he hadn't collapsed, though he was staggering now and looked disoriented. The last blow had moved him completely out of the kitchen and into the living room. She circled wider, to the side where his vision was impaired. He hadn't dropped either the baton or the belt, but the belt hand was still held to the eye she had damaged, blood trickling through his fingers. She moved in on him from behind and jumped onto his back, her fingers digging into his neck, searching for a carotid artery.

He yelled and shook his upper body. She could not believe how big and strong he was; she was hard-pressed to hang on. Robbins swung the baton over his shoulder, trying to catch her head, but she had it pressed against the side of his neck. Then he swung it around behind his back and found her, the stick catching her repeatedly on the calf. Ava tried to move her leg out of the way but started to slide down his back. She had no choice but to recover her grip, ignore the pain, and hold on even harder. 'Where is that fucking artery?' she shouted, her fingers lost in the mounds of flesh that protected his neck.

Robbins turned sideways and started to back up. Ava saw he was going to try to drive her into the wall. Her fingers pressed deeper, harder. She hit the wall and felt it give, but the momentum wasn't strong enough to dislodge her. He lurched forward. Ava could finally feel his legs starting to buckle. She clenched her fingers with every ounce of strength she could concentrate in them.

When they hit the floor, Robbins' head bounced with the impact. Ava slid off to the side and did a complete roll, coming to rest on her back about a metre away from him. Her leg was sore where he had beaten her with the baton. Her neck and shoulders ached from the belt strike; she knew there would be a welt. Her fingers felt stiff.

She turned to look at him. She'd never taken on anyone bigger or stronger. He twitched. *No*, she thought, *lie still.* He twitched again. His eyes opened, the bloody one nearest her, staring blindly. *What does it take?* she thought. He raised his head, shook his shoulders, and started to get up.

Ava scrambled to her feet and grabbed the baton, which had been jarred free when he fell.

Robbins was halfway up, his attention moving back and forth between her and the baton. 'Don't make me use it,' she said.

'Cunt,' he said, forcing himself to his feet.

She took out his left leg, the baton smashing into the kneecap with a sickening crack. He fell to the ground as if he'd been shot, letting loose a screech that tore through her head.

Ava's duct tape was in Seto's room. When she went in, he was awake and sitting up. His eyes bulged like a raccoon's caught in a flashlight, sweat pouring down his face. 'Lie down and don't move,' she said.

Robbins was still on the floor when she came back, but he was moving, trying to crawl towards his room. Ava got behind him and, avoiding the kicks from his good leg, grabbed his ankles and taped them together. That at least slowed him down. She thought about taping his wrists but wasn't sure she was strong enough to hold them together long enough to do it. She also wasn't sure that, even if she did manage it, he wouldn't eventually force the tape apart.

She went back to check on Seto. He looked even more panicked. 'You can sit up now, and turn around,' she told him.

He struggled to a sitting position, mumbling beneath his tape. She thought she could hear him saying, 'Don't hurt me, don't hurt me.' She undid his handcuffs and quickly taped his wrists together. Then she pushed him back onto the bed. 'Stay there and you'll be fine.'

Robbins wasn't moving as much. Maybe the effort to crawl had exhausted him, Ava thought. Still, she approached him cautiously, looking to see where his hands were. She slid one of the cuffs over his right wrist. It barely fit. Then she lifted his left arm and moved it across his back. He flinched and she felt the arm begin to resist. Quickly she yanked it towards the other, slipped the second handcuff on, and closed it. Then she reached again for his neck. He tried to twist away but she persisted, and finally she managed to put him completely out.

On her knees, Ava pushed herself back towards the bedroom. Easing into a sitting position, she leaned her back against the wall. She took deep, slow breaths, trying to calm herself down. But even as her body's tension eased, her mind raced with an anger that was directed mainly at herself – for having taken the Robbins brothers too lightly, for letting herself be blindsided. *Calm yourself*, she thought. *The worst is over*.

Then the doorbell rang.

Ava struggled to her feet. She had no idea who was there, but she wasn't going to open the door for anyone. She looked through the peephole. A young man in powder blue pyjamas was standing at the door looking concerned.

'Hello,' Ava said through the door, her voice hoarse with emotion that hadn't completely dissipated.

'I'm from the apartment next door. Is everything okay in there? I heard a horrible racket. I was just about to go downstairs to get someone,' he said, his face clouded with confusion.

'Please don't,' Ava said. 'My husband, he's epileptic. He had a fit, that's all. It was a bad one, even for him, but he's all right now. He would be mortified if he thought strangers were looking in on him.'

'It was a hell of a noise.'

'He's a big man and he hit the wall. It's passed. Please believe me, there will be no more trouble.'

She watched him through the peephole. He looked at least partially convinced. 'Thank you for your concern, though. It's really appreciated,' she said.

He took two steps back and looked around as if waiting for someone else to voice a complaint. 'Okay, no worries then. Like I said, I'm next door, in 310. If you need anything, let me know.'

'Thanks again,' Ava said, watching as he moved away, glancing back at the door.

She took a deep breath and turned. The apartment was a disaster. There was blood in several places on the floor and a cracked crater in the drywall she'd been backed into, and sometime during their struggle the coffee table had collapsed, two of its legs broken. There was no point in trying to clean it up. Robbins was on the floor and Seto was in the bed, and they weren't going anywhere. Ava knew she had better things to do and not that much time in which to get them done.

She had to step over Robbins to get into his room. A gun and a police badge were on top of his dresser. He was a sergeant, and still active. She figured he'd been crawling towards the gun. Her cellphone was in the bottom drawer, resting on some very large men's underwear. She took it out, turned it on, and walked into her own bedroom. Then she picked up her notebook and pen and took three sachets of VIA instant from her bag. The clock said six forty. She needed her morning coffee. She needed to think. The morning had barely begun, and Ava didn't need the day to get any more dramatic.

40

Ava stood by the stove watching the water boil, the mindlessness of it comfortably distracting. She made her coffee and went out onto the balcony. The sun was creeping up the side of the building and soon she'd be engulfed in it. She was thinking how pleasant it was outside when the *William Tell* overture called from the kitchen. She stuck her head through the door and looked at Robbins' phone until it went quiet. It was only a short reprieve, she knew. The Captain would call back soon, and she'd better be prepared to talk to him.

She sat on a chair and hoisted her legs onto the railing. She knew if she rolled up her pants the bruising would already be visible. *What a mess*, she thought. *What a fucking awful mess*. When was the last time, she thought again, she had misjudged a situation so badly? When was the last time she had misjudged a man so badly? Why hadn't she simply sent him the money in the first place and avoided all this chaos? Because it wasn't her nature to give in so easily, and besides, she hadn't trusted him to honour his commitments. And why hadn't he given her a chance to resend the money without all that unnecessary violence? Because that wasn't his nature, she answered herself again. He needed to hurt her. He needed to be dominant.

Ava finished her coffee and went back to the kitchen for another. She put two sachets into her second cup to really get a jolt. Then she picked up Robbins' phone and her own and returned to the balcony. She placed his on the table and pressed her voicemail key. There were more than twenty messages, most of them old. Uncle. Uncle. Uncle. Derek. Derek. Her mother. Mimi. Her mother. Uncle. Uncle. *He's worried*, she thought.

And then Andrew Tam. 'I need to hear from you,' he said, his voice a mixture of fear and anticipation. 'I have a meeting with my bank tomorrow morning, and I don't know what to tell them. You need to give me something, anything, that can help me hold them off. Please, Ava, call me. Call me.' Ava checked the time of his message. It had come in the middle of a Hong Kong night, right around when she was showing Seto to Bates, a few hours before Bates had sent the wire.

She scanned the other messages quickly. More of the same, until she got to Tam again. He sounded as if he was bouncing up and down. The five million had reached his account two hours before his meeting with the bank. As he was speaking, his emotions overcame him and he began to cry. *Well, at least some good has come of this*, Ava thought, listening to him say 'thank you' over and over again. As Uncle always said, they didn't just get people's money back, they got them their lives back. Now all she had to do was take care of her own.

The last voicemail was from Derek. 'I don't know if you have access to your phone yet. Just a heads-up – I have the information you wanted. Call whenever.' *You darling*, she thought, reaching for her notebook before calling him back. Then Robbins' phone jumped to life again.

The *William Tell* overture was rapidly becoming the most annoying piece of music she'd ever heard. She thought about not answering, even turning off the phone, and then instinctively knew that either of those choices would be wrong. Nothing good could come from putting him off. The last thing she needed was for him to go crazy on her, to do something unpredictable like calling in the cops or Morris Thomas and his boys. She needed to slow things down, not force his hand and have him speed them up. So she had to deal with him. She left the balcony, went into the kitchen, and sat down, her eyes looking out towards the harbour.

'This is Ava Lee,' she answered.

'Ms Lee?' he said.

'Yes, it's me.'

'I would like to speak to my brother,' he said.

He was cool, she gave him that. 'Your brother is indisposed.'

'I'll wait. Ask him to come to the phone.'

'Not that kind of indisposed.'

'I would still like to speak to him. Ask him to come to the phone.'

'He isn't in a position to walk.'

He paused. 'Then take the phone to him.'

'There isn't much point in that either, because I don't think he can talk.'

A longer pause. 'You're a nasty little thing, aren't you?'

Ava said, 'There is a French saying that applies to my

situation: "Be careful of that animal – it is very vicious. When you attack it, it defends itself.'"

'We could have a debate about who attacked whom, but I don't think that would help this situation,' Robbins said. Then he added, 'Is he alive?' as casually as if he were asking whether she had eaten breakfast.

'I think so. I haven't checked in the past ten minutes.'

She could hear him breathing through the phone but he didn't sound particularly stressed, and again she had to give him credit. 'Ms Lee, I hope you don't think this mistreatment of my brother changes your position in any material way,' he said.

'I wasn't thinking that far ahead when he was swinging a belt at me and threatening to break my bones with a baton.'

'Maybe that was ill-advised on his part.'

'He was simply doing what he was told.'

The Captain drew a deeper breath. 'You shouldn't have lied to me.'

There goes any concern for his brother, Ava thought. 'I accept that as a fair criticism, and I apologize for it. I also, if you remember, offered to fix the problem,' she said, offering her first peace token.

'It was perhaps silly of me not to accept, but I do have my pride and you did breach my trust.'

'And it was silly of me to have done that.'

'Is this the start of renewed negotiations?' he asked carefully.

'That's up to you.'

'Well, I think it could be. Forgive and forget, Ms Lee. Let's both of us forgive and forget.'

'I think that's best.'

He paused and then said slowly, 'Excellent. Now, of course, I still want my money.'

'That's a given, and I'm prepared to make that happen. I just need time to get hold of my people in Hong Kong and set things in motion ... in proper motion.'

'The full amount we agreed?'

'Of course.'

'Plus I'm going to have to look after my brother—'

'Nothing extra,' she said curtly, knowing she had to maintain some pretence of control on her end.

He didn't argue, but Ava knew she might not have heard the last about that. 'By my reckoning, it is sometime in the evening in Hong Kong. When exactly do you think you can execute the transfer?'

'You aren't the only one with a bank that provides out-of-hours service. The straight answer to your question is that I don't know until I talk to my people there. I have to reach them and they have to get to the bank.'

'Give me some rough idea of a time frame.'

'It may be a couple of hours before I know.'

'I'll give you an hour to reach them and get back to me with a schedule. When we have that, then we reassess our position.'

'I'm not sure what I can accomplish in an hour, but I'll go along with you as long as the door doesn't slam shut when the time is up.'

'I said we could reassess.'

Ava knew she wasn't going to do any better. 'That will do, thank you.'

'It's a good start anyway. Puts us back on the rails, so to speak,' Robbins said. 'But now, Ms Lee, I do have to say that we can't have a repeat of last night's document farce.'

'I understand that only too well.'

'I also don't mean to be overbearing or repetitive or unnecessarily threatening, but you have no passport and you aren't leaving the BVI without one. In fact, you aren't leaving until Morris Thomas says you can leave, and you can be certain that direction will come from me. You also have two men in your apartment, one who has been kidnapped and the other one – a local policeman at that – in what I presume is a deprived physical condition brought on by you. On top of those abuses, you have engaged in a fraudulent scheme with one of the leading banks on the island. Road Town is a small place. One phone call and you're minutes away from quite a pile of unpleasantness.'

'I do understand my situation,' Ava said.

'Still, there's no harm in my making it clear. I trust there's no offence taken on your part?'

'None.'

'So where does that leave us?'

'With me calling Hong Kong to urge them to get that wire out to you as fast as they can.'

'Exactly. And of course you'll call me the moment you have the details, and by the end of an hour even if you don't.'

'You'll hear from me either way.'

'Ms Lee, I await your call.'

Not a word of concern about his brother after the topic changed to money, Ava thought as she hung up. Blood ties must run pretty thin in Barbados.

She sat quietly for a minute. It had gone about as well as could be expected. He still had dollar signs dancing in his eyes, and he wasn't going to ease up on her until he had his money. He thought he had serious leverage, and in some respects he did, but only if she let time work for him. And when he got the money, was he capable of reneging on her? She had no doubt that it was, at the minimum, in the back of his mind. The thing was, she had no intention of hanging around to find out if she was right or not.

She went into her bedroom to fetch her toilet kit. She needed to get clean, take a quick shower, brush her teeth and hair. Dealing with the Robbins brothers made her feel dirty.

When she stripped, she saw that the red welt on her shoulder and neck was longer and wider than she'd thought. It would turn black and blue eventually. The side of her lower leg was throbbing and already discoloured. Thank God, she thought, he didn't catch bone, or she would be trying to deal with a break. She stepped into the shower, turned her face into the stream of water, and tried to think more pleasant thoughts.

Ten minutes later she was in the bedroom. She put her toilet kit into her bag, checked her cash stash, grabbed two more sachets of VIA, and headed for the kitchen. She made a coffee and then sat at the computer and began to search the British Virgin Islands and its Caribbean neighbours. She didn't have to look far.

It wasn't quite seven thirty when she sat on the balcony to call Derek, her notebook open to a clean page.

'Hi, Ava,' he said, his voice sleepy.

'I got your voicemail, thanks.'

'You're using your own phone again. Everything okay?'

'Looking up, anyway.'

'I was worried. Uncle too. He called to find out what happened to me. He said he had some guys in New York on standby but was waiting to hear from you before doing anything.'

'I'll call him after we're finished.'

'I located the girls.'

'I figured as much. Tell me what you found out.'

Derek had been thorough. As Ava reviewed her notes after they were finished, she began to feel that an element of control was finally back in her hands.

The cay below her window was beginning to come to life. Small offices were strung around the piers, most of them advertising charters and cruises. They were just starting to open up. *Hong Kong first*, Ava thought.

'*Wei*, Ava,' Uncle said breathlessly. 'Where are you?'

'Still in the BVI.'

'You are using your own phone.'

'Our situation has improved.'

'I was worried,' he sighed.

'I know you were. Sorry for that, Uncle. Now, did you get the two million I sent?'

'Yes, it came in yesterday morning, and Tam got his money too. My friend is grateful, although not as grateful as Tam ... But what about you? Did the phony wire work?'

'No.'

'Ava, I told you it was risky ... So now what, your Plan B?'

'There's a Plan C now.'

'Do we still send money to the Caymans?'

'No. Money isn't going anywhere.'

'Do you need my help in any other way?'

'No, I think I can manage.'

'Be careful.'

'As always.'

'I have men in New York, no more than eight hours away.'

She could imagine them. Two or three small Chinese men, tattoos peeking out from under their shirt collars, broken English, and US passports that might or might not pass rigorous examination. 'I don't need them, but thank you anyway.'

'Need them or not, you have to keep in touch with me, because if you go missing again for more than twenty-four hours I'm sending them in.'

'No worries, Uncle. I'll stay in touch.'

'When do you expect to leave that place?'

'Today, soon. I'll call you once I'm organized.'

'Any time. I'll leave my mobile on.'

41

The charter offices all looked about the same, and all of them seemed to offer identical services. So Ava chose the largest one, figuring that had to increase her chances of getting a boat.

'I'm spending the next week of my holiday on St Thomas, and I thought I'd like to get there by sea,' she said to the weather-beaten little man behind the counter.

'There are cruises you can join,' he said.

'I'd rather go alone.'

'More expensive.'

'I don't mind.'

'You want a bareboat?'

'A what?'

'You going to sail it? Skipper it yourself?'

'Of course not.'

'So you need a crew?'

'I need someone to sail the boat.'

'One way?'

'Yes.'

'We'd have to charge a two-way fee.'

'That's okay.'

'You care what kind of boat?'

'What do you mean?'

'You want a sailboat, a motorized boat?'

'I want to get there quickly.'

'A motorboat then.'

'If you say so,' Ava said.

'When do you want to leave?'

'Well, how long is the trip?'

'We're only going about fifty kilometres, so around two hours.'

'Then I'd like to leave this morning.'

'You need to be more specific.'

'Ten o'clock?'

He opened a ledger that was on the counter. 'Sure, but the only thing I've got available then is a Bavaria 35. It's expensive.'

'How much?'

'Round trip, figure six hundred dollars plus a tip for the skipper.'

'Cash okay?'

'Cash works.'

'Perfect. I'll be back here at ten.'

'I need a name.'

'Lee.'

'And contact information.'

She gave him her cellphone number.

'You'll need your passport to land on the US side.'

'Not a problem,' she said, reaching into her Chanel bag. 'Here's two hundred dollars as a deposit.'

The hour she had bargained with Robbins was almost up and she didn't want to call him from outside the apartment. She hustled back, taking a minute near the front door to see if there were any occupied cars lingering nearby, any people idling about. The area seemed clear.

The hour wasn't quite over when she settled into the kitchen. She used Robbins' phone to make the call. The Captain answered on the second ring. 'I can't tell you how pleased I am that you are prompt,' he said.

'I've been back and forth with Hong Kong, and the money is being organized as we speak. They tell me they're expediting it on an urgent basis.'

'What does "urgent" mean?'

'They're saying it should be in your account by five o'clock this evening. Not in transit, mind you, but physically in your Cayman Islands account. But Captain, you can't hold me to that; I'm just repeating what I was told. I can tell you, though, that I stressed and re-stressed the importance of its actually happening.'

'All very businesslike.'

'I insisted on having a timeline. I didn't want to have to give you generalities.'

'I think, Ms Lee, we are back on common ground.'

'I certainly hope so.'

She waited for him to ask for a copy of the new wire, her reply ready. Instead he moved on. 'How is my brother?'

Ava looked at the large, still body lying prone on the floor. He hadn't moved since she'd cuffed him. 'Resting.'

'Will he need medical care?'

'Perhaps, but not until the money is in your account and you've given me the green light to leave Road Town.'

'You have things in proper order, I'm glad to hear.'

So much for Jack Robbins, Ava thought again. 'I still need to make some plans,' she said. 'The flights out of here seem quite busy. There's one leaving for San Juan tonight at nine o'clock with some seats available. If you don't mind, on a contingency basis I'd like to reserve a seat on it.'

'I don't see any harm in that. What's the flight number?'

'American Airlines 4866, departing at eight fifty-five.'

'Fine.'

'And I'd appreciate it if you could let Mr Thomas know that those are my plans and arrange for him to have my passport dropped off later today at the apartment.'

'Once the money is in my account, I'll talk to Thomas.'

'I understand.'

'And you should probably assume you'll have to pick up your passport at the airport. He isn't a courier service, you know.'

'No problem.'

'Well, this has been a much better conversation, I must say.'

'For me too.'

'So now you have the rest of the day to kill. Do you have any plans?'

'I have to get out of this apartment for a while. I find that looking at your brother and Seto for hours on end is more than I can handle. I'll go for a walk, get some lunch. I'll keep your brother's phone with me in case you want to contact me.'

'Don't stray too far.'

'Have no worries,' Ava said.

When she hung up, she went online and booked the

American Airlines flight to San Juan. Then, using a different credit card and a different address, she bought a seat on American Airlines flight 672 leaving St Thomas at two thirty and arriving in Miami at five twenty, connecting with American Airlines flight 646 from Miami to Toronto at five past eight. She figured she'd be home just after midnight.

42

Ava decided to travel comfortably, in her running shoes, track pants, and the black T-shirt she'd slept in. She packed carefully, putting her jewellery and cash in the Chanel bag and then the bag into the bottom of the Louis Vuitton suitcase, surrounded by dirty clothes she'd neatly bundled up. The only expensive accessory she wore was the ivory chignon pin.

When she packed the Shanghai Tang bag, she remembered that she still had some chloral hydrate and the switchblade. She emptied the shampoo bottles into the sink. The chances were slim that anyone would have examined them, but it was foolish to take chances. She slipped the blade under the mattress of her bed.

Her Hong Kong passport and other loose ID went into the back pocket of her Adidas pants, which she sealed with the Velcro tab. The cash she needed for the boat, taxis, and meals en route was stuffed into her front pants pocket.

By nine thirty she was ready to go and saw no point in hanging around the apartment any longer. She left her bags by the door and paid a visit to Seto.

He was awake, his eyes opening and closing sporadically from the lingering effects of the drug. She sat him up. He motioned for her to remove the tape from his mouth. 'No, it has to stay on,' she said. He looked panicky again.

'Now listen to me carefully,' Ava said. 'I have to go out for a little while. The big guy you saw – Mr Clean – he's in the next room, so if I were you I wouldn't make too much noise. Nod if you understand me.'

He nodded.

'This is going to be over by tomorrow. I'm leaving then, and so is Mr Clean. We'll call the staff after we're gone and tell them where to find you. So until then, you behave yourself.'

He nodded.

'The last thing, and maybe the most important, is that you have to forget about me, about Andrew Tam, and about this entire affair. It never happened. You say one word and we'll find you and we'll hurt you. Do you believe me?'

He nodded.

Ava patted him on the cheek. 'And if I were you, I'd find another business. There are enough creeps peddling fish without you and that fat pervert of a friend of yours in the mix.'

As she left the apartment Ava took one last look back at Robbins. He still wasn't moving. Ava thought about dragging him into his bedroom but wasn't sure she was strong enough, and besides, what difference did it make where they found him? From the doorway she couldn't tell if he was actually breathing. Was he alive? She tiptoed close and reached down to feel the pulse in his wrist. It was racing along, maybe too fast. Well, it wasn't her problem any more.

Downstairs, Doreen was in the lobby behind the desk. 'I'm leaving today, heading for San Juan,' Ava said. 'My friends are still in the apartment but they don't need any maid service until tomorrow. Could you make a note of that, please?'

'That will be three days.'

'Just doing what they can for the environment,' Ava said.

She walked to the charter office and paid the man in cash, showed him her passport, and at five minutes to ten was aboard a Bavaria 35 heading out to sea. Ava looked back at the Guildford Apartments as the boat powered its way out of the harbour. She felt bad for the room maid who would stumble across Robbins and Seto next morning. Hopefully it wouldn't alarm her too much.

Road Town began to shrink into the distance. It was a pretty city, the white stucco buildings nestled against the greenery of the mountains encircling the deep blue harbour. She doubted she'd see it again. Revisiting old job locations was never a good idea.

She went below into the cabin when Road Town had become just a dot. About an hour and a half later the boat engines eased and Ava climbed back on deck to watch as they pulled into St Thomas.

The US Customs officer in St Thomas hardly glanced at her passport. She took a cab from the pier to Charlotte Amalie and boarded American Airlines flight 672 at two fifteen. At six o'clock she was eating a bowl of gumbo in the TGIF restaurant at Miami International.

She waited until seven to call Uncle. He was up already. Ava could hear Lourdes, his Filipina housekeeper of more than thirty years, asking if he wanted another cup of tea. 'I'm in Miami,' she said. 'I'll be in Toronto by midnight.'

'Thank goodness you are out that place. I didn't sleep well.'

'I told you, no worries.'

'Between you and Tommy Ordonez it has been a hard two days.'

'Don't mention Tommy Ordonez,' Ava said. 'I'm not home yet. I need to get home and I need to rest for a few days. So please, Uncle, not another word about Tommy Ordonez until I feel I'm ready.'

'All right,' he said, his reluctance obvious, but he knew how superstitious she could be.

'I just want to finish the Tam job, and it won't be finished until I'm in my own bed again.'

'Speaking of Tam, call him, will you? He wants to thank you personally.'

'He left me a voicemail already.'

'Ava, please. The man just wants to say thank you. You saved his business, his family's capital. Let him be appreciative.'

She reached Tam at his apartment. 'It's Ava. I got your voicemail. I'm just calling to tell you that I'm pleased things worked out.'

There was a long silence from the Hong Kong end. 'Andrew, are you there?' she asked.

'Sorry, Ava, I'm still in a bit of shock from yesterday. I was only a couple of hours from total disaster when the money came through. I had no idea it had been sent. I mean, you didn't communicate with me.'

Was that a complaint? she thought. 'I wasn't in a position to communicate directly. The best I could do was give Uncle at least an indication that the money was on its way.'

'He didn't pass that on.'

'What do you want me to say?' Ava asked. 'You got your money – what else matters?'

'Nothing. I'm sorry if I sound unappreciative.'

'In a day or two I'll send you our bank information. You can remit our commission then.'

'Yes, yes,' he muttered.

She felt another flash of irritation. They were always eager to agree to pay the fee when they thought it was their only chance to recover their money. Then when they had the money back, they tried to cling to every dollar of it. 'The fee is only half what we normally charge. Uncle waived his portion out of respect for your uncle.'

'We'll pay the fee, and Uncle's part as well, if you want,' Tam said quickly.

Ava knew she'd overreacted. Her nerves were still on edge; she needed to get home. 'No, just pay my part, but you should understand that Uncle did more than just waive his fee for a friend. At one point he advanced $300,000 US without any guarantee he would ever see it again,' she said, knowing that Tam would tell his uncle, knowing that the uncle would be forever indebted.

'They swam from China together,' Andrew Tam said, as if that explained everything.

Maybe it does, she thought.

43

It was a miserable night in Toronto. As the plane approached Pearson Airport from the west, Ava looked out and saw a sea of white slashed here and there with ribbons of highway that were struggling to stay black. As they started the final descent, the plane's windows became wet with sleet; the lights lining Highway 401 illuminated falling snow.

She coasted through Customs and Immigration, flashing her Hong Kong passport, and grabbed a limousine. The highways were slushy and the driver was being careful, not talking, focused on the road. The only time he spoke was when they hit a pothole pulling onto the Don Valley Parkway. 'Sorry about that,' he said.

She thought about Guyana and smiled. 'No problem,' she said.

Jack Robbins' phone had been turned off since she left Road Town that morning. She had thought about calling the Captain from Miami and quickly dismissed the idea as foolhardy. She needed to be on home ground, as far from him and his influence as she could get. She turned it on as the limo headed south on the Parkway, and was greeted by a barrage of messages. Ava checked the incoming numbers. All except one were from the Captain.

She opened the Shanghai Tang Double Happiness bag and took out her notebook, then hit CALL RETURN on Robbins' phone. 'Where are you?' he screamed.

'I'm riding in a car . . . in a snowstorm actually.'

He paused. 'I don't believe that.'

'I'm in Toronto, in a limo, trying to get home from the airport. I figure I'm about ten kilometres almost directly east of Olive Street.'

Ava could hear ice clinking on glass. He was drinking, his nighttime ritual. She waited for him to speak, waited for him to acknowledge the Olive Street reference. When he didn't respond, she began to read from her notebook.

'Ellie and Lizzie live in apartment 816 at 1415 Olive Street, about two blocks from Havergal. Ellie is in grade twelve, Lizzie in grade eleven. Ellie drives a blue Honda Accord, licence plate number BDAC 685. They leave for school at eight in the morning and are normally home by four thirty. My friend Derek, who, you might remember, did not meet me in Road Town, has been keeping an eye on them. If you need to know about their social lives, boyfriends and the like, sexual experiences even, he can find out. They seem like nice girls, Captain. It would be a tragedy if anything unfortunate were to happen to them. There isn't any reason for that to occur that I can think of, unless of course I find my life disrupted in any way . . .'

She could hear him breathing as he absorbed this new reality. 'Where are you?' he said deliberately, the rage tempered.

'As I said, I'm in Toronto, and I really am only about ten kilometres east of Olive Street.'

'How did you get out of Road Town, and—'

'What does it matter?' she said.

She could hear liquid pouring, the clang of ice swirling around his glass. Then he sighed as if he was giving in to something inevitable. 'There's no reason to involve my girls in any of this,' he said.

Ava said, 'That's my preference and, in my absence, Derek's. We don't want any reason to act otherwise. Although we would if the need arose, and you need to believe me when I say we would.'

'Leave my girls alone and you will never have to fear any action on my part.'

'You'll need to pass that message along to your brother too.'

'When he's functioning again, I will.'

'They found him?'

'Oh yes, they have him. When I didn't hear from you by nine, I sent in some of his men.'

'Is he okay?'

There was a long silence. 'He may be blind in one eye.'

'Yes, perhaps,' Ava said.

'He can't hear out of one ear.'

'That may pass.'

'And he's not going to be walking for a while.'

Ava thought about Jack Robbins standing over her with the belt and the baton, and moved on. 'How was Seto?'

'Groggy, confused. He says he can't remember how he got there or who brought him.'

'What do the police think happened?'

'They can't get anything out of him that makes sense.'

'Captain, I think it's best that your brother be equally

confused. I don't want to have to deal with long-distance police enquiries.'

'My brother won't talk to anyone unless I tell him to, and then he'll be following my advice.'

'And what kind of advice do you think you'll give him?'

'Seto has set an example that I think he should emulate.'

Ava looked out the limousine window as they exited the Parkway onto Bloor Street. The snow was falling harder now, the wind picking up. 'It seems we have an understanding, Captain.'

'Yes, I think we do, Ms Lee ... But tell me – humour me, please – where is the money that was supposed to have been sent?'

'There is no more money, you know that. You were paid $300,000 for services rendered. Be content with that.'

'Did you ever intend to send it?'

'You know, there was a chance that it would have been sent,' Ava said slowly. 'I honestly hadn't decided what to do until your brother tipped the scales. In effect, he – in reality, you – made that decision for me.'

'You were never going to send it. It was always a game with you,' he said.

'I don't see any value in second-guessing each other, Captain. You are $300,000 richer and I have a happy client. Let's leave it at that.'

'Yes, Ms Lee, maybe we should.'

'There is one last thing, Captain. I would very much like to have my Canadian passport back. I hate the idea that it's in someone else's possession and could be used for mischief.'

'Give me your address and I'll—'

Ava laughed. 'Yeah, sure. Look, have it sent to the bank in Kowloon to be held for pickup. And considering that I've already paid you $300,000, don't send it COD.'

Robbins hesitated and then said slowly, 'Ms Lee, I have to tell you that I wish our business relationship had ended on a more congenial note.'

'The only way that would have been possible from your end is if you had gotten your two million dollars. Me, I'm happy enough with the result as it is,' Ava said.

'You aren't entirely wrong about the money—' he began.

'Goodbye, Captain.'

'Ms Lee, if you're ever back in my neck of the woods—'

'Not a chance, Captain. Not a chance,' she said, closing the phone.

Ava saw the limo driver looking her in his rear-view mirror, and she realized that her end of the conversation must have sounded strange. 'What's the weather forecast?' she asked him.

'More of this,' he said.

She opened the window far enough to be able to stick her hand out. It was turning colder, the snow sticking to the ground. She tossed the phone out onto Bloor Street. It bounced twice before the back flew off. Traffic would take care of the rest.

COMING SOON

Read on for a preview of the next thrilling
Ava Lee novel, *The Fiery Gaze of the Tigress*

(1)

When Ava Lee woke up, the first thing she felt was a sharp pain shooting through her neck and shoulder. She stretched, causing the pain to become more intense, and then slowly relaxed her muscles. She knew from experience that the lashing she had endured wasn't going to cause any long-term damage.

She turned her head to look at the bedside clock. It was only 6 a.m. She had flown home to Toronto around midnight and had been in bed for less than five hours. She had thought that two melatonin capsules and a glass of Pinot Grigio would see her through the night, but the pain and a mind that was still a jumble of emotions were gnawing at her.

She lay quietly, hoping she could drift off again. After ten minutes she gave up and pulled herself out of bed. She kneeled to say a short prayer of thanks to St. Jude for her safe return, and then headed for the bathroom. Pulling off her black Giordano T-shirt, Ava turned so she could see her back in the mirror. The belt had hit her on the side of the neck and across her right shoulder, and then again on the same shoulder and partway down her back. The marks were a deep black and blue, yellowed at the edges. They looked worse than they felt, and in a few days they would start to fade.

Ava went into the kitchen, made herself a Starbucks VIA Ready Brew, and sat down at the small round table set against the window overlooking Cumberland Street and Avenue Road. She lived in the heart of Yorkville, the ritziest neighbourhood in downtown Toronto. Despite the early hour, the traffic below was barely moving as the January weather tried to decide if it was raining or snowing.

Normally she would have the *Globe and Mail* spread across the table, but she had been away for more than a week – travelling to Hong Kong, Thailand, Guyana, and the British Virgin Islands, tracking down and retrieving more than five million dollars that had been stolen from a client – and had cancelled the paper until further notice. So she opened up her laptop and turned it on to read the news online. That was a mistake.

After she signed on, Ava opened her email program, expecting to see messages from friends, a bit of spam, and not much else. She froze when she saw Uncle's name in her inbox. Uncle was her Hong Kong–based partner, a man in his seventies whose idea of high-tech communication was a Chinese knockoff iPhone he had bought for less than forty dollars at the Kowloon nighttime street market and used strictly for making calls. He had sent her two messages in the past eight hours; she couldn't remember receiving that many from him in the past year. She opened them. They were identical, simply stating that he needed her to call him. He didn't say it was urgent. He didn't have to – that he had sent two emails conveyed that fact well enough.

Ava groaned, went over to her hot-water Thermos, and made another coffee. She knew what he wanted to talk about. While she was in Guyana they had been offered a job by a Filipino-Chinese businessman named Tommy Ordonez. Ordonez was the wealthiest man in the islands. They had put him off so they could finish the job they were on. Ava had hoped he could be put off longer, because that job had turned nasty, with unforeseen complications. What was supposed to have been a straightforward tracking and retrieval of misappropriated funds had turned into extortion. She had prevailed, but not without difficulty, as the bruises and welts demonstrated, and not without stress, some of which still lingered.

Ava had turned off her cellphone the night before and thrown it into the bottom of her purse. She had intended to leave it there for a few days, or at least until she felt her head was in the right place. She went to retrieve it and saw that Uncle had called as well. She sighed. She had to call him back. She couldn't ignore two emails and a phone message without insulting him. Insulting Uncle was something she had never done – and never wished to do. It was just past six in the evening in Hong Kong, and Ava knew she'd probably catch him at a massage, an early dinner, or his Kowloon apartment.

'*Wei*,' Uncle said. Ava could hear his little dog yapping and his Filipina housekeeper, Lourdes, telling it to be quiet. He was still at the apartment.

'It's Ava.'

'You are in Toronto?'

'Yes, I got in late last night.'

'And you are okay?'

'Yes, I'm fine.'

'Good, I was worried about you . . . It is early there.'

'I couldn't sleep, and then I turned on my computer and saw your emails.'

'We need to talk.'

Ava wondered if he thought she was being critical of his persistence, and she felt a bit uneasy about being perceived as even mildly rude. 'No problem, Uncle. Is it about Tommy Ordonez?'

'Yes. He and his closest adviser, Chang Wang, each called me twice yesterday, after calling me twice the day before. I have been telling them they need to be patient.'

'And how did they react?'

'Impatiently.'

'Uncle, you did tell them we never do two jobs at the same time, and that I was still working on one?'

'Of course, but it only seemed to frustrate them more. Especially Ordonez. He is a man who does not think he should ever have to stand in a queue or have someone else's interests take precedence over his.'

'Did he say that?'

'He didn't need to. Ava, the last time I spoke to him he could barely contain himself. I could feel him eating his anger, and I know that if he had been talking to anyone but me he would have exploded.'

Ava finished her second coffee and, holding the phone to her ear, went to the counter and emptied another sachet into her cup. 'What do we know about the job, Uncle?'

'Not that much. Just that it is a lot of money, that it involves a Canadian real estate transaction, and that one of Ordonez's younger brothers, Philip Chew, is involved. They want to meet us face to face to provide the actual details.'

'Is it a firm contract?'

'If we want to accept it.'

'You haven't committed?'

'I thought it would be best for us to hear the full story before signing on.'

'What I don't understand, Uncle, is why, with all the resources and power they have, they need us in the first place.'

She had asked that question when the job offer was first made, and it had generated an awkward response from Uncle. Now he was just vague. 'They will explain everything when we are in Manila.'

'So you want us to go?'

'I told Chang Wang that we would discuss it with them, and they are insisting on doing that in person . . . I am told the sum of money involved is more than fifty million dollars. I think that is worth a trip to Manila, don't you?'

'Yes, of course it is,' she said, and then realized that Uncle had twice referred to Ordonez's right-hand man by both his family and given names. It was a form of respect he rarely used for clients, and she guessed there was some kind of bond between the two men. 'This Chang, Uncle, do you know him well?'

'He is from Wuhan, like me, and over the years we have done each other many favours. I would still have ten men rotting in Filipino prisons if it were not for him, and he would still be waiting for permits to build cigarette factories in Hubei province if it were not for me.'

Ava was accustomed to Uncle's Wuhan connections.

He had been born and raised in a village on its outskirts, and he and the other men from there who had escaped the Communist regime had remained intensely loyal to each other. 'And Chang hasn't confided in you about the nature of Ordonez's problem?'

'His first loyalty is to Ordonez. We need to understand and respect that.'

'Earlier you mentioned that Ordonez was restraining himself when he was talking to you. I didn't think you knew him.'

'Chang introduced us once, years ago, when I was at the top of my heap and he was scaling his. It was a passing encounter that seems more important to him than it is to me. I did not even remember the meeting until he mentioned it.'

Ava was now standing by the kitchen window. The falling rain was beginning to freeze onto it. She watched a car skid into the intersection below and slide into an SUV. She hated this kind of weather. At least Manila would be warm. 'Can you buy us an extra day or two?' she asked.

Uncle hesitated. She knew he didn't want to push her too hard. 'I would like to get there as soon as possible. But if you need to spend more time in Toronto, then I will deal with Chang Wang and Ordonez as best as I can.'

'Will they walk away from the deal if we delay?'

'I really don't know.'

'Well, I guess that's something we shouldn't risk,' Ava said.

'No, we should not. Their impatience could get the better of them.'

She did a quick calculation. 'If I catch the Cathay Pacific

flight late tonight, I can be in Hong Kong the day after tomorrow, early morning, your time. That at least will give me all of today to get caught up here, and I'll have a sixteen-hour flight I can sleep through.'

'Good. We can leave for Manila the morning you arrive. I will have those flights booked. We can meet in the Wing lounge,' Uncle said. 'I will let Chang Wang know right away that we are coming. Ordonez's office is near the Ayala Centre in Makati City. The Peninsula Hotel is nearby. I will have them book us rooms.'

'Okay, I'll call you when things are confirmed on this end.'

'Fine. And Ava, I think this is the right thing for us to do.'

She shrugged. 'Ordonez is a big man and it's a lot of money.'

'That does not mean we cannot still say no,' Uncle said. 'We will go and talk to them, and then you and I can discuss what we want to do. I have to tell you, I have a feeling that it will be worth it in the end.'

'Yes, Uncle.'

'Now I have to call Chang,' he said. As she hung up the phone, Ava tried to remember if she'd heard Uncle mention Chang's name before, and came up blank. That wasn't unusual. He had a network of friends and associates that spanned Asia, though his closest contacts were those who shared those long, deep Wuhan roots.

Is Ordonez from Wuhan as well? she wondered. She knew he was Chinese born, but nothing more specific than that. She'd find out soon enough, but her curiosity was far more aroused by the kind of problem a man as rich and powerful as Tommy Ordonez couldn't handle himself.

ACKNOWLEDGEMENTS

Ava Lee and her story came to me unexpectedly. When it was finished, I had no idea whether Ava and her life would be of interest to anyone else. To find out, I imposed her upon my children and friends, all avid readers. Their input and encouragement were invaluable, and I need to thank them.

Ava then found her way to Westwood Creative Artists, where she found support from Bruce Westwood and Carolyn Forde. Their enthusiasm was instrumental in helping Ava find a home. I owe them both a great debt of gratitude.

Home for Ava is House of Anansi Press. I want to thank publisher Sarah MacLachlan and the rest of her team for believing in Ava and for deciding they wanted to introduce her to the world.

Finally I must thank Janie Yoon, Senior Editor at Anansi, for her contribution to the final product. Janie is smart, dedicated, talented, persistent, and polite, much like Ava herself.

There is one attribution I need to clarify. 'People always do the right thing for the wrong reason' is referred to as one of Uncle's credos. In reality, I heard these words spoken many years ago by Saul Alinsky, the great Chicago community organizer, and they have stayed with me.

ACKNOWLEDGEMENTS